Amanda rushed in before she lost the nerve. "I don't want a divorce. I never did . . . Not really. I was so scared of being hurt that I didn't give our marriage a chance. Because of my fears I ended up hurting us both."

"Did it ever occur to you that I might also have been scared?"

"No . . . You never seemed . . ." She stopped, searching for the right words. "Roger told me that—"

"Roger? What does my brother have to do with this? Is he the reason you're here?" Zachary demanded, a muscle jumping in his tightly held jaw.

"No!"

"What did he do, beg you to come here today?"

"Of course not! I'm not here because of Roger. I'm here because I happen to be in love with you! Now will you shut up long enough to listen to what I have to say?" Her hand was on one hip while one high-heeled, booted foot tapped furiously on the linoleum floor.

Zachary looked doubtful. After a prolonged silence he asked, "You mean it?"

"About wanting you to shut up and listen? Absolutely."

"No. That you're in love with me?" His eyes searched hers.

"Yes," Amanda said quietly. "Very much so." Afraid to make a move toward him, she waited with her heart racing and a mounting sense of dread.

"Then why in the hell did you give up on us and walk out on me yesterday?" His arms were crossed over his chest.

"You expect so much from me. I was overwhelmed with fears and doubts. Honey, I'm sorry. I never meant to hurt you." She forced herself to ask while fighting back tears, "Am I too late?"

Other books by Bette Ford

FOR ALWAYS

FOREVER AFTER

ALL THE LOVE

"MAMA'S PEARL" in A MOTHER'S LOVE

AFTER DARK

ONE OF A KIND

ISLAND MAGIC

Published by BET/Arabesque Books

WHEN A
MAN
LOVES A
WOMAN

BETTE FORD

BET Publications, LLC
http://www.bet.com
http://www.arabesquebooks.com

ARABESQUE BOOKS are published by

BET Publications, LLC
c/o BET BOOKS
One BET Plaza
1900 W Place NE
Washington, DC 20018-1211

All Kensington Titles, Imprints, and Distributed Lines are available at special quantity discounts for bulk purchases for sales promotions, premiums, fund-raising, and educational or institutional use. Special book excerpts or customized printings can also be created to fit specific needs. For details, write or phone the office of the Kensington special sales manager: Kensington Publishing Corp., 850 Third Avenue, New York, NY 10022, attn: Special Sales Department, Phone: 1-800-221-2647.

First Printing: March 2002
10 9 8 7 6 5 4 3 2 1

Printed in the United States of America

I'd like to offer a heartfelt thanks to some talented writers: Carla Fredd, Beverly Jenkins, Francis Ray, Margie Walker, and Anita Williams. Your faith in me has helped me through a difficult year. Even though we live in four different states, good friends should never be taken for granted. Love you all.

One

"It's done," Amanda Daniels McFadden whispered aloud as she slowly put down the telephone with a far from steady hand. It was finally over, or at least it would be soon. A tear slipped past her lashes but she hastily wiped it away. "None of that."

A glance at the clock had her rushing into her leather coat, grabbing her purse, oversize portfolio and briefcase and hurrying out of her office door.

"Helen, if you need me I'll be—"

"Look, Mrs. McFadden," Helen Brown, her secretary, gushed. "Aren't they lovely?" She held up a crystal vase filled with dark red, heavily fragrant roses.

"Yes," Amanda said somewhat breathlessly. She did not need to look at the card to know who had sent them; nonetheless she accepted the small white card. Her eyes closed at the name scribbled at the bottom.

"Aren't you going to take them with you?"

"No," she said, swallowing with difficulty. "Please, put them in my office. I'm late for lunch as it is. If Roger calls, will you please tell him I'm on the way? Thanks. Helen, I'll be back after my meeting with Mrs. Williams."

"But, you've forgotten this." Helen handed her a small, slender, beautifully wrapped gold-embossed package.

Amanda took it, saying, "Got to run. See you," then hurrying down the short carpeted hall and through the outer door before any of her other employees could stop her.

Amanda's eyes burned from unshed tears and she was shaking so badly by the time she reached the elevator that she had to lean against the wall for support. After pushing the arrow marked DOWN, she shoved the unopened gift into the side pocket of her briefcase before she began taking slow, steady breaths in the hope of getting her emotions under control.

"I can do this . . . I can do this . . . I can do this," she repeated to herself until the elevator dinged, signaling its arrival.

Stepping into the elevator, Amanda acknowledged the two men inside with a nod. Her mind was not on the problem involved with running her own interior design studio, but with her recent conversation with her attorney, Jeffery Ross.

Today should have been a special one. The anniversary of her wedding day. Why, today of all days, did Mr. Ross have to send those papers? It wasn't the lawyer's error . . . it was hers. Amanda reminded herself that it didn't matter what day the papers arrived. They needed to be sent. It made no sense to put it off any longer.

She awoke alone as she did every morning. It was going to be that way from now on. More important, it was what she wanted. Soon, she could legally drop the McFadden from her name, then once again be plain Mandy Daniels.

She liked the sound of it, so warm and familiar, like a pair of worn, comfortable slippers.

The two men observing the golden-toned, African-American beauty would have laughed if they could have read her thoughts. She was tall, five-eight, and shapely, dressed all in dove-gray leather from her midcalf-length coat to her accessories, including chunky-heel leather boots.

Oblivious to the interest sent her way, Amanda searched the bottom of her purse for her car keys while struggling to hold on to the oversize portfolio and briefcase. Finally, she located and removed the heavy gold key ring with the costly letter *M* dangling from it. As she ran a French-manicured nail over the eighteen-karat gold charm with channel-set emeralds surrounded by diamonds, her thoughts were on the man who had given it to her.

"You're mine now, Mandy. You're a McFadden," Zachary had whispered huskily before he pressed his lips to the wide gold band he had placed there mere hours earlier, then covered her mouth in a hard, possessive kiss.

Not anymore, she wanted to shout. Stop it! She did not want to think about him, not today . . . especially not today. She had what she wanted. So why was she so sad, so out of sorts?

Shoving the keys into her pocket, Amanda instantly decided to buy a new key holder that very same day. While she was at it, she needed to start looking for a new location for her office, as well as her condo. Both were located in buildings owned by McFadden Realty.

Pulling on cashmere-lined gloves, she glanced at her wristwatch, then frowned. She was late. If she didn't hurry, Roger would be furious. Well, not exactly furious. Roger McFadden never really became angry with anyone. He was much too easygoing to let anyone or anything get under his skin for long, not even his stubborn older brother, Zachary.

Why was it so difficult to get Zachary out of her thoughts? They both had made a terrible mistake. Even if he did not agree, it was only a matter of time until he recognized there were no other options. If anything, he should be grateful she was finally releasing him from this pitiful excuse of a marriage.

"Hope the snow has stopped. It was great during the holidays for the kids, but enough is enough," the man closest to her commented.

Amanda glanced at him, surprised by his interest. She shrugged. "I suppose."

Dressed in the standard business suit and topcoat, he murmured, "After you," and held the elevator doors open, waiting for her to precede him into the underground parking garage.

Amanda mumbled her thanks, absently noting that he was average height with a clear, warm brown complexion.

"My name is Zachary Morgan. My law office is here in the building. You work in the building, don't you?" When she made no comment, he rushed on to say, "I mean, I'm sure I've seen you coming and going. Perhaps, we can have lunch someday?"

His name was all she really heard. She longed to yell at a complete stranger because of it, but caught herself before she completely lost it. The last thing she needed was an involvement with another man.

"Howdy, Mrs. McFadden. Anything I can do for you?" The security guard looked pointedly at the man at her side.

"Hi, Greg. How are you today?" she said as she slowed her steps. "I'm running late as usual. I suppose Roger has already left?"

"Yeah, he left about a half hour ago. You okay?"

"Fine. Thanks."

He smiled, touching his cap before continuing on.

To the man observing the exchange, Amanda said, "Mr.

Morgan, I'm married. But thanks anyway.'' She waved, turning toward the red car parked at the end of the next row. She mumbled to herself, ''Well, Zach, you do have your uses.''

Grandpa always said there were two things in life a man could always depend on—his horse and a woman being late. She nearly laughed out loud. That wonderful, wry old man may have had a point, at least when it came to her. Suddenly, she had to blink away tears. How she missed that stubborn, sweet man. Her grandfather had certainly believed in taking care of his own. He'd looked after her since she came to live with him when she was twelve.

After disengaging the alarm on her sleek red Lexus, her grandfather's last gift to her before his death, Amanda slid behind the wheel. Jake Daniels had died with the assurance that his beloved grandchild would be taken care of by the son of his oldest friend and neighbor.

She did not take time to warm the car on one of the coldest January days. After backing out of the parking space, she headed toward the well-marked exit ramp.

Her grandfather had not hesitated to take her in when her mother died. He had enjoyed spoiling her, believing that she had experienced too much suffering in her childhood. Although Jake had not been as wealthy as the McFaddens, he had managed his ranch and money wisely.

Jake had also seen to it that Amanda attended the University of Colorado at Boulder, then insisted on helping her start her own business fresh out of college. He had even gone so far as to rent office space in one of Denver's most prestigious professional buildings.

Her eyes misted with tears. She had loved him fiercely, and she missed him. She would have gladly given back all the gifts to have her feisty old grandfather back with her. None of the material things mattered. What was important was the deep love and sense of security he had given her, something her parents had failed to provide.

She was twenty-eight now and thankful that he had lived long enough to see how she had made a success of the design studio and even ventured into her own syndicated television show called *Elegant Designs by Amanda*. She also developed a line of plush home accessories, including stationery, fabric-covered books and photo albums, lamp shades, accent pillows and scented candles, all of which were sold in several exclusive boutiques around the city. The orders were so brisk that part of her business demanded more and more of her time.

She eased the car into the stream of heavy traffic on 17th Street, considered by some to be the Wall Street of the Rockies, with its impressive skyscrapers housing banks, investment houses and several major corporations and insurance companies. Relieved that the streets had been salted and cleared of snow, she headed north on Broadway to 18th Street where she traveled west toward Larimer.

No, she had not expected her business to take off as quickly as it had. Nor had she expected to be in the situation of having to send the man she had loved most of her life notice of her intentions to divorce him. What a terrible, heartbreaking mess.

Why had Zachary sent the roses and the gift? He knew their marriage was a mistake. One reckless night had changed both of their lives and ruined a perfectly wonderful friendship.

Amanda sighed wearily. She was tired. She had not slept well in days. January 23, their wedding day, marked the beginning of the most painful time in her life. She had lost not only her grandfather, but also her baby mere days after her grandfather's funeral. A double loss that she was not certain she could ever recover from.

Zachary had been supportive through it all, but Amanda

had been the one unable to cope. She had slipped into a depression; only her work had kept her going.

Releasing an impatient sound, she was disgusted with her inability to keep Zachary out of her thoughts and finally gave up trying. He, the oldest of three sons, had a strong sense of right and wrong. He never shirked responsibility.

He took over the family-owned, highly successful business, McFadden Realty, when his father had died suddenly ten years earlier. He had stepped down from an active role in the company as soon as his brothers were out of college and able to handle the business. Now, he spent his time on the ranch some 160 miles west of Denver, outside of Glenwood Springs, Colorado.

The problems in their marriage were certainly not his fault. If anyone was to blame for the dissolution it was Amanda. There was no way of getting around the fact that she was not capable of loving Zachary, or any man for that matter, the way a woman should love her man. Divorce was the only answer for them, and she was relieved that she had finally found the courage to get on with it. She had kept both of their lives in limbo long enough.

Amanda turned into the drive of the popular Italian restaurant situated in Larimer Square. Mario's was an antique brick structure like the other restaurants, shops and galleries in the area. The historic old buildings had been restored, as a reminder of the city's silver and gold rush days.

The morning had dawned cool and crisp, a beautiful day . . . a special day. It was their wedding anniversary. Zachary McFadden had been up well before dawn because he had been unable to sleep. So when the call came letting him know that his favorite mare, Penny, was ready to have her foal, he only needed time to pull on work clothes before he was on his way to the barn.

As he made his way back to the house several hours later, his stomach let him know it was long past breakfast, nearly noon in fact. He shifted stiff muscles beneath his heavy suede, fleeced-lined jacket. His long legs quickly covered the distance from the ranch yard, with him noticing the side garden that his mother was so proud of was blanketed by a fresh layer of pristine snow, onto the back porch and through the rear door that led directly into the mudroom.

After hanging up his jacket and Stetson and removing his boots, he entered the bathroom, off the kitchen. As he quickly shed his soiled clothes, showered and redressed in the fresh pair of worn jeans and chambray shirt stored in one of the cupboards, Zachary could not stop himself from wondering if Amanda had received the flowers and gift he had sent, and if she was angry because of them.

He had not made plans for the evening . . . an evening that should have been spent with his wife. No, he was not likely to forget anything connected to Amanda, including the losses they had both suffered this past year.

If left up to him, he would have liked to take her away for a few days to some romantic inn where they could be alone . . . where they could wake in each other's arms and make love, again and again. Hell, he would have settled for being able to see her today and personally give her the expensive bracelet he had carefully picked out for her.

But none of that would happen, not unless he broke his word . . . and that was something he was not about to do. At the very least he hoped she would appreciate the fact that he remembered their day.

"Morning, Margaret," he said as he entered the roomy kitchen. "Save me any breakfast?"

Margaret Armstrong, widow of one of the ranch hands, had been the housekeeper for the last fifteen years. She was a crisp, no-nonsense type of person, who was not afraid to speak her mind. Her pecan-brown skin was unlined and her thick black hair, flecked with gray, had been braided and coiled around her head. "Well, of course I saved you some food. I'll get it from the warmer. Foal came in all right?"

"Foals. Penny had twins," he acknowledged. He filled a coffee mug from the coffeemaker on the counter, before he made his way to the alcove at the side of the room and sank down into his usual chair. "What's this?" he asked, noting the special-delivery letter beside the newspaper at his place setting.

"Came a few minutes ago," Margaret said as she placed a plate of pancakes, scrambled eggs and bacon in front of him. "Need anything else?"

"No. Thanks," he said absently as he used his table knife to slit the bulky legal-size envelope open. "Is my mother in?"

"No, she and Miss Barbara had hair appointments and are going shopping in town. Left about half hour ago."

"Huh. Have you check in on. . . ." He stopped as he read the document. "Hell, no!"

"Something wrong?" she asked from where she stood in front of the opened refrigerator door, removing a pitcher of freshly squeezed orange juice.

"I'll say," Zachary snarled as he pushed back his chair. "Call down to the hanger. Tell Buck to get the chopper ready . . . now. I'm on my way." He was moving toward the mudroom.

". . . but, Zach, what about your breakfast?"

"You eat it."

"Good Afternoon, Mrs. McFadden. I believe your party is already seated. This way, please." The tuxedo-clad maître d' was all smiles as he led her through the crowded yet cleverly decorated dining room. The round tables were covered in pale blue linen and set with gleaming crystal and fine bone china. Tall palms and high-backed curved banquettes, upholstered in rich navy and green velvet print, afforded a certain measure of privacy.

Roger McFadden spotted Amanda as she approached, aware of the attention Amanda generally received wherever she went. Today was no exception. Several male heads skirted the palms to get a better view of her graceful curvy figure. He grinned. She was too levelheaded to care. She was one woman who used her brains and talents to get ahead, not her looks. Roger came to his full height of six-three, a welcoming smile warming his brown face.

"I could have drunk myself under this table waiting for you, Mandy. I've already had two of these. If you were any longer, I would be on the floor," he complained, as he took her hands and kissed a soft golden brown cheek.

Amanda reached up to give Roger a fierce hug. She saw so little of him these days and missed him terribly.

"Roger, please don't be angry with me. I'm so sorry. I had an appointment that took longer than planned. It's a good thing I didn't ask you to meet me in the lobby or we would have lost this wonderful table."

McFadden Realty was located on the top two floors of the office complex. It was only one of the buildings that the McFadden brothers inherited from their father. He had made a name for himself across the country. Zachary remained CEO, even though the day-to-day operations of the company were no longer his responsibility.

After Roger helped her with her coat, Amanda dropped gracefully down onto the booth. She smiled at the maître d', who had pulled the table out for them to be seated comfortably before replacing it and handing her a menu.

"Will you stop frowning at me?" Amanda teased. How handsome Roger was in his three-piece navy pinstriped business suit, every bit the corporate lawyer of the family-owned firm. He looked far different from the jean-clad kid she had grown up with. Although he was a year older, they had been friends as well as neighbors since middle school.

"You look great, except for those dark smudges under your eyes. Don't you sleep at night, girl?" Roger went on to scold, "Why haven't you called or dropped by the office? We do work in the same building." He did not give her time to answer even one of his demands before rushing on with, "I've dropped down to see you several times, but the well-trained Dracula lady you call a secretary claims you're out with a client every single time. Business must be booming." His skepticism was in his dark eyes.

It was true. Amanda did not bother making excuses. They both knew she had been avoiding him. And they also knew the reason why.

"Your strained marriage to my brother doesn't affect our friendship, Mandy. Peggy and I haven't so much as caught a glimpse of you in months. Why haven't you returned our calls? We both love you and miss you, honey." Roger had managed to strengthen the guilt she was feeling. "Zach was not the only one disappointed when you did not show up to celebrate the holidays with us. We're your family now."

"Please, don't. I have my reasons."

Even though Amanda longed for Roger's understanding, she was not about to ask for it. She still had to tell him about the divorce. But not yet; it would keep until after lunch. For now, she wanted to enjoy his companionship.

The three of them, including his wife Peggy, had been friends for so long. What Amanda had feared was that Roger and Peggy would turn against her because she was doing what she had to do in order to survive. After all, the two of them were a part of Zachary's family.

"Can we, please, talk about something more pleasant than me and my problems with your brother? How's my girl?"

Roger had married her dear friend right after college and

before law school. The three of them had attended the University of Colorado in Boulder.

"Very happy and very pregnant ... at last," he announced, without doubt an extremely proud father-to-be.

"How wonderful!" Amanda could not have been more pleased. They had been trying to have a baby for the past five years without any luck. "I'm so happy for you both. I'll call her today, as soon as I get back to the office. How is she feeling?"

"She's doing well, even though she has to stay off her feet as much as possible. We have been waiting on her hand and foot. Neither one of us is willing to take any risk with this baby." Recognizing what he had said, he hastily added, "I'm sorry, Mandy. I didn't mean to remind you of ..." He stopped abruptly.

Amanda shook her head, squeezing his hand reassuringly. "I'm fine ... now. And I'm very happy for you both."

She had been crushed when she had lost her own baby mere weeks after learning that she was expecting. It had taken quite a while to pull herself together emotionally. Even though she was much better now, there had never been any doubt how much she wanted that baby or how deeply she mourned the loss.

Roger nodded, then said, "Mother won't let her lift a finger. With so much pampering, she will be spoiled by the time the baby comes in the spring. I suppose there are advantages to living in one big household." He signaled the waiter. "Would you like a drink?"

The McFaddens shared a huge sprawling home in the mountains. Although all the members of the family had their own suites, they came together for meals. Since the death of her husband, Rebecca Hamilton McFadden had become protective of all her sons, but especially Zachary. While the lady had not been threatened when Peggy and Roger married, it was quite the opposite when it came to Amanda's marriage to Zachary. Able to trace her family roots back to the first freed slaves in the area, Rebecca had never approved of Amanda's own humble background. Nor had Rebecca welcomed her into the family.

Perhaps it was because Peggy had married the youngest of the McFadden brothers? But then again, Peggy took things in her stride and tended to get along with just about anyone, including their opinionated mother-in-law.

Mrs. McFadden made no secret of the fact she wanted Zachary to marry Barbara Hamilton, the distant cousin she had adopted years ago. Amanda could just imagine her mother-in-law's pleasure when she learned of the divorce.

"Mandy?"

"I'm sorry. What did you say?"

"Would you care for something to drink?"

"White wine, please."

"Peggy and I are planning a second honeymoon after the baby comes," he revealed with a smile.

"How wonderful," she said.

Because of the seriousness of her grandfather's illness, Amanda and Zachary had postponed their honeymoon. He had expected her to give up her condo in Denver and come to live with him on the ranch. It had been an uncomfortable arrangement. And she had left after only a few short weeks of marriage. They had never taken that honeymoon.

"You still haven't answered my question. Why have you been avoiding us?" Roger persisted.

Taking a deep breath, she said, "You know how much I treasure our friendship. I just had to get a few things settled before we talked. Besides, I could not come up to your office. At least not . . ." Her voice trailed away.

"What? You're afraid you might run into Zach? You know he doesn't come into the city unless there is a board meeting or a problem. You know as well as I do that Brad and I have taken over so our brother can devote himself to the ranch. Good grief, Mandy! That's no excuse.''

"If it weren't for Brad's degree in business management and administration, I would be lost. I spend half my time as it is on the telephone with Zach, getting his opinion on some new project. Whether he wants to admit it or not, Zach made more money for the firm during the five years he ran it single-handedly than Dad made. Zach has excellent instincts for the business; he just refuses to do anything about it.''

She shifted uncomfortably in her seat, unconsciously clenching her hands in her lap.

Roger laughed, warming to the topic. "Zach was wrong when he told Dad he was wasting his money sending him to get that degree in business rather than veterinary medicine. He was a natural at both. But Dad and Zach always did bump heads . . . too much alike if you ask me. Yet, Zach didn't hesitate when we lost Dad. Being the oldest has not always been easy, but he had no problem shouldering responsibility.''

The last thing she wanted to hear about was her husband's virtues. Besides, she knew what a giving and wonderful man she had married. It was one more reason why it was so important for her to give him back his freedom. He deserved that much and so much more.

"Can we change the subject?''

"Mandy, you're going to have to see Zach, sooner or later. Things can't go on like this for much longer.''

Two

Amanda shook her head. "You're wrong. I don't have to see him . . . not ever. Our marriage was a mistake from the very start." She bit her lip to keep it from trembling. "I lost our baby. There's no longer a reason for us to be married." She took a deep breath, trying to compose herself. "You, of all people, should know that. Zach and I faced it months ago."

She stared down at her menu without really seeing the print in front of her. Her stomach was in knots. Thoughts of what she'd lost and of her short, unhappy marriage did not ease the discomfort.

"Marriage is hard work. I know that. But when two people care about each other the way you two do, it can work out. I'm not saying it's going to be a piece of cake. Just start talking—"

"Stop it! And you wonder why I didn't want to see you?

I know how you feel. And I certainly knew you would try
to talk me into going back to Zachary. Forget it!'' Then she
closed her eyes as if she was trying to compose herself,
before she said, ''Roger, please . . . just leave it alone.'' Her
dark eyes pleaded for his understanding. Forcing a smile,
she asked, ''Shall we order? I'm starving.''

Food was the last thing she wanted, but she could not let
Roger see how vulnerable she still was to his brother. If
only she could stop caring about the man. It was almost
impossible, but it was something she had to do.

It was difficult enough knowing that she would be going
against her grandfather's last wishes. Jake had been pleased
about their marriage. It brought him a great deal of comfort
in his final days. She had to hold in the tears that lodged in
her throat.

As Amanda waited for Roger's response, her body was
tight with tension. She would like nothing more than to
remain friends with Roger and Peggy. She loved them both.
If only Roger would accept that both her and Zachary's
happiness rested outside the boundaries of their marriage.
It was too late for talking. There was nothing left to debate.
In a matter of weeks the marriage would be over.

Roger squeezed her hand before he signaled the waiter
that they were ready to order. She selected baked lasagna
and salad while Roger chose coleslaw, steak and cottage
fries.

Once they were alone, Roger said, ''Tell me about your
appointment. I hope it was not with Mrs. Frederick. The
lady is too much. After all your work she refused to pay
the bill because she changed her mind about her choices.
Naturally after the job was done. I still say you should have
taken her to court. With clients like that, you could be out
of business before the end of the year.''

She laughed. ''Thank goodness, she has been the exception. I've already spoken to my attorney about her. In fact,

just this morning he mentioned we could probably settle out of court. He spoke with her husband, and there's hope.'' She took a sip of her wine.

''So you talked to Jeffery Ross. Why all the secrecy? He has been your grandfather's lawyer for years, a good man,'' he commented, a puzzled frown wrinkling his brow as he studied her face. ''What's going on, Mandy?''

She nearly choked on the wine in her mouth. She was staring across the dining room at the tall, muscular man in a mud-spattered navy Stetson talking to the maître d'. She felt as if her heart had stopped beating, and her lungs certainly seemed to have lost their power to fill.

Zachary McFadden took long ground-eating strides toward them. There was no doubt about his mood. It was stamped on his bold African features, from the firm set of his square-cut jawline, the flare of his strong nose, the compression of his normally well-shaped mouth to the deep scowl that drew his black brows together—all announced how absolutely furious he was. His skin was the color of burnished copper.

Zachary was unmistakably the most attractive male in the room, Amanda decided in stunned dismay. At six-four, with broad muscular shoulders and trim waist and hips, he caught the interest of more than one female diner despite his less than crisp attire. She watched as he moved with a sensuous grace all his own. Everything outside of her very angry husband ceased to exist.

She had not seen him in nearly a year, yet his long, powerful body had not changed. His powerful legs were encased in faded jeans, his navy suede fleece-lined jacket was open to reveal a chambray work shirt, covering a broad chest. He looked as if he had just stepped down from his horse.

Who would believe he was a multimillionaire? His only

concession to the elegant restaurant was the removal of his Stetson. His thick black naturally wavy hair was cut short.

Roger grinned broadly, rising to slap his brother on the back. "Hey, Zach! I must say I'm surprised to see you in town today. I've been trying to get you into the office for the last three weeks." Roger noted with amusement that his brother had not heard a word he said. Zachary's jet-black eyes were devouring his wife.

He studied her with the same intent a panther devotes to its prey. His bold gaze focused on her small African features from her large chocolate-brown eyes, which had gone suddenly wide with apprehension, her small nose, her full enticing crimson-covered lips to her chin raised in defiance. Her creamy golden brown skin was flushed with hints of pink. His interest did not stop there.

As he took note that her thick black hair had been tucked beneath her silver-gray leather hat, his gaze touched the slender column of her throat, then moved down to the luscious round curves of her full breasts covered by a V-neck burgundy cashmere sweater set.

When his dark eyes finally returned to hers, Zachary spoke for the first time. "Hey, pretty girl." He leaned over the table to place a hard, punishing kiss against her trembling lips. When he drew back, his eyes held a dangerous glint of steel as if he dared her to deny his right to do that and more.

Amanda stared into the fathomless depths of his eyes, unable to think of a saucy rejoinder. What was he doing here, of all places? His flowers and anniversary gift this morning had been enough of a surprise.

More importantly, why had he kissed her like that as if they were not estranged . . . not on the brink of divorce? As if they were still lovers. She unwittingly pressed her fingers to her mouth, disturbed by the familiar taste and feel of his mouth on her.

Her senses still reeled from the familiar smell of his aftershave and soap, an outdoor, rustic scent like the man himself, combined with his natural, very masculine scent.

He was supposed to be on the ranch, over a hundred miles away. The Circle-M was one of the largest and most productive cattle spreads in this part of the country. Why wasn't he on it?

Roger was the first to break the lengthy silence. "Join us. I see our waiter with the appetizers. Have you eaten?"

Zachary, having slid onto the booth next to the dazed Amanda, said, "No, I haven't. I was in such a hurry to get into town that I didn't bother. Penny's foals were born during the night. Twin mares." He rested an arm along the top of the banquette, in order to comfortably accommodate his shoulders.

"Twins?" She smiled for the first time.

"How are they?" Roger asked.

"Mother and babies are doing fine."

She would have liked nothing better than to put some space between herself and her husband, but in order to accomplish that she would end up in her brother-in-law's lap.

There was no way she could ignore the way her husband's long length pressed against her from shoulder to hip, kindling memories she preferred to keep buried. Bittersweet memories of the two of them wrapped in each other's arms.

Scrutinizing Amanda, he asked, "How have you been?"

She tried to swallow the bite of cheese stick that seemed to be suddenly stuck in her throat before she forced herself to met his gaze and found her voice. "How did you find us?" She knew she should thank him for the flowers and gift, but she was nobody's fool. She did not want to arouse the formidable temper he was clearly struggling to control.

None of this was making any sense. Why was he angry?

Her plan to divorce him was hardly a surprise to him. They both knew it was long overdue.

They certainly could not continue to live as they had been with her in the condo in Denver and him on the Circle-M. They did not have a real marriage. There had never been a binding of hearts or blending of souls. The baby they had created was gone, ending their connection. She had to blink away sudden tears.

"Helen was a wealth of information," he said, referring to her assistant. "Mandy, you have not answered my question. How have you been?"

"I'm well. You certainly look fit."

She slowly began to relax. This was Zach. She had known him most of her life. While Roger had been the friend she had done things with and gone places with as a girl, Zachary had been the one she had run to with the problems that she could not tell her grandfather. No matter how complicated, including those first teenage crushes and doubts she had had about her own feminine appeal. Then there was the pressure of college classes, later the strain of starting her business.

Zachary had always listened. In fact, he was the one who had convinced her grandfather to let her try her wings. If it hadn't been for Zach's influence with Jake, Amanda might never have left the shelter of her grandfather's ranch. In Jake Daniels's day young women stayed at home until they married or died, whichever came first. If only they had not gotten married. Marriage had ruined a perfectly wonderful friendship.

"I don't like those dark circles I see under your eyes, Mandy," Zachary said. Without glancing at the menu, he quickly ordered coleslaw, a steak sandwich and cottage fries.

Amanda laughed. "You two still think alike." The brothers had always been close and she had always felt secure with the two of them.

They shrugged, grinning roguishly.

"I take it our Mandy has something to do with you being here, bro," Roger teased, his curiosity apparently getting the better of him. "Mind explaining to the hired help?"

"You didn't tell him?" Zachary arched a thick brow. "I'm genuinely shocked. My brother has privileges that even your husband was not allowed. Hell, I haven't been able to even see you since you left the ranch," he snarled bitterly.

"What is your problem? You're acting like a jealous fool! I have not seen Mandy in months. Our friendship is what it has always been," Roger snapped. Steering the conversation into safer channels, he inquired, "Did you have a chance to stop in at the office? I assumed you brought the chopper in?"

"Yes," Zachary said, sighing.

The McFadden Building had been designed to support a helicopter on its flat roof.

"Did you see Bradford? He mentioned this morning that he needed to contact you about the Florida property we purchased last month. It seems the local architect we wanted for the job is not available. Had a heart attack. Anyway, Brad thinks Anderson can handle a job of this scale. Remember, he designed those condos for us in Houston two years ago? What do you think?"

She was relieved. The switch to the unemotional matter of business gave her time to collect herself. It had only been since they became husband and wife that his attitude toward her had changed so drastically. He could be so possessive at times. And now he had actually accused her of having an affair with his own brother.

If he just had to accuse someone, why not Bradford? Amanda thought wildly. At least his middle brother was single. Evidently, Zachary didn't know that Bradford blamed her for the separation. Bradford barely spoke to her whenever they ran into each other in the elevator or the parking garage.

Amanda sighed dejectedly. Where would it all end? She was terrified their marriage would completely destroy the love and friendship they had always shared. If they did not correct this mistake and soon, there would be nothing left to save. Perhaps, it was already too late? How could she bear it if she lost Zachary for good?

"Here we are." Roger smiled as the waiter began dispensing plates.

Zachary, the husband, was far removed from the strong, supportive Zach she had grown up adoring. He had been a man while she had been a gangly teenager. He was ten years older than Amanda, but he had always been there for her.

Even though he had a life of his own, he always made himself available to her. He offered his muscular shoulder to cry on when she experienced some disappointment or offered an understanding ear when she needed to talk.

Everything was different now. He insisted she accept him as her lover, something she simply could not do. She was unable to cope with his potent male charms and the sheer force of his sexuality. Amanda did not want Zachary in her bed.

"You're not eating. Would you care for something else?" Zachary asked as he eyed her barely touched plate. Both men were nearly finished with their meal.

Her stomach was filled with tension. So much so that she had barely managed to swallow a few forkfuls of her meal. She could not force it down, unless she wanted to be sick. She ended up pushing her plate away.

"I'm not hungry." Unable to ignore the question uppermost in her mind any longer, she asked, "Why don't you go ahead and say what's on your mind, Zach? I know you're furious. I assumed you received the papers announcing my intentions to file for a divorce."

"What!" Roger gasped.

"Yes, I heard from your Mr. Ross," Zachary hissed out

between clenched white teeth. "But this is neither the time nor the place to go into the details of our marriage. We will talk later, at home."

"We have no home," Amanda insisted irrationally, suddenly furious with him. "I don't know when I'll see you again, except in court." Zachary could make her lose all objectivity and logic in the blink of an eye. She hated to lose control of her emotions, thus giving him the upper hand.

Zachary had no such compulsion. He snarled, "And whose fault is it that we have no home? Certainly not mine!" His nostrils flared with his mounting rage.

Consciously, she knew he would never hurt her; nonetheless Amanda trembled involuntarily. Zachary's quick temper was something she had never been comfortable with. It could flare without notice.

Amanda had seen it in action when Zachary discovered one of his men had misused one of his animals. He had gone after the man with clenched fists. She had been stiff with terror. Until now his anger had never been directed at her. Their upcoming divorce had evidently changed all that.

Paralyzed with fear from the harshness of his tone, she was sent back to that hidden place, deep inside herself, when she was still a girl and vulnerable. Flashbacks of her father in a drunken rage filled her head. Hated thoughts of when her father took his frustrations out on her mother and Amanda when she tried to protect her mother from his blows. That fear had never completely disappeared.

It was dormant within her until a particular pitch in a man's voice sent it spiraling through her system. When Amanda heard that chilling tone in Zachary's voice, she had to bite her lips to keep from screaming; beads of perspiration covered her forehead and unshed tears burned her eyes.

"Control that temper of yours, man. Can't you see you're scaring the hell out of Mandy?" Roger hissed, glaring at his much taller and heavier older brother.

Zachary sighed wearily before leaning back against the seat. He said nothing as he struggled with his emotions.

"Look, I have an appointment. I have to get out of here. Do you need a ride?" Roger asked, reaching for his wallet.

"No, thanks. Let me take care of the check. I barged in on your meal. Besides, it's not often I'm allowed to feed my own wife," Zachary said softly, his voice tinged with bitterness.

"Are you okay, Mandy?" Roger hesitated, watching her closely.

"I'm fine." She smiled weakly, managing to control her discomfort. She ignored her husband completely as her system slowly returned to normal.

"Are you going to stop in before you head back?" Roger asked Zachary.

"Yeah. Mandy can give me a lift," he announced arrogantly.

She made no comment, but clenched her small hands together in her lap. She hated this . . . hated every bit of it.

Roger leaned over and kissed her cheek. "Stop being a stranger, you hear?"

Amanda nodded. "Take care and give Peggy my love."

"Bye."

Once they were alone a pungent silence lingered. Zachary sipped his beer while he studied his wife.

Their waiter broke the quiet when he asked, "Would either of you care for something more? Perhaps you would like to see our dessert tray?"

"Mandy?"

"Coffee, please."

"I'll have the same." Zachary reached into his pocket and pulled out a thin gold cigar case and lighter.

"I thought you'd given those up?" she reprimanded.

"There are a lot of things about me you have not been interested in knowing this past year, including my preference in movies, plays, food and sex. Celibacy doesn't agree with me.''

When he saw her wounded expression, he swore beneath his breath. Taking Amanda's small hands in his work-calloused ones, he said, ''I hate the distance between us. We can't even carry on a simple conversation.'' He caressed her fingers. ''I'm sorry I lost my temper earlier. This isn't only hard on you. I've missed you, sugar.''

''I don't like the way things are between us, either.'' She looked up at him, pleading for understanding. ''I can't stand it when you're cold and furious with me. Zach, it hurts so much. I did what I thought was best for both of us. I never meant to hurt you.''

He lifted one hand to run a lean finger over her high-sculptured cheekbone, following the curve down her jawline to the sensitive hollow at the base of her throat. ''You ask too much of me,'' he said in a deep throaty whisper.

Shivers of awareness ran down her spine, ignited by his touch. Fear rushed up to block out the pleasure. ''Please . . . don't,'' Amanda whispered as she moved just out of his reach. She was shaken not only by his caress, but by the fact that he still wore the wide gold band she had placed on his hand on their wedding day.

She dropped her gaze, concerned that she had just added insult to injury, but she could not help it. She had seen the muscles along his jawline throb rhythmically as if he were grinding his teeth in mute frustration.

Zachary said, ''Let's get out of here. We can talk at your place,'' as he crushed out the cigar he had only just lit.

''The coffee?''

''We have to talk, Mandy.''

''I can't,'' she confessed, glancing at her watch.

''Why the hell not?'' he demanded, ignoring the hot drink the waiter had just placed in front of them. ''Check, please.''

''Zach! I have a business to run,'' she hissed impatiently.

"I'm sorry, but I have an appointment with a client this afternoon."

"Then we can talk tonight over dinner. Where would you like me to make reservations?" He reached into his pocket and pulled out a money clip. He dropped a large bill on the table.

"My appointment isn't at the office, Zach. I'm seeing my client in her home in Cherry Hills. I can't have dinner with you. I have plans." Amanda shoved her arms in the sleeves of her coat before he could assist her and completely missed the hardening of his jet-black eyes.

"Are you saying you have a date?" He stood, with feet spaced firmly apart, his jaw jutting stubbornly.

Amanda took a deep breath before sliding gracefully out of the booth, placing her bag over her shoulder. When she met his eyes, she said, "Christopher Black is a business associate, not a date. What is wrong with a simple business dinner?"

"Not a thing." He smiled suddenly. He took her elbow to steer her out of the restaurant. "You will give me a lift to the office, won't you?"

"Of course."

She did not want to admit even to herself that she was thrown by his sudden change of mood. This new casual attitude bordered on indifference. She certainly did not want him angry with her, but she did not welcome his indifference either. What was with him? Or had he just stopped caring about her altogether?

"Your stub, Mrs. McFadden?" the parking attendant requested while he glanced at the tall man adjusting his Stetson low on his forehead at her side.

"Do you want to drive?" Amanda looked up at him with laughter dancing in her dark eyes.

"Naturally. I know better than to get into a car with you behind the wheel, pretty girl." Zachary threw back his head and roared with laughter, almost losing his hat in the process. Her driving skills had been a bone of contention between them for years.

She arched her brow. "I don't see what is at all funny, Zachary McFadden. I'm a good driver, now. And even if I might have been a lousy driver once, and I stress 'if' . . . it's your fault. After all, you're the one who taught me all I know on the subject." Laughing in spite of herself, she asked, "Do you remember the time I barely missed the fence only to hit the barn instead? Granddaddy was fit to be tied."

They both laughed at the incident.

"If it was not for that pile of hay you hit first, we never would have made it." His chest rumbled with amusement. "Jake was furious with both of us for weeks. But I never did understand why I had to pay for the barn and the repairs on his old Buick when you did the damage."

"It was your fault. Besides, I was grounded for a month and had to clean out every stall in that old barn until, quote, 'I learned the value of property,' " Amanda reminded him indignantly.

"How was it my fault? You were behind the wheel, sugar."

"If you had let me drive your car, it would never have happened," she insisted, then giggled when his black brows shot up in disbelief.

"Have you demolish my Porsche? No way!"

They both knew his navy sports car was his most prized possession. He had gotten a new one every year and refused to let anyone else drive it.

The bright red car was brought to a halt in front of them. Zachary helped Amanda inside, fastened her seat belt, closed the door and tipped the attendant, before he came around to slide behind the steering wheel. After adjusting the seat to accommodate his long legs and securing his own seat belt, he eased the car out into traffic.

They rode in silence for a time. When he glanced over at her after stopping for the traffic light, he discovered tears glistening on her lashes and slowly trickling down her cheeks. He said nothing, but he pulled over into the first available parking space.

Amanda, lost in memories, was not aware of what he had done until he unhooked her seat belt and his strong arms came around her, bringing her against his broad chest.

Three

"It's all right, Mandy. I miss Jake, too."

Amanda sighed heavily, leaning into Zachary's hard frame, thankful that he understood without explanation. As she closed her eyes, allowing the grief to wash over her, she found comfort from his strength. He had also loved her grandfather.

"Cry, Mandy. Get it out." His cheek rested against hers when he said, "Jake was a special man. I'm proud to have been his friend. He took my side when I had to stand up to my father. Jake understood that I had to do what was right for me, even when Dad didn't. I regret that it caused a rift between the two old friends."

She nodded, stroking his cheek reassuringly. "Grand-daddy believed in you. He knew you were a good man. And he never blamed you for what happened between him and your dad."

He paused, before he admitted, "I regretted it, but at the time, all I could think of was how important it was to me to prove myself to my father. Andrew McFadden was a hard man."

"And you did. You made a success of the ranch."

When he lifted her chin the hat covering her hair fell off, causing her thick black curls to spill down past her shoulders. He ran his fingers through its ebony softness. His voice was gruff with emotion when he said, "I know it has been a tough year, sugar. Too damn many losses."

She struggled for composure. The loss of the baby was one they shared. She knew he had wanted that baby as much as she had. He was an honorable man. He always did what he believed to be right, including marrying the expectant mother of his child. He had done right by her. Now it was her turn to do right by him and give him back his freedom.

When she moved away, she saw the damage she had done to his shirt. She brushed at the stain. "I'm sorry. I've gotten makeup on you."

"Doesn't matter," he answered as he took a clean linen handkerchief from his pocket to dry her mascara-smeared eyes and damp cheeks.

"I'm surprised you can sit next to me. I rode Sierra out to the airstrip." He referred to his favorite stallion.

"I'm accustomed to your somewhat horsy smell." She giggled, then said around a deep sigh, "Oh, Zach. You have no idea how much I've missed you." Then she began searching her purse for a compact and lipstick to repair the damage.

"So why divorce me? Mandy, you haven't given our marriage a chance. You're after the easy way out." He lifted her chin until she met his gaze; then he said, "We can make it work, given time, pretty girl."

Pulling away, she insisted, "Nothing can change the past. You know as well as I do that we married for the wrong reason. I should never have let you talk me into it. I should have followed my first instincts and raised the baby on my own. Now look what has happened. We don't have anything. Not our baby . . ." She swallowed back tears before she could continue. ". . . not a marriage. There is nothing left to hang on to."

"Mandy, we both wanted that baby and mourn the loss. Instead of bringing us closer, you pushed me away. And I allowed it. I thought I was giving you the time you needed to heal." His mouth was taut when he said, "But unlike you, I have no regrets about our marriage. Have you given this any real thought? Or are you acting on pure emotion?" His hands were balled into fists when he snapped, "Damn it, today is our anniversary. Doesn't that mean anything to you? Why did you have to do this today?"

"That was an unfortunate mistake. But you are wrong. I've thought of little else. I can't give you what you need. It would be better for us to go ahead with the divorce. Don't you see? We never fought until we got married." She dropped her lashes before she said unhappily. "We loved each other . . . now we can hardly stay in the same room without fighting. Zach, please. I need you . . . but not as my husband."

A muscle played in his jaw when he said, "We can't go back, Mandy. You're no longer the girl you once were. And I'm not your big brother. You're a woman . . . my woman. Accept it!"

She closed her mouth in mute frustration. It was pointless to try and reason with this mule-headed man. He just refused to accept that there was a vulnerable part of herself that she could not share, even with him. No matter how much Amanda loved and trusted Zachary, she could not let him make love to her again. It would leave her too vulnerable, too dependent on him. She could never give a man that kind of power.

Technically, she was still a child when she looked down at her mother for the final time. Amanda silently vowed that she would never put herself at a man's mercy. She was not like her mother. Nor would she be totally dependent on any man, thus leaving herself weak, unable to function when he walked away, as her father had done. Never.

"I said—"

"I heard you. And the answer is no." She busied herself with uncapping a tube of lipstick.

Before she could apply the crimson color, he angled her face toward his own. His kiss was hard, punishing as if he was claiming what was his alone. He used his tongue to push between the seams of her soft lips and plunge into the moist sweet cavity beyond. He groaned as he stroked her tongue with his own . . . again and again.

Amanda offered no protest as wave upon dazzling wave of pleasure rushed over her. Each new surge of his tongue was hotter than the last until she pressed the aching tips of her breasts against the firm muscles of his chest.

"Oh, Zach . . ."

Annoyed by the thickness of his jacket, she shivered with relief when his hand moved inside her coat, under her sweater, to cup her silk-and-lace-covered breast. She moaned in pleasure when he squeezed her softness. Trembling in reaction, her hands slid up until she could caress his dark, hair-roughened cheek.

"Sugar," he whispered.

Amanda came to her senses when she felt Zachary's hand slide under the hem of her skirt to caress the sleek smoothness of her nylon-covered inner thigh. She recalled not only where they were, but more importantly, what she had allowed him to do.

"Don't . . ." she said as she freed herself. Hugging the opposite door as she fought for control, she hissed at him, "You know I hate it when you touch me intimately." Her hands were balled in her lap. She was furious at him but even more so with herself. "You know that!"

How could she have been so weak? How could she have let him practically take her in broad daylight in the front seat of her car?

Whatever Zachary had been about to say to her, he swallowed it. He swore beneath his breath, gunning the motor before he set the car into motion. The veins in his neck throbbed as if he were grinding his teeth while he expertly handled the car. His gaze did not waver from the road ahead.

When he eased to a stop in the no-parking zone in front of the McFadden Building, he said almost casually, "What time will you be free this evening?"

Shivering, she imagined the two of them alone in the condo. If what happened in the car had taken place in the privacy of her home it would not take much to envision the two of them in bed together. She was not about to let that happen.

"Ten-thirty . . . eleven. Why?"

"We have a few things to discuss, Mrs. McFadden."

"No!" Then in a much softer tone, she said, "I—I—I mean, not tonight." Amanda was determined to keep this conversation as painless and businesslike as possible. "Let's leave it for a few days. Perhaps we can have lunch next week . . . on Tuesday?"

"Fine." He nodded. "Shall we say twelve at my club?"

Astonished by his easy acceptance, she decided not to question it. "Yes, that will be fine."

He looked down, briefly fingering the jewel-covered chain hanging from her key ring. "I see you still use it. I'm surprised, since you no longer wear your wedding rings."

He opened his door, stepped out and then walked around

the hood of the car to the sidewalk before entering the building, leaving her staring after him.

Amanda was home but too exhausted to do more than slump against the steering wheel. It had been one long, draining day. Her afternoon appointment had not gone well. Unable to keep her mind on what she was supposed to be doing, she had to ask the poor woman to repeat herself several times.

It wasn't like her not to be on top of her career. She had worked too hard to get where she was to fall apart like this. Her professional reputation was at stake.

What was the matter with her? Nothing like this had ever happened before. But Amanda knew the answer. She had been thrown by Zachary's appearance in Mario. She needed no reminder that today was their anniversary. She certainly could have done without the flowers and gift he'd sent that morning.

A year ago they had had a small private ceremony in the hospital chapel with only family present. Amanda's grandfather had been gravely ill, but despite the chemotherapy he was receiving, he had insisted on standing up with her. Their guests were members of Zachary's family.

The reception had been a luncheon in one of the private rooms in the Brown Palace Hotel. They'd decided to postpone their honeymoon because her grandfather had been much too ill for them to go away, even for a few days.

What a horrible mess. It looked as if it would not be an amicable divorce. Well, at least Zachary had given her a little time before she had to face him again.

Should she ask her attorney to join them for lunch next week? If Jeffery Ross was present, there could be no misunderstanding about her intentions. And this afternoon's mistake could not happen again. There was nothing Zachary could do or say to change her mind. Their marriage had ended months ago when she left the Circle-M and moved back to Denver. Their divorce was a natural progression for them. Zachary should not need convincing, but now was not the time to worry about her soon-to-be-ex-husband.

It was almost seven and Christopher would be picking her up within the hour. Why the man claimed he could not have a business meeting with her at his office during business hours was a mystery to her. There was no denying that the two of them worked well together.

Christopher was a top-notch architect, specializing in renovating and restoring older houses. He had been so impressed by Amanda's work that he approached her to work with him. Once he had completed the exterior and interior structural changes, he called her in. Amanda planned the color schemes, selected wallpaper, drapes, flooring, fixtures for both the kitchen and bathrooms and the lighting fixtures . . . all designed to enhance the home's beauty.

Once Christopher sold the house, at a handsome profit, he paid Amanda well for her work. More often than not, the new owners were so impressed by her work that they commissioned her to finish the interior design.

Christopher always insisted on taking her out to an expensive restaurant for their consultations. Although he was a bachelor, he knew Amanda was off-limits. She made no secret about her marital status. Unfortunately, he also knew that she was separated from her husband.

Their relationship was a mutually profitable business arrangement. On occasion, he let it be known he would not object to a more personal relationship with her. She adamantly refused.

Amanda had not moved a single muscle to enter the magnificent marble and glass high-rise condominium complex where she had lived for the last six years. The impressive building housed a gym, along with indoor and outdoor swimming pools, tennis and racquetball courts, game rooms, saunas and club rooms, as well as valet parking.

"No one's going to carry you inside?" she mumbled aloud, then giggled at the thought of the very correct doorman's reaction if she drove up to the entrance and asked for that particular service.

She had gone back to her office before heading home to pick up additional work. She often worked out of her home office for a few hours in the morning, preferring its peacefulness to the hectic pace of the design studio that included two assistants who were constantly in competition with each other, plus a secretary who loved to mother her. Since she had added the signature accessories, she'd also had to increase her staff to assemble the products. She never seemed to get everything done.

Gathering her briefcase with the laptop inside, the heavy portfolio brimming with sketches and fabric samples and her purse, Amanda scrambled out of the car.

Even the hiring of Yolanda James, an old college classmate, as art consultant had not completely taken the pressure off, but it had helped considerably. It was amazing how Yolanda could look at one of her sketches and instantly know which piece of artwork would dramatize what Amanda had created. Sometimes it took Yolanda only a few hours but occasionally it took months to find the perfect piece of art.

If Amanda's workload did not ease up she would have no choice but to hire another full-time designer. Yet, the problems of running her own interior design studio were not the reason why she felt as tight as a coiled rope. Her estranged husband was responsible for that.

If only she knew why Zachary was fighting her on the divorce. Their marriage had never been a real one. It was nothing like what Roger and Peggy shared. Why couldn't he see that?

After collecting and stuffing her mail into the outside pocket of her briefcase, Amanda punched the numbered elevator button with more force than necessary. There was no point in pretending that Zachary had not been far from her thoughts the entire day, a complete waste of her time.

She should be concentrating on what she would wear to dinner. In all honesty, she did not care what Christopher thought of her. She simply did not think of him in a personal way.

If it were left up to her, she would stay home, take a long hot bath, brush her hair until her scalp protested, then curl up on the sofa, wrapped in nothing more than a warm velvet robe, and read the latest Walter Mosley novel. She had read every one of the "Easy" mysteries. Nothing relaxed her more than a quiet evening at home with a good book and the soothing rhythm of jazz playing in the background.

"At last," she murmured when the elevator doors opened on her floor. There were only four condos on each floor, each one spacious with a glorious view of Denver's skyline. She had moved into the high-security building to please her grandfather. And it was yet another choice piece of prime real estate owned by the McFadden brothers. Technically, her soon-to-be ex-husband was her landlord.

"Hi, Amanda," her next-door neighbor called as she emerged from her place.

"Hi, Joan. How are you?"

Joan Braddock was the owner and manager of the Braddock Gallery. The two art lovers had a great deal in common. Amanda had bought pieces from Joan's gallery from time to time. Since they both lived alone, occasionally they dined out, saw a movie or went to the theater together.

"I'm just fine, but I bet you're on top of the world." Joan giggled. After locking her door, she grinned from ear to ear as she tucked a blond curl behind her ear.

"Huh?"

"If I had a hunk like that moving in with me, I'd be turning cartwheels. I thought you said you're married?" The other woman's curiosity had clearly gotten the best of her.

"I am. What are you talking about?" Amanda was just too tired to exert much effort toward solving the puzzle.

"You tell me! Or have you and your husband reconciled? Oh, hell! Do I ever sound like the number-one nosy neighbor? Look, I'm sorry, hon. It's just not every day I see such a big, beautiful man with real muscles, and a genuine cowboy, too. You're lucky, whoever he is. Sure, he looked as if he just parked his horse at the curb . . . but who cares?" Joan laughed, running to catch the elevator before it left without her. "See you. Call me when you're free. That is, if you're ever free again." Joan waved as the elevator doors closed behind her.

Amanda had stopped in the center of the carpeted hallway and stood there too stunned to take another step. She just stared at the solid oak of her front door at the end of the corridor.

"No!" she hissed. It could not be. Zachary could not have moved into the condo without so much as a word to her. Only a few hours before, the man had readily agreed to meet the following week in order to discuss their divorce. Readily? Docile?

"That rat! That low-life snake!" Amanda snapped. Even he didn't have the nerve to move into her home without telling her. Knowing him as well as she did, she had no doubt that he had the nerve to do exactly as he pleased.

"Zachary McFadden, I will break both your arms for

this!'' she fumed as she marched forward to insert her key into the lock, certain it could be no one else. Burglars did not move in, they moved you out.

By the time she stepped inside the foyer, carpeted in the lush celery green that ran thoughout the condo and matched the silk-covered walls, she was shaking with rage.

After flicking on lamps as she walked, she spared no more than a glance at the huge crystal vase of dark red roses but unceremoniously dumped her things on top of the glass-top walnut side table and into one of the cream velvet Queen Anne chairs that flanked the table. Nor did she need to look into the large oval antique gold-framed mirror above the table to know her face was hot with fury and her heart raced with unexpected anticipation.

''Just what does he think he's trying to pull? Calm down, Mandy girl,'' she mumbled aloud. She would not go in yelling her head off. She had to calm down in order to handle this rationally. She couldn't possibly win if she was too upset to think straight. The problem was she felt as if her blood were boiling in her veins.

She took several deep fortifying breaths before she was able to hang her coat in the closet. Glancing inside the sun-yellow kitchen on her right as she walked down the central hallway, Amanda confirmed what she already knew, Zachary had made himself at home. A coffee mug and dirty dish sat in the sink of her spotlessly clean kitchen. It remained spotless because she seldom had time to make more than coffee and toast.

She entered the darkened living room that opened off the entranceway. Although furious, she was relatively composed. She switched on lamps as she went.

She was proud of her home. She had worked hard to make it as plush and comfortable as she could afford. Her eyes moved over the large semicircular, sectional forest-green velvet sofa that faced twin Louis-XVI armchairs, done in cream damask. A collection of Nigerian Igbo ancient shrine figures were placed on one end of the tall table behind the sofa.

The large living room displayed her love of mixing modern furnishings with period pieces. She did not spare even a token glance at the wall opposite the sofa where her favorite piece was located, the fruitwood slate-front colonial desk. Next to the desk was the cherry-wood armoire housing both a portable bar and a stereo system. Between the two hung an oil painting by one of Denver's up-and-coming black artists, Matt Cummings. She enjoyed his bold use of color and the strong lines of the Nigerian men at work depicted in the piece. Above the sofa was a large oil painting depicting a breathtaking mountain-high sunset.

She stood in front of the floor-to-ceiling glass doors with a spectacular view of the Denver skyline, pausing only long enough to close the pale green silk drapes. The throw pillows on the sofa and the armchairs were made from ukara cloth from Nigeria.

Nothing was out of place. And there was no sign of him. Moving down the central hallway, past the dining area, she paused to turn on the lamp in the small den on the right, furnished with a comfortable deep-cushioned sofa and oak shelving running the entire width of the room that was brimming with books, plants, stereo equipment, CDs, videos and an oversize television set and DVD player.

Her heels were soundless on the thick carpet as she halted at the open door on the left to peek inside her home office. A drawing board stood in the center of the room, and a series of drawer cabinets had been built into the wall holding her sketch pads, swatches of material, wallpaper, and carpet samples. A small brass daybed was positioned beneath the picture window, upholstered in a rust and green jungle print and topped with matching throw pillows. Where was he?

Her steps slowed as she approached the closed double doors at the end of the hallway. Her bedroom was decorated in classic French provincial furnishings. The queen-size bed was centered along the far wall covered in a cream velvet comforter trimmed in pale green. The dust-ruffled pillow shams were also done in the cream edged in pale green. A brass clock quietly ticked on the nightstand.

He was not physically present, but he had been there. A black leather toiletry case rested on the top of the dresser. A navy toweling robe was on the bench at the foot of the bed.

She inhaled deeply before she opened the door to the walk-in closet. Her lips compressed as she stared at the rows of men's slacks, jeans, shirts and matching ties, as well as shoes and boots, that were neatly stored beside her things.

Amanda was trembling so badly by the time she returned to the bedroom that she had to sit down in one of the armchairs near the windows. She didn't bother to draw the pale green silk drapes.

She could not get past the indisputable fact that Zachary had indeed moved into her home. Numb with shock, Amanda was not conscious of the passage of time.

Suddenly she hissed aloud, "Damn you, Zach! How could you? How could you do this to me! And where are you?"

She wanted him there so she could scream at him . . . hit him . . . vent her outrage. One thing she knew for sure was that she was not about to let him get away with this even if he was determined to make their pitiful excuse for a marriage work. Well, she was equally determined to put an end to it. She had to move on with her life. She would divorce him whether he liked it or not.

Restless, she paced in front of the windows. Surely, he did not believe she would keep quiet and just go along with him? No way! He would be lucky if she didn't toss his things in front of the elevator. It was what he deserved.

She jumped when she heard the doorbell. Christopher! As she hurried toward the foyer, she debated her next move. How could she calmly go out when her entire life was falling apart?

Four

"Hey, beautiful." Christopher Black beamed. He was one of the most handsome African-American men that Amanda had ever met. His look was so sophisticated, downright suave that she often wondered if he spent hours in front of a mirror. He was also a very eligible bachelor.

The young ambitious architect owned his own firm, which was a rarity for someone only thirty-two. Women chased Christopher wherever he went, and his name frequently appeared in the Mile High City's society columns.

"Hi, Christopher. Come in. I'm sorry but I'm running late." Having decided to go out and try to forget she even knew Zachary McFadden, Amanda forced a smile as she said, "Just give me a few minutes to change. It has been one of those days."

"No problem. I'm early," Christopher said, shrugging out of his overcoat.

Quickly hanging it in the hall closet, she paused long enough to say, "Make yourself a drink. I won't be long," before heading down the hallway toward her bedroom.

"Our reservations are for eight-thirty. I'm sure they'll hold our table," he said confidently, watching the sway of her hips as she moved. "Can I help?"

"Very funny. I think I can manage on my own," she tossed from over her shoulder.

Closing the bedroom door firmly behind her, she was not about to let Zachary spoil her evening. Nor was she going to sit home brooding over his unwelcome intrusion into her world. She would deal with him later.

She changed into a mandarin-collared, cream silk jacquard dress with long sleeves that clung in all the right places, black silk cording forming the decorative frog accents along one shoulder. After stepping into black snakeskin pumps, she selected a small ebony snakeskin purse. With a cream cashmere shawl with black trim over her arm, she moved to the small vanity table tucked into the corner of the bedroom.

She chose square enameled earrings rather than the black highly faceted, oval onyx earrings surrounded with princess-cut diamonds her husband had sent her last Christmas. Pinning her hair up into a smooth coil at her crown, she let loose curls frame her face.

It was while she was touching up her makeup that she noticed the envelope propped against the mirror. Her name was written in bold masculine script. Her hands were far from steady as she unfolded the single sheet inside.

Sugar, sorry that I missed you. I'm having dinner with Brad. Have a nice evening. See you later. It was signed *Zach.*

A sharp sound of exasperation slipped out. There wasn't one word of explanation as to why his things were in her closet. Anyone reading it would assume it was an ordinary note from a husband to his wife, explaining his absence for a few hours.

Only there was nothing remotely ordinary about her marriage to Zachary. And if he thought for a single minute that he could waltz into her home any time he chose, he was dead wrong. Just wait until she saw him. She had a few things to say to him.

"Amanda? It's quarter past eight," her guest called from outside her door.

"Be right out, Chris." She smiled as she applied a vibrant red lipstick, knowing how much he hated the shortened version of his name. It probably took him longer to get ready for an evening out than it normally took her. Good grief, she was being nasty.

Christopher was not the problem. She had been unconsciously comparing him to another man with a quick easy smile that made the small lines near his ebony eyes crinkle and whose voice was deep and gravelly.

It was Zachary's quick wit, his relaxed manner that was so disarming. Clothes did not define him. He was the same whether he wore a pair of old jeans and a cotton shirt or a beautifully tailored tuxedo made especially for him to a charity ball. He possessed the rare ability of being comfortable with himself.

"Why, Zach? Why are you doing this?" she mumbled aloud.

"Darling, did you say something?"

Startled, she realized she had forgotten all about Christopher.

"I'm ready." She forced a smile as she opened her door. She had to work to hide her discomfort that Christopher was waiting on the other side of her bedroom door.

"It was well worth the wait," he crooned, leaning over to place a kiss on her cheek, but she moved so swiftly past him that his lips barely grazed her skin.

"Let's get going. My portfolio is on the hall table," she said as she opened the closet and took out her black velvet evening coat.

She flushed when she looked inside for his coat. She had been so upset when he arrived that she had hardly given him more than a token glance.

Holding a soft black leather man's overcoat, she asked, "Is this yours?"

"No," Christopher said sharply, causing her to really look at him.

No, that couldn't be his since he wore a brown three-piece suit. She quickly replaced the leather to hold out a dark brown fine wool overcoat.

"How about this one?" she asked, hoping to appear unconcerned that he now knew there were several men's coats in her closet.

"Thanks," he said tightly, accepting the garment without voicing the obvious. He held her coat for her, then draped her shawl around her shoulders before following her out, her heavy leather case in his hand.

It was not until they were in the car on the way to the restaurant that he asked, "Whose clothes are those, Amanda? I did not realize there was someone new in your life. What happened to that estranged husband of yours?"

She whipped her head around to glance at him. Having to put up with even one possessive male this day was more than enough for her. She was not about to take on another, especially when he had no rights where she was concerned.

"I don't believe it's any of your business as to who I choose to sleep with," she snapped.

Her response set the tone for the evening. Although pleasant, she was all business, refusing to so much as joke with him. She showed him the sketches she had done for the two houses he was currently renovating, and jotted down the changes he wanted in a small notebook. She politely thanked him for two new clients.

"There is no need for you to thank me. Your work speaks for itself. The clients insisted that only you could complete what you start." Frowning, Christopher asked, "Are you sure I can't tempt you with dessert? There is no need for us to rush."

Amanda quietly said, "Thanks, but no." The thought of what was waiting for her at home was reason enough for her to leave.

"Darling, I know I owe you an apology. I had no right to make that remark in the car, regardless of my interest in you. You're a beautiful woman. And I was jealous. I don't like you seeing other men."

"I've made no secret of the fact that I'm married." She sighing tiredly. Evidently the lack of sleep and stress of the day's events were catching up with her. "I've had a very full day. Please, take me home."

"Coffee?" he prompted.

"None for me."

She was more irritated than angry. There was only one man who had the ability to make her boil with fury. She was not looking forward to the fight ahead of her. And there was no doubt in her mind that she would have an argument on her hands when it came to getting her point across to her arrogant husband.

Neither of them said much during the long drive back to her place. Christopher broke the silence when he pulled into a parking space close to the entrance of her building. "Darling, won't you accept my apologies? Can't we continue our friendship?"

Amanda, absorbed in wondering if Zachary had returned to the condo while she was away, glanced at Christopher. "What did you say?"

Christopher repeated his request, ending with, "We work well together."

She did not bother waiting for him to open her door. She got out of the car and started toward the entrance.

They were in the elevator when he asked, "Why are you so angry? I simply asked you a question."

"We're business associates, nothing more. Christopher, if you prefer to take your business elsewhere, I understand. But I have never led you to believe there could be more between us. It would be best if we met from now on at my office. That way there won't be any cause for misunderstanding."

"Don't punish me. Please, don't let what happened earlier come between us. Can I come in for a quick drink so we can talk this over?"

They had reached her door by this time. Searching in her purse for her key, she was not looking at him. "Evidently you didn't hear what I said?" Quite frankly, she was too tired to consider even a moment more of his company.

He reached out to caress her cheek. "I heard everything. You have just had a very bad day. I certainly understand that. It has been . . ."

Before she could locate her key the door opened. Amanda was not the only one who looked surprised. Christopher took a hasty step back from the taller, broader man who filled the doorway.

"Hey, pretty girl. Forget your key?" Zachary smiled, showing even white teeth.

Before she could answer, Zachary leaned forward to brush her mouth with his own. When he lifted his head, she inhaled quickly, struggling to catch her breath. She missed the hard assessing look the two men exchanged.

"Good evening. I'm Zachary McFadden, Amanda's husband." He offered his hand.

Christopher, having recovered his composure, shook hands. "Christopher Black. Look, I think I should be going."

"Nonsense. Come in, have a nightcap before you go." His invitation surprised them all. "Did you have a pleasant evening, sugar?" He took her coat as well as Christopher's.

After retrieving her portfolio from Christopher and placing it on the armchair in the foyer, she managed to smile as if nothing unusual were happening.

"Yes, how was yours?"

Zachary had changed into navy wool trousers and a pale blue cashmere crew-neck sweater that seemed to enhance his dark good looks. She tried to ignore her awareness of him as he clasped a hand around her waist and urged her into the living room.

"Have a seat, Chris," Zachary said. Giving Amanda an easy smile, he then said, "How much fun can I have without you?" He placed a kiss on her nape before she could walk away.

She could not suppress a shiver as she sank gratefully onto the sectional sofa.

"What will you have, Chris?" Zachary asked.

"Scotch, if you have it. Neat." Christopher took a seat across from Amanda in one of the armchairs.

"Sugar?" Zachary asked. "White wine?" His eyes danced with mischief.

"Sparkling water with lime, please," she said, eyeing him suspiciously. He was up to something, that much she was certain, and enjoying himself in the process.

"I understand from what my brothers have told me, Chris, that you've made quite a name for yourself." Zachary handed the other man his drink before he gave Amanda hers and seated himself beside her. "You've designed some impressive houses around the city. And the houses you have renovated, I understand, are something to be proud of."

"Thank you." Christopher flashed a relaxed smile.

"I only speak the truth. Have you considered branching out?" Zachary paused before he quizzed, "Designing condominiums, office complexes and shopping malls?"

Amanda noted the amusement quirking Zachary's mouth.

"Why do you ask?" Christopher asked with apparent surprise.

Zachary said, "My brothers and I are looking for a new architect to design the resort complex we are interested in building in Florida. The architect we originally hired was taken ill and can't take on the project."

"I don't understand. I thought you were a rancher?"

"You didn't tell him who I am, sugar?" Zachary quirked a black brow.

Amanda said tightly, "I did not think it was important. My relationship with Christopher has nothing to do with you, Zach."

"Your relationship with any man has everything to do with me, Mandy," Zachary told her quietly. He smiled at Christopher when he said, "I'm a rancher, but my brothers and I jointly own McFadden Realty."

Annoyed that Christopher's surprise seemed to give Zachary an enormous amount of satisfaction, Amanda had to bite her lip to remain silent.

"I take it you've heard of us?"

"Naturally. Who in this part of the country hasn't? I didn't connect the company to Amanda." Christopher looked as if his favorite lollipop had been snatched out of his reach. He rushed to say, "I can assure you, nothing personal is going on between myself and Amanda. Our relationship is entirely a business one."

She looked from the contents of her glass in time to see a look of concern on Christopher's face and a smirk on her husband's. She did not know which one she wanted to smack more. It was pointless to try and warn Christopher that

Zachary was making a fool of him. Zachary was merely dangling a carrot under Christopher's nose.

"I'm well aware of that, Chris. If I thought you had a personal interest in my wife, you would be out on your ear. You see, where my wife is concerned, I can be a jealous man."

Amanda did not utter a sound. She was too angry to trust what might come out of her mouth. She glared at her husband, thoroughly infuriated with his manipulations.

"You've made yourself clear. And I know how you feel. If Amanda was my wife, I'd feel the same way," Christopher said, making no effort to even so much as look at his hostess.

She was losing what little respect she had for Christopher. Not twenty minutes ago he had declared his very personal interest in her. Apparently, his career was his number-one consideration.

"Good," Zachary said with a grin. "Now about that complex in Florida. Why don't you call my secretary tomorrow to set up an appointment with my brothers and me? Who knows? It may prove mutually satisfactory." He handled the other man with finesse, so much so that Christopher did not seem to recognize what was right in front of his face.

"Yes, I will do that." Christopher beamed.

"You don't mind traveling?" Zachary asked.

"Not in the least."

"Wonderful. Our sites are all over the world, although we tend to develop more property in the southwestern portion of the country."

"That's not a problem. I think I should be going." Christopher rose to his feet. He offered his hand. "Thank you, Mr. McFadden." The prospect of working for such a prosperous and well-established firm would be a huge boost to a small firm.

Zachary stood, shaking hands.

"Good night, Christopher. Thanks for a delightful evening. We must do it again, soon.'' Amanda's smile was enticing, deliberately taunting both men.

To her amazement, Christopher's gaze swiftly moved from her to Zachary. He nervously shifted from one foot to the other as he waited for the other man's response.

Zachary said casually, ''I'll see Chris out, sugar. Be right back.''

Zachary did not try to hide his amusement when he closed the door behind the other man. In fact, he knew it had mushroomed into a roguish grin by the time he returned to the living room.

''Christopher is certainly no fool. He dove for that offer like a hog after a bushel of corn. Is he any good?''

''Does it matter?''

''I won't hire him if he doesn't know his business.''

''He's good.''

Zachary watched her closely. Her entire body had seemed to bristle with anger. She sat with arms folded over her heaving breast, her legs crossed at the knee while one foot swung agitatedly back and forth.

He was prepared for an argument but none was forthcoming. Evidently, she had more important matters on her mind than her business associate's ambitions.

He teased, ''Where is your sense of humor? Your friend and I both got what we wanted. Surely, you aren't angry because I offered him a job?'' When she glared at him without bothering to respond, he walked over and ran a finger soothingly down her cheek to the tip of her oval chin. ''The choice was his. He could have refused.''

Disturbed by her continued silence, he assured her, ''You won't lose business because of him, you know. Your work stands on its own merit.''

Even though she was pleased by the compliment, she

pulled away from his caressing touch. Her voice was edged with a certain amount of bitterness when she said, "Don't touch me!"

Clenching his jaw, he had to struggle not to show his emotions. He knew she was upset with him. He had expected no less from her. Nevertheless he was hurt when she flinched away from him.

He said as evenly as he could manage, "Perhaps a little music will raise the temperature in here. If I'm not mistaken I'd say it's below zero."

He went to the open armoire that also housed the stereo system and a selection of CDs. Soon the mellow, warming tones of piano and saxophone filled the electrically charged atmosphere.

When he faced her, she looked directly into his eyes. Her chin raised a notch when she said, "Why are you here, Zach? What are your things doing in my closets . . . in my bedroom?"

There was not a single doubt in his mind that Amanda really did not want to hear his answer. He wondered if she would ever be ready for the unvarnished truth. She had built so many defenses around her heart . . . so many against him that he doubted his own ability to reach her. Unfortunately that was only part of the problem.

He had been waiting an eternity for her to accept him as not only her husband but also her lover. This past year had not exactly been easy for him. It had taken all his resolve to keep his word and give her the time she requested. He had slept alone for nearly a year, longing for her . . . needing her. Each morning he awoke feeling more alone and needy than the day before. Yet, he had kept his word.

Her little anniversary surprise had changed all that. Those papers had simultaneously crushed him and freed him from his promise. Amanda was determined to put off seeing him. And he knew she was interested in one thing, fortifying herself against every single tender emotion she had for him. He was not about to let that happen.

"Zach," she persisted, "I asked why you're here."

"You're here, pretty girl. That should be answer enough."

"That's it!" Her dark eyes shot daggers at him.

"Yeah," he said evenly, folding his arms over his broad chest.

"That's not good enough." She glared at him. "Zachary McFadden, did you hear anything I said to you at lunch? I don't want this marriage." Amanda practically screamed, "You have no right to be here!"

With tightly clenched teeth and hands balled at his sides, it took him a moment before slowing his breathing, thus easing his heart rate enough that he could start thinking with his head instead of reacting to his emotions.

When he spoke, he chose his words with care. "Who has more right? Christopher Black? That clown could barely keep his hands off you. If I hadn't opened that door when I did—"

"Christopher has nothing to do with you moving into my home," she interrupted, jumping to her feet. "Zach, this is about the two of us and you know it." She began pacing back and forth, then finally came to a stop in front of him.

He could not stop himself from taking note of how utterly beautiful she was in her fury. Her chin was raised, her small nostrils flared daintily, her full breasts strained against the confines of her dress. But this was not about his desire for her. It went deeper than physical need.

She was as essential to him as the air that filled his lungs and the food that nurtured his body. She was vital to his well-being and he was not about to stand idly by and watch her walk out of his life. He had never run away from a challenge in his life. And he was not about to start now.

"You're right. It's about the two of us. Did you really think I would quietly go along with your plans? Think again.

It ain't gonna happen. I've had enough of waiting for you to honor our marriage vows.''

He ran a hand restlessly over his hair before he said with a scowl, "I was a damn fool ever to agree to it in the first place. You're not the only one who lost someone important to them this past year. Mandy, I not only lost my baby and my mentor, but I also lost my wife."

They stared at each other for a time.

When she spoke her voice was just above a whisper. "Zach, what are you trying to do to me?"

"Do, Mandy?" he quizzed. Zachary pulled her into his arms, molding her soft body against his hard length. His face was so close to hers that he could feel her heat through their clothes. He ran a soothing hand up and down her back as he said against her hair, "You haven't given me or our marriage a chance. I'm not walking away until you can convince me otherwise."

She sighed heavily, allowing herself a moment more in his arms. Pushing herself away, she said, "Zach, this isn't some sports game we're discussing here. This is my life! I won't stand for it. Do you hear me!"

Five

"No doubt everyone on this floor can hear you," he said dryly.

"Zach? You can't do this."

Although he had allowed her to move away from him, he followed her across the room. "It isn't that hard to understand. In fact, it's downright simple. I intend to honor the commitment I made to you on our wedding day. I'm keeping my word." He ran a trembling hand over his jaw. "Everything happens for a reason. The pregnancy and our marriage were not planned. Even though I was also hurting I gave you the time you asked for. Can you give me less?"

Tears filled Amanda's dark eyes. She bit her bottom lip as if to hold back a tremor. She swallowed before she said, "That's not fair. You're trying to make me feel guilty. I won't let you."

"You have not let me be your husband . . . your lover. Can you honestly tell me you have no feelings for me?"

"We tried to make it work. You know we did! But it all fell apart." Her hands were trembling as she wiped the moisture from her face with the back of her hand.

Zachary quickly eliminated the space separating them. His eyes bore into hers. "We didn't try at all. You living in Denver and me on the ranch is not trying."

"You agreed to the separation."

"I agreed to give you time to get over Jake's and our baby's deaths." He walked to the desk and took out the envelope she had delivered to him that morning. His voice was rough with temper when he said, "I never agreed to this." He tore it in half, then in half again before he threw the pieces down. "Hell, no!"

She slowly backed away as if she was afraid of him. She was quiet for a time, as if she was giving him time to quiet his temper, and also to ease her own discomfort.

Although she looked as if she was frightened, she said, "I thought you would welcome having your freedom back. We can't go on the way we have. It's no way to live. You're a virile man. Aren't you tired of living like a monk?"

"I feel as if I should thank you for not insulting me by assuming I would go to another woman for what you won't give me," he snapped.

She closed her eyes and said, "Stop it!"

"Stop what?"

"Zach, we don't love each other, not like we should."

His voice was filled with bitterness when he said, "Mandy, I have never stopped loving you. When did you stop loving me?"

"You know what I mean." She turned her back on him, unable to bear the pain she saw in his eyes. Moving back to the sofa, she sank into the soft cushions, kicking off her shoes before she tucked her legs under her.

"I'm afraid I don't. What exactly did you mean?"

"I've always been able to count on you, been able to talk things over with you. Now all that has changed. Zach, you're not the same . . . I'm not the same. Why must everything be so darn complicated?"

He stood in front of her, his long muscular legs braced apart. The veins in his throat pulsated when he said quietly, "It all changed the day you became mine. You didn't answer me. When did you stop caring about me?"

She looked at him, wondering how he managed to shatter her defensives. Reaching for his hand, she brought his work-roughened palm to her cheek, moving it against her face.

"Oh, Zach, you know I love you. I always have. Why else did I call you when I found out my grandfather was dying? I knew you would come that night. I knew I could count on you, trust you with my fears . . ."

"And I betrayed that trust when I lost control and took you that same night," he rasped painfully.

"You make it sound as if it was rape. It was consensual and you know it."

"I hate the way I took advantage of your vulnerability. When we kissed, my brain stopped functioning and my body took over." He sighed wearily. "It was as if my common sense suddenly shut down. All I was thinking about was how much I wanted you and how long I'd waited to have you in my arms. Nothing else seemed to matter." Zachary was scowling when he said, "I ended up hurting you."

"No," she corrected. After taking a deep breath, she continued, "We were both hurting that night. You were as upset as I was, by the possibility of losing Granddaddy. And we made the mistake of looking for comfort in bed. There was no blame."

"You ended up pregnant. If I hadn't . . ." His voice trailed away before he cleared his throat and went on to say, "I talked you into marrying me even though you wanted to raise the baby on your own.''

"Our marriage may have been a mistake, but I never, not once, regretted that precious baby we made that night. How could I?''

The pain from that loss was unmistakable, and it was something they both felt. It was there in dampness in both their eyes.

Zachary broke the silence when he said, "Thank you.''

"We've both been hurt. I want to put an end to the hurting. Yes, I love you, but I'm not in love with you and you're not in love with me. I can't give you what you need.'' Her eyes were like twin pools of misery as she stared up at him.

He sank down onto his haunches so he could study her beautiful face. His voice was raw with emotions when he asked, "What do you think I want, pretty girl?''

"Oh, Zach, you're such a wonderful man and you need a woman who can love you the way you deserve to be loved.'' After clearing her throat she gave voice to her thoughts. "You, my love, need someone who can challenge you mentally, as well as make love to you without anything getting in the way. I'm not that woman.'' She stroked his cheek. "Please, honey, accept this for both our sakes.'' As difficult as it was to put into words, she managed to whisper, "You know as well as I do that I can't satisfy you sexually.''

Zachary could not believe what he'd just heard. How could she even say those things to him? It was as if she had not been there with him when they made love that first time. It was crazy.

He had lost it that night for one reason . . . it was Amanda in his arms. She was what made it earth-shatteringly sweet for him. Losing control was something that had never happened before with him, not even when he was an untried kid. All he could think about that night was burying himself deep inside her. Their friendship had not entered into the equation. He almost laughed with self-mockery. That was the trouble, he had done very little thinking at all.

"You, Amanda Ann Daniels McFadden, satisfy me more than any woman has ever come close to doing. I can't get the sweet taste of your skin out of my mind. Nor can I forget how it feels to be inside your delectable body. No, sugar, it's not possible for me to forget how perfectly you gloved me. Believe me, when I say I tried. But I can't stop wanting and needing you."

He chuckled wryly. "One thing you've never done is bore me . . . far from it. You're wrong. Mandy, you are the one who challenges me in every way. I have no desire to replace you in my bed or my life."

"Then you must be planning on becoming a monk."

"No." He shook his head. "But no one else can possibly take your place. I'm willing to wait for sexual fulfillment. If nothing else, I know how to bide my time."

"I told you I can't—"

"It happened . . . it can happen again. Mandy, give us the time we need to live together in order to give our marriage a chance."

"Zach, how long are you willing to wait? A year? Two? Perhaps ten? Come on! We're both entitled to more from life."

"It took years for me to prove to my father that the ranch could be profitable. And it was worth the backbreaking work and the never-ending hours of blood and sweat to make it happen. I'm not afraid of a challenge, Mandy. Hell, I waited almost six years after Dad's death until Roger and Brad were able to take over the business before I could return to the ranch full-time."

"But—"

"No buts. I'm prepared to invest my time and energy in

making our marriage a real one." Watching her closely, he went on to say, "You're worth any inconvenience it may cause me to live in Denver with you."

"Zach—"

"No, let me finish. I've given you nearly a year to get over the losses in our lives. Now I'm asking you to give me that same consideration. You owe me that much."

Amanda needed to put some space between them. She needed to think. She walked to the French doors, parted the drapes, opened the doors and stepped out onto the balcony. Cold air rushed over her as she gazed out into the star-filled sky.

She hugged herself while wondering how she could do what he asked. Even as a girl she had never entertained romantic fantasies. How could she even formulate those kinds of thoughts when her earliest memories were of watching her father inflict pain on her mother?

She wanted no part of love that could also hurt and destroy. Zachary was not a fairy-tale prince sent to sweep her off her feet. He was an active man, physically fit, big and very strong. He was also warm and generous. She had no doubt in her mind that he would never hurt her physically . . . emotionally was an entirely different issue.

He could hurt her so much more, if she allowed herself to fall in love with him. She had lost control of herself in his arms. Forgetting everything but how he made her feel. Deep inside she feared she was capable of loving the way her mother had once loved her father . . . unconditionally. She turned at the sudden sound of the door behind her opening.

Zachary draped her shawl over her shoulders before he shoved his hands into his pockets. He said close to her ear, "Mandy, I'm asking for a chance."

"We tried before . . ." She broke off, unable to finish. Tears spilled down her brown cheeks. She averted her face while silently praying that Zachary would not suspect she was referring to the day she miscarried. She didn't want him to think she blamed herself for the loss.

When she shivered, he caught her hand and urged her back inside. He closed the doors. "You're freezing."

"I'm . . ." She could not go on.

Amanda encircled his waist, rested her cheek against his chest. Zachary simply held her, one hand moving over her back, the other hand slowly removing the hairpins from her hair to massage the tight muscles in her nape. Amanda did not protest until he kissed the sensitive place behind her ear before he tongued the lobe, then took it into his mouth to suckle.

"Zach . . ."

"It's okay, sugar." His mouth followed the curve of her jawline, then trailed up to her soft trembling parted lips, covering them with his. He pressed tender kisses, one after the other.

When Amanda's lips opened beneath his, Zachary groaned huskily, stroking her tongue with his own. He eased into the depths of her mouth to relish the sweetness within.

"Sweet, so sweet," he murmured against her lips.

Reeling from the impact of his hot, seductive kisses, she couldn't stop the way a part of her responded to the sensuous assault on her senses. Without conscious thought, she moved deeper into his arms, unwittingly seeking more of his caresses as he moved his hands up and down her silk-covered arms, then moved them down the slope of her back.

Zachary gathered her against him, pressing her soft, full breasts into the warmth of his chest. Her breasts seemed to swell, the nipples suddenly pebbly hard, boring into his chest.

"Mandy . . ." he said huskily, into her ear, moving the hard proof of his arousal against her.

Suddenly horrified by what she had let happen, Amanda

pushed against his chest, struggling to put some distance between them. She had been too close, dangerously so of losing her head. She knew better than to let her guard down with him. She had paid dearly for giving in to the strength of his masculine charms.

Zachary caught her hand, holding on to her. "Pretty girl . . .''

Amanda knew how close she was to giving in. She yanked her hand away as if she could not bear his touch a second longer. "I won't sleep with you. Not now, not ever. You know how much I hate sex!"

Zachary quirked a black brow. "That's what you prefer to believe but we both know that's not true."

Lifting her chin, she said, "You were there. You know what a mess I made of our marriage. Zach, you did all the giving and I had nothing to give in return." She shuddered. "Do you have any idea how selfish that made me feel? Knowing that I'm empty inside?" Her eyes were quickly flooded with tears. She brushed them away impatiently.

"That's not how it was between us. You were going through a very difficult time. An unplanned pregnancy, a new husband with his own set of demands, not to mention a very sick grandparent. Plus you had a business to run while commuting over a hundred miles a day. It was too much. You were overwhelmed."

He shook his head. "You're not frigid, sugar. You feel . . . you feel things very deeply. Perhaps that's what frightens you? It certainly is worth considering."

"You're wrong," she said while wondering if he were correct.

No matter what was said it did not change the facts. There was no question that she was her mother's daughter. Her mirror confirmed that every blasted day. But it was up to her. Amanda was the only one who could save herself from her mother's tragic fate. She couldn't afford to take any risks. It was best that she not crave a man's touch, not love him so much that she could not imagine life without him in it.

She whispered, "I'm not like . . ." She stopped abruptly, then said, ". . . that." She had nearly said she was not like her mother.

"Just because you don't want those emotions does not mean they are not there. Mandy, listen to me. I'm not inexperienced, I know when a woman wants me. And, baby, I know you felt that desire in the past . . . you will again if you let it happen. Stop fighting me. Just let it be."

Amanda was so agitated that she was practically wringing her hands. "Leave it alone. I *really* don't want to talk about this anymore." Her entire body was stiff with dread.

"Okay . . . okay." He held his hands palm up in front of him before his voice softened and slowed. "Calm down. Let's deal with one issue at a time."

She scowled at him. Evidently the fact that she said "hate" left a bitter taste in his mouth because he flatly refused to accept her claim. She certainly needed no reminder that he had enjoyed women.

Over the years he seemed to go from one empty-headed beauty to the next. Yet, he expected her to believe all that changed? Ple-e-ease. She was not so naive that she believed Zachary McFadden had done without sex during their lengthy separation. What did he think, she was stupid? His sex drive was too strong for her to swallow that for a minute.

Amanda quickly pushed the unpleasant thought away, unwilling to remember how she used to tease him about his active love life before their involvement.

A man's sexual appetite didn't change when he married, did it? Not hardly, she sniffed. Now that Zachary's manly hunger was directed at her, Amanda knew she would never be able to cope with the full force of his masculinity.

"Mandy, caring about each other is not a weakness. It can't destroy you. You certainly can't die from it."

Making an effort to square her shoulders before she said, "It has been an extremely long day, Zach. We can settle this in the morning." She could not quite meet his gaze when she mumbled, "I will make up the daybed in my studio for you." She didn't bother to glance back as she headed down the central hall.

"Thanks, but that won't be necessary. From now on I'll be sleeping with you." He had been following the seductive sway of her hips, until she stopped abruptly and whirled to face him.

"I told you I'm not having sex with you, Zachary."

"I did not ask you to. But we will sleep in the same bed. I'm asking for the same amount of time I gave you, Mrs. McFadden."

"Don't . . . do this to me," she pleaded with him. "If I could sleep with you, I would never have spoken to my attorney about divorce."

"We sleep together from now on. I won't try to make love to you for now. But I'm not about to give up . . . not by a long shot."

"We're discussing my life . . . my sanity. Damn you, Zachary. I won't have sex with you . . . ever."

A muscle jumped in his cheek when he said, "I'm not giving up on us. We stay together until we're both convinced, one way or the other. We owe it to ourselves to try." He was looking into her eyes when he said, "Trust me, Mandy. I won't hurt you, not ever. Now go to bed. I'll be in later, after you're asleep. You won't even know I'm there."

Amanda was not sure if his tone had been deeply soothing or she was too tired to fight anymore. Either way when he gently turned her toward the bedroom door, she did not protest.

Once she was inside, she closed the door behind her a

leaned back against its solid support. She wondered if she had actually felt his lips on the back of her neck or if she had imagined it.

Seeking the comfort of a hot scented bath, Amanda tried not to think, concentrating on the mundane task. More importantly, she tried not to anticipate what the next hour might bring.

Zachary asked for her trust. Something she had always given him without conscious thought. She had trusted him to have patience with her . . . to teach her how to dive, to teach her how to fish and cook over an open campfire.

She had also trusted him to help convince her grandfather that she was old enough to move out on her own. And she had trusted him to keep his word that he would not contact her when he agreed to the separation. Was this any different? Could she trust him with her body and her heart? She sighed wearily. Unfortunately there weren't any easy answers.

"What to do? What to do?" she grumbled to herself, scrubbing her skin so hard it hurt.

Finally, she hauled herself out of the tub to wrap herself in a dark green bath sheet. After brushing her hair hurriedly she braided it into a single French plait and pulled on a cream-colored satin nightshirt over her head. The lace ruffled-edge hem stopped at the knee and the wide sleeves were gathered into cuffs and edged with lace.

Leaving the bathroom as neat and tidy as she had found it, Amanda crossed the thick carpet on bare feet. For a long moment, she stared longingly at the queen-size bed before turning her back on it and going soundlessly to the door. Opening it a crack, she listened.

The soft melodic tones of Tracy Chapman's "Matters of the Heart" filtered through the otherwise silent apartment. ﹍﹍ made her way quietly into her home office.

﹍﹍lling off the floral coverlet and placing the back ﹍﹍ the floor, she found everything she needed in the cupboard. Quickly making up the single bed, she shivered as she snuggled between cool crisp sheets and beneath a single blanket. Closing her eyes, she forced herself to concentrate on nothing more stimulating than regulating her breathing. She didn't need flannel sheets or a down comforter, both of which were on the other bed.

Zachary was a bright guy. He wouldn't have any trouble figuring out where she was or why she had opted not to sleep beside him. It would take more than a kiss on her nape to convince her to attempt a reconciliation. He might not realize it but she knew him well enough to know that he'd never be happy in a sexless marriage. She could not even imagine such a thing.

He needed a warm, sensuous woman who would be willing to turn a blind eye to his domineering male arrogance and his mother's need to be first in her sons' lives. She would never be that woman.

Even if she were able to someday overcome her fear of being dependent on a man for her well-being, she would never give up her career. She had worked very hard to make a success of her business.

She didn't want to make her home on a vast isolated ranch in the mountains. She simply could never be his adoring sex kitten or a mealymouthed daughter-in-law to his domineering mother. Not ever!

Curling into a tight ball, she wrapped her arms around her raised knees. She lay on her side with her back to the door, trying to make herself relax rather than listening for his footsteps.

He could stay up all night listening to music if he liked. From now on he was the enemy. They no longer shared any type of connection. Their friendship was a thing of the past.

She had made the biggest mistake of her life when she had married her best friend and because of it he was lost to her. Brushing at slow trickling tears, she pressed her face into the pillow.

Even though he could be so stubborn, she could not stop herself from worrying that she was not being fair to him. Was she being selfish, yet again? The question whirled repeatedly inside her head. She had hurt him once today by sending the divorce papers on their wedding anniversary. There was no doubt about the hurt she saw in his eyes again this evening.

She could not count the number of times he had been there for her. Whatever she needed or whenever she needed him, he had been there. She had always been secure in the knowledge that he believed in her.

It had been Zachary who had flown to Denver to tell her that her grandfather had been hospitalized. He had taken her to Jake's bedside. He had been at her side as the once strong man had grown weaker and weaker.

He had also helped her find the courage within herself to face the fact that her grandfather was dying quickly and to respect his last wishes. Jake had not wanted to be hooked up to the machines that could prolong his life. He wanted to go quietly and peacefully while Amanda had not wanted to let him go.

Zachary had done all those things and more. He had arranged the wedding while she sat by her grandfather's side refusing to leave. She had lived in that hospital those last horrible weeks, leaving only on her wedding day at her grandfather's insistence.

In the warmth and comfort of her husband's arms, she had for once forgotten everything. She rediscovered the intensity of physical release. Zachary had taken her back to a world that was a kaleidoscope of colors and feelings, a place that left her temporarily content and tranquil. They found that magical place together, not once or even twice, but several times during that first night of marriage. But in the wee hours of the morning the hotel telephone had rung. Jake Daniels had died in his sleep.

The next few weeks were a nightmare for Amanda. As one day had run into the next, her only relief from the darkness of grief had been Zachary. He had been her tower of strength ... her best friend. He had made no sexual demands on her; in fact, he asked for nothing except to be at her side and to share her loss.

Her grandfather had left her his ranch and house, plus a sizable number of stocks and bonds. Amanda had cried when she heard the news, cried as she had not been able to do when she'd learned of his death or at his funeral. She had wept because her grandfather was lost to her ... the dear old man who had given her a home, but more important, Jake Daniels had loved her as much as she had loved him.

Less than a week after Jake's death, Amanda had suffered another devastating loss. While she had gone out riding alone, needing the solitude, her horse had stumbled and Amanda had been thrown. She had hit her head and lain there weak with pain, unable to rise, unable to summon help. When Zachary had found her hours later, she was barely conscious, numb with shock and grief, and very angry with fate ... with herself. So angry that she had shut herself off from everyone, especially Zachary.

She had never been able to share the pain of losing her baby, not even with her husband. He had reluctantly agreed to give her time to adjust to all the changes in her life. He had kept his promise not to see her or call her until she was ready.

Sighing unhappily, she found herself wondering if she could do this one thing for him. Could she give him the chance he asked for? Didn't she owe him that much?

Even though she did not like the high-handed way he had forced her into this dilemma, that did not change the facts as far as she was concerned. He deserved this chance, she thought, and she didn't have the heart to refuse to give it to him. The problem was, could she find the courage to follow this through?

In spite of how furious he had made her today, she still loved him. There was no doubt that her vulnerability to him would only escalate, considering the circumstances. How was she going to cope with the changes that were bound to take place? More important, how was she going to protect herself from making the same mistake that had led to her mother's destruction?

She was so lost in thought that she failed to hear the door open or him cross on bare feet to the daybed.

"Zach!" She jumped when she felt the hardness of his chest as his arms encircled her from behind.

"Scoot over," he grumbled.

Six

Amanda's nerve endings tingled with awareness as Zachary's hair-roughened thighs pressed against hers. He snuggled even closer to her, lying with his head on her pillow. His warm breath fanned her temple.

"What are you doing here?"

She nearly turned toward him but thought better of it at the last second. It was difficult enough with him at her back. His heat seeped through her nightshirt, warming her, while his clean male scent filled her nostrils. He smelled like the pine-scented soap he preferred.

Ignoring her question, he asked one of his own. "Why are you still awake? Have you been thinking about us?"

"What else?" she said around a weary sigh.

"Well?"

"My decision can wait. What are you doing in here with me?" Judging by his bare hair-roughened chest and limbs, she was afraid to find out just how little he was wearing. There was no mistaking the hard pressure of his erection against her back.

"I'm here to sleep, but now that's impossible until you tell me what you've decided."

"Did anyone, besides me, ever tell you that you're stubborn? In my opinion, that's your number-one character flaw. You really should do something about it, Zach."

"Your decision," he persisted.

"I owe you."

He did not say a word, and, unfortunately, she could not see his scowl.

"Now will you kindly remove yourself from this bed? Sex has no part of this agreement," she was quick to clarify.

His arms tightened around her. Then he said, "Where you're concerned, I can't afford to have a hell of a lot of pride. We've both said enough for one night. Let's get some sleep."

"You shouldn't be here."

He yawned. "It's late. Now be good and shut up." Running his hands down her arms, he said, "You're shivering. Cold?"

She had been before he had climbed into her bed. Now that his vibrant warmth surrounded her, she felt as if she were encased in a furnace.

"Why aren't you in the big bed?"

"Big? Hardly. It's too short, like this one. But I can survive a few nights until we can buy a king-size bed. Now let me sleep. I don't know about you, but I have to get up early tomorrow."

"Zach!"

"Will you be still! Or are you trying to arouse me? I assure you, if you keep wiggling your behind against me you're going to get more attention than you're interested in at the moment."

She stiffened. "I did not invite you in here."

He sighed heavily before answering, "You agreed to try. That means from now on we sleep together. Now if you aren't comfortable here, we can try the sofa in the den or the kitchen floor . . . I don't really care as long as I can get a few hours' shut-eye."

"Let me up, Zach. I'm not sharing this tiny bed with you."

His arms tightened around her, chuckling, "You chose this bed, pretty girl."

She was angry. Only, she was unsure whom she was angrier with, him or herself. When she decided to sleep here, she certainly had not planned on sharing the space.

"I mean it. Let me up," she said in a near panic. "I can't breathe with you smothering me this way. You're too big."

He rose without further protest, but before she could let out a sigh of relief, he gathered her up against his chest. He carried her into the other room.

"Zach . . ."

After he placed her unceremoniously on one side of the queen-size bed, he snapped, "We have an agreement." Going around to the opposite side, he climbed in, pulled the bedding up to his shoulders and turned his back on her. "Good night."

Zachary had never had a problem rising early. His internal alarm clock seldom caused him to oversleep. He sighed deeply, enjoying the feel of his wife in his arms. He would like nothing better than to stay right where he was. Sometime during the night, she had wrapped a shapely thigh and arm across his body. Her head rested on his shoulder.

His heavy shaft told him what he already knew, that it had been too long since he had been inside his woman. Nearly a year of celibacy had taken its toil on his self-control. He had always prided himself on being a man ruled by his head, not by his penis.

Amanda had agreed to give their marriage a chance. For that he was overwhelmingly grateful. He also suspected she had no idea how badly he wanted to make their marriage a real one. He would not entertain the possibility of failure.

Her dinner with Christopher Black had certainly thrown him, although he had recovered quickly. He was not about to let jealousy divert him from his ultimate goal. He wanted more than a real chance to make their marriage work. He also wanted her love.

He knew it would take all of his resolve not to rush her, but to give her the time she needed. He could not afford to let his own nagging doubts interfere with what had to be done. And he hoped she would not keep him waiting too long.

He suppressed a groan as she snuggled even closer. Her soft, satin-covered breasts pressed into his bare chest and her silky thigh caressed his skin. He swore beneath his breath, knowing he had to put some space between them now or end up breaking his promise. Careful not to awake his wife, he gingerly eased away and soundlessly padded across the carpet into the bathroom.

Amanda woke with a start, uncertain of what had disturbed her. A glance at the bedside clock had her scowling in disbelief. Four-thirty! It was far too early for her to be awake. She jumped when the closet door opened and Zachary walked into the bedroom.

"Sorry, didn't mean to wake you," he said quietly, coming over to stand beside the bed.

"You scared me," she accused in a breathless rush. "Are you leaving?" she asked, taking in his jeans and denim work shirt. He carried a pair of well-worn cowboy boots.

"Yeah. Some of us don't get to sleep in." He dropped into one of the armchairs near the windows to pull on the boots.

Covering a yawn, she wiggled beneath the goose-down comforter. "You call seven sleeping in?" she asked, referring to the time her clock was set to go off.

He stood and began tucking his shirt into the waistband of his jeans. "I do." He grinned as he walked over and leaned down and tucked a wayward curl behind her ear.

"Please, don't. Touching was not part of our arrangement." She shivered, reacting as if he had done far more than move her hair out of her eyes.

He stiffened momentarily, then without a trace of emotion asked, "Cold?"

"Freezing. I suppose that was what woke me," she said, determined not to internalize the glimpse of hurt she thought she saw in his dark eyes.

"So I do have my uses," he pointed out. "I'll raise the thermostat before I leave."

"Thank you."

Her gaze moved up the length of his jean-clad thighs, lingering on the distinctly masculine bulge; then, as if realizing what she was doing, she blushed, quickly bringing her eyes upward, past his trim waist and wide chest and broad shoulders before she reached his eyes.

"You get up this early every morning?" She tried to remember what time he rose during the brief time they were first married. "Everybody I know is asleep at this hour. This is not the Circle-M."

He chuckled. "Tell me this isn't Jake's number-one cow girl talking." Then he leaned over to kiss her lips, but she turned her face and his lips grazed her cheek instead. "I've a ranch to run. I don't intend to change my job just because I've changed my address. You're not married to a businessman with regular nine-to-five hours, pretty girl. You got yourself a genuine cowpoke.''

He crossed to the dresser, pocketing his wallet and keys before strapping a leather-banded watch on his wrist.

When he moved toward the doorway, she said, "Wait . . ."

"I'm already late. Why don't you try to get some sleep while you still can or you're going to be too tired to go into the office? Don't hold supper for me. I'll probably be very late. Oh, do me a favor . . . buy a king-size bed.''

"Are you really going to commute back and forth between here and the ranch?''

"That's the plan. I brought a car yesterday so I can drive to the office, collect the chopper and fly back to the ranch. Tonight, I'll reverse the process. Get some rest.'' With that he was gone.

Amanda listened, wondering if she heard the refrigerator door close before she heard the front door closing. She sighed, then punched the pillow several times, trying to get comfortable. When that did not work, she began to take deep, slow breaths until she realized that she was breathing in his scent. She frowned, wondering if their bodies had touched during the night.

Her cheeks were hot when she recognized that she was on his side of the bed, cradling his pillow. Quickly scooting over, she decided he was right. What was needed was a much larger bed.

After tossing and turning for a while, she gave up trying and decided to use the time constructively. Armed with her laptop, a bulging portfolio and a large mug of strong black coffee, she spent the next few hours working in her home office. By the time she reached the downtown office at ten, she had already put in half a day's work.

She took time off at noon to go shopping for the new bed and bedding. Zachary was not the only one wanting to put some additional space between them. She paid extra for the assurance she did not have to spend another night worried that she might have slept in her husband's arms.

She also arranged to have her bed moved to her storage area in the condominium basement until she decided what to do about it. She left for home early, something that rarely happened. She could not relax until the new brass king-size bed was in place.

Later after a long shower, she changed into a pair of silk pajamas, brushed her hair and arranged it in a loose topknot. She prepared a simple meal of sweet potatoes baked with brown sugar and cinnamon, a leg of lamb and mixed salad greens.

As she ate, her eyes repeatedly went to the wall clock. She had to remind herself that she was not waiting up for Zachary. After preparing a plate for him, she covered it with clear plastic wrap, placed it and the rest of the leftovers in the refrigerator. After cleaning the kitchen, she curled up on the couch in the den with the latest Yolanda Joe novel. The trouble was she could not concentrate.

Around nine-thirty she gave up all pretense of reading and turned on the television to a program on the food channel. Even Emeril could not stop her from listening for the sound of a key in the lock.

She was wasting time speculating on whether Zachary would return or if he had changed his mind about staying in town with her. What did it matter? If anything, she should be relieved that he hadn't returned. She had not invited him to stay in the first place. They both were used to conducting separate lives. When they lost their baby, they'd lost their connection.

Not once during the past year had she wondered what he was doing or with whom. Well, that was not exactly accurate. She had thought of him. She just hadn't done anything about those thoughts. How could she when she no longer felt free to contact him?

In the past she would reach for the telephone, then remember that what he chose to do with his life no longer had anything to do with her. If he needed a woman for sexual reasons, she was the last person who should offer objections.

He didn't have to look far. His distant cousin, Barbara Hamilton, another member of the McFadden household, would do anything to please Zachary.

Stop this! She needed no reminders that she had no hold on her husband. There had been nothing sexual between the two of them since their wedding night.

Covering her face with her hands, she knew the last thing she needed to be doing was to worry about Zachary's sex life. They had lived apart for nearly a year.

Why had Zachary complicated things by moving in with her? Couldn't he see that his being here was a waste of time and emotion? Sighing tiredly, she decided that eventually he would have no choice but to accept that what they had didn't even come close to resembling a real marriage. Their unnatural situation could not begin to meet either one of their emotional needs.

How long could any red-blooded man put up with no sexual contact in his marriage? A month? Two? Perhaps six? Eventually, Zachary would have no other option but to accept what she had tried to make clear from the very beginning. She made a much better friend than wife. She hoped he realized this before it destroyed the respect and love they had always shared.

When the brass clock on the wall unit chimed ten times, she chewed her bottom lip, trying to remember his exact words that morning. Zachary said he would be late. But this late? What if something had happened to him? What if his helicopter had crashed? He could be lying dead somewhere and she would never know. Maybe she should turn to the all-news channel?

"Enough of this!" she scolded herself.

Nothing had happened. He knew how to take care of himself. He'd probably decided to have dinner with his family, then relax in the library with his mother and Barbara. Amanda had no difficulty visualizing Rebecca McFadden leaving the two dear hearts together.

His mother was too smart to openly matchmake. Oh, no. She would never risk discovery. Mrs. McFadden was like a slippery old fox, taking subtle steps toward her ultimate goal, replacing Amanda with Barbara as her daughter-in-law. Barbara was certainly no threat to Mrs. McFadden's matriarch position in the McFadden household, while Amanda was too independent to be controlled.

Amanda had no illusions concerning her mother-in-law. The woman couldn't stand her. His mother had come right out and accused her of getting pregnant in order to trap her oldest son.

Zachary must have inherited her determination. The woman was not about to give up on her plans. It was only a matter of time until the lady succeeded. In order to do that, her manipulations had to be subtle, done behind his back. He was too strong-willed to let anyone run his life, not even his beloved mother.

Fed up, Amanda reached for the telephone, then drew back her hand before she could lift the handset. No, she couldn't call. She didn't want him thinking she doubted him. Their agreement was less than a day old and they were both still feeling their way. What she needed was a distraction.

Perhaps she would call Peggy? No. This was the younger woman's time to be alone with her husband. Mrs. McFadden gave Roger and Peggy little enough privacy as it was. Besides, what could Amanda say? She was calling because she did not trust her husband?

"Hey, pretty girl," Zachary called from the foyer. "Where are you?"

"In the den," she called back.

There he was, his big frame filling the opened doorway. He dropped a kiss on her forehead before he sank into the armchair adjacent to the sofa, and stretched his long legs out in front of him.

"You look beat."

"Yeah," he said wearily, unbuttoning his shirt and running one hand tiredly over his chest.

Relief rushed over her. Even though he looked exhausted, he was back and well. The knowledge warmed her. She had to force her eyes away from his body.

"How was your day?"

"Good. Can I get you something?"

"A beer, but I can get it myself," he grumbled, with his head back and his eyes closed.

"Just stay there. I'll get it."

Amanda was in desperate need of a diversion. Suddenly, she was overwhelmed by his sheer masculinity. She was mumbling to herself long before she reached the kitchen. She had to stop, pull herself together before she really did something stupid. Zachary was just a man, no different than any other. But even as the thought raced through her head, she knew she was lying to herself.

There was nothing ordinary about Zachary McFadden . . . that in itself was becoming a real problem. She was aware of him in ways she would never have thought possible just a few days ago.

By the time she returned with the large glass mug of imported beer, she felt as if she was in control of her wayward thoughts. She placed it in his hand since he hadn't opened his eyes. "Here."

He grunted what she took to be thanks.

"Bad day?" she asked, beginning to feel sorry for the man.

"Mmm."

She did not give herself time to think about it, just reacted to his tiredness. Moving behind his chair, she began kneading the tense muscles in his neck and wide shoulders. As she massaged his bronze flesh, she smiled when he groaned.

"Feels good?"

"Oh yeah." He sighed, eyes closed. His deep voice had dropped even more, making it slow and sexy, causing her heart rate to quicken. When she finished he caught her hands, brought them to his lips before she could move out of reach. He placed a kiss in the center of each soft palm. "Please . . . don't stop."

Her hands were far from steady and she was afraid to touch him, again. She laughed. "Oh, no. I'm not going to spoil you." Deciding a change of topic was needed, she asked, "Have you eaten?"

"If you call a sandwich on my way to the chopper eating. No time," he said as he pulled off his work boots.

"What do you mean, no time? It's nearly eleven." Her hands settled on her hips.

"I know." He took a long sip of his drink, heavy lids covering his dark eyes, as he stretched comfortably back against the cushions. "I got back around six, went straight to the office. My brothers had a mound of work waiting for my okay."

"No wonder you're exhausted. What are you trying to do, kill yourself?" She didn't wait for him to answer. "While you're burning the midnight oil, both of your brothers are probably home relaxing. You shouldn't let them take advantage of the fact you're here in Denver."

He chuckled. "It's called payback. The only time I've shown my face in the office for most of the past year has been for board meetings." He shrugged. "I've even missed a few of those."

"That's no excuse for taking advantage of you. What?''

Zachary had been studying her. He sent her a slow, sexy grin. "Come here." When she didn't move, he snagged her hand and pulled her down onto his lap.

Seven

Before Amanda could form a protest, his kiss was warm, enticing as he enjoyed her soft, full lips. Zachary took his time, as he savored her sweetness. He didn't force her lips open, but he did trace her bottom lip with his tongue, causing a moan to rise in her throat and for her to unwittingly open for the hot caresses of his tongue.

She trembled, waiting for him to deepen the kiss even more, but he surprised her when he eased away. Amanda studied him, puzzled by his withdrawal.

He laughed throatily, before he said, ''No point in starting something I can't finish.''

She quickly got to her feet. ''Excuse me. I'll get your meal.''

Scowling, she hurried into the kitchen and tried to ignore the way her knees were shaking as she pulled out the covered plate from the refrigerator, placed it in the microwave and began setting the table. She whisked the freshly made salad dressing, filled a water glass . . . in short, did everything that she could think of that would take her mind off the man in her den. When the microwave's bell sounded Amanda jumped, then scolded herself, before she called him.

"Smells wonderful," he said, walking past her to the sink, and washed his hands before he sat down at the table. "Talk to me while I eat."

She nodded because she didn't trust herself to answer verbally. She was as nervous as a lovesick teenager on a first date. It made no sense.

"Did you go back to sleep?"

"No. After you left I tossed and turned until I finally gave up. So I got up and worked until it was time to get ready for the office."

She realized that she was disturbed by his withdrawal. Should she accept his explanation? Or was there another reason? Maybe he was tired of waiting? Who knew? The male libido was a total mystery to her.

Her experience with men was limited. Naturally she had dated over the years, but she managed to keep men at a distance . . . never letting any of them get but so close. She had only been intimate with one man, and that was Zachary.

Tonight, he hadn't prolonged the kiss nor had he taken it beyond a certain level. She couldn't stop herself from speculating on whether he was simply tired of her refusals. She should be grateful for his control. After all, it was what she wanted.

"Sorry I woke you this morning, pretty girl." His voice was like a deep, throaty caress.

"No need to apologize."

Eyeing his plate, he asked, "Did you make this?"

"Of course I did." She cocked a saucy brow. "What are you implying?"

"Not a thing. Just wondered if it was carryout." He still made no move to raise his fork.

"It's not carryout. Would you care to inspect the trash for boxes?"

He bowed his head, praying, "Lord, please help me." His dark lashes lifted toward the heavens before he cautiously raised his fork.

Hands on hips, she hissed, "Zachary McFadden. I don't believe you brought the good Lord into this. If you have something to say about my food, be a man. Just say it."

"Now, sugar . . ."

"Don't act innocent with me . . . you . . . you low-down rotten snake. I know what you're going to say. And I don't want to hear it. If you don't eat I—I—I—I . . ." Having failed to come up with something really horrible to threaten him with, she pointed a menacing finger at him.

Zachary roared with laughter. "Mandy, calm down. I'm hungry enough to give it a try, but my memory is long." He grinned sheepishly. "Wait until I tell Roger you had nerve enough to cook me a meal."

Exasperated, she warned, "If you don't taste it, I'll never speak to you again. Or I will be the one telling Roger who hid his dress boots on his and Peggy's wedding day."

"Now that is wrong. Okay, okay, I'll keep my mouth shut. Mandy, don't pretend you don't understand my reluctance. Girl, you damn near killed me the last time you fed me. That's something a man never forgets . . . stomach cramps and all." His eyes gleamed playfully.

Her lips quivered with amusement, even while she tried her best to glare at him. Unable to hold in the giggle a second longer, she had no choice but to let it out.

When she recovered, she said, "I was sixteen! And I might add it's unfair of you to remind me of it. Besides, it was the first time I prepared an entire meal all on my own. I only made a few mistakes. It could have happened to anyone.'' She insisted, ''My biggest mistake was inviting the two worst food critics in the state to dinner. You and Roger were *soooo wrong!*''

''Ha! It was nearly my last meal. Roger and I were sick half the night. Poor Jake.'' He shook his head. ''He was the brave one, having to eat your cooking for years. Every time you were home from college, you tried some new fancy dish on him. The man was a steak-and-potatoes kind of guy. No wonder he was so cranky.''

''Very funny.''

''Funny? I am serious. Remember the roast? It was burned clear through to the center. And those scalloped potatoes with cheese . . . good grief. Pretty girl, how did you manage to scorch the cheese without cooking the potatoes? And man, that chocolate cake.'' He shuddered at the memory. ''Salt instead of sugar. Man, I almost gave up eating for a month. And to think I married the cook.'' He tried to look pitiful when he asked, ''Do you really expect me to eat this, darlin'?''

Amanda, having folded her arms beneath her breasts, had tried to forget the absolute mess she had made of that meal. What made her really mad was that he hadn't exaggerated. It had been awful. Both Roger and Zachary had never let her live it down.

''I do.''

The noise he made deep in his throat was anything but favorable. She waited, knowing he was in for a treat. Although it had taken years of persistence on the part of Kate Jenson, her grandfather's housekeeper had managed to teach Amanda to cook.

Amanda had also taken several advanced cooking classes at college. Although her grandfather preferred simple country fare, he had indulged her and sampled some of her complicated dishes. After that first fiasco, neither Roger nor Zachary was willing to dine at the Danielses' unless Jake assured them that Kate and not Amanda had prepared the meal.

It seemed like an eternity before her husband managed to move his fork from his plate to his mouth. Placing a tiny bit of fragrant sweet potatoes into his mouth, he tested the texture and flavor with his tongue before chewing thoroughly and finally swallowing. He didn't say a word until after he tasted the leg of lamb and mixed green salad.

"Mandy," he said with genuine surprise, "this is delicious."

She hid a satisfied smile behind an indignant huff, going back into the kitchen. She collected crystal glasses, chilled rosé and a bowl of mixed fresh fruit. When she returned she found he was well into his meal and showed signs of enjoying every morsel.

She poured the wine before she made herself comfortable across from him. She tucked her long legs under her. During the entire process, she steadfastly ignored his efforts to gain her attention.

"Mandy, don't be that way. You know I didn't mean to hurt your feelings."

She purposely remained silent while concentrating on taking a sip from her glass. It would serve him right if she stopped speaking to him altogether.

He swore beneath his breath before he took her hand. He whispered, "Will a kiss make it better?" When he looked into her eyes, he accused, "You're a fake." There was no mistaking the playful glimmer in their velvety brown depths.

"You deserve to be punished."

Her breath seemed to catch in her throat as she fought the magnetic pull of his potent male charm. He was too close. She could smell his dark, coppery skin. He favored a rustic, woody masculine scent. His gaze centered on the fullness of her dark pink-colored lips. Her throat was so dry she licked her lips, causing his gaze to practically scorch her from the heat. There was no doubt in her mind that he wanted her.

His dark head was bent toward hers, but he surprised her when he did not attempt to kiss her. One lean finger traveled a slow path from the shell shape of her earlobe down the side of her throat, then farther down to the fine bones creating the hollow at the base of her throat.

He inhaled deeply before he said huskily, "You're exquisite. You were made to enjoy a man's touch, created to give and receive pleasure. Your skin is so incredibly soft . . . to touch, to taste."

Before she realized his intent he unbuttoned the row of fabric-covered buttons down the front of her top. Caught in the sensuous trap of his low deep voice, she could not so much as lift a finger to stop him or utter one word of protest.

His work-roughened fingertips journeyed down the natural valley between her lush breasts and continued down to the sensitive swell to her stomach. He traced the indentation of her navel.

Amanda's head filled with erotic memories of this man's caressing every inch of her bare body, leaving her aching for more. She had known the heat of his hands being replaced by the even hotter wash of his tongue. His mouth had touched the entire globe before he lingered on the aching tips. She had nearly lost her mind when he took the nipple into his mouth to suck. Closing her eyes, she had no difficulty recalling how beautiful he had made her feel . . . how adored. Amanda had worked to push the memory from her mind, but it was all coming back no matter how hard she tried to repress it.

"Zach . . ." she whispered, trembling with longing.

She ached for his touch . . . his hot mouth. She released a pent-up breath when finally he stroked the curve of one aching breast before he took it into the warmth of his hand. Then, he tenderly squeezed her softness, before he stroked her taut nipple.

He made no move to take the peak into his mouth, nor did he tease it with the edge of his teeth. He worried the highly sensitive ebony crest with his thumb.

Her small teeth sank into her bottom lip as he turned his attention to the other breast. She ached with desire so much so that she could not do more than whimper for what she craved.

Close to her ear, he groaned, "I've missed you, pretty girl."

There was no past or future for her . . . there was only now. Desire raced through her system, leaving her weak with need and her body tightening from his tender caresses. Shivering uncontrollably, she wanted not only his hands on her body but his mouth, his tongue . . . all of him. Yet, she could no more ask for what she needed than she could fly.

Zachary's breath was quick and fast, yet he began fastening the silk top. Once every single button was closed, he pressed a hard, all-too-brief kiss on the inside of her wrists.

"I know," he said. "Leave you alone."

Amanda blinked rapidly as if she could not comprehend what he had said. She pressed a hand over her lips as if she could hold in the denial. For once he was wrong, that was not what she wanted. But she would not . . . could not plead with him to finish what he started. She would rather cut out her own tongue. How could he not know what she wanted . . . what she needed? It had been so long since they had made love.

She was so caught up in her own battling emotions that

she missed the mixture of blatant male satisfaction and raw hunger shimmering in the depths of his dark eyes. When she did manage to look at him, through the concealing thickness of her lashes, she was disconcerted. He casually finished his meal as if there had been no interruption.

Her breathing was still elevated as she silently questioned his behavior. He had never called a halt to their love play in the past. Why the sudden change? She was the one who always refused. What was different about tonight?

Zachary was straightforward in whatever he took on, from his business dealings to the way he ran the ranch . . . straightforward in his sexual desire. There had never been any doubt of his intention when he wanted to make love . . . until now.

It was as if he had suddenly decided she was no longer worth the effort. Although the thought was disturbing it would not go away. Perhaps it was as simple as he claimed. He was either fed up with her refusals or just plain tired of her.

She honestly could not blame him if that was the case. Was this how he felt when she pushed him away?

"Roger and Brad were impressed by your business associate's portfolio. Chris was in this afternoon. I gather he's rather anxious to start this new project. I must say his work was excellent. But then, I knew you wouldn't work with anyone whose skills were not exceptional."

"If that was a backhanded compliment, then you can keep it," she snapped.

"Are you still upset about this deal? I promised your work would not suffer because of it."

She was upset, but it had nothing to do with Christopher and everything to do with the changes in Zachary's behavior toward her.

"My business dealings aren't your concern."

He studied her for a moment, then said, "It's late, sugar.

I think I will turn in.'' He rose, gathering his empty dishes and utensils. He carried them into the kitchen.

She didn't move, but listened to the sounds of him running water in the sink to wash up the few remaining dishes. What if he was biding his time? Surely, he wasn't waiting for her to make the first move? If that was the case he'd have an extremely long wait. He was only here because he refused to admit their marriage had failed.

She was not blind to his sexual appeal. Her husband was not only a handsome man, but also a wonderful catch. She was aware that women found him attractive.

After flicking off the kitchen light, Zachary paused beside her chair long enough to brush her cheek with his lips, murmuring good night, then walked off toward the bedroom.

What kind of game was he playing? Would he be waiting for her in bed? She heard the faint sound of the shower being turned on. Enough! she chided herself.

After she turned off the lamps in the living room, she lingered in the den, uncertain of what to expect. If only she knew what he was up to, then she could gauge her behavior accordingly.

She watched television far longer than she normally would have. She was exhausted when she finally made her way to the bedroom. Her stomach seemed to curl on a hard knot of tension as she hesitated just inside the open bedroom door.

The room was lit by the lamp on the dresser, leaving the bed in shadow. Her bare feet were soundless on the carpet as she avoided looking at her husband. She went into the walk-in closet, pulled a pink satin nightshirt from the bureau. When she was ready for bed, she slowly returned to the bedroom.

After switching off the lamp, she refused to so much as glance his way until she reached her side of the large bed.

Zachary was lying on his back, his chest bare, the comforter stopped at his waist.

Her brown eyes flashed a mixture of shock and disappointment as she watched his deep chest rise and fall with his breathing. He was sound asleep.

Amanda's office, decorated in shades of cream with slight touches of leaf green, gave the appearance of an elegant nineteenth-century sitting room with its combination of a French sofa and English chintz-covered armchairs. A beautiful Nigerian ceremonial robe was hung above the sofa. It was a colorful composition of reds, golds and rusts.

The only concession to modern design was the large glass-topped table centered along the opposite wall and serving as her desk. A drafting table was tucked between a set of floor-to-ceiling windows. In place of filing cabinets, a huge armoire filled one corner of the room and held essentials. Both workstations were situated on the cream-colored Aubusson floral area rug.

"How much longer? How much can any sane woman put up with without losing her mind?" she grumbled aloud as she paced.

She couldn't seem to concentrate on anything. She should have been working on the new print for the line of home-decor accessories. Instead, she stared out the window. She could not get past the reality of having the most annoying, hard-muscled and copper-skinned man in her bed every night.

This craziness had been going on for two weeks. She did not know how much more of it she could take. Not that she saw that much of Zachary. He generally left before she got up and turned in before she did most nights. She was exhausted from staying up late into the night reading or watching television in the den, until she was certain he was sleeping.

The worst part of it was that she woke every single morning on his side of the bed, her cheek pressed against his pillows. What was her problem? Why couldn't she stay on her side of the bed?

Even more annoying to her was that he slept in nothing more than pajama bottoms that usually rode low on his hips. It was winter, for heaven's sake.

The one and only morning she had awakened before her alarm went off, Zachary was walking out of the bathroom with only a towel around his lean hips. He casually dropped the thing on the carpet before he stepped into a pair of navy briefs. Even though her face was hot, she kept her lids lowered. She certainly didn't want him to know she had been watching him. From the top of his head to the soles of his feet, he was all male.

After a quick knock on the open door, Yolanda James said with a wide grin on her smooth chocolate-brown face, "Hey, girl, got a moment?"

"Hi." Amanda smiled, going over to offer a hug. Yolanda and her husband, Jackson, were both old college friends. He had majored in business while Yolanda had majored in art history. "Sit down. I haven't seen you in a while. How was your and Jackson's trip to Las Vegas?"

"Exciting. We had a ball. Saw all the shows." Yolanda took one of the cream velvet-covered armchairs in front of the desk.

"How much did you lose?"

"I'm not telling. It was fun. And so hot."

"Sounds wonderful. Any place warm sounds like heaven, this time of year. Did you have a chance to look at the pictures of the Randolph home?"

"I did. I found a watercolor that I think will be perfect over the fireplace in the great room and another that might

work in their foyer. Both are at the Braddock Gallery. I also
stopped in at the Merrill Gallery on Seventeenth, but I didn't
see anything I liked nearly as much. The colors were fabulous
. . . all mauve and pinks with just a touch of burgundy. It
is one of Kellogg's, done in the last stages before he died.
Do you have time this afternoon to run down to lower
downtown to the art district and take a look?''

Amanda perched on the edge of the desk, but was only
half listening.

When she didn't answer, Yolanda prompted, ''Mandy?''

Amanda blinked rapidly, embarrassed that she had not
been paying attention. ''Sorry,'' she mumbled, before she
went over to the first set of windows that looked down on
the street. ''I missed half of what you said. I can't keep my
mind on anything lately.''

Yolanda eyed her curiously. The two women had more
in common than their love of art and interior design.
Although they were as different as night and day, they were
both survivors of abuse.

''Does this have anything to do that gorgeous cowboy
you married?''

Amanda kept her back to her friend. She had had lunch
with Yolanda not long after Zachary had moved into her
place. Amanda had ended up telling her more than she
intended. It was not that she didn't trust Yolanda to keep it
to herself. It had more to do with Amanda's tendency to
keep her problems deep inside.

''Yeah'' was about all Amanda was willing to admit.
''But it's complicated.''

Walking over to the door, Yolanda closed it. When she
turned, she leaned back against it. ''I have a couple of hours
before my next appointment. So talk.''

''There's not a lot to tell. Zachary asked for a chance to
prove we can make a go of it. I felt I owed him that much.

Now it seems we're stuck with each other, including sleeping in the same bed without sexual contact.''

Yolanda quirked a beautifully shaped brow. "Sounds tough. Now tell me again, how are you giving this a real go-round, when you won't let the man get next to you?"

"What makes you think I'm the one who hasn't changed?"

"Get real. I'd bet money that the brother isn't the one embracing celibacy."

"No, he isn't. It's what I insisted on, and it's driving me nuts. Yolanda, I don't know how much longer I can take it. I'm fighting my feelings because sex will only lead to vulnerability and loss of control. I can't handle that."

"Listen to me, girl." Yolanda took her hand and led her over to the sofa. Once they were both seated, she said, "Every man is not like your father, or my mother, for that matter. There are good people out there. Some who don't get off on using you or taking advantage of your weakness. I believe those were your words when we talked about my fears before I married Jackson."

"That's different."

"What's different? You can give advice, but not take it? Come on, Mandy. If I can get past the fear, so can you."

Amanda glared at her friend. "It's not the same and you know it. It was easier for you to trust a man because your abuser was female. It's not the same for me."

"Easy? That argument is full of holes and you know it. First of all, it wasn't easy for me to develop a friendship with you, but I managed it." Yolanda scuffed. "None of it is ever pain free, girlfriend. It is very difficult to love, especially when you've been hurt badly as a child." Yolanda squeezed Amanda's hand. "It was my mother, but, honey, it took me a long time to trust anyone, especially that man. Even longer to let Jackson see how deeply I felt about him. But it happened. And I've never been happier."

"Yolanda." Amanda smiled at her. "You know how happy I am for you, but—"

"It can happen for you."

"How?" Amanda shook her head, unhappily.

"Zach has been your best friend for years. You already trust him . . ." Yolanda persisted, ". . . more so than I think you even realize. Take it a step at a time. Go slow. When you're ready, take it to the next level. But tell him what is going on with you."

Amanda hung her head, studying her hands. "I hear you here" —she pointed to her head—"but not here." Her hand rested over her heart.

Yolanda frowned at her. "If you had no feelings for the man, you would certainly not let him into your bed every night. That alone takes an incredible amount of trust."

Amanda nodded, knowing Yolanda was right. It had taken a great deal of faith for her to sleep beside him each night. Not once had she tried to stay awake all night, worrying that Zachary would take advantage of her during the night. If anything, she was more worried about her own resolve. Zachary would never force her. That was not his way.

"Just because I can sleep beside him doesn't mean I'll ever feel the way I need to feel to make our marriage a real one. I'm not in love with him."

"Sure you're not."

"I'm not." Amanda didn't want to feel what her mother felt for her father. She shuddered at the thought of it.

"If you don't love him, then why are you having trouble divorcing him?"

"I didn't say I didn't love him. I'm not in love with him. Besides, he's the one who doesn't want to let go."

"I don't get it. Is Zach pressuring you to have sex with him? Is he insisting on his marital rights?"

"No," she admitted somewhat dejectedly.

That was what bothered her the most. Zachary had not put his hands on her in weeks.

"What again did you say was your problem?"

Eight

"Zach is handling this whole situation better than I am." Crossing her arms, it was several moments before Amanda candidly said, "I want . . . him to hold me." She closed her eyes to hold back the tears and swallowed before she could say, "I want him to hold me every night. I want it so much it scares me. I might be making it happen during the night."

"Making it happen? How?"

Amanda rose, moving restlessly from the desk to the drafting table to the window and back again. She blushed with embarrassment when she admitted, "I wake up on his side of the bed every morning with my head on his pillow. We're sharing a king-size bed, Yolanda. I have no idea how I manage it."

Yolanda couldn't stop the laughter rising in her throat.

"It's not funny!"

"Yeah, it is," she giggled. "You would be on the floor

if I told you the same thing." Yolanda took a deep breath to calm herself before she asked, "Have you ever thought about asking him?"

"Asking what? If I throw myself at him during the night? Never!"

"It's the only way."

"No."

"Okay. Okay." Yolanda grinned. "Zachary is a great guy and you know it."

"He deserves someone who can love him. And that isn't me."

"So you're telling me you can handle him being with another woman?"

Amanda lifted her chin stubbornly. "I offered to give him his freedom, remember?"

"In theory, yeah. But I never thought you'd actually go through with it. Jackson and I went through some tough times, but he hung in there with me until I got it together. Zachary sounds as if he is in this for the long haul." Yolanda paused before she said bluntly, "Maybe he just doesn't have the qualities that you need from a man?"

Amanda merely looked at her friend because right then she did not trust her feelings. When the telephone rang, she was grateful for the interruption. "Excuse me. I have to take it. Gloria is at lunch."

Amanda handled the call as quickly as she could. "Sorry about that. Come on. Let's get out of here and take a look at those paintings."

Amanda reached for her wool hat and coat. She needed the cool crisp air to clear her head.

"Mandy?"

"No more. Let's leave it for now."

"Okay. But please, promise me you'll think it over before you make a decision. No matter what you said, I don't believe you would calmly sit back and let another woman take your husband away from you.''

Avoiding the other woman's eyes, Amanda whispered, "I promise."

Amanda had no idea what had awakened her but even before she opened her eyes, she knew she was in her husband's arms. Her arm was clasped around his lean waist, her thigh was tucked between his and her head was cushioned on his shoulder.

"Oh, no," she moaned.

Pushing a wave of ebony hair out of her eyes, she saw that he was asleep and she was on his side of the bed. When she tried to cautiously disengage herself without waking him, she found her hair was trapped beneath a muscular shoulder.

A glance at the clock made her groan unhappily. It was eight-thirty. Why was he still here? Normally he was long gone before she had to get up. And there was no way she could get up without waking him.

"Zach?"

The trouble was she was a little too accustomed to him being in the condo with her. So much so that she was beginning to wonder if she could even sleep if he wasn't beside her. A chill raced down her spine.

"Zachary . . . wake up."

He grumbled in his sleep, tightening his hold on her, thus easing her onto his chest.

"Zach! Wake up. We're late."

"What time is it, sugar? Seems like I just closed my eyes," he complained as he absently ran a hand down her spine until he was cupping her buttocks.

"It's not your eyes that concern me. Stop that."

There was no way she could fail to notice the hardening

of his sex against her bare stomach. Bare? Her gown had evidently risen during the night.

He chuckled, his black lashes lifting enough to inspect her tousled beauty. He moved her up along his upper torso until he could nestle his face in the scented place between her neck and shoulder.

"Some things are beyond my control."

"Let go." She shivered. "I have an appointment at ten."

"A kiss, first," he groaned, his breath warming her throat.

As sensation after sensation raced down her spine, Amanda pushed against the hard wall of his chest in an effort to free herself. But she managed to bring herself even more firmly against him, the hard tips of her breasts aching from the contact.

"You've got to be kidding?"

Just the feel of his arousal was disturbing. With her thighs splayed there was no way she could avoid the long length of his erection. Her feminine muscles tightened in response.

When she tried to move away, he held her fast. She closed her eyes, hoping he couldn't feel her damp heat as her body prepared itself for his invasion. She physically longed for what her mind told her she had no business wanting.

In the blink of an eye she was no longer on top of him, but on her back beneath him, inhaling his masculine scent. His open mouth was moving down her throat to the hollow at its base. His tongue felt rough and hot on her highly sensitive skin as he tasted her. With unhurried ease he opened the small buttons lining the front of her gown.

Breathlessly she whispered, "What are you doing?"

"You know exactly what I'm doing," he said huskily.

"I don't want this."

"I can tell by how fast you are breathing and how hard your nipples are. They're like ripe blackberries urging me to taste them."

He dropped his hand as he covered a lush globe, gently

squeezing her softness, then stroking the dark peak with work-roughened fingers. She trembled in response.

Before Amanda could formulate even a token protest, Zachary had dropped his head to take the highly sensitive nipple in his mouth. He licked her, over and over again, causing a moan to escape from deep in her throat. He brought her aching nipple into the heat of his mouth to apply heart-stopping suction. She barely managed to control a scream but was unable to contain the trembling . . . the enjoyment. Desire rushed over her, until she was consumed by it as excitement raced through her system, settling in the pulsating waves in her woman's center.

"Zach . . ."

"Hmmm," he groaned as he sucked harder. When she whimpered, he asked, "Does it feel good, baby?" as he squeezed the other nipple, before his hand moved down her soft body. He caressed her stomach, then moved lower to the lush dark curls shielding her sex.

Amanda opened her eyes, struggling against her own need and what little rational judgment that remained.

"Don't . . ." was all she was able to manage as he cupped her mound.

"Don't what? Don't stop?" he said into her ear an instant before he took one long-awaited kiss after another . . . each deeper than the last as he squeezed her fleshy moist folds.

She moaned against his mouth and was sobbing by the time he opened the soft folds and he slid a blunt finger inside her damp sheath while he sucked each hard peak in turn. Amanda gasped his name as he pressed the heel of his palm against her clitoris and lost her struggle to gather her defenses. All she could do was hang on to Zachary. He didn't stop until she came apart in his arms, sobbing his name as she climaxed.

Before she could catch her breath, he kissed his way down her body until he could wedge his shoulders between her thighs. He placed sizzling-hot kisses along her thigh. She held her breath when she felt him open her to his kisses and then the hot, persistent strokes of his tongue. He laved her again and again. With burning lungs and heart rate pounding in her ears, she cried out when he intensified the pleasure by concentrating on her clitoris. Her second release was more powerful than the first and seemed to go on and on.

As she gradually recovered her equilibrium, Zachary rose, pressing his open mouth between the place where her shoulder and neck joined. His voice was gruff with desire when he said, "Don't ever tell me you're frigid again."

When she was finally able to make her brain function, she realized that her husband's breathing was as quick and uneven as hers.

"Zach ..." Amanda whispered. She watched him through the thickness of her lashes, acutely aware of his long powerful body. His hands were laced on his flat stomach inches above the thick, jutting length of his penis. Although all he wore was low riding, pajama bottoms there was no doubt what lay beneath the thin silk. She yearned to touch him, offer herself to him, to take him inside her body and ease the emptiness deep inside, yet she hesitated.

He looked at her then, his eyes hot with molten desire that he made no move to eliminate. His voice was almost casual when he said, "Aren't you late?"

"Yes." She blushed.

She had no idea why, but it hurt knowing he not only did not expect her to do anything to ease his need but that he did not want her to.

She managed to ask, "What about you?"

"I have a board meeting this morning. I'll put the coffee on while you shower." He rose from the bed, disappearing into the bathroom for a few moments. When he returned she still had not moved. He said gruffly, "You have ten minutes to finish in the shower or we share.'' Then he disappeared down the hall.

Some fifteen minutes later, Amanda stood in front of the large bathroom mirror wrapped in an ivory bath sheet with her hair in electric rollers, applying makeup when her husband, in all his natural glory, walked into the room. Her eyes went wide before she quickly averted her gaze, determined to ignore the play of firm muscles in his wide shoulders and arms, which tapered down to lean waist, firm hips and powerful legs. There was no excess flesh on his copper-bronze body. Or any doubts about his erection.

She nearly poked herself in the eye with a mascara wand when Zachary casually planted a lingering kiss on the back of her neck before he entered the shower stall. Had she ever felt more selfish and less like a woman?

It was over a hurried breakfast that he invited her to have a late lunch with him. She had been so absorbed in trying not to notice how devastatingly handsome he was in a charcoal-gray suit, dove-gray silk shirt and gray and navy striped tie that she nearly missed the invitation.

''Aren't you going out to the Circle-M today?'' she asked as she sipped from her coffee mug. She had done no more than taste the French toast and bacon he was enjoying.

''Not until later this afternoon.'' He studied her bent head. ''I like the outfit, even though your legs are covered.''

She had chosen a tailored beige wool pantsuit. The jacket buttoned almost to the base of her throat. The front of her hair had been caught into a clasp at her crown and the rest had been left to cascade down past her shoulders.

Her only jewelry was a pair of mabe' pearl with gold-rimmed earrings, and her wedding rings that she had put on for the first time since their reconciliation. The four-karat square-cut diamond engagement ring was surrounded by emeralds and set in gold. It was topped by a polished wide gold band.

"Would you like to come along? It's been a while since you've been in cow country and even longer since you've been on a horse."

They looked into each other's eyes. They both knew the last time she had been on a horse had been the day she had been thrown and suffered a miscarriage.

Although he had never blamed her for the accident, his mother had not been so generous. Rebecca Hamilton McFadden insisted that it was Amanda's reckless behavior, going riding alone, that had caused her to lose her baby.

She was the first to look away. "Not today," she said softly.

"We both lost a baby that day, Mandy. Why won't you talk to me about it?"

Although she looked at him for only an instant, there was no way she could fail to notice the pain in his dark eyes. Eventually, she whispered, "I can't. It still hurts."

"Sharing the pain may not make it go away, but it makes it bearable. I wanted our baby, too. I was looking forward to being a father for the first time." When she made no response, he sighed heavily, then changed the subject. "At least come to the ranch with me. You'll get to see Peggy."

"I can't." After glancing at the wall clock, she said, "It's late. I need to get out of here. I'll see you, what, about one-thirty?"

"I'm not sure. It will probably be after two. I'll call later this morning." A frown creased his brow.

She practically bolted from the table, unable to remain a second longer. She nearly jumped out of her skin when she discovered he was behind her. She accepted his help with her cashmere, camel-colored trench coat.

"Thank you," she mumbled, grabbing her purse and portfolio from the hall table. "Zach, you don't have to drive me in. Why don't you finish your breakfast?" She tried to smile, but failed.

"Fine," he said tightly.

Before she could get out the door, he gently pulled her backward against his chest. "Mandy," he murmured close to her ear, "I know it still hurts, but please never forget I share the pain. Even though our baby was not planned does not mean it wasn't deeply loved." As if he felt her trembling in his arms, he tightened his hold on her arms. "When you're ready to come to the ranch, we'll face it together."

She nodded, trying to swallow her tears. She did turn around and hug him. "I'll remember," she said, before she brushed her lips against his, then stepped back. "Gotta run. See you later."

She was working at the computer when the telephone on her desk rang. "That better be Zach," she mumbled aloud. It was after two and she was starving. "Amanda Daniels McFadden," she said, as she automatically clicked the SAVE icon on the screen.

"Hi, little bit," a heavy male voice rasped into her ear. "It's been a long time. I've missed you."

She grasped the handset so tightly she nearly broke a nail while wondering if she were having a nightmare. It had been years since she heard his voice.

"Little bit?"

"Daddy?" she said in disbelief. "Is that you?"

"Yeah, it's me . . . your old dad. How's my little girl?" Sebastian Daniels sounded as if he were in the habit of calling daily. "I hope I haven't caught you at a bad time?"

"No . . . yes." She faltered, unable to believe she was speaking to the father she hadn't seen or heard from in nearly sixteen years. Struggling to collect herself, she managed to say, "I'm surprised to hear from you."

"I'm in Denver. I just heard about Dad's death," he ended lamely.

What did he mean? How could he have just heard that her grandfather, his father, had died? Jeffery Ross, the family attorney, had been trying to locate him for over a year.

She stared at the telephone unprepared for the sudden rush of feelings . . . unpleasant feelings she did not want to experience ever again.

"Amanda? You still there?"

"Yes. . . ." Years of anger, bitterness and resentment replaced the shock she felt when she realized who was on the line. This was the man who had callously walked out on them and left them to fend for themselves. He had broken her mother's heart . . . time and time again with his verbal and physical abuse.

Her so-called father had left her mother so dependent on him that she did not want to live without him in her life. Nothing was enough, not even the love of her only child.

"I'd like to see you, little bit. Can we have a little supper together and visit?"

Amanda, having winced at the almost forgotten endearment, made no response. Sebastian Daniels was the very last person she wanted to see . . . ever.

He was a nasty drunk. Unfortunately, he was drunk more than he was sober. It was not unusual for him to backhand her mother or Amanda, if she got in his way. Her mother had not been the only one hurt by his rages.

Amanda had suffered more than the physical pain her father inflicted on her young body . . . he had crushed something vital within her. Her father had nearly destroyed her faith in men . . . making it nearly impossible for her to trust a man or give him her love.

She shuddered as a flood of unwelcome memories washed over her. The last time she had seen her father, her mother had to be hospitalized to recover from the injuries she'd suffered from his last beating. Amanda had also been recovering from the broken arm she had gotten when she tried to stop her father from killing her mother. He'd been so out of it that Amanda wondered if he even remembered why he had been so enraged.

"Please, Amanda," Sebastian pleaded, "it's important to me to at least see you while I'm in town." He rushed on to say, "Dad told me about you over the years when we talked on the telephone. I never seemed to be in one place long enough to establish a permanent address. Always moving on," he rambled, then said urgently, "little bit. . . ."

She was not sure when the trembling had started. It was so intense that her teeth were practically chattering. She held on to the desk as if she were afraid she'd fall out of her chair. Tears ran unchecked down her face, clogging her throat.

Zachary chose that moment to knock on her open door before he peered inside her office. "Hi, pretty girl. Sorry I'm late. But the . . ." He stopped, taking in her dazed brown eyes, pale face streaked with tears. Closing the door, he crossed to her. "What is it, my love?"

Nine

Amanda was in his arms without being conscious of moving. She couldn't formulate the words necessary to explain, so she simply hung on to him with all her might.

Zachary gently took the receiver she held clenched in one hand and said, "Hello? This is Zachary McFadden, Amanda's husband. Who am I speaking to?"

She didn't listen to his side of the dialogue. She buried her face against his throat, her arms around his waist. Zachary was the only stable thing in her life and she could not bear to let go of him. The warmth of his body seemed to penetrate her numbness. Gradually the quivering stopped, and she felt as if she could breathe again.

After replacing the handset in its cradle, he guided her over to the sofa. He held her, his hand moving soothingly over her back.

"Go ahead, cry, pretty girl . . . if it will help," he urged.

"Cry!" she bristled, suddenly furious. "I won't ever shed another tear over that drunk. That miserable coward! That abuser!" she screeched, jumping to her feet. "I detest the man!"

Tears streamed down her face, almost blinding her as raged spilled forth. "Why did he call me? It's too late for my mother . . . too late for Granddaddy. If he really cared, he would have been here when my grandfather and his own father needed him. All those months of suffering. Where was Sebastian Daniels then?" She paused for breath. "I've buried my mother because of him. Now that Granddaddy is gone he shows up . . . wanting me to welcome him with open arms." She shook her head vehemently. "What does he want from me now? He is supposed to be contacting the lawyer, not me."

Zachary made no response, although his concern was on his strong African features. It was his quiet strength that had a calming effect on Amanda.

Looking into his eyes, she insisted, "I don't want to see that man . . . not ever!"

"It's entirely up to you."

After blowing her nose on the handkerchief he had given her, she asked with a frown, "You think I should, don't you?"

"Yes. I do."

"But why?" She didn't give him time to answer, but began telling him things that she had told only her grandfather.

"Living with my father was like living with a rattlesnake. I never knew what to expect. He used to taunt my mother, calling her names. Sometimes, he would get so drunk he didn't know what he was doing or saying. He used to hurt me when I tried to stop him from hitting my mother. He would slap me so hard my ears would ring. Once he hit me so hard I flew across the room and crashed into the wall.

"The last time he hurt me he broke my arm. I was trying to stop him from killing my mother . . . she was already unconscious . . . she couldn't even feel his blows . . . but he wouldn't stop. When he started kicking her, I couldn't stand it anymore. Zach, I was so scared, but I had to stop him."

Zachary was also shaking but with rage as he came over to her and just held her, stroking her arms and shoulders. "I'm so sorry, love, that you had to go through something like that."

She was trembling so badly she would have fallen if Zachary had not been holding her. "I bet my father didn't tell you why he beat her that day, did he?"

"No, he didn't. But you don't have to—"

"Oh, but I do. He nearly killed my mother because she wouldn't give him the money she had hidden to buy food and pay our rent. Daddy was so out of control that day that he took the money . . . not caring what he had left behind."

"Mandy, you don't have to—" he broke in.

She shook her head. "Let me finish. I want you to know the kind of man that calls himself my father. Zach, I was the one who called for help that day, not him. I thought she was dead, but she survived that time."

She pushed away, then began moving restlessly around the room. "My father left us soon after that. My mother kept asking for him. I was afraid to tell her the truth, but I was too young to keep a secret like that for long." A sob caught in her throat, and she had to pause before she could go on. Eventually, she said, "It was not long after she was home from the hospital and I was back in school that everything changed. It began like such an ordinary day, but it was not how it ended. I got her breakfast before I went to school that day . . ."

Amanda took a deep, fortifying breath. Even though more than a dozen years had passed it was nearly impossible to put all this into words.

Zachary caught her hand in his, shaking his head. "No, Mandy—"

"Let me finish . . . please. I need to tell you."

"Okay."

"I stayed late that day. I wanted so badly to be like the other kids. I knew I was supposed to come straight home after school. But when Marie Hunter asked me and three other girls to her house to listen to her new album, I forgot about having to go home . . . forgot my mother was sick and needed me." A single tear slid down her cheek.

"I just wanted to be like the other girls. It felt so good pretending that they liked me. That I was just like all of them . . . that afternoon. l wanted that so much," Amanda whispered.

"I wanted my family to be like theirs . . . one that didn't have a drunk as a father, who said he loved us, yet hurt us over and over again." She quickly swallowed a sob. "I stayed and laughed and danced with the other girls.

"I—I—I—I d—d—didn't get home until late. When I walked into the house it was so quiet . . . too quiet. I called my mother, but she didn't answer. She wasn't in the kitchen preparing our meal or in her bedroom resting. That's when I got really scared." Amanda unconsciously rubbed her arms as if she could still feel the chilling terror she had experienced that day.

"I stood between the two bedrooms, not knowing where she could be. It was as if no one was there . . . not even me. Then I saw it . . . the blood. It was on the floor. I was standing in it." Tears spilled down her cheeks. "It was her blood, Zach."

"Oh, baby." He gathered her close, his arms around her waist, allowing her to lean on him.

Amanda accepted his support, but she had to tell him . . . had to finish. She rushed on to say, "She was dead. She had slashed her wrists with a razor blade. She loved him so much that she didn't want to live, not without him." Burying her damp face against his throat, she said, "Sh—sh—she f—f—f—forgot about me. It was as if I didn't matter. My father was everything to her. Everything!" Her entire body was quivering when she choked out, "That's the man you want me to sit down and eat with!"

"I'm so sorry, baby. So sorry you had to go through that." His voice was rough with emotion. He pressed a kiss against her forehead. "Jake told me some of it. But I had no idea how bad . . ." He stopped, moving a soothing hand over her slender back.

"Over the years, he never called me. Never talked to me. Now because he wants to see me, I'm supposed to go running to him like a good little girl. Well, I'm not his little girl anymore."

"It's over, my love. He can't hurt you . . . I won't let him," he said quietly. "He will have to go through me to get to you."

It was a while before she was composed enough to stand on her own. "You still think I should see him, don't you?"

"Yeah. See him, then forget him."

Amanda looked at him with large grief-stricken eyes, then pushed against his chest until he let her go and dropped down onto the sofa as if the air had been knocked out of her. Covering her face with trembling hands, she began to cry as she had not let herself cry in years.

"Mandy, don't," he said as he sat beside her and took her protesting form into his arms. He held her until she quieted.

She used his handkerchief to dry her face. Eventually she asked, "What did you tell him?"

"That we would meet him tomorrow for lunch. He's staying at the Marriott's Residence Inn on Zuni Street. But don't worry about it. I'll go. He has to be told about Jake and what it was like for him in the end."

''That's Mr. Ross's job, not yours.''

''It should come from family. Ross can give him the provision in Jake's will later.''

''He deserves nothing!''

''He is still Jake's son. And as his son, he deserves whatever Jake wanted him to have,'' Zachary persisted, squeezing her hand. ''Hungry? How about a nice juicy steak?''

''I'm not.'' All she felt was drained . . . of both emotion and energy.

''Well, I am. I'll eat your steak and mine. Go fix your face while I make a reservation.''

Too tired to argue, Amanda went through the door behind her desk. The bathroom, although small, was done in shades of green. She reappeared a few minutes later looking and feeling better, although there was nothing she could do about her swollen lids.

To her amazement, she was able to relax and enjoy the meal made bearable by Zachary's lighthearted banter. He flatly refused to discuss anything more serious than her first hiking trip through the mountains with him and his brothers and Peggy. He soon had her laughing at those bumbling attempts to put up the tent and having to fish for their supper.

It was not until late that night as they lay in bed, Amanda's back pressed against his chest, enclosed in the warmth of his arms, that she reluctantly agreed to have lunch with her father. Zachary held her until she fell asleep.

Amanda woke alone the next morning in a far from pleasant mood. She had slept fretfully. It took all her strength just to get out of bed. She decided to work in her home studio rather than go into the office and inflict her rotten mood on others.

Even though she had her laptop, she could not concentrate on the work she had brought home the night before. After she had laundered, folded and put away several loads of clothes, she was still looking for something to distract her.

She dressed in a tailored navy pantsuit, then restlessly moved from one room to the next. Why hadn't Zachary called? She had no idea if he had gone into the office or if he'd flown out to the ranch. As the clock moved toward noon, she managed to worry herself into a fine temper, certain that he would not keep his word and she would be forced to deal with her father alone.

When Zachary walked in the door, she greeted him with, "Well, you certainly took your time!"

He dropped his sheepskin jacket on a chair in the foyer and was dressed in a black shirt and jeans. He quirked a brow but made no verbal response. He did place a tender kiss at the corner of her red-gloss-covered mouth before he pulled back to look into her troubled gaze.

"Stop worrying. It'll be fine, I promise. He can never hurt you again. Remember, you're not that scared little girl anymore, are you?"

"No, I'm not." She smiled for the first time that day.

"Ready?"

"Yes."

Amanda's heart was racing when they entered the restaurant, Denver Chop House, where Sebastian had arranged to meet them.

"You're doing fine," Zachary whispered, taking her cold hands into his. Although she looked perfectly composed, he knew of the harsh emotions she fought to control.

"I know what you're trying to do," she warned him, then whispered, "I have—"

"Good afternoon," the restaurant's hostess greeted them with a smile.

Zachary answered, "Good afternoon. We're meeting Mr. Daniels for lunch."

"This way, please."

Amanda, having not seen her father since she was a child, wondered if she would have recognized the man.

A thin, stoop-shouldered, bent man hastily got to his feet. At barely six feet, Sebastian Daniels was only a few inches taller than Amanda. His hair was steel gray now, and his brown creased face and dark eyes reflected the damage that years of hard drinking had caused him.

Sebastian was nothing like the hardworking man who had sired him. Although he seemed to be sober, his unsteady hands made Amanda suspect his abstinence was a recent occurrence.

"Amanda." Her father smiled, holding out his hands to her. He flinched when she made no effort to touch him. Embarrassed, he rushed on to say, "You're so beautiful, little bit ... just beautiful. You must be Zachary?" He offered his hand.

"Yes," Zachary said, shaking his hand.

Other than to politely thank her father for the compliment, Amanda had nothing to say. Once they were all seated, she fought the slight weakening of her resolve. Here was the father she had once loved with blind devotion, despite his abuse.

When the waiter asked if they were ready to order, both men looked expectantly at her. All she was interested in was getting lunch over with; nonetheless, she ordered a chicken salad. She did not listen to the men ordering, but reminded herself that this was not about feelings. It was about the truth.

She could not so much as look at him without remembering the way he had harmed her mother. The last time she saw him replayed in her mind. He was packing to leave them. She had pleaded with him to stay. She somehow knew that his leaving would devastate them both. He was still her daddy, and she loved him then, even though she had bruises on her face and her arm was in a cast because of him.

She had clung to her father, begging him to stay. She remembered sobbing, asking, what was she to tell her mother? It was only after she had lost her mother that her feelings for him had changed. Her mother's suicide had affected her deeply . . . still did even after all these years.

"So," she said, once they were alone. "Where have you been all these years?"

It was the anxiety that she saw in her father's eyes that broke through one of the protective layers of hostility that Amanda had carefully wrapped around her heart over the years.

She was willing to listen as he began recounting his life. Strangely, his voice held no resentment but seemed to contain a certain measure of regret. Amanda was shaken when he admitted that he had caused many of his own problems.

She could not believe her ears when her father admitted that he was an alcoholic. She gripped Zachary's hand beneath the table, having to bite her lip to hold in a bitter retort. She had lost her belief and trust in him.

When Sebastian confessed that he had stopped blaming others for his own shortcomings and had started to straighten himself out, Amanda couldn't help wondering if he truly believed that just because he admitted his drinking was a sickness he could not control, he could change the past. If that was the case he was wrong. His drinking had destroyed their family.

She was shocked that she felt anything for him . . . even relief when he confessed that he had stopped drinking and sought professional help. She said nothing. In fact, she had little to say during the entire meal.

Zachary expertly maneuvered the conversation to Jake,

explaining their own long-standing friendship and recounted details of Jake's illness and death.

At this point, she was unable to remain silent any longer. Although she could not address him as father and certainly could never forgive his ill treatment of her mother, she stated, "I'm sorry about your difficulties. And I know that Grandpa loved you and that love never stopped, no matter how many years went by without hearing from you."

Sebastian said gruffly, "Thank you, little bit. Do you think you could—"

"Don't ask anything more of me. I don't know if I can ever forget what you did to Mommy or to me. Maybe, you really did not intend to hurt us. Nevertheless, you did just that. But that's not why we're here." Her voice faltered; she was choking on the turbulence of her emotions. When Zachary gently squeezed her hand, her eyes briefly met his, conveying her thanks.

She managed to say, "I don't know your plans, but I want you to understand that even though I hope you can find some happiness, I don't want you in my life."

The tears she had been holding inside were dangerously close to the surface. Unwilling to let that happen, especially in front of this man, the source of so much pain, she quickly excused herself. She whispered in her husband's ear that she would wait for him in the car, before she hurried out of the crowded restaurant.

Tears were streaming down her face by the time the car was brought around and she slipped inside. Furiously wiping her face, she decided that her father had already caused the Daniels women more than enough grief for one lifetime. Everyone who loved him had suffered because of it . . . her mother, his own father and herself.

"You okay?" Zachary asked when he joined her.

She rested against the soft gray leather seat with her

eyes closed. Her exhaustion was apparent when she nodded, biting her bottom lip to halt its betraying tremors.

"Mandy?"

"I'm fine," she managed with difficulty.

"You're not fine," he said tightly, but started the motor and set the car into motion without saying more.

It was only after he had pulled into a parking space in front of the condominiums that she said tiredly, "I really should go into the office to at least show my face for an hour or so."

"Your assistant can handle things for one day. You're in no condition to work after what you've been through today."

She did not have the energy to argue when he came around and opened the door for her. By the time they reached the condo, she had roused herself enough to notice that Zachary had said no more than a few words during the drive back.

He had been so kind, so understanding through this entire ordeal. She mumbled her thanks when he slid her coat from her arms and hung it in the hall closet. When he joined her in the living room, she turned to him, realizing how much she owed him.

"Zach, I appreciate all you've done to get me through that meeting with my father. I'm not sure I could have managed it on my own. Thank you."

When she slid her arms up around his shoulders and lifted her face to press a kiss on his bronze cheek, his face twisted into a grimace. He stepped away from her before her soft mouth could do more than brush his skin.

Zachary's dark eyes flashed with temper. "I don't need your gratitude, damn it."

He walked into the kitchen while a shaken Amanda sank down into one of the armchairs. She shot him an inquiring look when he returned carrying a bottle of beer in one hand and a tall glass of cola in the other. Without a word he handed the glass to her.

Confused and surprisingly hurt, she had no idea what she had done to set him off. Yes, she had been somewhat self-absorbed since her father had called the day before, but she had not meant to take it out on him.

His mouth was compressed and his dark eyes were brooding when he met her questioning gaze. He snapped, "Don't look at me like that!"

Ten

Sebastian Daniels was disappointed. Well, he had tried
... that should have counted for something. As he stared
dishearteningly at his barely eaten lunch, he decided he
should be thankful that his rich son-in-law had picked up
the lunch tab.

It hurt that even after more than a dozen years, his little
girl did not want anything to do with him. Amanda had
certainly done well for herself, she had married a McFadden.
And it was not just any of the brothers but the oldest and
wealthiest of the bunch, from what he had heard. But then
she had the old man backing her.

Even though it had been nearly thirty years since he had
spent any time in Glenwood Springs or on the Double-D,
he could not fail to take notice that the McFadden name
was still respected throughout the state. His old man had
certainly put stock in the name.

Sebastian scowled. It was hard to believe that Jake Daniels was gone. Hard to accept that finally he no longer had anything to prove to anyone. None of it should have mattered anymore.

His mother had died when he was born. Sebastian and his twin brother, Danny, had been raised by their father on the Double-D. The running was finally over. There was no one left to care what happened to him, not even his Darlene.

"Would you care for something else, sir?" the waiter asked.

Sebastian shook his head, but stopped suddenly. Then, he said, "Yes. Scotch, neat."

"Right away, sir."

Sebastian's hands had started trembling as soon as he placed the order. What was he doing? But he knew exactly what he wanted. Or did he?

He had been clean now for six months after nearly dying in a Vegas hospital. He had no choice, flat on his back, but to face the fact that if he wanted to live he had to stop drinking. The doctor warned him that his liver was almost completely destroyed.

He wasn't ready to leave this earth, not yet. There was so much unsettled in his life. He had been marking time until his old man relented and handed over the reins of the Double-D to him. That had not happened as long as Jake Daniels had lived. He'd only learned of his death when he called the ranch last week and the old housekeeper had passed on that news.

He refused to be haunted by the old man's belief that he had killed his twin brother. Yet he still had to deal with the fact that his only child didn't care if he lived or died. Amanda, apparently, blamed him for her mother's death.

Sebastian hastily got up before his drink arrived. Dropping a bill on the table before he left the restaurant as quickly as possible on unsteady legs. Even though his hotel was nearby, he didn't even try to make it on his own. He hired a cab. He did not breathe easily until he was inside his room.

He swore heatedly. Why wouldn't his girl give him a chance? Yeah, he certainly had made his share of mistakes. Hell, he was not proud of them. It was true he had been drinking heavily through the worst of it. Hell, he didn't remember half the things he had done. Often he lost days, even weeks at a time.

How could Amanda still hold him responsible for leaving when he had done what he thought was best for her and Darlene? Sebastian didn't need to be reminded that he had been out of control . . . out of his mind, blinded by rage because of his own failings.

Back then, he would start the day with a shot of scotch. It had been downhill the rest of the day. The more he drank the angrier he became. He barely remembered hitting Darlene until his daughter was on the telephone calling for an ambulance, much less breaking Amanda's arm when she tried to stop him.

It had taken a long while for him to straighten himself out. Sebastian had had to get in touch with the old man in order to find his own family. Only then had he finally learned the extent of the damage he caused. Darlene was dead and Mandy was living with Jake on the Double-D. The news had sent him into a downward spiral that had lasted, not months, but years. Eventually, he had ended up in the hospital. Unfortunately, he had not been able to stop even then. He was drinking because his father was raising his daughter. He hated the way the old man passed on his holier-than-God attitude. He didn't need any reminders that he was responsible.

Pacing in front of the windows, Sebastian wondered if there was anything he could do to get Amanda to just listen to his side of things. Not that he had a clue how to make amends.

Exhausted he sank down into an armchair, covering his face with trembling hands. He had never meant to hurt his little girl or Darlene. He hadn't meant any of it.

Amanda snapped, "Zach, what is your problem?"

"I'm not a damn saint! I have my limits."

"Why are you angry? I only wanted you to know how I feel. I certainly didn't mean to insult you. What is so wrong with me expressing my appreciation?"

Zachary stared at her. How could she even ask the question? His pulse had gone wild, his heart racing from a combination of rage and raw need. His entire body had pulsed. It was all he could do not to show her exactly how he defined that appreciation.

She of all people should know what was absolutely critical to his well-being. What he needed was her . . . only her. Why else would he have put himself through the sheer torment of trying to sleep night after night beside her?

She had no idea how many hours he worked, just so he could sleep when his head hit the pillow . . . More often than not it hadn't helped. He had to take ice-cold showers, rather than the hot ones he needed to ease the ache from sore muscles. The relentless hunger never went away. It nagged him, testing his self-control. Whenever they were together, he was semiaroused . . . aching with desire.

Living with Amanda was getting to Zachary. Frankly, he had no idea how much more he could take. He woke every blasted morning with a pulsating erection and Amanda's soft sweet body draped over him. It took all his resolve to keep his word and gently ease her body away from his, rather than slide between her soft, silky golden-brown thighs.

He had always prided himself on being a man of his word. Both his father and Jake had taught him and his brothers that a man who did not keep his word was not a man.

Thank goodness, there had only been one morning when he had nearly lost it. It was the morning they had both overslept. When she woke him, he had been more than ready to give her the hard loving they both craved. Technically, he had kept his word . . . just barely.

He had simply done what he'd been longing to do . . . he had given his woman a release from the sexual tension eating him alive. He had caressed and sucked her pretty breasts, then caressed her hot, dewy mound until she had gone wild in his arms. She had climaxed not once, but a second time when he had tongued her sweetness as he had been longing to do for a very long time.

Just the memory of her cries caused his body to harden and ache for more of the same. Hell, yeah, he had wanted to take their love play to the next level, but Amanda had looked at him with a combination of raw fear and feminine desire. Her fear had been like a slap in the face. Somehow he'd managed to move away from her, without finishing what he started.

She had no idea what that sacrifice had cost him. It had taken a huge chunk out of his self-esteem and his manhood. His word was not something he gave lightly. It would only take a word from her to release him from the promise. But Amanda had not asked for his lovemaking.

There had been no way he could conceal his desire. He nearly laughed out loud when he recalled how shocked she had been when he walked into the bathroom a little later. Hell, he wanted her to see what she had done to him. His shaft had been heavy with desire, his scrotum tight with need. She had felt him when he kissed her nape before he stepped into an ice-cold shower.

A mixture of frustration and anger nagged at him. The very last thing any man wanted from his woman was her gratitude. And that was all she was offering.

"Zach, I asked—"

"Everything is wrong with it," he hissed through clenched teeth.

He put his untouched bottle down with so much force it was a wonder it did not break, and walked toward her with long, determined steps. Before Amanda could do more than blink, Zachary took her glass, placed it on the coffee table and pulled her against him. Holding her by her shoulders, he stared down into her large dark eyes.

"What . . ." was all she got out before he crushed her mouth beneath his own.

His lips were hard, punishing. When she whimpered in protest, his mouth instantly softened, but he did not let her go. He took what he needed . . . his tongue moved insistently over her sweet lips until she opened to accept the full thrust of his tongue. She trembled as his mouth branded Amanda his.

"Let's not pretend. You know exactly what I need from you, Mandy. Gratitude doesn't have a damn thing to do with it."

When his mouth returned to hers, he stroked her tongue with his own, tasting and teasing until she went limp against him, soothingly meeting his erotic caresses with her own feminine warmth.

One large hand glided down her back to the base of her spine. He thrust her hips into his while his other hand moved up to the ripe swells of her breasts. He gently squeezed, enjoying the softness of the silk-covered globe. When he worried her tight nipple, it was all he could do not to unbutton her suit jacket and take her hard blackberry peak into his mouth to suck. Just as unexpectedly as he had taken her into his arms, he released her. His breath was as rapid and uneven as hers.

His black eyes were full of self-loathing when he said,

"I'm sorry. I didn't mean to do that." He rubbed his hand over his dark wavy hair. "You've been through enough today without me trying to force you into something you aren't ready for."

Unable to look at her without touching her, Zachary turned away, shoving both hands into his trousers pockets. He used his breathing to slow his runaway heart rate and the tremor in his legs. There was not much he could do about the discomfort between his thighs.

Zachary waited, listening to her rapid breathing, but she said nothing to ease his impatience with himself. Finally he broke the emotion-charged silence, saying, "Why don't you rest this afternoon? I'm going to work out at the gym for a couple of hours. Later, I'll be at the office if you need me." He walked toward the bedroom, but he paused long enough to say, "If you're up to it, I'd like to take you out to dinner this evening?"

She answered without looking at him. "Dinner will be fine. What time?"

"Eight. Wear something pretty. We're going out dancing later." With that, he disappeared down the hall.

Amanda still had not moved when he returned with a leather duffel bag in one hand.

"See you later," he called as he closed the front door quietly behind him.

"This has to be about sex," Amanda mumbled, as she restlessly picked up one object after another, without paying attention to what she was doing.

There could be no other explanation, just when they seemed to be getting along so well. Yes, there had been a tremendous amount of pressure for both of them since he'd moved into the condo. Perhaps she had not given enough thought to how all of this was affecting him? It was at his insistence that they had been sleeping side by side for weeks now.

There was what happened the other morning. Zachary had pleasured her without expecting anything in return. What about his needs? He was a virile man. She had felt his desire, experienced his passion. Yet, he had not demanded that she return the favor. And she had been left feeling guilty and incredibly selfish, almost as if she were the one taking advantage of him.

One thing she had gained from seeing her father again was a reminder that her husband was nothing like him. She could find no fault with the way Zachary treated her or his understanding of her situation. In a few short weeks she had come to rely on his quiet strength. But it looked as if he were being driven up a wall by sexual frustration. Had living with her day after day proven to be more of a hardship than he had anticipated?

If that was the case, then she had been right from the beginning when she'd warned him that this arrangement couldn't possibly work. The fact that she might be proven right didn't bring even a hint of satisfaction.

Amanda had cared about Zachary far too long. She did not want to be the source of his unhappiness. Her parents' marriage had certainly not shown her how a marriage should work.

Zachary expected too much from her. If only she were like Yolanda. The girl was a survivor. Yolanda had lived through similar bouts of physical and emotional abuse, but despite that she had been able to find happiness with a wonderful man. She had been lucky enough to have gone against the odds and learned to love; more importantly, she had learned to trust.

Was it possible for Amanda to do the same? Did she even have the courage to try? Or was she so afraid of being hurt to take the risk? Unfortunately wishing was not enough. Life just didn't work that way.

Amanda dressed with particular care, hoping to boost her spirits. She admitted to herself that she also wanted to please her husband in some small way. She hated the look of self-loathing she had glimpsed on his face.

She selected a simple, high-neck red sheath that left her back bare to the waist. She put on the diamond and ruby cluster earrings that Zachary had sent her for her last birthday and his anniversary gift, a lovely ruby and emerald and diamond floral motif bracelet that she had placed in a drawer and never worn. She felt bad that she hadn't even thanked him for either gift. Her grandfather would be ashamed of her callousness.

Pushing that unpleasant thought away, she stepped into red and black snakeskin heels. After collecting the small, matching evening bag, she decided not to put her hair up but brushed the thickness to one side, leaving the ebony curls to cascade down one side of her face and her back. She checked herself in the full-length mirror and decided she had done her best.

When Zachary arrived, he acknowledged her belated thank-you with a nod of his head and seemed pleased that she wore the jewelry. He complimented her and seemed to be in a much better mood than when he had left the condo. In fact, it was as if he had set out to both charm and entertain her.

He had made a reservation at a small supper club in the lower downtown area that had a reputation for both fabulous food and a Caribbean band that swung from hard rock to the more seductive rhythm and blues with a bit of sultry reggae thrown in the mix.

Zachary was clearly the most handsome man in the room, Amanda decided as she sat across from him at a small linen-draped dinner table, lit by candlelight. He had changed into a navy suit that he teamed with an ivory shirt and tie.

"Enjoying yourself?" he asked, leaning back in his chair.

"Very much so." Amanda offered a relaxed smile.

They had shared a delicious meal of tossed salad greens with a wonderful honey-mustard dressing, new jack potatoes and succulent prime rib.

"Any room to share a slice of double-chocolate fudge cake with me?" she asked.

"Share?"

She laughed. "It's too much for one person."

He grinned, reaching across the table to play with her fingers. "I might want to eat it all."

"Don't be selfish," she coaxed, dropping her thick lashes.

Zachary grinned, his dark eyes caressing her face. "I can be bribed."

"Forget it. I want the cake and you can watch me eat it." She laughed, signaling the waiter.

A deep chuckle started down in his chest. When the waiter arrived it was Zachary who ordered the decadent dessert and two forks.

"Did I tell you how beautiful you look tonight?"

"Yes, but I don't mind if you repeat yourself." She flashed him a teasing glance.

"Stop flirting with me. I might get the wrong idea," he said, somewhat breathlessly, lifting her hand over to his mouth and brushing his lips over her knuckles. He turned her hand and then placed another kiss in the warm center of her soft palm.

Her eyes went wide, and her heart suddenly skipped a beat. Before she could think of a response their waiter appeared with their dessert. Amanda smiled her thanks as he put the plate in the center of the table where they both could reach it. When she looked at Zachary again she had herself under control.

"Good?" She watched him taste the dessert.

"Mmm," he agreed, his dark eyes touching her. "I may eat it all."

"You better not," she warned, taking a forkful. "Sinful," she moaned in pleasure. "I know I shouldn't, but I can't help myself."

"Why not?" he asked as he helped himself to more.

"I can not afford another half inch on these hips."

He grinned. "You won't hear me complaining."

She opened her mouth to respond, but before she could, she heard someone calling his name.

"What a fabulous surprise!" Barbara Hamilton laughed as she approached the table.

The twenty-two-year-old beauty didn't spare Amanda so much as a glance. Petite, she was everything Amanda was not, pampered, spoiled and adored by the entire family, and she exuded self-confidence.

"Hi, sweetheart. Out on the town?" Zachary rose to his feet to kiss his distant cousin's cheek.

"Hello, Barbara," Amanda said, quietly putting down her fork. She suddenly lost her appetite.

"Mandy." She forced a smile. "Pretty dress."

"Who are you with?" he asked.

"Friends . . . Carol Hunter and Madeline Ross. See, they're waving."

"Oh, yeah," he said, acknowledging them with a nod.

"I won't keep you. Are you are going down to the club on the lower level for dancing?"

"Yes, we planned to," he answered for them both.

"Save me a dance." She kissed him and was gone.

When he sat down, he eyed Amanda curiously. She had stopped eating and was sipping coffee. "What's wrong?"

"Nothing. You finish it."

His brow was creased in a frown, but he finished the

dessert. He shocked her when he asked, "Why don't you like Barbara?"

"What makes you think that?"

"You were enjoying yourself until she came over. Now you've gone all cold on me. Come to think of it, I can't recall the two of you ever having a conversation. I know she is young and a bit spoiled, but that's not a crime."

Her full lips thinned with annoyance. His distant cousin was hardly her favorite subject. Her mother-in-law had made no secret of the fact that she believed Barbara would make him a much better wife than Amanda.

"Mandy?"

"We're not friends. Let's leave it at that."

"But why? Barbara has had a difficult life. Like you, she lost her parents at such an early age. If my family hadn't taken her in, she would have ended up being sent from one boarding school to the next." He paused, watching her closely. "I just don't understand it. You two are close to the same age. Both of you love shopping and pretty things. Why can't you be friends? You're family."

She couldn't very well say that she would never be a friend with a woman who wanted her husband. "Zach, just leave it alone."

Unfortunately, he was not about to let it drop. "I know Mother had a wild idea that Barbara and I were well suited at one time, but that was before our wedding. I'm glad she's gotten over that one. It was a ridiculous idea. Barbara is much too young for me, but she would be perfect for Brad."

"Your brother?"

"Yeah. The way those two argue there must be something going on between them." He laughed. When the waiter asked if he'd care for another cup of coffee, Zachary asked for the check.

He was wrong. His mother had not changed her mind.

Oh, no! Rebecca McFadden was not about to let a little thing like his marriage stop her.

Once he had settled the bill, he rose and came around to her chair. "Ready to work off some of that food on the dance floor?"

Amanda couldn't seem to resist his smile and returned with one of her own. "Yes." She made up her mind that she was not going to let Barbara spoil their evening.

The band and dance floor were on a lower level. The club was nearly full, but he found a small candlelit table near the dance floor.

Amanda relaxed for the first time in weeks. She moved easily to the steel drums, laughing with enjoyment. When they sat down to catch their breath, she did not protest when he held her hand in his.

Yet, when she spotted Barbara moving toward their table, Amanda excused herself and headed toward the ladies' room. She used the time to run a comb through her hair and freshen her makeup.

When she returned to the table, she was pleasantly surprised to find Zachary waiting to lead her back out onto the dance floor. He pulled her into his arms. They moved to the beat of the slow, sultry music. She closed her eyes and leaned her head on his shoulder. His arms tightened around her small waist. She was disappointed when the song ended and he suggested they leave. They both had had a long day and had to get up early in the morning.

As she gazed up at the star-filled wintry night, she admitted to herself that she was glad Zachary wouldn't be leaving her at the front door. There was no getting away from the fact that Amanda truly enjoyed his company.

Even though he showered first, she did not put off getting ready for bed until she was certain he was asleep. For the first time since he moved in with her, she wasn't dreading the night ahead. Her stomach was not tight with tension at the thought of sharing the bed with him. She was changing, getting used to having him beside her.

Her heart skipped a beat when she returned to the darkened bedroom and discovered that he was still awake. She did not turn and hurry back into the den to waste time until she knew he was asleep . . . not tonight.

As Amanda lay in the dark with her back against his chest, his arms around her waist, she wondered if she was growing a bit too dependent on him. No one had to tell her that what the two of them shared would not last.

Just this afternoon he had kissed her long and hard. How much longer? How long did she have before he'd had enough? She wasn't fooling herself, she knew that Zachary had his limits.

After a time, she whispered, ''Zach, are you asleep?''

''Almost. What is it?'' he said close to her ear.

''Do you think he has really stopped drinking?'' She didn't explain whom she meant . . . she didn't have to.

''I don't know, sugar. But your father did mention that he wanted to see you again.''

''What did you tell him?'' Her entire body had stiffened with dread.

''That it's your choice. I warned him that he won't ever see you without me.''

''You don't trust him, do you?''

''I didn't say that,'' he murmured, absently caressing her midsection. ''Don't worry. He won't get a chance to hurt you again.''

''I'm not afraid of him . . . not anymore. I just don't want him in my life. He has hurt the Daniels women enough. It ends with me.''

''Given time you might get used to the idea of him being in Denver, might . . .''

''So you don't think he'll leave when he gets the money?''

"I don't know." He dropped a kiss on her nape before he said, "I don't want you to be surprised if he calls again."

"I have nothing more to say to him. Why can't he just leave me alone?"

"That's easy. He wants to be in your life. I can't blame him for that," he said softly.

Determined as she was to push Sebastian Daniels out of her thoughts, it was a while before she realized that Zachary was asleep and she was able to sleep.

Eleven

Sebastian didn't see the people he pushed past as he left the McFadden Building. He had just completed his business with Jeffery Ross, his father's attorney. It had not gone well.

He was shaking, shaking from out-and-out rage. He hadn't bothered to stop at his daughter's offices on his way to the lawyer's office, knowing she would not welcome a visit. He had called her twice this week and had not gotten through.

He no longer wanted to see her. How could she? He hadn't believed it at first. He had never imagined that his own baby girl was capable of betraying him this way. It was a huge mistake on her part.

How had she managed it? How had Amanda twisted the old man around her finger in order to convince him to leave her the Double-D? Oh, Sebastian knew she blamed him for her mother's death. But he never suspected that she would take her vendetta this far. What was worse, she had not said one single word about it at lunch. It was probably because she knew she was wrong. Instead of apologizing to her, he should have slapped her down.

He failed to notice the darkened clouds or the fresh layer of snow underfoot as he moved aimlessly down the sidewalk. It was much colder than it had been when he entered the McFadden Building. Yet, he didn't notice the cold and the odd looks he received because he made no effort to button his coat or cover his exposed head and hands.

How could his little girl have done this to him? His only child had managed to completely turn the old man against him. Why else had the old bastard left her the ranch? It was not as if she needed the money. How could she be married to a McFadden?

"Damn it!" he snarled.

The Double-D was his. It was his birthright. He was Jake's only living son. It certainly proved what he'd always known. The old man had never loved him the way he had his older brother, Danny.

Danny was older by an hour. Their mother had bled to death after Sebastian had been born. Jake secretly held his younger son responsible for the loss. There had never been a time during his growing-up years that Sebastian hadn't felt the difference in the way his father treated them. It was subtle, but it was there nonetheless. And it never stopped hurting. The only person Sebastian had felt close to had been his twin.

Danny was long dead. Yet, Jake had never forgotten that Sebastian had been behind the wheel when his twin had been killed. It had happened on their seventeenth birthday. They'd gone off to celebrate with friends. They had too many beers. Danny had been in no condition to drive. Of the two of them, Sebastian had been steadier on his feet so he was behind the wheel of their father's old truck.

When a deer had darted out of the darkness on the country

road a few miles from home, Sebastian had not seen it in time. He had swerved, slamming into the side of a tree. Jake had been the one who had found them. He had taken one whiff of his son's breath and added shame on top of blame.

"Hey, watch it!"

Sebastian stared at the man, not even realizing he had nearly walked right over him. "Sorry," he grumbled, suddenly aware of his surroundings. He got the shakes the instant he spotted the neon sign of Andy's Bar and Grill two doors down the block.

Unconsciously licking suddenly dry lips, he shoved unsteady hands into his pockets, suddenly noticing the bitter cold and blowing snow. When he felt the cashier's check in his pocket, his anger returned in a blind rush. He took the dozen or so steps that would put him at the entrance of the bar.

He had no idea how long he just stood there, looking through the glass door into the dim interior, imagining not only the warm interior but a fiery heat in his belly, followed by the blessed relief that liquor never failed to give him. He could forget what a disappointment he had been as a son, as a husband and as a father. He didn't have to try to prove himself to anyone. He would drink until he numbed the pain and replaced it with a sense of strength and power.

"You coming or going, buddy?" a man said from over his shoulder.

As if suddenly realizing that he was blocking the doorway, Sebastian stepped aside, but then he had always felt as if he had been in the way. The old man had mourned Danny, never seeming to care that he had another son.

When the door swung closed, Sebastian found himself inside the bar. The smells of smoke, stale cigars and spilled beer were all there to welcome him back. He felt as if he had come home.

"What can I get you?" the bartender asked, as he gave the cracked-tile bar a quick wipe with a damp, stained rag.

"Scotch . . . neat," Sebastian said, as he straddled a barstool. One drink was all he needed, just enough to forget about strangling his own flesh and blood.

How much did he need to forget the wrong done to him this day? Two, three drinks? How could he forget that his father did not believe in his own son's innocence?

The only reason he hadn't been arrested was that the old man was a friend of the sheriff. The car crash was later ruled an accident, and Sebastian had not been charged. It had been a rough year, but Sebastian had left the Double-D when he turned eighteen and never looked back.

After he and Darlene had married, she had been the one to contact the old man. Over the years she maintained the contact, something to do with having no family of her own. She insisted that Amanda needed to know her people. Darlene had even taken the girl to the ranch during the summers. He had never gone with them. He took pride in not paying for those trips. Let his old man foot the bill if he wanted to see the kid.

As the years passed, Sebastian had found that the only way to keep the memories at bay was with a bottle. Alcohol had a strange effect on him. It allowed him to forget the sound of his twin's voice in his head. It also gave him strength, thus allowed him to feel like a man.

The bartender plopped the shot glass on the bar, waiting expectantly.

Sebastian pulled out a fifty-dollar bill. "Keep 'em coming."

He saw no reason to stop, that is, until he put Darlene in the hospital that last time. He knew he had busted up her bad, and he got scared. She had nearly died. She would have died if Amanda hadn't called for help. He didn't even remember hitting his daughter. He was too far gone. With

Darlene just lying there not moving, he had sobered up instantly, aware of what he had done.

Like a coward, he had run, knowing Darlene would never forgive him, not this time. He'd scared himself, afraid she wouldn't recover from his drunken rage. He had gone on a major binge. It was months before he had finally built up the nerve to call home. He found the number had been disconnected. He had no choice but to contact his old man. That was how he had learned that his wife had died and Amanda was living with his old man on the Double-D.

That loss had started him drinking again. And he had not stopped for more years than he cared to count. He worked because he needed to keep a bottle in his pocket and a roof over his head. The only thing that had saved him this last time was ending up in the hospital, near death.

Amanda had more than a dozen years to worm her way into the old man's heart. He swore bitterly. He felt as if his own flesh and blood had stabbed him in the back. What was money compared to the Double-D?

Sebastian cradled the glass in his hands, his fingertips caressing the smooth surface. He inhaled deeply before he threw back his head, downing the contents. A comforting heat seeped all the way down to his toes, warming him as nothing else could, providing the long-awaited solace he desperately needed.

"Hell, yeah," he grumbled to himself. This was exactly what he needed. "The little witch certainly didn't need the ranch." As far as he was concerned she was no longer a Daniels. She was a McFadden now.

"Amanda?" Gloria Dain called as she hurried into the large workroom where Amanda was working at one of the sewing machines. The room was filled with noise while a soft jazz played in the background.

Anna Atkins was at the serger and Margaret Clark was at the embroidery machine. They were making and monogramming table linens and napkins for the Hollingsworth Hotel. Jennifer Bond, Kelly Robert and Betty Singleton were working at tables covering picture frames, hat boxes, blank-page hard-covered books, pen and pencil holders, photo albums and book covers with hand-painted silk fabrics Amanda had designed, part of the home-accessories collection that was scheduled to go into several of the upscale boutiques. Amanda didn't look up from the ruffle she was stitching onto yet another throw pillow that would be displayed in the Boykins' bedroom.

"What's wrong? Did Mrs. Moore call again about her drapes?" Amanda dropped the last pillow onto the pile.

"No, thank goodness." Gloria eyed the pile of pillows filling the wide silk-lined basket. The lipstick-red oriental fabric was embroidered with gold thread.

Gloria waited until she had Amanda's attention, then waved the glossy trade journal at her boss. "I found that oriental brass chest that Mrs. Boykins has been looking for to complete her sitting room."

"That's wonderful news." Amanda stood, stretching tired muscles in her back and legs before she glanced at the glossy photograph. "Mmm, I think you're right."

Gloria beamed. "I've got to get on the phone to the gallery. I will die if they sell it out from under me."

Amanda smiled as she started down the hallway toward the reception area and the offices. "They wouldn't dare, that is, if they value their lives. Has John finished those shelves at the Boykinses?"

Gloria and her husband, John, had worked for Amanda for several years. John was a highly skilled carpenter.

"Yes, he's on his way back. He planned to stop at the upholstery to check on those armchairs for the Boykinses' sitting room. The snow is probably slowing him down."

They paused in the reception area where Helen Brown was on the telephone.

"Stop worrying, you'll get the chest. And you're right, it will complete the look we're trying to create. I wonder how Mrs. Grant is coming with those drapes."

Gloria teased, "As long as they're red, Mrs. Boykins will love them."

Amanda laughed. "She is crazy about the color."

"Gosh, it's good to hear you laugh. You've had us a bit worried lately," Gloria said, as she followed Amanda into her office.

"What? Have I been down in the mouth?" Amanda asked, as she sat down in the chintz-covered chair behind the desk.

"Not that . . . just a bit self-absorbed, if you know what I mean. Is there something I can do for you?"

"No, but thanks. I'm fine."

"I can't help noticing that you're wearing your wedding rings again. The reconciliation going well?" Gloria asked curiously.

Amanda absently fingered her rings. When she looked at Gloria, she smiled. "We're trying."

"I'm glad. In the ten years John and I have been together, we've certainly had our share of ups and downs. Hang in there." Moving toward the open door, Gloria called from over her shoulder, "Keep your fingers crossed that I can get that chest," before she hurried to the office she shared with the other assistant.

Amanda didn't bother looking through the telephone messages Helen had left on the desk. She didn't even spare a glance at the array of photographs on the desk, of the newly purchased resort complex in the south of France.

She had no idea why she was not excited about the upcoming Bendini job. A chance to fly to Nice in order to design the interior of one of the world's plushest resorts with no restrictions on cost should have been a dream come true. So why wasn't she thrilled?

Mr. Bendini had been highly pleased with the work she had done, first with his historic family home in Denver, then his town house in New York just last year. Both residences had been pictured in *Architectural Digest*. He had also recommended her to several of his wealthy friends. She had been grateful and had gained an international reputation. Yet, all she could concentrate on was her personal problems.

Would Zachary even bother to object if she took off for the south of France? Knowing him, she doubted it. He had always supported her in her career, long before they married. He'd probably help her pack.

Pushing back her chair, she crossed to the windows that overlooked the downtown streets and stared at the snow that was coming down in earnest. It had been snowing on and off all day. The ground was layered with a thick blanket of snow that had slowed traffic considerably.

She had been so caught up in her own problems that she failed to recognize they were in the midst of what looked to be blizzard conditions. Within the last few weeks she had grown used to sharing her home with Zachary. Lately he, on the other hand, had spent more time away than he did with her. In fact, she saw little of him these days.

The weekends were the worst. He spent Saturdays on the ranch, claiming he was catching up on paperwork, and Sundays he went skiing with his brothers in the mountains. Although he still slept beside her during the week, they had not done anything together since the night he'd taken her out to dinner and dancing.

She knew she had no business feeling neglected. It wasn't as if she wanted him to treat her like a real wife. Her whole point in agreeing to this arrangement was to prove to him they were two drastically different people who didn't want the same things from life. Time seemed to be proving her right.

So why wasn't she relieved? It was not as if he was pressuring her to make love. The only time they'd even come close was the morning she'd overslept.

Thank goodness, there had been no repeat of what happened that morning when he came so close to making love to her. Although he had held her a few times, there was nothing sexual about it. Zachary had offered comfort, nothing more.

Even though she had confessed to Yolanda how much she longed to sleep in his arms, she had never shared that with Zachary. She couldn't, especially when she didn't ever want to be vulnerable to him.

Not that it mattered anymore. These days she was the one hugging her pillow, yearning for more. She told herself again and again that she should be thrilled that he was ignoring her; instead she had never felt more isolated or alone.

Evidently, Zachary had reached the point where he no longer found her desirable. Why else was he spending so much time at the ranch? Then there was Barbara, just waiting for their marriage to fall apart.

Amanda was alarmed by her burgeoning awareness of the man who slept soundly while she tossed and turned most of the night. It was as if she had become her own worst enemy. How could she rest when she was keenly aware of his muscular bronze frame? He wore no more than pajama bottoms, regardless of the outside temperature. He may not have changed, but she certainly had.

Their sleeping arrangement was slowly driving her up a wall. She tossed and turned night after night. She had tried everything she could think of to stay away from him, from sleeping on the very edge of the king-size bed, thus risking falling on the floor, to placing a pillow between them.

Regardless of what she did, without fail, she woke on Zachary's side of the bed, with no idea how she got there.

It was not as if her determination had wavered. She flatly refused to cave in to her awareness of him. Sexual gratification could only lead to emotional dependency and weakness. She had only to remember her mother after one of her father's beatings to cool her lustful thoughts.

When she was a little girl, she remembered asking her mother how she could forgive her father for hurting her again and again. Her mother's answers were always the same: when Amanda grew up and fell in love, then she would understand why. But she'd never understood. At her mother's grave site she had vowed that she would never love anyone so deeply and so completely that she would take her own life because of the loss.

The crazy thing was that even after more than a dozen years, her father claimed he had loved his family. Amanda's hands were balled into fists as she recalled her father's confession. They were lies, every single one of them. It had taken all her resolve not to scream that love didn't have a damn thing to do with the pain. She would be plain stupid if she hadn't learned something from a childhood of watching her father systematically destroy his own family. Amanda had always prided herself on being nobody's fool.

"Oh, Zach . . ." she murmured aloud.

If things did not change between them soon, she would drop somewhere from sheer exhaustion. Come to think of it, Zachary hadn't been looking so great either. He had begun to look gaunt from his dual responsibilities of running the ranch and the family business.

"Mrs. McFadden?" Helen knocked on the open door. Although Helen was a grandmother, who was raising a teenage grandson, she wore her haircut into a low natural and didn't look a day over thirty.

"Yes, Helen," Amanda said, slowly turning from the

window. She smiled at her secretary, who after years of working together insisted on addressing her formally.

"Two messages from Mr. Sebastian Daniels."

"Thank you" was all Amanda said, but her brow was creased in a frown.

Her father was just not going to leave her alone. He made a habit of calling her at the office. What she could not understand was why. She had learned from her lawyer, Jeffery Ross, that her father had met with him and received the money from Jake's estate. Why hadn't he left town? What could be holding him? She had made herself clear. There would be no tender reconciliation between the two of them.

Helen cleared her throat before she went on to say, "I just heard the weather report. We already had seven inches of snow on the ground and another eight inches is expected before morning. Would you mind if we left early? It's after three, and if the staff doesn't leave soon, we may not make it home."

Amanda blushed with embarrassment. "Of course. Would you tell the others?"

Where was her mind? Here she had been staring down at the street, yet the urgency of the situation had not registered.

"Are you all right?"

"Yes, I'm just a little tired." The excuse sounded lame even to Amanda's ears, but it was the truth. "Thanks."

"You are leaving also, aren't you?"

The concern in the other woman's voice caused Amanda to smile. "Yes, I'll lock up and leave as soon as I make a call."

Worried that Zachary might try flying in during the storm, Amanda waited until she was alone before she went to the desk and punched the number to the Circle-M. As she nervously listened to the telephone ring, she wondered if she should be calling Roger instead. He might know

Zachary's plan. That was silly. It was far simpler to call her husband and speak to him.

"McFadden residence."

"Hello, Mrs. McFadden. How are you?" As Amanda instantly recognized her mother-in-law's voice, her heart sank.

"Amanda? Is that you?" Rebecca Hamilton McFadden asked icily.

"Yes. May I speak to Zachary, please?"

"I'm well, thank you," Mrs. McFadden sarcastically announced. "My son isn't in. He's out on the range," she ended coldly.

"Please tell Zach I called." Amanda did not need to be reminded that the older woman felt as if she was unsuitable for her eldest son.

"I must congratulate you. But then you are a clever little thing, aren't you?" Rebecca said, rather than replacing the receiver. "Zachary could never resist a challenge, even as a small boy. It won't be long before he realizes that you deliberately lost his baby. You were unbelievably reckless." Her voice exuded confidence when she said, "It's only a matter of time until he realizes you're all wrong for him."

Wiping away the sudden rush of tears, her body taut with tension, Amanda insisted, "You have no right to speak to me that way."

Why did she let the woman pull her strings, as if she were a brainless puppet? Her mother-in-law's venom was certainly no surprise and this was not the first time. It happened her first day home from the hospital after her miscarriage.

"You trapped my son into marriage and you tell me I have no right?" Rebecca huffed with indignation. "Young woman, I love my son. And so does Barbara. Those two would have been married by now, if you had kept your dress down."

Amanda gasped, shaking with rage. Before she could collect herself to respond, her mother-in-law said, "More than likely Zachary won't be able to make it into Denver tonight. I wouldn't hold a meal for him, if I were you."

"Good-bye." Amanda hung up before she said something she would really regret later.

She was smarting from the other woman's attack. She sat with her arms wrapped protectively around herself as the old insecurities, along with impotence, bubbled inside her. She should have hung up the instant that horrible woman came on the line. Rebecca McFadden was hateful and just plain mean.

"How could she?" Amanda hissed as she reached for a tissue to dry a fresh bout of tears. How could she think for even a moment that Amanda had deliberately tried to hurt her own baby? How could anyone be that hateful . . . that downright cruel?

Was it all because Zachary's mother did not believe Amanda's lineage was equivalent to her own? Amanda suspected that was only part of the reason. For some reason his mother saw Amanda as a threat to her own place in the McFadden household.

Zachary owned the Circle-M, including the ranch home he shared with his family. He had bought the place from his father back when his father considered the ranch more of a liability than an asset.

Zachary had worked hard during the ensuing years to prove to his father that he was wrong, not only about the ranch but also about him. He, like his father, had a knack for making money, something the entire family had benefited from over the years.

Mrs. McFadden was naturally cool to anyone outside her family and social sphere. The day Amanda married Zachary, that coolness had turned into out-and-out hostility. Mere minutes before the ceremony she had told Amanda that she was making a serious mistake and that she would never be welcome in her home.

Unfortunately, his mother had kept her promise. Mrs. McFadden had done everything within her power to make Amanda feel unwelcome at the Circle-M. Naturally, his mother kept her hostilities hidden from her son.

If Amanda lived to be a hundred, she could never forget her mother-in-law's words that fateful day when she had been the most vulnerable, "You think by gaining my son's name you had it all. You couldn't be more wrong. You lost your only leverage when you lost that baby. You've lost the money, the house and the man." Mrs. McFadden barely took a breath before she went on to say, "This is my home and you will never be a member of this family. You will always be an outsider."

"I'm going now," Helen said, from the open doorway. "You won't be long, will you? The others have all gone."

"I'm leaving soon. Go ahead. I'll see you in the morning." Amanda absently waved, forcing a smile.

Once she was alone, she sagged in the chair behind the desk. She could not stop herself from speculating on how much her mother-in-law knew about their so-called reconciliation. Had Zachary told her it was only a temporary arrangement?

Not for the first time, she wondered if his mother had shared her beliefs with Zachary. Did he think that she'd deliberately hurt their baby? Surely, he would have mentioned it to her?

Why was she tormenting herself this way? Zachary would never believe such a thing. He knew how desperately she wanted their baby . . . how much she still suffered from the loss. No, even her mother-in-law could not be so heartless as to suggest such a thing to her own son.

"Calm down," she cautioned herself. She was overreacting. They had shared the loss ... grieved together. His mother was trying to hurt her, trying to make trouble.

"Zachary." Just thoughts of her proud, exasperatingly stubborn, strong-willed husband brought a smile to her face. He was not one to discuss the intimate details of his marriage with anyone, even his beloved mother.

Amanda might not be able to make love to him the way he needed, but she did believe in him and she trusted him. And she was so thankful that she did not have to share a house with the woman. There was not a house big enough to hold the two of them peacefully.

The sound of the telephone interrupted her thoughts. "Daniels Interior Designs. May I help you?"

"You still there?" Roger's voice came over the line.

"Hi, shouldn't you be on your way back to the ranch while the roads are still open?"

"I'm spending the night in the city. What are you still doing in the office? You should be home by now."

"Roger, did you call to fuss at me? Or is there another reason?" She laughed, feeling much better.

"Just checking up on family. Zach would have my hide if I did not make sure you're okay. Need a lift home?"

"No, thanks. I have my car. It's out there somewhere buried in the snow. Besides, it's not far to my place, but you know that, I might add. I could walk, if I had to. Where are you, anyway?"

"In my office. Brad and I are sharing the penthouse tonight," he explained. "Would you like to have dinner with us?"

Amanda had forgotten about that spacious three-bedroom apartment on the top floor, which the brothers used occasionally. Zachary had lived there during his stint in the city. She also recalled how much he had hated it ... no horses or cows.

"Thanks, but not tonight. You're right. I should be getting

home. Do you think Zach will fly in this weather?'' She tried but failed to keep the anxiety out of her voice.

''I doubt he will be able to get clearance. Have you spoken to him?''

''No.'' She shuddered, recalling her conversation with her mother-in-law. Amanda was not about to share that information with Roger, or Zachary, for that matter. ''He was out on the range when I called.''

''Hmm. I hope my brother has sense enough not to try to fly or drive in. He can be a bit mule-headed at times.''

''Peggy tells me that trait runs in the family,'' she attempted to tease, even though the thought of Zachary being at risk scared her. ''What if—''

''He's fine, Mandy. Stop fretting. You'll hear from him before long. Get your coat and boots on, I'm driving you home. When big brother calls, I want to be able to reassure him that you got home without a problem. We McFaddens look after our own.''

She felt obligated to say, ''I'm not a child.''

''And I know how much you hate driving in that white stuff. I'll meet you in the lobby in ten minutes.'' Roger hung up, without giving her time to come up with yet another objection.

Amanda gave in. Roger was right. She had never liked driving in the snow, but that was not enough to keep her from doing what had to be done. Why worry about it when she did not have to? That decided, she began collecting her things.

Twelve

The short drive took more than an hour with the traffic barely moving. They passed an accident where one car had plowed into the back of another. Visibility was limited because of the high winds. Several drivers were on the side of the road, waiting for a tow truck to dig them out, which was not surprising, considering the blowing snow and the height of some of the snowdrifts.

Amanda invited Roger in for a hot drink, but he refused, saying he was eager to get back to the penthouse, into some warm, dry clothes, and call Peggy. Amanda kissed his cheek, then hurried out of the howling wind into the warmth of the lobby.

Pausing to collect the mail and a newspaper, she was grateful that it didn't take long for the elevator to arrive. She did not bother to change from the gray flannel slacks and green silk blouse she'd worn to the office that morning.

But she did unpin and brush her hair, in hopes of easing the beginning signs of a tension headache.

In warm fuzzy slippers, Amanda moved restlessly around the living room, continuously eyeing the silent telephone. She wasn't about to call the ranch again, although she did call Zachary's cell phone number without any luck. She suspected that he had either forgotten to turn the thing on or there was a problem because of the storm; either way, she could not reach him.

She was so worried because she could not reach him that she did not bother to do any of the things she normally did at the end of the day such as preparing a meal. She was not interested in food. Instead, she sat down on the carpet beside the French doors where she could watch the snow. It was a beautiful scene especially when she was inside and out of the storm. For the unprotected, it was a nightmare.

Shivering with her arms wrapped around upraised legs, she rested her chin on her knees. Even though she was cold, she could not work up the energy to check the thermostat.

Amanda told herself that she wasn't worried about her husband. She should not expect him, not in this weather. Yet, she could not get away from the fact that for the first time in two months Zachary would not be coming home to her.

She had no idea how long she sat brooding over the incredible sense of loneliness she was experiencing. This was ridiculous. She should be used to being alone . . . used to the quietness of her home.

It seemed as if Zachary had taken control of her thoughts just as boldly as he had moved into her home. The simple truth was she not only missed him, she was furious with him as well.

Why hadn't he called? Told her something? What if his mother had not told him that she called? Or worse, what if Mrs. McFadden told him that she had called and was not expecting him tonight? If that was the case, he had no reason to call.

"You are pitiful," she chided herself.

Amanda had promised him a year, but her resistance was weakening, a bit more each day. Good grief. They had a full ten more months to go. Would she come out of this with her heart whole? Was she underrating her own resilience? Was it possible for her to make love with him and still survive emotionally? She had been asking herself those questions for weeks with no clear answer.

To fall in love with him was just too risky. It would bring dependence and loss of control. One thing she was certain of was that making love with him would not alter the situation between Amanda and his mother. Nor would it make their problems disappear.

She watched the sky, dark and heavy with clouds, and listened to the howling wind as it pelted snowflakes against the glass doors. The room was illuminated by the distant streetlights and moonlight.

He was not coming. Perhaps she should be grateful that she would be able to sleep without worrying about getting too close to him during the night. This respite might give her time to build her defenses against him. She needed the time. He was . . .

Suddenly a lamp was switched on. Zachary stood inside the pool of light.

"Zach!"

"Why are you sitting in the dark?" he asked as he advanced toward her.

"What are you doing here?"

He grinned. "I live here, or have you forgotten? It's cold in here." He went over to the thermostat and adjusted the setting. When he turned, he lifted a black brow. "Shall I come down or are you coming up?" His warm dark eyes feasted on the length of her curvy limbs and golden brown beauty.

"Come down." She smiled, not bothering to hide her relief.

He sat down behind her, reaching out a hand to lift the soft curls from the side of her neck, and pressed a warm kiss there. "Have a hard day?" He began to knead the tight muscles in her neck.

"Mmm," she moaned softly, letting her head drop forward. "Not a bad day, just a long one."

His work-roughened hands moved to the soft pads of her shoulders to gently knead, then stroked and finally caressed her through the silk blouse.

She tingled with pleasure, and found herself drifting back toward the solid wall of his chest. She closed her eyes, wanting him to touch her, taste her. What was she thinking?

Abruptly, she straightened as she recognized what she was allowing to happen. She shifted away, just out of reach. Sex would not change anything, other than increasing her vulnerability. If she was not extremely cautious, she would wind up begging him to make love to her.

"Mandy—"

Her voice was not quite steady when she interrupted, "I didn't think you were coming. You didn't call. You didn't try to fly, did you?"

He scowled, not bothering to hide his disappointment. He rested his hands on muscular thighs. "I took the Jeep. How did you get home? I didn't see your car in the lot."

"Roger brought me. He and Brad are staying in the penthouse." She glanced at him through the thickness of her lashes.

He wore navy cords and a heavy burgundy cable-knit sweater. He stretched out beside her, bending one leg at the knee, and rested his back comfortably against the wall.

"You look tired. Have you eaten?"

"I'm tired, sugar. But I'll survive."

"Are you hungry?"

"Not for food, if that's what you're offering," he said with a touch of impatience.

"What is that supposed to mean?"

"I think you know perfectly well what I'm hungry for, Mandy." He rose smoothly to his feet. "Excuse me, I need a shower." He left without a backward glance.

Amanda knew. She was just as tired of their silent war as he evidently was. Even though she understood his frustration, it still bothered her. Instead of being angry with him, she was annoyed with herself. She was feeling too much. Unable to sit still a second longer, she got up and put on a CD before going into the kitchen.

She prepared a salad, then began washing and dicing green onions, mushrooms and red bell pepper, before she grated cheddar and Muenster cheese. Then she cracked half a dozen eggs in a large mixing bowl and began whipping them with a whisk. In a little more than fifteen minutes she had the table set for two.

"What is this?" He eyed the place settings on the leaf-green tablecloth as she lit lemon-scented tapered candles.

She looked at him, taking in the fact that all he wore was a pair of low-riding jeans, faded from frequent washing. His chest was bare.

"I'm hungry," she quipped, forcing her eyes away. "You're welcome to watch me eat," she said, returning her attention to the stove where she dropped a generous pat of butter into the hot skillet.

She tried to ignore the sparks of desire that caused her breath to catch in her throat. For a moment, she had almost reached out and traced the mat of dark hair on his chest to where it narrowed at his midsection, then disappeared inside his jeans. She forced herself to look away from the prominent ridge of his sex and ignore the urge to press her face into the bronze hollow at his throat and taste his dark skin while inhaling his clean male scent.

He leaned against the counter. His six-four frame suddenly made the kitchen seem unbearably small. She could feel his eyes on her.

"What are you making?"

"An omelet . . . my favorite."

"Aw, come on, pretty girl. Stop rubbing it in," he said huskily, coming over to stand behind her. "If I had a choice I would prefer to be inside you," he said, close to her ear, his hands spanning her waist, moving her back until she rested against him.

"You *don't* have a choice," she insisted, trying to take a side step away from him. He held on to her.

"My point exactly," he groaned deep in his throat. Then he dipped his head in order to worry her earlobe with his tongue, savoring the taste of her sweet-scented flesh before he moved away. "Can I do anything to help?" he asked as he watched her add the vegetables, then the eggs and cheese.

You can leave me the hell alone, she longed to yell at him, but instead said, "Uncork the wine, please. It's chilling in the refrigerator."

"You know I don't expect you to cook for me every night. You have enough to do with running your business. We need to hire a housekeeper."

"No!"

"Why not?" He held the corkscrew in one hand and the bottle of red wine in the other.

Within minutes she placed two perfectly formed fluffy omelets on their plates. "I don't want a stranger in my home."

Carrying the plates to the table, she returned for the salad bowl while Zachary filled their glasses.

"Is there anything else you need from the kitchen?"

"No. Thanks," she said, taking the chair he held out for her.

"Now that we're together, you do need extra help. You've been cooking, cleaning, washing clothes, plus maintaining and operating a business. Enough is enough."

"I do not want a housekeeper. Please say grace so we can enjoy our meal."

She was not about to admit that she could not stand the thought of another woman doing the things for him she enjoyed. Sure, it was extra work, but that did not matter. She was not willing to turn over the few privileges she had as his wife. She was not able to be his lover and give him the physical pleasure he craved, but she could take care of his other needs. Amanda was not about to let him snatch that away from her.

How could she possibly explain this to him? How could she make him understand? Frankly, she was not sure she understood it herself. She hated the way she felt about herself, as if other women knew the secrets of pleasuring their men while she didn't have a clue.

How much longer would he be able to put up with her refusals? Judging by his comment in the kitchen, not much longer. He was losing patience with her. Furthermore, she couldn't even hold it against him. Before too much longer she would be alone again. She trembled involuntarily.

"Still cold?" he asked, as he helped himself to another serving of salad.

"No. I'm fine," she said.

"My mother has always had help in the house. And she prides herself on keeping a lovely home. She would never—"

It was the wrong thing to say. Amanda had had enough of his mother for this day. She interjected agitatedly, "I'm not your mother. This is my home, not hers. I don't want a housekeeper."

His eyes bore into hers, while a muscle danced in his cheek. "I'm hiring the housekeeper in the morning. That's the end of it," he said emphatically.

"Whatever you say, darlin'." She smiled sweetly, halting the movement of her fork in midair.

He took in the bewitching depth of her lovely eyes, red-gloss-covered full lips and the flare of her delicate nostrils as she jutted out her chin.

"And?" he prompted.

"I will fire her the instant she arrives for work. Soooo, if you must hire someone, go ahead. I can't stop you. But be warned . . . the woman won't last a day."

He made an impatient sound in his throat. He lifted his wineglass and downed the contents. "You're enough to drive a saint to drink!"

"How could you?" she cried, averting her face so that he could not see how badly he had hurt her.

"Oh, hell," he said, when he realized what he had done. "Honey, I'm sorry. I didn't mean that the way it sounded." He sighed heavily. "Sometimes you make me angry enough to chew nails."

When she refused to look at him, let alone accept his apology, he angrily refilled his glass and resumed eating. The veins along his jawline throbbed rhythmically as if he were clenching his strong white teeth rather than chewing.

The meal continued in silence. The tension was so thick, she felt as if it were suffocating her. She could not overlook the stubborn set of Zachary's jaw or his tightly compressed mouth. Fury flickered in the onyx depths of his eyes. She gave up all pretense of eating.

"Zach . . ." She stopped, a knot of unhappiness locked in her throat.

He lifted long dark lashes to look at her. He also did not seem to be finding much pleasure in the meal. "Yeah?"

"Please . . . don't be angry," she whispered.

Her dark eyes were wide with appeal. She could not explain why she suddenly felt like crying or why his anger disturbed her so much. Nothing was making much sense tonight. One second she was deliberately provoking him, the next she longed to curl up in his lap and tuck her face in that place between his shoulder and his neck. Why did it have to be so complicated? If only she did not care so deeply.

Pushing back his chair, he said quietly, "I have my limits, Mandy."

She surprised them both when she whispered, "Will you . . . please . . . just hold me?" She moved on trembling legs toward him, even though she was afraid that he would refuse.

There was no hesitation on his part. He pulled her down onto his lap, placing an arm around her waist. She let out a deep sigh, resting her head on his shoulder, her nose pressed against the side of his throat.

He said nothing, making no move to ease the tension between them. He didn't press her into his chest or kiss her. He did nothing to convey how he felt about her wanting to be close to him. In fact, he sat quietly as if he was waiting for an explanation.

"Zach, don't be this way. Taking care of the condo is something I want to do . . . need to do." Amanda slipped her arms around his neck, stroking the hair that grew at his nape.

Suddenly, she realized she was not frightened by his anger. She didn't like it, and she certainly was upset because of it, but not afraid. It was exhilarating knowing she was slowly conquering some of her fears.

He shifted until he could study her face. His gaze lingered on her lips when she dampened them with her tongue.

He swallowed before he said quietly, "I don't want you exhausted from working. Don't you think I can see those shadows under your eyes? I know you toss and turn most nights. It's not until dawn that you finally relax enough to allow your body to get the rest it needs.''

She blinked in dismay. She was tired most days. As she sagged against him, her soft breasts pressed into his chest and she let out a deep breath. She wasn't about to tell him the reason she couldn't sleep had nothing to do with being overworked and everything to do with him sleeping beside her.

Absently, her fingers slid over the firm muscles of his hairy, coppery bronze flesh. The caress was an indulgence on her part. She relished the tautness of his rib cage, her hand momentarily resting on his tight stomach.

He caught her hand and held it in his own. When she looked up at him, his dark eyes were glazed with sexual need.

His voice had deepened when he said, ''You've managed to cool my temper, but in the process you have taken on more than I'm sure you bargained on.''

Sensual awareness spiraled from the pit of her stomach as he shifted, allowing her to feel the strength of his erection.

''Zach . . .''

Before she could even formulate a protest he took her mouth in a hard, lengthy kiss. Amanda tried but failed to gather her thoughts. She couldn't think as she filled her lungs with his warm male scent. Her lips parted, expectantly yearning for the searing hot caress of his tongue against her own. That particular caress was not forthcoming.

She moaned in protest when he did not deepen the kiss, but unwittingly rubbed the aching tips of her breasts into his chest. She quivered at the sound of his husky groan. Only she needed more. When his mouth moved enticingly against the softness of her lips, she wrapped her arms around his neck.

''Please . . .'' she urged.

Hungry for the taste of him as well as the feel of his hard

strength, she slid her tongue into his mouth. She explored the smooth surface of his white teeth, then moved on to the fleshy inside of his bottom lip before she pulled his lip into her mouth, to suckle.

Trembling from her sweet assault, he shifted her body until she straddled his heavy-muscled thighs. She was close but not close enough. He slid her forward even more until their bodies came into oh-so-sweet contact; only then did he give her what they both craved, the deep thrust of his tongue against hers. His erection pressed insistently against her plump mound as his tongue played with hers.

Eventually, they had no choice but to part as they struggled to fill their lungs with air. He looked into her lovely chocolate-brown eyes with sizzling-hot ebony eyes.

"Mandy . . ." he said as his long fingers moved into her dark, thick curls. The sudden ringing of the telephone cut through the smoldering heat of desire.

"I should get that," she whispered breathlessly.

Zachary looked anything but thrilled by the intrusion. He took her mouth in another seductive assault on her senses.

"Honey . . . it might be important," she managed to say as she tried to put some distance between them.

He held her fast, ignoring the insistent jingle of the telephone.

"Zach . . ." she said against his lips.

"Let the machine get it," he said as he tantalized her mouth with his.

She moaned, "I turned it off when I got home."

He kissed her again and again, but the telephone continued to ring.

"Honey, let me go."

"Why, so you can use it as yet another reason to keep me at a distance?"

Amanda had no ready response. Finally, she said, "It

obviously must be important or it would have stopped by now. What if there's an emergency?''

Frustrated, he said, "Then by all means, go.''

She hurried into the kitchen, picking up the extension on the wall. The last thing she wanted was to make him angry but that was exactly what she had done.

"Hello?''

"It's about time! I was beginning to think you had died or something.''

"Hello, Barbara,'' Amanda said impatiently.

"Let me talk to Zach.''

Amanda glared at the telephone. She was close to hanging up, but thought better of it. What was it with the McFadden women? "Just a second.''

He was scowling when she handed over the handset, taking care not to touch his skin.

"It's your lover, Barbara.''

Momentarily shocked into silence, he stared at her.

Amanda fumed, suddenly certain that he had to be getting sex from somewhere. He most certainly was not getting any from her. She snatched the plates from the table and hurried into the kitchen.

"What in the hell!'' he snarled, pushing out of his chair. He stepped into her path before she could reach the sink. "You had better explain.''

She lifted her chin in an effort to stare him down. "I'm not stupid, Zach. You're a virile man. You proved that before the telephone rang. Barbara is beautiful and willing. And you've been spending a lot of time at the ranch. What more is required?''

He was careful not to touch her. He was too angry. "Don't ever accuse me of something unless you can be damn sure you can back it up, Mandy McFadden,'' he said between clenched teeth. "I haven't given you one reason to doubt me. I don't operate that way. Damn it, you know it.''

She took in the muscles working along his jawline, the unyielding line of his compressed lips. There was no mistaking that he was livid.

She wondered if she had jumped to the wrong conclusion. Could she be mistaken? What if she was assuming the worst because of her own insecurities? Or was this a result of her unpleasant conversation with his mother?

Zachary had a strong sex drive, there was no question about that. That did not necessarily mean he was susceptible to Barbara's delectable charms. But there was no doubt that Barbara wanted him and was ruthless enough not to care that he was married.

The woman lived in his house, for goodness' sake. And she was more than willing to make herself available to him whenever he wanted. His own mother had said as much. But Zachary was not underhanded about anything. He was too straightforward to waste time with subterfuge. And he was certainly not afraid to go after what he wanted.

There was a husky quality to his voice when he said, ''Don't use Barbara to keep me away from you.'' His hand moved from her wrist to stroke the inside of her arm below her elbow. He turned a fleeting touch into a sensuous caress.

With downcast lids, she said, ''If I'm wrong, I apologize. Hurry . . . Barbara is waiting.''

''If?'' He was not satisfied with the concession.

''The phone . . .''

Reluctantly, he removed his hand and returned to the next room to pick up the handset from where he'd dropped it on the carpet.

She would not have thought it was possible for her to agree with Mrs. McFadden. But in this case his mother was right. Barbara would have been Zachary's wife by now, if Amanda had not gotten pregnant.

Amanda and Zachary had turned to each other in a moment of weakness and shared pain. And because of that night they had changed the course of both their lives. But she wasn't naive enough to think just being married to her would stop him from desiring another woman.

For now he felt obligated to make a go of their marriage. His stupid male pride would not let him do less than what he believed was right. He intended to make a go of their marriage, even if they both had to suffer because of it. Sooner or later, even he would have to admit the truth. They were playing at marriage.

Unfortunately, Amanda's resolve was weakening with each new day. She wanted him . . . she wanted him to make love to her even when she knew their circumstances were all wrong for any kind of lasting union. Thank goodness she was not one to act on her instincts.

She turned on the radio in an effort to drown out the sound of his voice as she began cleaning the kitchen. Why had he come into the kitchen to take the call? The last thing she wanted was to hear his side of the conversation as he consoled poor Barbara.

She was up to her elbows in suds when he said, from behind her, "Mandy, do you honestly believe I'm low enough to sleep with my own cousin, then casually come home to my wife? Or was I right? Is this yet another way to keep me at a distance?"

"Just forget I said anything." Channeling her energies into washing a wineglass, she said, "It doesn't matter. We both know you're just passing through."

"Mandy, I—"

"Can't you understand I don't care where . . ." she said agitatedly. "Just forget I—" She then cried out in pain. "Ouch!"

"What have you done?" He lifted her hands out of the water.

She watched as blood gushed from an open cut. In her

agitation she had snapped the stem off the wineglass and the crystal had sliced across her palm.

Zachary placed a clean dish towel on the cut and folded her fingers tightly over it to stem the flow of blood. "Come on," he ordered, retaining his hold on her wrist. "I'll clean it in the bathroom."

"I can do it myself." She fought a wave of dizziness as throbbing pain shot up her arm.

"For once in your life, shut up." Before she realized his intent, he pressed his broad shoulder into her stomach, then straightened, lifting her off her feet.

She gasped, "What are you doing?"

"Be still," he cautioned as he carried her draped over his shoulder through the dining room, down the hallway, into their bedroom and the connecting bath. He set her down on the counter beside the sink.

"If you—"

"Hush and let me take care of you for a change," he said as he shoved her hand palm up under running water. Finding the first-aid kit behind the mirrored cabinet, he gently probed the wound.

"Ouch! That hurts," she complained.

"I have to make certain there isn't any glass still inside, sugar," he soothed. "It will only take another second. Now be a big girl and don't pout," he teased, smiling at the way she had jutted out her bottom lip. "This is going to hurt." He saturated a gaze pad with disinfectant.

"It already hurts."

"Hold still," he said as she jerked her hand away before he could disinfect the area. Holding on to her wrist, he said, "Sorry, sugar."

"Do you think I'll need stitches?"

"No, I don't think so." Wiping away her tears as she bit her lip, he whispered, "I'm almost done." He quickly cov-

ered the wound with a thick gauze pad before he wrapped
it with a strip of gauze and tapped it in place. "All finished."

"Thank you." She blushed in embarrassment, knowing
she had behaved badly.

"Don't mention it." Watching her closely, he began,
"About Barbara, I—"

"No. Please, I don't want to talk about it anymore. It
really isn't any of my business, especially since . . . well,
you know."

He cupped her chin so she could not look away, then said
between tightly clenched teeth, "Everything about me is
your business. What made you think I want Barbara? She's
like a sister to me."

"Because you . . ." She stopped abruptly. "Doesn't
matter."

"Because what?" He stubbornly refused to drop it.

"Forget it. I don't know about you but I'm exhausted.
All I want is a long soak in the tub and then to go to sleep,"
she said wearily.

There was no way she was going to tell him that he was
the reason she thought what she did. He slept beside her
night after night without even reaching for her during the
night. What else could she think under the circumstances?

"Go ahead. We can talk while you take your bath."
Zachary crossed his arms over his chest, not taking his eyes
from hers.

Thirteen

Amanda's head shot up as she looked at him as if she doubted she had heard him correctly. When she could speak, she said, "I'd like some privacy."

After sliding off the counter, she kicked off her heels, then used the uninjured hand to open tiny buttons on one cuff but the other one proved to be more difficult.

"Why? I have seen and tasted every inch of your sweet body, Mrs. McFadden." His mouth quirked upward at the corners.

"Go away!" she said, both physically and emotionally drained. She had taken as much as she was about to from this stubborn man for one night. She didn't want to think about him, or Barbara, for that matter.

As if she had not spoken he walked over to the large cream marble bathtub, maneuvered the brass taps until water poured full force into the tub. Picking up the bottle of her floral-scented bath oil from the small basket of toiletries she kept nestled on the back rim of the tub, he dumped a good portion of the contents into the rushing water.

"That's too much." She watched a huge mountain of foam appear beneath the flow.

He shrugged, replacing the bottle. When the tub was nearly full, he turned off the tap. "My lady, your bath awaits." He bowed gallantly, his eyes twinkling with humor.

"You think this is funny, don't you?" She had no intention of undressing in front of him, not that she was getting far on her own.

His response was to finish unbuttoning the tiny pearl buttons lining her blouse. When she tried to pull free, he held her still, until the blouse could be slipped off her shoulders and arms. When he unbuttoned and unzipped her slacks, she could not keep still a second longer.

"Will you stop!"

"I've had enough of your orders, Mandy. You're still right handed, which means you can not undress, or wash yourself, for that matter, without getting that bandage wet."

"I can do it!"

With one hand trembling with nerves and the other throbbing with pain, she slid her slacks down her hips and with his help stepped free. She was left standing in nothing more than a pair of sheer-to-the-waist panty hose and a satin teddy. The very brief, pale green lace-edged garment was cut high at the thigh, offering Zachary a breathtaking view of long shapely legs and sweetly curved hips, the low-cut bodice barely covering her full breasts.

She tried and failed to ignore his sudden intake of air as she eased the straps down her arms but held the bodice in place. She was all too aware of him in nothing more than low-riding jeans. The mirrors that lined the walls behind the large, wide-rimmed tub revealed far more than she wanted to see.

"You can go now," she persisted, glancing at him from over one shoulder, unaware of just how provocative the move was.

His dark brooding gaze was generating more heat than the furnace. The only move he made was to cross his arms over his broad bare chest. Judging by his stance he was not going anywhere any time soon.

She managed to wiggle out of the panty hose, but was stopped by the front clasp of the built-in demi-bra on her teddy. When his hands made short work of the clasp she scowled but didn't say a word. She blushed hotly when the teddy fell to her waist, then eased it down her hips without his help. She walked around him to the tub, keeping her face averted.

Perching on the wide rim, she was forced to admit, "I forgot my hair." She pulled the thick curls over one shoulder.

"What do you need?" His voice had deepened.

"There are hairpins in that glass-covered bowl on the vanity in the bedroom."

"Pretty please," he drawled, humor gleaming his gaze.

Her cheeks were already hot with embarrassment, when she mimicked, "Pretty please."

His chuckle could be heard even as he disappeared into the bedroom. He was back in no time with the pins resting in his large palm.

"Thanks," she murmured, suddenly breathless as he stood so close they were almost touching. She tried to twist her hair into a loose knot at her crown, but some of the curls slipped down.

"I'll do it." Zachary twisted it into a rope, then secured it at her crown. "It's not pretty, but I think it will hold."

Holding her small waist, he guided her down into the tub. Still blushing, she felt his hot lingering gaze move down her throat, her shoulders, to the top swells of her breasts visible above the foam.

"Thanks," she mumbled.

Zachary removed a thick towel from the stack on the built-in shelf at the one end of the tub. He also found the lighter she stored on the shelf. First he rolled the towel so that she could rest her hand on it; then he leaned over and lit the row of candles nestled in small crystal glasses along the rim.

"Comfortable?" he asked, after replacing the lighter and lowering the overhead light.

"Yes," she lied. How could she be comfortable with him in the room with her? She watched in disbelief while he dropped down to his haunches beside the tub. She bit her bottom lip to contain the tremor. Surely he didn't intend to stay and bathe her? Just the thought of his dark hands moving over her gave her goose pimples.

"If you get me a plastic bag out of the kitchen, I won't get the bandage wet."

When he didn't answer but reached for a bar of the floral-scented soap she preferred, her heart began hammering in her chest. Her eyes challenged his, but he made no move to touch her.

"You're beautiful." His eyes smoldered with desire when he asked, "How much longer, pretty girl?"

She swallowed the lump that had suddenly formed in her throat, knowing perfectly well what he meant. She had been asking herself that same question for days . . . no, weeks. Unfortunately, she did not know the answer. Nevertheless, she could not prevent herself from studying his copper bronze throat and his starkly handsome African features. Her eyes lingered on his well-shaped, full lips.

His voice was barely above a whisper when he said, "We sleep together every night without really being together. It is not enough. I need more. I need you, sugar. Don't you need me?" He did not wait for an answer. "You're my woman and I am your man. Make love with me.'' His eyes bore into hers.

"Zach . . .'' She faltered. ". . . y—you promised.'' She placed her bandage hand on his throat near the hollow where she could feel his heart racing, her pink-lacquered fingertips attempting to soothe, stroking his pulse point.

"When are you going to stop punishing me for something that happened between two other people?''

"I'm not.'' Her voice was shaky even to her own ears.

"Every time you look at me, you remember him. You're punishing me, and yourself, for a past that has nothing to do with either one of us. I'm not Sebastian Daniels, Mandy.'' His voice was gruff with emotion when he went on to say, "Don't you know by now that I could never hurt you the way he hurt your mother? I most certainly couldn't walk out on you . . . not ever. Stop tormenting us because of their mistakes.''

He was wrong . . . so wrong. Yet, the hurt was real and it had never completely gone away even after so many years. She closed her eyes as if she could shut out the pain of the past and the starkness of the truth.

Finally she confessed, "I've never even seen the kind of marriage you want. Even when I moved in with my grandfather, it was years after my grandmother had passed.''

Tenderly, he stroked her cheek. "What happened between your parents is over. Nothing you say or do can change what happened.''

"I know that.''

"Then why won't you let yourself trust me? Believe in my love for you.''

"I trust you.''

"No, sugar. You've lumped me in the same category as your father.'' Tilting her face, thus forcing her to meet his scrutiny, he said, "I have not had sex with Barbara or anyone else. You are my wife and I will continue to honor the commitment I made to you on our wedding day." He paused. "I'm not saying I'm sporting a halo." His voice deepened even more when he admitted, "I'm hungry for you, Mandy McFadden, and I've had it with waiting."

Unable to bear the anguish mirrored in his eyes, she whispered, "Please try to understand—"

"Understand! Hell, no!" he said, fresh out of patience. "I need you. More to the point, I know you want me. Why else do I wake up every morning with you in my arms? Haven't you wondered why you wake up on my pillow every morning? Or did you think I could drag you across the bed without waking you?"

She dropped her head, bringing her legs up to her chest as if she could escape by curling herself into a ball. He said no more but lathered his dark hands with floral-scented soap and began to smooth over her nape and shoulders. She kept her eyes closed as he stroked lower, down her back. She trembled when his hands moved into the water, stroking the silky skin at the small of her back, the flare of her shapely hips.

"So soft . . . so beautiful," he said close to her ear.

His mouth was close to her damp throat, but not close enough. She trembled with longing as she thoughtlessly turned, pressing the hard, aching tips of her breasts into his well-muscled chest.

"Zachary," she moaned.

Sliding her arms around his neck, she surprised them both when she brushed her full lips shyly against his. When he parted his lips but did not deepen the exchange, she was the one kissing him, thrusting her tongue into the heat of his mouth.

He groaned, gathering her still closer, suckling her tongue. Suddenly he pulled away. "Open your eyes, Mandy, and look at me."

Her heavy-lidded eyes were as rich as sweetened, dark

chocolate, hot with desire as she stared at him. A part of her wanted to look away, protect herself, but deep inside she knew she was safe. She had never known a woman could want a man as badly as she wanted Zachary. Nothing else mattered.

He rose, taking a bath sheet from the heated towel bar, and held it for her. Her heart beat wildly in her chest as she slowly stood, sudsy water cascaded down her golden length. He steadied her as she stepped over the rim of the tub onto the thick rug. The warmth of the bath sheet could not compare to the blazing hunger in his gaze as he wrapped it around her and tucked the end between the full swells of her breasts to secure it.

"I need the words," he said quietly, brushing his knuckles gently along the side of her face. "It has to be a mutual decision. It won't work any other way."

She could feel the strength of his desire against her stomach. Even though he was fully aroused, he was clearly in control of his emotions. She did not give herself time to consider, she reacted to heat of her own need. She kissed his collarbone before she said, "I can feel how much you want me. That should be enough."

His entire body stiffened. "No, Mandy." He dropped his hand, turning away from her.

"Where are you going?"

"Does it matter?"

"Zach, don't—"

"Then tell me what I need to hear." A muscle jumped in his cheek and his hand rested on a lean hip.

Amanda dropped the towel, letting it fall, and quickly moved to encircle his taut waist. "I want to be with you. I want you to make love to me."

A shudder shook his body as he tightened his arms around her, content for the moment just to hold her as he pressed his face against her warm, scented throat.

"Oh, sugar. I need you, badly," he whispered an instant before he led her into the bedroom. A single bedside lamp lit the room. He yanked the bedding back before turning to her.

Her breath caught in her throat as he unzipped his jeans, shoved them down his legs and stepped free of them. He was so darn sexy, all six feet four inches of him.

It had been so long since they had been like this. He hesitated as if he expected her to back down, something Amanda was not about to do. Pressing her lips against his throat, she tasted him with the velvet heat of her tongue. She could hear the pent-up air he slowly released.

"Mandy . . ." he sighed, an instant before he crushed her to him in a bone-tightening grip. "It has been too long. Tell me now if you're planning to change your mind while I still can stop."

Beyond speech, she shook her head. She felt him tremble, his heavy shaft pressed against her stomach as he pushed a muscular leg between her thighs.

Amanda lifted her face toward his, seeking his sizzling-hot kisses. Zachary covered her mouth with his own, parting her soft lips in order to stroke her tongue with his own. Shivers of need raced up and down her spine as the kiss went on and on.

When their lips eventually separated, he dropped his head to sample the sweet curve of her jaw, then down to the soft flesh of her neck. When he teasingly captured her earlobe, he traced the delicate shell-like curve until her breathless moans urged him to take it into the warmth his mouth to tenderly suck the lobe.

Her heart was pounding like a drum when he guided her down onto the bed and came down beside her. She welcomed him into her arms, clinging to him, opening for more of his hot, hungry kisses. He devoured her mouth before he moved down her body, enjoying the taste of her soft golden skin.

He paid particular attention to the generous outer curves of her breasts. He kissed each breast, and only then did he take a tight nipple into the heat of his mouth. He tasted her as if he were savoring a succulent drop of sweet chocolate. She whimpered as he began to suck her nipple, drawing it deep into his mouth.

"You're so sweet . . . so sweet," he whispered huskily.

"Ohhhhhhh . . . ." she called out as each new sensation increased the pleasure. Deep inside her womb, she felt the tug of his mouth, causing her to press her soft mound against the hard length of his thigh.

"Not enough . . . too much," he said, around the hard peak.

"Harder . . ."

As he gave her what she needed, her nails dug into his broad shoulders. She cried out in distress when he left one damp nipple and moaned in pleasure when he turned his attention to the other.

"I need you . . ."

"Not yet. I want you ready for me . . . wet for me," he crooned as his caressing hands traveled down her body to squeeze her lush hips.

She trembled when he explored the petal-soft skin of her inner thigh, but cried out, panting in anticipation when he cupped and squeezed the plump folds of her mound. She moaned as his fingertips moved through the thick curls, parting her legs even more. He fondled the soft curls of her sex. She cried out his name when he slid a large calloused finger deep inside her damp sheath, filling the emptiness.

"Oh . . ." she whimpered her enjoyment.

He whispered her name as he worried her nipple gently against his teeth while continuing to stroke her sweet heat. "You like that, don't you, sugar?

"Oh yes . . ." When he increased the friction, she moaned, trembling with desire.

"Zach . . . I need you . . . all of you. Ple-e-ease!"

"I intend to please you, pretty girl," Zachary crooned against her throat as he gently stroked a thumb over her clitoris.

Amanda tossed her head from side to side as he quickened the caresses while suckling a hard nipple. He didn't ease up until she cried out his name as her body quivered from the force of her release.

"So sweet," he murmured, moving up in order to take her mouth in a hard, tongue-stroking kiss.

When Zachary allowed Amanda the liberty of breath, she dragged in much-needed air, before she pressed a series of kisses along his throat, tonguing the sensitive spot behind his ear before moving down to his bronze chest. It had been so long since she had granted herself the luxury of touching him . . . caressing his dark warm skin.

He had a firm, heavy-muscled upper body from the physical labor he did on the ranch and long, taut-muscled thighs from long hours spent in the saddle. She paused to worry his small ebony nipples, first with her fingertips and then the warm wash of her tongue. His quickening breath and hoarse moans gave her as much pleasure as she gave him.

Longing to pleasure him, she smoothed her hand down his taut rib cage and over his concave stomach. Circling his navel, she moved her fingers into the crisp black hair surrounding his jutting hard shaft. When she stroked his long, thick length, he rasped her name. He caught her hand, holding it still.

Her questioning eyes met his. "You don't like my touch?"

Zachary placed a kiss in the center of her palm. "More than you can possibly know, but I doubt I can hold on to what little control I have left. It has been so long . . . too long."

"Let me . . . please." She pressed her lips against his throat.

He nodded his consent, unable to refuse her anything. He closed his eyes at the acute pleasure of her soft hands on his throbbing penis. He nearly lost it when she explored the highly sensitive, broad crest, smoothing the moisture she found there over the glans. Zachary showed her how to curl her small hands around his steel-hard sex in order to give him the long, hard strokes he craved. The sweetness of it caused his entire body to tighten, and he begged her to stop.

Snatching her hand away, she whispered, "I'm sorry. I didn't meant to hurt you."

"You didn't . . ." he barely got out as he pulled her up his long body until she could meet the hard-driving force of his hungry mouth. She was gasping for breath when he rolled her beneath him. "I need to be inside you . . . now," he groaned into her ear as he positioned himself between her golden thighs.

Even though he was shaking with need, his kiss was tender as he stroked her with the broad head of his sex. He fought his own sense of urgency to give her time to adjust to the feel of him inside her moist heat. She opened herself even more to him wrapping her legs around his waist glorying in his strength. It was while he stroked her clitoris that she sank her nails into his shoulders, holding back a scream. She wanted . . . no, needed more of his hard length.

"Zach . . . please. I need you . . . all of you. Now!" she said, arching her back.

He flexed his hips, pushing forward, giving her his entire thick length. They both called out from the pleasure of it. She protested when he pulled back, tightening her legs around him trying to keep him deep inside where she needed him the most.

"Trust me, sugar," he said around a heavy groan. He lifted her leg, placing it over his shoulder, opening her even more to his deep penetration. He plunged, then pulled back, only to repeat the movement again and again.

Amanda gasped out his name, clinging to him, instinctively tightening around him. Zachary gritted his teeth as her inner muscles milked his pulsating shaft. He was close, too close to completion. His heart raced as he quickened his strokes, propelling her toward her own release. He slid a hand between their bodies, to gently squeeze her taut nipple and then her aching clitoris again and again.

"Love me . . . love me," he moaned into her ear as he sent her hurling into a breath-stealing climax, groaning as her slick inner muscles eliminated his last measure of control. He crooned as his big body shook in a series of convulsions as he reached his own climax. They clung to each other, both of them wet with perspiration, while their breathing gradually slowed.

A generous smile tilted the corners of her mouth. Amanda had never felt more womanly . . . or more complete. She didn't need the words. She knew she had satisfied him, and that alone gave her a deeper sense of accomplishment and feminine confidence than ever before.

Fourteen

Zachary tenderly brushed Amanda's lips with his own. "Sorry. I didn't mean to crush you beneath me." He rolled onto his back, bringing her with him, settling her over him. Running a calloused finger down her cheek, he whispered throatily, "You okay? I lost it at the end. Did I hurt you?"

"No." She teased, "Did I hurt you?"

"Not hardly, sexy lady." He chuckled, pressing warm kisses against her full, lush mouth.

When she shivered, he reached down and pulled the flannel sheet and down comforter over them both.

"Better?"

She nodded, burying her face between his shoulder and neck, touched by his thoughtfulness and overwhelmed by the intimacy they had shared. Resting in his strong arm, she hummed to herself, wondering if all couples feel this sense of closeness after making love. Had her parents ever felt this way?

"What are you humming?"

Although somewhat embarrassed, she confessed, "Just a song my mother used to play on the record player and we used to sing around the house when I was little. I don't know what made me remember it."

He smiled, kissing her cheek. "When a Man Loves a Woman"?

"Yes. The original was by Percy Sledge," she admitted, surprised that he recognized the song.

Zachary's arms tightened around her, bringing her even closer to his warmth. She was silent for so long that he asked, "You aren't going to sleep on me, are you?"

"Mmm . . ." was all she could manage. Despite everything they had just shared, there was a part of her that she needed to keep hidden.

When he rose she complained, "Where are you going?"

"We're going to finish what we started."

Before she could sort that one out, he scooped her up and carried her into the bathroom.

"The water is cold." She shivered as she sank down in the tub resting her back against his front, nestled between his long legs.

"Give me a minute," he said, kissing her neck before turning on the hot water and the whirlpool jets. "Better?"

"Mmm." She closed her eyes, trying to push her nagging fears away and concentrate on nothing more than the heat of his large body against hers.

Zachary massaged her shoulders, moving down her sleek spine until she began to relax. She moaned when he cupped her hip. He caressed the length of her thighs, before he parted them, giving him unlimited access to her feminine secrets. With blunt fingertips he traced the puffy feminine folds, parted them to find her warmer than the temperature of the water around them.

Amanda's breathing accelerated as she arched back, resting her head on his shoulder. His breathing was as quick and uneven as hers as he cupped her breasts, as if weighing their cushiony softness, then rhythmically tugged the tight nipples between his thumbs and forefingers.

"We can't—"

"Can't what, sugar? Make love again?"

"Yes . . ." she said around a breathless moan.

"No doubts tonight, my love. Let's forget everything and concentrate on enjoying each other," Zachary whispered close to her ear, pressing a kiss to the sensitive spot just below, causing her to tremble with sexual tension.

He heard her moans and felt her body quiver as he concentrated on one thing, fingering her aching bud. When she called out his name, he knew she was close to climaxing but trying to hold back.

"Let go."

She caught his hand. "Not again."

"Again and again," he insisted gruffly, with renewed desire. He turned her until she straddled his thighs and could take him deep inside. He showed her how to move in order to pleasure them both. It was quick, urgent as Amanda raced with Zachary toward completion. Once more they were speeding toward the ultimate pinnacle and they reached it together, sharing a shattering sweet release.

"I can't get enough of you," he groaned as he kissed her again and again.

She clung to him, her eyes closed and her hands around his neck. When she angled her chin so she could see his eyes, she asked. "Why was it different that time?"

He did not try to suppress a grin. "We're different every

time. Come on, we better get out of here before we both shrivel up.'' He kissed her wrinkled fingertips. ''Besides, I need to change that bandage. Is your hand hurting?''

She smiled. ''I'm feeling no pain. And I don't want to move. I'd rather stay right here all night.''

Even though he'd like nothing better himself, his practical nature prevailed. He roused himself enough to get them out of the tub, dry off and rebandage her injured hand before they went to bed.

As he dozed with his wife's head on his shoulder, her arm flung across his waist, he knew he was more content than he had been in a very long time, if ever. He wasn't foolish enough to think that the next day or the one after that would be different. Amanda was a long way from admitting that she was in love with him or that she even wanted their marriage to work . . . a very long way.

Amanda stirred when light kisses landed on her forehead, cheeks and down the side of her neck. Leisurely, she stretched her arms above her head, slowly lifting her lashes.

''Morning.'' Zachary smiled as he sat beside her on the bed.

Her eyes traveled across his chest, partly covered by a beige cotton shirt. Her face went hot as she recalled the previous night and what they'd shared.

They had made love once more before they'd fallen asleep. Was it any wonder she felt so relaxed, almost languorous? Surprisingly, her awareness of him had not diminished one little bit.

''Good morning.'' She pushed her hair out of her eyes.

He gave her a slow, sexy grin. ''No need to ask if you

slept well. I finally gave up waiting for you to awake and decided to take matters into my own hands.''

She returned his smile, inhaling his clean male scent and sandalwood aftershave. Sunlight spilled in through the open drapes.

"What time is it?" she asked as she eased herself up into a sitting position, causing the comforter to fall to her waist.

"After twelve." He grinned, watching her blush when she realized she was nude.

She yanked the sheet over her breasts, tucking it under her arms. "I slept past noon? I couldn't have."

"You did. Obviously you needed the rest," he said as he placed a heavily laden tray across her lap. "Your breakfast, my love."

Her eyes locked with him for an instant when she realized that he had called her his love. "Zach, this is wonderful, but I've got to get dressed. I have to get to the office. I'm surprised Helen hasn't called. Why are you still here? Don't you have a board meeting today?"

"Hold on. We aren't going anywhere today. According to the weather report, there's more than a foot of snow on the ground and it is still coming. Everything is closed and not much of anything is moving out there today."

"Oh! I assumed the roads would be cleared by now."

"It's still coming down. Your food's getting cold." He picked up his own heaping plate and coffee mug from the tray, making himself comfortable on his side of the bed.

She combed her fingers through her tousled hair. "I'm a mess."

"You're gorgeous with your hair messy, your lids heavy with sleep and your lips swollen from my kisses."

Embarrassed by the compliment, she decided to change the subject. "It smells delicious. I didn't know you were so handy in the kitchen."

"I have my moments, especially when all I have to do is open a box and read the directions." His eyes sparkled with humor as he cut a blueberry pancake with a fork and held it out to her. "Open."

Accepting the offering, she chewed. "Mmm. Good." She realized she was hungry, having eaten little the night before.

She set the tray on the bed between them. "Be right back." Covering herself with his short toweling robe that was on the bench at the foot of the bed, she hurried into the bathroom. Feeling refreshed after making a quick use of the shower, brushing her teeth and her hair, she dug into her breakfast.

He teased, "Very nice, but totally unnecessary. There was a time when you didn't mind going a week or so without a bathroom and a toothbrush."

Laughing, she said, "I was fourteen the first time Peggy and I went hiking with you and your brothers. And even back then, believe me, I missed my bathroom. Washing in a cold mountain stream and going behind a bush has absolutely no appeal."

He laughed. "You've gotten your bandage wet. How is the hand?"

"Better." She sipped from a glass of freshly squeezed orange juice. "Thanks."

"You don't need that robe, even if it does look better on you than me."

"Did you sleep well?" She wasn't quite ready to examine what happened between them the night before and most certainly was not prepared to discuss it.

"Without a doubt," he said as he took a sip from his coffee mug.

"Did Helen call?"

"Yeah. I gave her permission to call your employees and inform them that they're off with pay until the weather clears."

She merely quirked a brow at him, knowing she would have done the same thing.

His eyes were on her when he said, "We need to talk."

"Let's not. Mmm, this is delicious, Zach."

She concentrated on her breakfast rather than the disappointment on his face. It should be enough that she had pleased him. She was not ready to explore her own emotions. She was afraid of what she might find.

Depositing his empty plate on the tray, he disappeared into the bathroom only to return with the first-aid kit.

"Now?" she asked with a fork halfway to her mouth.

"When you're done."

She tried to prolong the meal, but finally had to give up when she could not force down another bite. After he had replaced the bandage she found the courage to ask, "What did you want to talk about?"

He placed the tray on the dresser, then settled beside her on the bed with the morning newspaper. He was silent so long that she was beginning to wonder if he'd changed his mind.

"Zach?"

"You're regretting making love, aren't you?"

"No. Are you?"

"That depends." His gaze searched hers. "We didn't use protection. We should have discussed it before it happened, but then neither one of us was doing much thinking."

Reluctantly, she admitted, "There was no need. I'm taking birth control pills."

"Since when?"

"A few days after you moved in."

"You decided this without consulting me?"

"It wasn't planned. I went to a regularly scheduled appointment with my gynecologist. I talked with her while I was in the office. Besides, if I had told you beforehand, we would have only ended up in an argument . . . just like now.'' She avoided his piercing black eyes.

"You decided—"

"Yes! I couldn't take the chance. I've already had one unplanned pregnancy. I don't want another.''

"So why didn't you tell me, Mandy?''

"Isn't it obvious? I didn't think you would understand. Besides, we were not even . . . you know.''

When he started laughing, she did look at him sharply. "What is so funny?''

"It's good to know that you realize our making love was meant to happen.''

She studied him from beneath the thickness of her lashes as he reclined on the pillows, the newspaper in one hand. His other hand was behind his head, his bare feet crossed at the ankles. He wore a pair of faded black jeans and his shirt unbuttoned nearly to his waist.

She could not seem to stop herself from remembering what they shared during the night. There was no doubt that she had wanted him as much as he had wanted her. It was a waste of time trying to analyze why they had made love last night of all the nights they shared.

Surprisingly her awareness of him was just as powerful now as it had been the night before. He had shattered her defenses. Yes, there was a storm raging outside, but the one inside her was more powerful than the one that had brought the city to its knees.

"Aren't you worried about your precious cows?''

He grinned. "They're being taken care of. The men were out early this morning. We're holding our own.''

"You called the ranch?''

"Of course.''

"I was surprised you bothered to come back during the storm. I was sure you'd rather be at the ranch than here where you can't take care of things personally.''

"I'm where I want to be. Besides, I have a very capable foreman, who knows his job. If I didn't trust him, he wouldn't have kept the job for ten years."

"I see." She placed her empty mug on the nightstand and picked up an emery board. She sat with her legs curled under her.

"I doubt it," he said thoughtfully as he stretched out an arm and pulled her against his side. He sighed when she pressed her face between his neck and shoulder.

Not only had she allowed him to make love to her twice last night, but she had turned to him during the course of the long night. Through her caresses she had urged him to take her once more to that wondrous place.

"It looks like we might be stuck inside for several days, sugar," he remarked, still studying the newspaper.

She punched his arm with her fist, then yelped. "Ouch!" The pain made her realize that it was her injured hand she had hit him with.

"Did you hurt yourself?" A teasing light shimmered in his eyes.

"Yes!" she huffed. "Go ahead, read the newspaper. Like I care."

He tossed the paper onto the floor, then rolled over, pinning her beneath him. He laughed. "You'd like my attention, my love?" His head descended until he could sponge her plump bottom lip with his tongue, then take her lip into his own mouth to suckle.

"Maybe," Amanda said when she could speak. She turned her face away so that his mouth landed on her cheek.

He groaned as he held her still to accept his hot kisses. "Mmm, you taste like maple syrup." Between kisses, he confessed, "I've been wanting to do this all morning."

"Oh, Zach . . ."

Last night had been vastly different from their first time. Her heart had been so heavy with fear for her grandfather back then that she hadn't been able to come close to reaching the heights he had taken her to last night. Even their wedding night and the days following had been marred by worry and later grief.

As shivers of pure excitement rushed over her, she opened like the delicate petals of a flower, seeking not the warmth of the sun but his masculine heat. His caresses were fast becoming habit-forming, necessary to her well-being, but she refused to dwell on that . . . not now. She closed her mind to all but the way her husband was making her feel. After only one night of his lovemaking, she was powerless to prevent herself from responding to his blatant masculinity.

The intrusion of the telephone ringing caused them both to hesitate. Amanda reached for it before he could stop her. "Hello?"

Zachary took it away from her, intent on hanging up, but the sound of his brother's voice stopped him. "Roger? What's wrong?"

"What is it?" she asked.

He said into the receiver, "What! When? Hang on. I'm on my way." Then he put down the telephone and rose from the bed.

"What happened? Where are you going?" she asked as he rushed into the walk-in closet.

"Hold on a second," he called from over his shoulder.

"What happened?" She scrambled into an upright position.

When he returned, he had pulled on thermo underwear and heavy-corded slacks. He carried a wool shirt and a pair of wool socks.

"Zach . . ."

"It's Peggy. She fell down the stairs . . . she's bleeding. They called her obstetrician and he wants them to bring her into the hospital. They're on the way."

"No!" She sank back down. Painful memories of the day she lost their baby rushed over her.

"I'm sorry to leave you like this, but I've got to get Roger to the hospital." He finished dressing as he talked. "He's in a bad way. There is no way he can get out there in this mess, but he's determined to try. If the weather clears just a little, I can take him up in the chopper. If not, we have to take the Jeep."

Tears rolled unchecked down Amanda's face as she pressed her fingertips against her lips, trying to hold in the anguish.

Pulling on socks, he muttered impatiently, "Where are my damn boots?" His frowning gaze swung to his wife. "Mandy." He rushed over and gathered her against him. "I know this is particularly hard on you. All we can do is pray and believe that Peggy and the baby are going to be okay." He placed a kiss against her temple.

"I'd hate for her to go through . . . what I went through." When she saw the pain in his eyes, she amended, ". . . what we went through. They've waited so long to have this baby."

"I know. I've got to go, my love. I'll call as soon as I hear something."

"Wait! I'm going with you."

"No, I'm not sure if we can fly in. We may have to take the Jeep. I can't take a chance on you being with us if we get stuck somewhere between Denver and Glenwood Springs. I'll call as soon as I can. And, Mandy." He hesitated, brushing her lips with his. "Pray." With that he was gone.

* * *

The call from Zachary came well after midnight. Peggy would be all right. It had been close, and she had not lost her baby, but she would have to spend the remainder of her pregnancy in bed.

Fifteen

"Ten long and empty days!" Zachary grumbled to himself as he dropped into the chair behind his desk. Ten nights without Amanda. One damn problem after another had kept him at the Circle-M. He swore impatiently. And now the family thing this weekend. How much more of this could he take?

It was different this time, vastly different than the more than ten months they had been separated. She had been in a bad way and he had no choice but to give her the time she requested. The only way he had kept going was by his belief that some day they would be together again.

He'd had no other choice but to force the issue by moving in with her. And he was fooling himself into thinking their reconciliation had brought drastic changes. There were problems, but this was the first time they had slept apart for any length of time. Judging by his temper, he was not handling it well. Phone calls were not doing it for him. He needed more. He needed his woman.

One thing was certain, he was not about to spend another night without his wife. With that decided, he reached for the telephone at his elbow.

"Daniels Interior Designs. How may I help you?"

"Helen, this is Zach. Is Mandy in?"

"Yes, Mr. McFadden. Just a moment, please."

He waited impatiently, drumming his fingertips on the top of the desk.

"Amanda Daniels McFadden, may I help you?"

"You certainly can, sugar. I miss you like hell, pretty girl," he said huskily, then asked, "Are you busy?"

"Zach . . ." she said around a sigh.

"Yeah. You sound tired." His voice deepened almost gravelly. "Are you up to your eyebrows in work?"

"In people is more like it. Where are you? At the condo?"

"Why? Would you rush home for an afternoon of loving?" His pulse quickened at the mere thought.

"Zachary!" she scolded softly.

"What do you expect from a highly frustrated cowpoke, who's been without his lady for ten long days and very lonely nights? I ache for you, love," he whispered. When she did not respond, he sighed wearily. "Nothing to say?"

"I can't at the moment," her voice barely above a whisper.

He couldn't help wondering why she couldn't talk. Was it because she was not alone? Or was it that she had taken advantage of his absence by fortifying her defenses against him?

"Are you in the city?" she quizzed softly.

"The Circle-M. It looks like I won't be able to make it in again this weekend. Come to me, love. Come for the weekend. Barbara's birthday party is tomorrow night, and

I can't get out of it. Peggy has been asking for you." He paused before he added, "I need you with me."

There was a prolonged silence before she asked, "Peggy home from the hospital?"

"Yeah. Roger brought her home this morning." Zachary struggled with his emotions. He reminded himself that she was not alone. "She said thanks for the flowers you sent to the hospital. Will you come?" he persisted.

"Can we talk about this later?"

"I want you here."

Amanda whispered, careful not to be overheard, "You know your mother and I don't get along."

"What does my mother have to do with this? This is between the two of us."

"Zach—"

"Don't Zach me, Mandy McFadden," he said tightly, his temper rising. "Stop making excuses! I want you here with me this weekend." He went on to say, as if she had not just refused to come, "You can drive in with Brad after work."

"I'm very sorry, darlin', but that is not convenient." Her voice was dripping with honey.

"We both knew there would be times when I couldn't make it into Denver. This is one of them. There has been one problem after another with the herd, plus I have family responsibilities."

"Hold on a minute, please," she said sweetly.

He was pacing the length of the fireplace adjacent to his desk when he heard her say, "Gloria, I'm sorry. This is going to take longer than I expected. May I get back to you?" There was another lengthy pause before she said to the other woman, "Thanks. Please, close the door behind you." Then Amanda came back on the line. "Zach, you have no right to make demands on me."

"Who has more right?" he snarled impatiently. "Evidently, you've forgotten that you happen to be my wife. When in the hell are you going to start acting like it?''

''When the place freezes over!'' she returned angrily, slamming down the telephone.

''Just who does he think he's talking to? He can't order me around!'' Amanda fumed.

Just because they had made love did not given him the right to act as if he owned her! Why in the world would she want to go to Barbara's party? Ple-e-ease! She was no more eager to see Barbara or his mother than they were to see her.

When the telephone rang, she said as calmly as she could manage, ''Yes, Helen?''

''Mr. McFadden, line three.''

''Please tell him I'll have to call him back. Thanks.'' Amanda infused a touch of regret into her voice solely for her secretary's benefit.

Determined to put her stubborn husband out of her mind and take care of the demands of her business, she got up and walked down the hall to Gloria's office.

After she finished, she turned her attention to the sketch she had started earlier. Unfortunately, her eyes involuntarily went to the end table where a Waterford crystal vase held two dozen long-stem, dark red roses. They were from Zachary, a fragrant reminder that he had been thinking of her. Had he really missed her as much she had missed him? How could he? He had little Barbara to keep him entertained. And he expected her to chase after him? No way, no how.

How did the man manage to be so arrogant, mule-headed and at the same time thoughtful and tender? There was no doubt about it that he had a stubborn streak that was more than a mile long and over a yard wide. At the moment, she was not sure if she would rather kiss him for sending the flowers and his wonderful nightly calls, or hit him over the head with the vase.

It was not until after she left the office for the day that she began to have second thoughts. Maybe she should have gone with his brother? She hadn't seen Zach in more than a week. And she'd missed him so much. Was she wrong not to go?

Zachary wanted her with him. It was the only time he had asked anything of her since they had reconciled, and she felt terribly guilty for refusing.

By the time she reached the condo she knew that if she had gone with Brad she would not have had to spend yet another long weekend missing Zachary. Nor did she have to wonder what new stunt Barbara was using to gain his attention.

The condo had been quiet ... much too quiet without him. Not that he made a great deal of noise, but she missed their talks and his teasing. Even when they disagreed, he had always listened to her views.

Why had she been so quick to refuse? She hadn't given herself a chance to even think about it. What was she afraid of? That she would find out there was really more between Barbara and Zachary than he was admitting? Or was it that she simply didn't fit into his life? Unfortunately, there were no easy answers. At the most unexpected times she found herself longing for the feel of his long, muscular body against hers, his hot kisses. Enough! Amanda chided herself. She did not want to remember.

After letting herself into the condo, she left her things in the foyer, and walked past the mail that had been stacked neatly on the table.

"I'm glad you decided to come home on time for a change," Zachary said as he came from the kitchen, a coffee mug in his large, long-fingered hand.

Amanda jumped, pressing a hand to her racing heart. "Zach! You scared me!"

His eyes moved over her, taking in the cream wool slacks and a pink cashmere sweater set outlining her shapely curves. Her hair was caught in a loose knot at her crown and she wore pink mother-of-pearl and gold earrings.

"I thought you were . . ." Her voice trailed off as she took in the way his dark brown cords hugged his long legs and the cream cable-knit sweater complemented his dark good looks.

"I'm here to pick up my wife," he said quietly. The muscles along his jaw jumped in his cheek but he made no move to touch her.

She didn't need to be told he was angry . . . furious was more like it. Nothing in his manner or casual tone reflected his mood. Nonetheless, she felt his anger. She had come to accept that he would never lift a hand against her. She was no longer frightened by his temper. What she felt was regret that she had pushed him into coming.

She preferred to see laughter in his jet-black eyes and a smile on his generous lips, and then there were his kisses. It had been ten long, empty days since they had been together and all she was so conscious of his masculine appeal that she had failed to respond to his announcement.

"Let's go."

"I beg your pardon?" she managed to say, flicking a pink tongue over her dark-rog-tinted lips.

His gaze momentarily centered on her soft mouth; then he cleared his throat before he said, "You heard correctly. Your bag is packed and in the car. Get your coat. My mother is holding dinner for us." He turned and walked back into the kitchen.

She simply stood there, not believing she heard correctly. Then she followed him into the kitchen. She watched him pour what was left in his mug down the sink and rinse out the mug. "What is going on here? Why is it so important that I come with you to the ranch? I assure you that Barbara won't be upset if I miss her party." She glared at him. "As long as Barbara is happy, nothing else matters, right?"

"Mother has been planning this party for Barbara for months. Besides, we both know that Barbara is not the issue between the two of us." He cupped her elbow and propelled her back into the foyer. He picked up her purse, shoved it into her hands and collected their coats from the closet.

"I don't like your attitude."

She could not believe he was capable of treating her this way. What was worse, she couldn't understand why she wanted to be with him. She had vowed when she left his mother's home that she was never going back. Nonetheless, her heart rate hadn't slowed since she first caught sight of him. She had been unable to think of little else all afternoon outside of him.

He'd shrugged into his brown suede jacket, thrown a fur coat over her shoulders, before he urged her out the door. He locked it behind them.

"Why can't y—" Her attention was focused on the stubborn set of his jaw and tightly compressed lips, so much so that she failed to notice they were not alone.

"Hi, Amanda," her neighbor said, as she locked her own door. "I haven't seen you in a while. How have you been?"

Amanda turned with a start, her face hot with embarrassment. "Joan! It's good to see you." Noting the way the other woman was eyeing Zachary, Amanda asked, "Have you met my husband, Zachary?"

"No, I haven't." Joan smiled warmly, offering her hand.

"My pleasure, Ms. Braddock," he acknowledged smoothly, his anger masked behind a polite smile. He shook her hand before he ushered the two ladies toward the elevator.

Amanda silently fumed as she recognized that she had

not told him Joan's last name. He had evidently taken more than a passing interest in the building.

"Nice to meet you," Joan answered. "That was some snowstorm we had the other week. I sure hope it's the last big one of the season, although I doubt it. Are you a skier, Zachary?"

"Yes. And you?"

"I'm a city girl. My art gallery takes a great deal of my time." She looked pointedly at Amanda as they entered the elevator. "Amanda, I love your coat. Is that sable?" Joan exclaimed.

Amanda glanced down. She was indeed wearing a very expensive three-quarter-length, hooded sable coat. One she had never seen before.

"It was a belated Valentine's gift," Zachary explained to the curious Joan and his stunned wife as they rode down together.

"Lucky you. You both must come over and see the new exhibit at my gallery. It's a Flagstone at his best." Joan went on chattering about the local painter who was just starting to gain international acceptance.

Amanda was too caught up in her own thoughts to respond. Joan walked with them out of the building. Although the streets were clear of snow, the air was cold and crisp. Zachary's Porsche was parked next to Joan's yellow Blazer.

After saying their good-byes, he held the door for Amanda, waited until her seat belt was fastened. He walked around the hood and slid under the steering column. Once he secured his own seat belt, he turned the key in the ignition.

"Zach . . ." She touched the hand resting on his thigh. "I want to thank—"

"Don't thank me for the coat, damn it. If you can't say you've missed me or you want to be with me this weekend, then don't bother being polite. I want a hell of a lot more from you than that.'' His voice was edged with bitterness as he headed toward the interstate.

She jerked her hand back, struggling to sort through her tender emotions. It hurt knowing he didn't care that she was touched because he had taken time to select something so lovely for her. The expense of the gift didn't matter . . . his intent to please her did. Nor could she tell him how much it meant to her that despite how busy he was, he had come for her himself.

If it were not for his mother, Amanda would not have objected to spending time on the ranch. She sighed unhappily. How would it all end? And how much more of this could either one of them take? More important, why was his hurt and anger so upsetting?

Her eyes filled with tears, for she was finally able to put a name to her confusing emotions. The truth hit her all at once as if she'd been smacked in the face with it. It was not welcome, but it was just there. Amanda suddenly realized that she was undeniably, deeply in love with her own husband.

She had nearly stopped breathing when he had suddenly appeared in the kitchen doorway. If not for their disagreement, she would have rushed into his arms, locked her arms around his neck and lifted her face to his.

Instead she was stiff with a mixture of fear and dread. She didn't want this! Didn't need it! Yet, the emotion was so powerful that she couldn't help wondering if she loved him as much as, if not more than, her mother had once loved her father. Was this how it felt? This overwhelming need? Now that she could finally put a name to what she felt for him, she was terribly shaken.

Turning as far away from him as the seat belt would allow, she stared out the window. Unfortunately, she could not see anything beyond her troubled thoughts. What now? Could she keep her feelings hidden? Did she have a choice?

She closed her eyes, knowing that whatever she did, she must never let him guess her feelings.

Deep in thought, she didn't notice that they had exited the interstate some time back. The white-coated mountain walls soared thousands of feet into the darkening sky, providing a perfect backdrop for the Circle-M, nestled between the foothills of the River National Forest and the rich grassland flats, outside of Glenwood Springs.

Despite the sheer panic that had seized her as she discovered her feelings for Zachary, the lure of the land touched her very soul and seemed to welcome her back. She let down her window just a bit to inhale deeply. The night air was crisp, sharp and filled with the scent of pine that no bottle could duplicate.

She had not realized just how much she had missed the stark beauty of the mountains. They passed mile upon mile of blue spruce, providing a lush green to the otherwise barren winter foliage. In the spring and summer the narrow-leafed cottonwoods and the giant aspens would flourish and were often flanked by willows and thimbleberries.

In a few short months the foothills would be brilliant with blooms, the scarlet sumac, purple daisies, lavender locoweed and of course her personal favorite, the wine-red wild roses. She also enjoyed the autumn when the treetops were aflame with colors ranging from lemon to burnt amber and the sky on a clear day was a rich, luscious blue.

When he turned onto the private road that divided the Circle-M, she was surprised to see the herd so close to the house. She almost laughed at the thought. Close by Colorado standards meant a good twenty or more miles away.

Under normal circumstances, she would have reminded Zachary of how she and Roger used to follow him on horseback, eager for his attention, or how they used to enjoy the most breathtaking sunsets. But there was nothing remotely normal about the heavy silence in which they had traveled.

He slowed the car as the road curved sharply to the left. Amanda shifted against the soft leather bucket seat, trying to relieve some of the tension that had built up inside during the long, uncomfortably silent drive. Her anger had long since dissipated. In its place was a single concern.

How was she going to keep her feelings to herself? Yes, for the first time in her life she was in love. And no matter how much that tiny romantic part of her yearned to welcome the tender emotions, her cautious nature and the painful lessons learned from her family stopped her cold. She wasn't like her friend, Peggy. She was Darlene Daniels's daughter.

Being in love meant she must continue to be the distant wife, and she would do it gladly. She would do whatever it took to keep Zachary at a distance. She needed no reminders of how very responsive she was to his male charm, his hypnotic smiles, and his dark seductive eyes.

She was no fool. She had learned at her mother's knee what it was like to be used by a man and then discarded like a broken doll. In her parents' case, her mother had been used and abused until she could no longer live without her husband. Not even the love of her only child had given her reason to go on living.

Falling in love was hardly the cure-all that the romantics claimed. Love, in Amanda's opinion, was the absolute worst thing that could have happened. If she were not extremely careful, loving Zachary could mark the end of her independence, her self-respect and most importantly, the end of what made her unique.

If she was to survive, she had no option but to protect herself in every way she could. Instead of turning to him, she kept her gaze averted from his hard profile. There was nothing to say . . . nothing that could change the deep emotions lodged in her heart. As long as Zachary was busy nursing his brooding anger she was safe.

"How much longer are you going to pout?" he demanded in a low menacing growl as he shifted gears.

He handled the sports car as he did everything, with skill and casual ease. His long-fingered bronze hands glided along the steering wheel as if he were caressing it. The last night they been together he had caressed, kissed and licked every inch of her body.

Flushed with embarrassment, she was infuriated with herself. She had to stop this. She had no business longing to have his hands on her body, yearning for the feel of them smoothing over her bare skin. It had to end now, especially when she knew where those kinds of thoughts would lead. Anger was much safer.

Amanda reminded herself that she had every reason to be angry with him. She was the one forced to spend time with the mother-in-law from hell. Rebecca McFadden detested her and was probably plotting her downfall at this very minute.

Zachary swore. "Are you planning to give me the silent treatment all weekend? Because if you are, let me warn you, I've had as much of it as I intend to take."

"And I have had as much of your temper as I intend to take," she shot back. Even though she was aware that in a very real sense she was teasing a tiger, she was not about to back down.

He seemed angrier than he had been when she had hung up on him, angrier than when they were at the condo. Apparently a hundred plus miles of complete silence had not done a thing toward easing his temper.

It was not as if she exactly welcomed his anger, but she was not about to risk her sanity by falling into his arms either. She made a hasty promise to herself that under no circumstances was she to forget he wanted more from her than she could afford to give.

When they rounded the bend, she saw the well-lit house

resting on the top of a hill, bordered by trees on one side. It was an impressive house, a huge two-story colonial field-stone structure. As they pulled to a stop in the wide circular drive, her sense of dread intensified.

He helped her from the car as if he expected her to bolt. She filled her lungs with cold night air.

He sighed heavily while he absently rubbed the soft fur covering her shoulders. "Mandy, it shouldn't be this way. We have—"

She interrupted, "Zach, you've gotten me here. What more do you want . . . my soul as well?"

"Not your soul, sugar," he whispered close to her ear. "Just your love . . . only that." His mouth covered hers in a hungry kiss. "I've missed you so damn much. What's so wrong with wanting to be with my own wife or needing to make love to you?"

"This is not about me. If it was, you would not have disregarded my feelings. Your only concern is for Barbara." Amanda walked away, heading for the front door.

Judging by his harsh expletive, she had successfully antagonized him all over again. She did not need to be told she was toying with fire, but she had no other option. She either kept him angry or she would have to deal with his irresistible sexuality.

"Zachary, you're back. Good evening, Amanda." Rebecca Hamilton McFadden opened the door seconds before Amanda could turn the brass knob. Mrs. McFadden's smile did not reach her cold, dark eyes. "It's a pleasure to have you here, dear."

Both women knew why she had made the comment. Zachary was a step behind with her overnight case in hand.

Mrs. McFadden was faultlessly tailored in a pale blue silk dress with triple strands of perfectly matched black pearls around her thin neck. She had the ability to make Amanda feel like a giraffe, all neck and legs, next to her petite, almost doll-like frame.

Even the fine lines on her classic-featured bronze face could not detract from her ethereal, almost fragile beauty. Mrs. McFadden was adored and protected by all three of her sons.

Sixteen

"Thank you, Mrs. McFadden. How have you been?" Amanda knew what was expected of her.

"I'm quite well, thank you. Come in." Her smile deepened when she focused on her eldest son. "Son, you need not bother yourself with that. Mansfield can do that. After all, that's what we pay him for," she announced haughtily.

"No trouble, Mother. Don't fuss." Zachary's voice had softened as he paused to kiss his mother's cheek, after closing the door behind them.

They stood in an impressive marble foyer, which flowed into a wide central hall with rooms opening on both sides, a sweeping staircase curving upward in a wide, graceful arch.

"Be right back," he said.

As Amanda watched him ascend the stairs she could not help wondering what he had put inside that bulging case. She was here for one weekend, not a month.

"Come into the library, Amanda." Mrs. McFadden walked away, her head held high.

"Mandy! How good to have you back, child." Mrs. Armstrong, the housekeeper, approached with a welcoming smile. She was wheeling a service trolley filled with finger sandwiches and a heavily laden sterling silver tray.

Amanda's smile was instantly warm and genuine. Margaret Armstrong had always been kind to her, and that was something she would never forget, considering how difficult it had been to return to this house after she had lost their baby.

"It's good to see you, Margaret. You're looking well." Amanda gave the other woman a hug before she handed over her coat.

She turned in time to see the tightening of her mother-in-law's mouth as she eyed the luxurious fur.

"Do you like it?" Amanda asked her mother-in-law. "It was a gift from Zachary." She did not expect an answer and did not get one. She wondered, yet again, how the two of them were going to reside under the same roof even for a weekend.

Mrs. McFadden led the way through the first door on the right, into the large book-lined library where the family gathered in the evenings.

Amanda's feet sank into plush, rose carpet. Twin cranberry brocade sofas faced each other in front of a brick fireplace. A fire burned welcomingly in the grate. Burgundy, high-back soft leather armchairs with ottomans were positioned around the long room forming conversational groupings.

Mrs. Armstrong placed the silver tray with sterling coffee and tea server on the low mahogany table between the sofas and positioned the brass trolley close to Mrs. McFadden, where she had made herself comfortable at one end of a sofa.

"Coffee? Tea?" Mrs. McFadden said, dismissing Mrs. Armstrong with a flick of her long, perfectly manicured hand.

"Tea, please," Amanda requested.

"Sugar? Cream?"

"No, thank you." Amanda found it virtually impossible to relax in her mother-in-law's presence.

"Well, will you look who's here. How are you doing, darlin'?" Roger said as he strolled in.

He placed a kiss on his mother's cheek, then smiled at Amanda, giving her a hug before he sprawled on the sofa next to his mother. Roger was casually dressed in gray slacks and a pullover sweater. Despite his smile he looked tired.

"I'm fine, but more important, how is Peggy?"

"Much better. We're certainly glad to have her home." Roger accepted the steaming cup of coffee his mother offered. "I'm glad you came. Peggy is anxious to see you. Maybe you can stop in for a visit with her after dinner?"

"I'd like that. How are you managing?"

"Better now that I've gotten her home and out of that hospital." He tiredly rubbed his jaw.

"My poor darling." Mrs. McFadden beamed as she patted Roger's hand. "Son, you're exhausted. You haven't had more than a few hours' sleep since Peggy went into the hospital."

"Don't worry, Mother. This is one night I'm sure I will get a full night's rest." Roger smiled at her before he asked, "Where is Zach?"

"Right here," Zachary said, with a smile on his face as he entered the room, eyeing his wife. "Speaking of sleeping well, I know I will with Mandy beside me." He sat down beside his wife, resting his arm along the back of the sofa, encircling her shoulders. "May I have a cup of coffee, Mother?"

"Of course, son," Mrs. McFadden said sweetly to him,

even though her lips had compressed slightly. Both men were unaware of the look of disapproval she sent Amanda's way as they discussed the ranch, but Amanda was uncomfortably aware of it.

"Will you look at this? While I work my butt off, you two lounge around all day drinking coffee and relaxing in front of the fire. What's up with that?" Bradford McFadden demanded, as he walked into the library.

"Really, son," Mrs. McFadden scolded. "You know I can't stand that kind of talk."

He shrugged, not the least put out. Bradford was a tall, slender man who shared the same coppery bronze coloring as his brothers. Like the other two, he was strikingly handsome, but he was several inches shorter than his brothers. Dressed formally in a black business suit, he looked every inch the well-paid executive. His brothers grinned, not the least bit put out by his taunts.

"Darling, come join us." Mrs. McFadden beamed, apparently delighted to have all three of her sons at home.

"Mother," Bradford acknowledged, kissing her forehead before turning his attention to his sister-in-law. "Mandy, you're as beautiful as I remember. Is this a short visit or are you back for good?" He didn't wait for a response but continued dryly, "Zach certainly has been running himself ragged, between the ranch and Denver. Save us all from independent women."

"Shut up, Brad," Zachary cautioned as he'd felt Amanda stiffen beside him. "Make yourself a drink. You could use one."

Bradford shrugged. "Just stating my opinion."

"You can keep your opinion to yourself," Roger offered. "How was the meeting with Harrison?"

Loosening his tie and opening the button close to his throat, he said as he walked to the array of crystal decanters on a side table and poured himself a drink, "Lousy. He's holding out for more money. Must have read that stupid article in *Fortune* about Zach's holdings.''

Zachary lifted a brow, but didn't comment.

With drink in hand, Bradford asked, dropping down on the arm of the sofa beside his mother, ''Where is Barbara?''

''She's having dinner in town with a friend,'' Mrs. McFadden explained.

At the mention of Barbara's name, Amanda felt Zachary's eyes on her. She shifted uncomfortably. She didn't know Bradford as well as she knew Roger and Zachary. He had always seemed somewhat aloof, even as a boy.

There was no question about his loyalty toward his family. He had never said so, but Amanda knew he blamed her for the failure of her marriage to his brother. Whenever they ran into each other in the McFadden Building, he barely spoke to her.

''Peggy home?'' Bradford inquired.

''Yeah. She's resting. It has been a rough ten days, starting with that last storm,'' Roger said.

''You can say that again.'' Zachary's hand tightened on Amanda's shoulders.

''Are you going out again after dinner, Zachary?'' Mrs. McFadden's concern was evident. ''Why must you continue with this? You have been out all night, every night this week, existing on hardly any sleep. And today, when you should have been sleeping, you drove into Denver to get Amanda. Bradford could have just as easily brought her out to the ranch. There was no reason for you to go.'' Mrs. McFadden paused, long enough to catch her breath, then added, ''Darling, surely you can leave the chore of hunting that wild coyote to your men?''

''It's my responsibility, Mother,'' Zachary said firmly.

''You've been out hunting for a wild coyote?'' Amanda asked with genuine horror in her voice. ''Why didn't you tell me?''

"There's nothing to tell. This ranch is my problem, just as the office is Brad's and our legal dealings are Roger's. If I'm lucky, we can trap him without bringing him down. We think he is wounded, that's why he's hunting on the ranch." Zachary's tone indicated that the matter was not open for discussion. Looking at his mother, he asked, "Everything all set for the party tomorrow night?"

As if on cue, Mrs. McFadden said with a wide smile, "Perfectly. Barbara is going to be so pleased. We should have a full house."

Shaken by the discovery that Zachary had been out looking for a dangerous animal, Amanda said, "Please, excuse me. I need to freshen up before dinner." She placed her cup on the coffee table and rose gracefully. "Please, don't get up."

Amanda did not so much as glance her husband's way as she headed toward the staircase. She couldn't look at him, not when she didn't know exactly what she was feeling. All she knew was that she was upset. The thought of him going out looking for a wild animal did not sit well with her. He could have been mauled to death and she would not have known. Why hadn't he told her? She shivered, terrified of what he'd faced night after night. She could not bear it if anything happened to him.

What was wrong with her? She felt as if her life were falling apart. The knowledge that she was hopelessly in love with her husband didn't help matters. Not only did she love him, but she didn't dare reveal her emotions. It was too much. How was she supposed to cope? She was only just beginning to accept the depth and strength of that love.

During the drive she had been deliberately feeding her husband's temper, hoping to keep a measurable distance between them. Now he was furious with her, and she didn't want him to go out with his mind on their argument, and not on what he had to do. How in the world was she supposed to undo the damage?

Pausing on the second-floor landing, she stood outside the first door on the left. Reluctantly, she turned the brass knob to enter the suite of rooms she had once shared with Zachary.

As her eyes went around the sitting room she recalled how much she'd liked it. A roomy, butter-soft, taupe leather sofa and high-back navy leather armchairs that blended with both the glossy hardwood floors and the luxurious oriental area rug in shades of tan, bone and taupe with touches of russet tones. Brass lamps were positioned on mahogany end tables and were shaded with rust pinch-pleated silk. The drapes at the wide picture window were also rust, and a cozy fire burned in the screened grate.

She stopped on the threshold of the comfortably furnished bedroom. The floor was covered in a lush, taupe carpeting. A king-size bed was centered against the wall on a raised mahogany platform between floor-to-ceiling bookshelves filled with books, spanning a wide range of subjects.

It had always amazed her how extensive her husband's interests were and how well read he was despite his busy schedule. Picking up the book on the nightstand, Amanda smiled as she read the title on the spine, *The African-American Century* by Henry Louis Gates Jr. and Cornell West.

An oversize carved armoire was tucked into a corner, while a mirrored dresser and large-screen television set were all positioned on the wall opposite the bed. Both the drapes and down-filled comforter were in rich velvet, in a geometric pattern in shades of copper, taupe and navy. Deep-cushioned navy armchairs shared a plush matching ottoman. One door led into a walk-in closet, the other led into the connecting bathroom.

Even though she had first come here as Zachary's bride,

she hadn't come with a carefree or joyful heart. The painful loss of her grandfather had been too fresh and it had been quickly followed by another even more crushing loss ... that of their baby.

Zachary had shared her grief and listened when she needed to talk. He had made no sexual demands. More often than not, he had asked for nothing more than to hold her throughout the long nights.

He was going hunting tonight while he was angry and disappointed in her. What could she say to him? She couldn't very well tell him the truth. Her reluctance to come today had nothing to do with how she felt about him, but everything to do with his beloved mother. But Amanda was the one who had needlessly hurt him.

What could she do? Was there anything that she could say to stop him from going after that wild animal tonight? Hardly. He was determined to do what needed to be done. It was one of the things she loved about him, one of the things that made him so dependable and at the same time so infuriating.

There was no point in fooling herself. There was nothing she could do to stop him from going after that coyote. But there had to be something she could do or say to make up with him before he left.

She took a quick shower and changed into a deep purple silk sheath that she knew he liked. She left her hair around her shoulders, then reapplied her makeup before rejoining the others. She was disappointed that there had been no opportunity to speak privately to Zachary.

She could tell by the way he did not look into her eyes that he was still angry. He was almost broodingly silent during the meal, only responding when asked a direct question. If it hadn't been for Roger's enthusiasm that Peggy was home, the entire meal would have been intolerable.

They were leaving the formal dining room when the sound of his men's voices carried down the hall from the kitchen.

"It sounds as if you're being paged, big bro," Bradford said with a grin.

"Yeah, it does," Zachary said casually.

"Be careful, son," his mother urged.

"Don't worry, Mother. He knows what he is doing," Roger said reassuringly.

When Zachary turned to leave while the rest of the family continued on into the library, Amanda was momentarily stunned that he planned to leave without so much as a good night to her. She hurried after him. Hurt, anger and fear were all mixed together when she called his name.

He paused, slowly turning back toward her. His face was closed, devoid of emotion. "Yes?"

Brought up short by lack of warmth in his eyes, Amanda studied him with large troubled eyes. This hard, unyielding man wasn't the man she had adored since childhood, the man she so recently discovered owned her heart.

"You're still angry with me," she said softly, moving forward until she stood directly in his path. When he made no effort to deny it, she moved even closer. "Please, don't leave this way," she whispered as her slim arms glided beneath his and encircled his trim waist. She pressed into his deep chest . . . craving his reassurance.

He released a throaty groan, tightening his arms around her and drawing her even closer to him. He dropped his head until his cheek rested against her temple.

"I have damn good reason to be angry with you. What do you expect? You fight me at every turn. And you keep throwing Barbara in my face when you know there's nothing romantic between us. When I asked you to come spend the weekend on the ranch with me, you refused without giving it any consideration."

"It's not like that," she said, trying to make him understand what she couldn't put into words.

"Did our last time together mean anything to you, Mandy?"

He didn't even try to conceal his disappointment. Did he care so much? Or was her imagination running away from her? If only she knew she could trust him with her heart. And what if she was wrong?

Exasperated by her silence, Zachary demanded, "Why are you in my arms? Evidently, I was wrong about what we shared."

"That's not true."

"Mandy . . ."

A man's laughter from the back of the house forced her to say, "I don't want you to go out angry with me." She reached up to press her mouth against his throat. "Please, be careful."

He tightened his hold on her waist, saying, "I wish I understood you, lady. You're unwilling to give me your love or trust in my love for you. Yet, you're here now, asking me to be careful."

Her lips brushed his chin when she whispered, "Kiss me . . . please."

She did not have to ask twice. He angled his head so that his firm lips covered hers in a hard, hungry kiss that was much too brief.

"I have to go. Get some sleep," he said, then stepped back and hurried out.

Pressing unsteady fingertips against her trembling lips, she realized that she had not been thinking but feeling. Her emotions had taken control, overshadowed all else, including her own reservations.

Even though she had probably only further complicated a complex situation, she was glad that they were at least on speaking terms. If nothing else, he could now concentrate on the problem of the wild coyote and not their problems. She said a silent prayer before she passed the library to mount the stairs.

"Mandy, hold up," Roger called, coming out of the library. "Are you okay?" he asked, when he reached her, placing an arm around her shoulders.

She shrugged. "I guess."

They climbed the remaining stairs together. "It doesn't take a genius to see that you and Zach had an argument. He was as tight as a drum, ready to explode, while you refused to so much as speak to him. Can I help?"

"We talked. I don't like the idea of him out there in the dark looking for some wild animal. I didn't want him to leave angry."

"Zach is tough. He can take care of himself." Roger chuckled, before he said, "My guess is after a sweet send-off, he'll be eager to get back to you."

She blushed. Changing the subject, she asked, "Do you think Peggy is up to a quick visit tonight?"

"From you, absolutely." He grinned, opening the door of the suite across from Zachary's.

The rooms were similar in design, but had been decorated in shades of rose from a rich burgundy to palest pink. The sitting room housed a sofa, twin armchairs and a desk in front of the windows, which overlooked the front of the house.

"You decent?" Roger called as he peeked into the bedroom. "You've got company."

"Great!"

Peggy McFadden was propped up in a huge canopy bed covered by a lovely quilt. She'd been watching the television in the built-in cabinet across from the bed. She was a small, slight woman in her last trimester of pregnancy.

"Hey, girl," Amanda said with a wide smile as she crossed the room. "Look at you! You look great."

"What I look is huge. It's about time you showed your face." Peggy held her arms out to her longtime friend and sister-in-law.

"You look wonderful," Amanda said as they exchanged hugs and kisses. "It's so good to see you at home. How are you feeling?"

Amanda noted that her coffee-tone complexion glowed from happiness despite the dark smudges under her pretty eyes. Although she was tiny in stature, Peggy had a warm and loving spirit.

"I'm so glad to be home. I hated that hospital," she said, patting the place beside her slim hip. "Sit by me."

"Peggy Marie, you scared us all. You will take better care of yourself," Amanda scolded. She patted Peggy's round tummy at the same time holding back tears.

Amanda was not about to let her own painful memories spoil this special time for her friends. For so long she had been self-absorbed, and in the process had neglected two of her dearest friends. Amanda hadn't seen Peggy since she moved back to Denver.

"Don't start! I've heard all I care to on the subject of my health from the worrywart over there," Peggy complained, pointing an accusing finger at her husband.

From where he lounged in the armchair, Roger merely gave her a playful smile. His dark eyes caressed his wife's short curly natural, her high cheekbones and her soft lips before he turned his attention to the television program.

"Oh, Mandy, I have missed you. I'm so happy you came for the entire weekend. We can talk and talk and talk." Peggy laughed, holding Amanda's hand. "I loved the flowers you sent to the hospital. Thanks. They were beautiful."

"You're more than welcome. I only stopped in tonight to say hello. It's late and you need your rest."

"But you just got here."

"There are no buts about it, darlin'," Roger interrupted.

"The doctor said rest, and I intend to make sure you do just that. If I have to stay home and watch you, I will."

Peggy made a face at him.

"Would you like a snack? You didn't eat much dinner," he said.

"I ate as much as I could. Will you stop fussing?"

"You've given me one bad scare, Peggy McFadden. I can't take another one. Behave," Roger warned.

"I'm being good. Now stop worrying."

They stared into each other's eyes for a few moments as if they had forgotten Amanda was in the room. Their love and devotion to each other was unmistakable.

"Roger is right," Amanda said as she rose. "I'll stop in tomorrow and spend part of the day with you. We can have that talk then."

"Promise?"

"Yes, I do." Amanda leaned over and kissed Peggy's cheek. "Sleep well. Good night, you two. Don't get up, Roger, I can see myself out." She waved before hurrying out.

Peggy, like Amanda, had a degree in fine arts. Unlike Amanda, she had never pursued a career in design. Roger wanted her home and so she happily devoted herself to him and her sculpting. The two had talked about building a home of their own on the ranch. Amanda had no idea why it hadn't gone further than talk, but she suspected it had a great deal to do with Mrs. McFadden.

Whereas Peggy had learned to cope with their domineering mother-in-law, Amanda had never tried. The few weeks that she lived in the woman's house had convinced Amanda that even if she and Zachary had not married for the wrong reason, they would have had no real privacy.

Amanda knew she could not live under the same roof as his mother after the cruel way the woman blamed her for the loss of her baby. Never again! It had been so painful that Amanda could not share the accusation with anyone, especially not her husband.

She never wanted to come between Zachary and his mother. The McFaddens were a close-knit family, which was something Amanda admired. It was best left unsaid.

As she finished unpacking she laughed at the number of things Zachary had packed for the weekend. There were three pairs of wool slacks and coordinated sweaters, three skirts and matching blouses, two dresses, three evening gowns, high-heel shoes and a mountain of lingerie and a robe but no slippers, nightgowns or panty hose. Thank goodness, she could wash out the pair she had on. How could a man whose own wardrobe consisted mainly of work clothes give her such a wide variety?

Opening one of his drawers, she helped herself to a pair of his silk pajamas. She was amazed that he had so many pairs, and all of them were silk, navy and looked brand-new. He no doubt received a new pair every Christmas.

She giggled, imagining his reaction to receiving yet another pair for his birthday. What an idea. She would give him three new pairs, all in bright red. Her eyes sparkled as she took the top and left the bottoms on his side of the wide bed.

She sobered suddenly. By his birthday next year they may not be together. Imagining life without Zachary brought no tilt to her lips or excitement into her eyes. There was no point in avoiding the truth. Their marriage was temporary. Next January twenty-third would be the end of their arrangement.

After a long soak in his bronze tiled bathroom, she put on the pajama top. It stopped at midthigh and she was forced to roll the long sleeves up. She tiredly settled between the flannel sheets, under the down-filled comforter. Knowing she would not be able to sleep, she reached for the book on the nightstand and began reading.

It was after two in the morning when she fell asleep with the bedside lamp on and the book propped on Zachary's pillows. She did not stir an hour later when he slid in beside her and switched off the light.

Perhaps she sensed his presence because Amanda curled her body toward his, seeking his warmth. When she opened her eyes, late the next morning, she was alone.

Her face was pressed into his pillow and the pajama bottom she had left for him was gone, confirming that they'd shared the bed at some time during the night.

She was disappointed that Zachary had not awakened her. Apparently he was still angry. And even though he knew she would have welcomed him into her arms and into her body . . . it hadn't mattered.

She dropped her face into her hands. It hurt knowing that he had not tried to correct what was wrong between them. And she had no idea how to go about fixing the problem herself. Perhaps it was already too late?

Seventeen

"It is so good to have you here," Peggy repeated yet again that afternoon, as she squeezed Amanda's hand. The two women were in her cozy sitting room.

"If you say that one more time, I swear I will scream. We've been talking for almost two hours. I think it's time I let you have a nap."

Although Peggy looked better than she had the day before, Amanda did not want her to overdo.

"Honestly, you're beginning to sound like my husband. I'm in my flannel pajamas, lying down with my feet up and covered by a quilt. If that's not resting, what is?" Peggy pouted. "I'm used to working. I have not been inside my studio in weeks." She had converted one of the downstairs rooms and often spent hours there sculpting.

"I have to admit, you've been good. We just worry about you, darlin'."

"Enough is enough!" Peggy complained. "I haven't moved since Roger carried me to this chaise longue."

"Forgive us! We love you and want you to have a healthy baby," Amanda said with both her hands on her hips. "If that means not sculpting or even helping Margaret with the washing, then you do it!"

"Mandy, I'm sorry. I didn't mean to fuss or remind you of your loss. I wasn't thinking. Forgive me."

"Don't worry about it. I'm much better. It's just that none of us want you and Roger to go through what Zachary and I did," Amanda ended quietly.

"I know."

"Try to be patient with us when we get a bit protective of you and that precious baby. Now, let's think of something to keep you busy."

"You're starting to sound just like her." They both knew the "her" she referred to was their mother-in-law. "All I need right now is for that 'woman' to come in here administering her loving care," Peggy snapped impatiently, then shrugged her shoulders. "I know, I'm being simply hateful. I'm just so tired of being in this house. I'd almost convinced Roger that we need a place of our own; then this happened."

She hesitated before she revealed, "Mandy, I can't stand it. The doctor warned that I might have to be in bed for the rest of the pregnancy. By then, I'll definitely be a loony bird."

"You're only making it harder on yourself." Amanda came over and gave her a hug before she said, "We both know what it's like living in her house. But you can't dwell on it right now. Just forget about our dear sweet mother-in-law and concentrate on the baby. I know!" she said excitedly. "If you like, I can bring you some pattern books for baby clothes. We can get out the old knitting needles and have lots of little clothes ready and waiting for that little girl you're going to have."

"Little boy. My stubborn husband is the one who wants a girl." Peggy smiled dreamily. "Come down here so I can give you another hug," she instructed, then did just that. "Thanks. See why I love you? Mandy, it's a wonderful idea and so much better than thinking about the fact that not only do I have to stay in bed, but I have to give up making love with my husband."

"How's Roger taking it?" Amanda asked, making herself comfortable once more on one end of the sofa.

"He's not happy about it, but he's not complaining either. He's taking it like he does most things, in his stride. I'm the one that loves to complain, according to my dear husband."

Amanda giggled. "Life is never dull with you around."

"How could it be with three gorgeous men and the queen witch to keep things interesting? And let us not forget the ohhhh-soooo-lovely spoiled Barbara."

"Peggy? What is this? You've always gotten along so much better with our mother-in-law than I ever did. Did something happen? Have you two had an argument?"

"Nothing that uncivilized. I'm just so tired of having to deal with her every single day." She sighed. "I want a home of our own, not merely a few rooms. And I want to be able to cook what pleases me. If I want to have romantic candlelight dinners with my husband, seven nights a week, I should be able to do that without explanation to anyone. Mandy, I want to be able to go shopping and spend all of Roger's money without comment from anyone, except from him. We haven't had any privacy since Roger was in law school in Boston. I want to pick out my own baby's clothes, furnishings and wallpaper."

Peggy paused to catch her breath. "Maybe it's being pregnant that has me so emotional? Lately, being in this house has really gotten on my nerves. And I will never forget how hateful Mrs. McFadden was to you when you lost your baby ... all behind Zachary's back, naturally. I don't blame you for leaving this house and not ever wanting to come back. Did you ever tell Zach what she said to you? The only reason I haven't told Roger is that you made me promise.''

"No! There was no point. Like his brothers, Zachary adores his mother.'' Amanda shook her head. ''Besides. I could never hurt him like that. At the time, it was simpler for me to move back to the condo and get my life back on track. I wasn't exactly thinking straight when I left here.''

"Simpler for whom? Mrs. McFadden? Barbara? Certainly not you and Zach.''

"Calm down, Peggy. It doesn't matter anymore. And you're right, a woman deserves to have some privacy, especially in a marriage. It would have been different, if Mrs. McFadden were a kind, thoughtful person. We both know better. She's determined to run her sons' lives and be sneaky about it.'' Suddenly chilled, Amanda ran her hands over her cashmere-covered arms. ''But this doesn't help your situation. Now isn't exactly the best time for you and Roger to build that house you two once talked about. After the baby comes, then make your move. For now you have enough to do with keeping your spirits up, so please try to relax and enjoy this time. Peggy, you can't afford to let anyone or anything keep you from having a healthy baby.''

"I know, you're right, but it's getting harder and harder to live in this house,'' she said unhappily. ''Oh, Mandy, I do miss our talks.''

"Me too.''

"Mrs. McFadden has been so unfair to you. If I live to be a hundred I will never understand why she detested you. It stared from the moment you came into this house as Zachary's bride. Why? Because you were not the one she handpicked for him?'' Peggy shook her head, saying, ''Just be careful. You can't let her destroy your marriage, especially now that you and Zach have found each other again. He loves you so much.''

Amanda rose, going over to the large picture window. She did not see the mountains in the distance or the rolling snow-covered range.

"You don't understand how things are between us. I wanted a divorce, he didn't. Now we are both trying to make it work, but . . ." Amanda shrugged her shoulders, having run out of words to explain her feelings. It was so complicated.

"Have you been able to let him see into your heart?"

"If only it were that simple." Amanda's thoughts drifted back to the night of the storm. Nothing else mattered as they made love for the first time without anything overshadowing it . . . not the grief of the past or the problems they now faced. They'd concentrated on each other during that night.

He had wakened her the next morning with even more kisses and breakfast in bed. She only had to close her eyes to recall the way he had made love to her. She'd been unable to hold back even a small part of herself. Her responses had been heartfelt. There had been nothing hurried about the way they had loved . . . their entire focus had been on one thing . . . giving pleasure.

She frowned, comparing the vast difference between that morning and this one. She had overslept and Zachary had been out on the range when she had gone down for breakfast. She'd immediately lost her appetite and settled for toast and a cup of hot tea.

Later she had had lunch with Peggy in her rooms. In fact, she had not seen her husband all that day. Peggy was the one who had told her that Zachary and his men had captured the coyote. The animal had been sedated and taken to a wildlife reserve that morning.

Was he still angry with her? Was that why he hadn't wakened her? There had to be a reason why he'd made no effort to spend time with her. After all, he had insisted she come. Yet he had left her to her own devices.

"Mandy?"

"We're trying to work things out. But it hasn't been easy. So much has gotten in the way," Amanda said quietly.

"Love is all that matters. Zach is in love with you. Have you shown him the love you have for him?"

Was it true? Could Zachary be in love with her? He had never said it quite that way. What if it was true? It might change everything. Did she have the courage to risk being vunerable?

"I can't. Not yet."

She was only just beginning to understand what she felt for him. Her newly discovered feelings had certainly made her sensitive to his needs. Just last night she had been petrified that he would be injured. This morning she had been hurt because he had left the suite without a word to her.

What if Peggy was right? Surely he'd expect her to move back to the ranch? Could she cope with living under that woman's roof? Just the thought made her shudder. No! This was not about Mrs. McFadden. It was about the two of them.

There was no doubt about the fact that she was very much in love with him. There could be no other explanation for why she continued yearning for him. Just last night, she wanted nothing more than to feel the hard length of his body pressed against hers and to know he was safe.

Loving him could only lead to more complications. She had no choice. She had to find a way to conceal her emotions. For all she knew she could be a mere step away from repeating her mother's tragic mistakes. Had her mother felt this same overwhelming need that Amanda was now experiencing? Or were there varying degrees of love? Just how bad did it get?

What if her feelings continued to grow? Would she eventually relinquish a vital part of herself because of the way he made her feel? She couldn't even count the numerous times since their reconciliation that she'd reminded herself that she must not forget the painful lessons learned at her mother's knee. Yet, she had gone ahead and fallen in love with him anyway.

Although Amanda knew she was very different from her parent, if Zachary left her today, she would be just as devastated as her mother had once been. That single thought was terrifying.

Peggy's voice broke into her thoughts when she said, "Mandy, I'm worried about you. Keeping all that pain locked inside isn't healthy. Please, remember that I'm here for you whenever you need to talk."

Offering a somewhat shaky smile, Amanda said, "There's no easy solution. It certainly doesn't help that my father is back in town."

"What does he want?"

"Who knows? The first time he called my office I nearly lost it. Thank goodness, Zach was there. I could barely speak when I heard his voice after so many years; all those memories rushed back. It was horrible," Amanda confessed as she sat down on the sofa.

"I can imagine."

"He wanted me to see me. I refused but Zach felt it was important for me to at least see him. I couldn't have done it without Zach at my side." Amanda shook her head. "It was the most painful meal. I was so upset at the time. I'm still not sure what I said to the man. Can you believe, he had just learned about Granddaddy's death?"

"What?"

"Mr. Ross had been trying to locate him all this time."

"Was he sober?"

"Yes . . . or rather he appeared to be. But he was very shaky. Claimed he was sorry about the past."

''It took him long enough. It's been over ten years since he saw you last.''

''He calls me at the office, when I least expect it. I can't get him to stop.''

''Has he threatened you in any way?''

''No. And please don't mention this to Roger. I don't want Zach to feel obligated to confront my father.''

''Why not?''

''Zach knows how I feel. All I want is for Sebastian Daniels to go back to wherever he came from. I don't want him in my life.''

''Maybe he's changed? Maybe if you and Zach sat down with him again there might be some way to repair the damage?''

''How can that happen when I don't trust the man? He wants something from me. I just don't know what.''

''Mandy, you have to tell Zach about the calls.''

''I can't.''

''You have to.''

''It's humiliating. It was bad enough that Zach had to meet him. Believe me when I say being his daughter is nothing to be proud of.''

''Unfortunately, we can't pick our parents. You have to tell your husband about the calls, if for no other reason that Zach deserves to know you're being harassed.''

''Peggy, you have to calm down.'' Amanda went over and took her hand.

''I don't like this.''

''I don't either, but it isn't worth you getting upset. My father is going to go away, like he always does. He never stays long.'' Amanda flicked her hand. ''Problem solved. I just have to wait him out.''

''What if you're wrong?''

''I'm not. There is nothing here to hold him. My grandfather left him enough money to keep him in liquor for some time to come. That's all he cares about."

"I can only hope you're right. But eventually, you are going to have to tell Zach about his calls."

"I will, I promise. Now you have to promise that you won't say anything to Roger about this. Give me a chance to work it out on my own."

Peggy nodded. "For now I can keep my mouth closed."

"Thanks."

"I'm so glad you came this weekend, but I hope you don't find being here too painful."

"It hasn't been easy. Neither one of us can change what happened. I'm so much better than I was when I left this house last year. But more important, I'm so happy for you and Roger. You two have waited so long for this."

Peggy beamed with happiness. "We'll always be friends, even if we haven't seen each other very often these days."

"That's my fault."

"No, it's not. It can't be helped."

"So tell me," Amanda said. "Do you know the baby's sex yet?"

"No, we decided to wait."

"Which do you want, a little boy that looks like your handsome husband?"

"Oh, yes." She laughed. "Or a little girl . . . just so long as it's healthy. Mandy, I need to ask a favor."

"Uh-oh."

"Are you planning to go skiing with the others tomorrow?"

"I haven't thought about it. Besides, I haven't been asked," Amanda admitted candidly. "Who's going?"

"Barbara, Zach, Brad and Roger, if I can get him to go. They go most Sundays. Zach probably assumed you would be going along without being asked. That's just like a man. Are you going?"

"Why, would you like me to stay here with you?"

"Please, Mandy. I would really like for Roger to go. He hasn't had any fun since I fell. If you don't volunteer to stay with me, he'll stay home whether I ask him to go or not. He can be so stubborn."

Amanda laughed. "I believe it runs in the family. I'd love to stay and visit with you. It's no hardship . . . believe me. I can't remember the last time I went skiing. I assure you, I can live without watching Barbara make a play for my husband."

"Girl! Don't pay her any mind. She has a thing for Brad, only no one is supposed to know, but we all do. Everyone, that is, accept Brad and Mrs. McFadden. If I call the yarn shop in town and tell them what we need, Roger can pick everything up this afternoon. We can start knitting tomorrow."

"Roger will go pick up what?" he asked as he walked into the sitting room. He paused to give his wife a quick kiss before he flopped down on the sofa beside Amanda and kissed her cheek. He was dressed casually in beat-up jeans and an old college sweatshirt.

"You need a shower." Peggy wrinkled her nose.

"I've been out on the range mending fences all day. A little sweat is good for a man. So what do you need?"

"Knitting supplies. If I call now, I'm sure you will have time to pick them up before the dinner party, won't you, darling?" Peggy smiled, batting her eyelashes playfully at him.

He complained, but agreed easily enough, a smile dancing in his eyes. "You two have a good visit?"

"Yes," they both said at once, then laughed.

"You have not been on your feet, have you?" he asked Peggy.

"No, I have not! Ask Mandy."

"She's behaving. If you two will excuse me, I think I'll find my husband. Have you seen him?"

"He's probably in the office in front of the computer." Roger leaned back and propped his feet on the coffee table.

"Mandy, stop back later this evening. I want to see your dress for the party, okay?"

"Will do." Amanda smiled, getting to her feet. "See you both later."

Amanda suspected that Zach was still angry with her. Since her earlier attempt at easing the discord between them had apparently failed, she had to think of something else. It was amazing that in such a short time she'd gotten used to being with him. She'd missed him. She even missed their occasional disagreements.

After making a brief stop across the hall to run a quick brush through her hair and touch up the copper-tinted lipstick, she went looking for him. She didn't bother changing from the peach V-neck cashmere sweater and brown wool slacks.

Zachary's office was situated toward the rear of the spacious house. Evidence of preparations for the party was all around. The catering staff was hard at work preparing for the night ahead.

Amanda smiled as she pictured him in his private domain, which was almost spartan compared to the rest of the house. Bare maple hardwood floor, huge mahogany desk positioned in front of the floor-to-ceiling picture window. His most prized possession, his computer, was placed on the curved table against the far wall surrounded by built-in maple bookshelves. Unless he had made changes, the only cozy features were the huge, deep-cushioned black leather sofa and armchairs with ottomans.

His door was open when Amanda crossed the threshold. She issued a startled gasp at the sight of Zachary standing beside his desk with Barbara in his arms.

The shapely beauty had wound her arms around his neck and was running kisses over his lean cheek, down to his mouth. Zachary, as far as Amanda could tell, wasn't protesting. Far from it, with his head bent toward Barbara's, his hands were clasped on either side of Barbara's waist. Neither seemed aware of their audience.

"Oh, Zach! I can't believe it!" Barbara exclaimed.

"What do you think you're doing!" Amanda snapped, causing Barbara to turn with a start and Zachary's head to jerk up.

"Amanda!" Barbara said as she slowly slid her hands from his shoulders and down his chest in a blatant caress.

"Yes, Amanda . . . his wife," she hissed as she crossed the room. "I suggest you take your hands off my husband. Now!" Her eyes were hot with temper as she lifted her chin haughtily. Her dark curls bounced around her shoulders, her small nostrils flared indignantly, her breasts rose as her breathing quickened.

Amanda was unaware of the way he studied her. A slow smile spread across his dark face, which he quickly masked when she sent him a challenging look.

Her hands were balled on both hips as she glared at her husband. "You better start explaining fast, and it better be good."

"Amanda, really. I had no idea you were so insecure," Barbara said while taking a cautious step backward. "I was only thanking Zach for my birthday gift."

Amanda walked right up to the other woman, saying, "I don't care what you were thanking him for. Keep your hands off him. He's mine! And I will not tell you again. Now, get out of here before I forget I'm a lady."

Barbara's velvety brown complexion took on a decidedly gray tinge as she looked from one to the other. Zachary, having folded his arms across his chest, apparently wasn't the least bit put out by Amanda's threats.

"Zach!" Barbara wailed.

"You heard the lady. Get out." He issued the order calmly, his eyes on his wife. "And, Barbara, close the door behind you."

Barbara evidently knew when she had been defeated, for she pivoted on her heels and left them, slamming the door behind her.

The instant Amanda heard the door close, she yelled, "How dare you come back into my life, only to mistreat me! If you don't want me, why didn't you just sign the divorce papers and leave me the hell alone? If you wanted that spoiled little witch, I most certainly would never have stood in your way."

It was only when she paused to catch her breath that she realized his shoulders were shaking. In fact, his eyes were lit with laughter. As she stared in disbelief, his chest rumpled with mirth. He was laughing at her! Her last ounce of control snapped. She didn't think . . . she just reacted.

"Damn you!" she said, as she hurled herself at him.

He caught her, sobering the instant he saw tears in her eyes as she pummeled his chest, determined to hurt him as he was hurting her. Her body shook with violent sobs as she lashed out at him.

He did not try to stop her, but endured her blows until she was exhausted, slumping against him. He held her around the waist, supporting her in strong muscular arms.

"Are you ready to listen to me now?" he asked, tenderly tucking curls behind her ear.

Amanda was trembling so badly she would have fallen if he had not been supporting her. The last thing she wanted was to listen to anything he had to say. Yet, his closeness, his tenderness was unnerving, especially after seeing him only minutes earlier with Barbara in his arms.

"Let me go," she choked out brokenly. "I don't want you touching me . . . not ever."

"You can forget that, love. No one else has a right to touch you, no one but me. I'm yours, as you so loudly declared, much to my pleasure. And you, my love, are mine. We're not about to split up over some stupid misunderstanding."

"I said let go," she persisted, her voice a bit firmer as she regained control over her emotions.

He urged her as far as the leather sofa before he did as she asked. Too weak to protest, she sat down and concentrated on nothing more than taking deep, slow breaths.

"Mandy, there is an explanation." He stood with his hands shoved into his pockets.

Eighteen

Glaring, she hissed, "I will not be married to a man who can't keep his hands off other women. We haven't made love in over a week. Is that the problem? How could you go running off to that woman's arms after what we've shared?"

She didn't give Zachary a chance to respond before hurrying on to say, "The last time we were together you made love to me! If I'm not enough for you, you're welcome to her. You're worse than one of those stupid cows out there." Gesturing wildly toward the range, she snapped, "You're certainly no better than a horny bull! Do you hear me, Zachary McFadden? I want a divorce!"

"Well, you're not getting one, you little fool!" he snarled. "Are you ever going to stop comparing me to Sebastian Daniels? Why can't you get it through your pretty head that he and I are not the same kind of man?"

"That's not what I was doing!" she nearly screamed at him.

"You, my darling wife, can't see what's right in your face. What do I want with Barbara?"

Then he dropped down beside her, cupping her face so she couldn't look away from him. "Barbara is a kid! Hell, she's even younger than you are, Mandy. I gave her a check for her birthday, enough for that new car she has been wanting. She was only showing her gratitude. Besides, she has been in love with Brad since she was sixteen."

"But your mother wants—"

"What does my mother have to do with this? This is our life we're discussing here. Either you trust me, or you don't. I'm sick of you throwing Barbara in my face every time you get ticked. Stop using her as an excuse to keep us apart." He hesitated for a moment, then candidly admitted, "It has always been you. For the last ten years, I've been worried about what man you would decide to give your love to. I can't even tell you how much it meant to me the night I discovered I was the first."

"What? Why would—"

"This is not about Barbara." Frustrated, he ran a hand over his hair. "Maybe I should be grateful that you finally got around to wondering where I've been getting sex this past year? We both know it sure ain't been from you, lady."

She blinked, her astonishment etched in her small African features. "I got your point."

"Have you? I doubt it."

"You brought it up, so answer the question. Where have you been getting sex from?"

His eyes locked with hers when he said, "I've been celibate. I haven't been near another woman since we made love that first time. And you're so right, I'm as horny as a bull . . . only for you, pretty girl."

Celibate. The word seemed to echo inside her head. She

told herself that she had no right to be pleased that he hadn't been with anyone else. It didn't change the fact that he was her husband. And it was her right, no one else's, to take care of his needs. Only last night she had ached for him. If he had reached for her, she would not have refused.

Even now she was tempted to raise his hand to her lips and kiss the wedding ring that he always wore, even when she had stopped wearing hers. Instead she asked, "Why didn't you wake me when you came in during the night or even this morning before you left the suite?"

"You know why. I was angry."

"Are you angry now?" she asked softly as she slid forward so that her arms could glide over his shoulders and encircle his neck.

"Not exactly." His eyes were on her generous mouth.

"Please, don't be. Honey, I'm sorry. You're right. I jumped to the wrong conclusion." When she placed a lingering kiss on his wide firm lips, he groaned deep in his throat. "Please do me one favor ... keep cousin Barbara out of your arms."

"You got it. Oh, my love," he whispered huskily, parting her lips for the eager thrust of his tongue. He found, then savored the sweetness inside. "Haven't I shown you that it's you I want. Don't you know I can't get enough of you?"

"Well ..." She blushed.

He chuckled. "If you would like me to prove it, I'd be more than happy to accommodate you."

"Ple-e-ease."

He moved until he was sprawled back against one end of the sofa, her hips nestled between his parted thighs, her breasts rested on his chest. His mouth settled on the sensitive place on her throat as he unfastened the small mother-of-pearl buttons lining the front of her sweater. Baring the lush curve of her lace-covered breasts, he rubbed his face against the full swells as he unclasped her bra to cradle her softness in large palms.

"You are so beautiful," he whispered huskily, rolling her erect nipples between his fingertips.

"Zach," she moaned, forgetting all about their disagreement, his mother. All that was important was the searing heat he created deep inside.

When she got his flannel shirt opened to kiss the flesh she had pummeled earlier, her soft tongue sent sparks of pleasure shooting through them both. He groaned deep in his throat as he ravished her mouth hungrily, suckling her tongue. He caressed her round bottom, lifting her against his rock-hard penis, annoyed by the multiple layers of fabric that separated them.

She trembled, feeling the heat he created even through their clothing. She sighed in relief when he released the button at her waist and eased her zipper down.

"Mandy," he growled, turning his attention to her breasts, to lick a searing hot path toward her nipple. He lifted her until he could take her nipple into his mouth and repeatedly love the dark hard peak; then he suckled.

She bit her lips to hold back the scream rising in her throat. Zachary increased the suction until she quivered in his arms as she spiraled toward a quick release. Afterward, she went limp in his arms.

"I should have awakened you last night. I wanted you then. I want you now."

"Honey . . ." She tried resisting, using the endearment without conscious thought. Pulling away from his drugging kisses, she grabbed his busy hand that had managed to glide past the elastic lace top of her panties to slide his fingers into the soft curls covering her sex. When he squeezed her slick mound, she whimpered, barely managed to say, ". . . not here."

His response was to roll her toward the back of the sofa

and beneath him. He eased a muscular thigh between hers and pressed hot kisses along her throat.

"We can't . . ." she persisted breathlessly.

"Why?" He stopped to stare into her eyes, his burning like twin ebony flames.

"Zach . . ." she soothed, kissing his cheek, his mouth, ". . . we are in your office, remember? Anyone can walk in here. There is no lock on that door."

As if to prove her point there was a brief knock on the door before his foreman opened the door.

She was not sure which of them was more embarrassed, the big older man or herself, for they both blushed when her head popped up. Thank goodness, the back of the sofa faced the doorway and Zachary's upper body covered hers. Nothing could hide the embarrassment on her face or her messy hair and her lips swollen from Zachary's kisses.

"Sorry, boss." Josh Barton began backing out. "I'll wait in the hall."

"You do that," Zachary snarled with impatience.

Once the door was closed, Amanda pushed him away and began straightening her clothes. "I told you," she whispered in exasperation. "Do you think he saw anything?"

"Stop worrying. My body was covering yours," he said, putting his own clothes to right. "Okay?" At her nod, he went to open the door.

"What do you want?" Zachary barked, going over to his desk. He ran an unsteady hand over his hair. There was nothing he could do about the blatant outline of his arousal.

The man didn't move his eyes from his boss's angry face. "The men delivered the coyote without incident. And Parker's here with that . . . ah . . . new feed mixture you ordered. Where should I have the men put it?"

"The south barn for now. You needed me for that?" Zachary sent the other man a hard look.

"Your signature." Joe Barton gave Zachary the purchasing order he'd been holding.

Zachary scribbled his name, then advised as his foreman hurried toward the safety of the door, "Next time, make sure you wait until I give the okay for you to open that door. Better yet, get a man up here to put a lock on the damn thing."

"Yes, sir!" The older man grinned, quickly closing the portal firmly behind him.

She collapsed on the sofa unable to hold in the giggles that rose in her throat. Zachary joined in, stretching out on one end of the sofa, using her lap as a pillow for his head.

"That was close. I suppose this room could use more than a lock. What it needs is your touch. You know, a lamp or something? What do you think?"

"Well, perhaps a dark blue area rug with touches of cream," Amanda said as she stroked his naturally wavy close-cut hair. "An oil over the fireplace, then cream wallpaper flecked with navy in silk. A plant in the far corner and perhaps—"

"Hey, wait a minute."

"You don't like plants?" she teased, tracing the line of his generous mouth.

"I have more on my mind than redecorating my den," he crooned, his voice deepening as he looked up at her. His eyes lingered on the generous curves of her breasts before they moved on to her pretty mouth and finally came to linger on her sparkling brown eyes. "Do I need to make an appointment?"

"An appointment?"

"Oh, yeah. It may be the only way I can get you alone, behind a locked door without being interrupted. Shall we say ten o'clock in our bedroom?" Zachary's eyes smoldered as he waited for her response.

"Are you serious?"

"Absolutely. Ten?" he repeated.

"What about the party tonight?" She tried to ignore the quickening beat of her heart.

"What about it?"

"That is why we're here this weekend."

"We've been apart for too many long empty days and nights. If ten o'clock is too early, how about ten-fifteen?"

She laughed. "That's not much better."

Gently cupping her nape, he guided her face down toward his waiting mouth. He helped himself to a series of light butterfly kisses before he said huskily, "I don't intend to wait an instant longer, pretty girl. We can make our excuses. A roomful of people is not my idea of a good time."

"Honey . . ."

She forgot what she had been about to say when he licked her lips, tracing the generous curves of her mouth. He didn't stop there, he slid the tip of his tongue into the very corner of her mouth, causing her swollen nipples to harden even more, aching for more.

Evidently he only wanted to play, for he teased her repeatedly with just that tender stroke of his tongue. Impatient to once again experience the full thrust of his tongue against her own, she moaned deep in her throat as she parted her lips even more and rubbed her tongue against his.

That seductive assault on his senses was his undoing. He wasted no time in devouring her sweetness. He groaned his enjoyment, a hand moving to worry the tip of one breast.

"Zach . . ." she moaned. "If we don't stop, someone else will get an eyeful."

He chuckled, getting to his feet, then tugged her up. "Eleven?" he haggled, as he hooked an arm over her shoulders and led her out the door and toward the central staircase.

Mounting the stairs together, she reminded him, "Honey, I am spending the night."

"Not taking any chances. For all I know, you'll want me

to wait until the house is cleaned and everyone is tucked into their respective beds.''

Amanda teased, ''That shouldn't take too long.''

Once they were inside his suite with the door closed, he backed her up against the door. ''You tease, but I am dead serious. I feel as if I've done nothing but wait this past year.'' Nestling the tender spot at the base of her throat with the hot wash of his tongue, he persisted, ''Twelve?''

Quivering in excitement and awareness that he was close to losing his temper caused her to say, ''I'm not putting you off. It's not my fault that tonight is little Barbara's birthday party. I would still be in Denver if you had left me alone.''

She knew almost instantly that she had said the wrong thing. His big body had gone taut with tension and he dropped his hands to his sides. He would have backed away if she hadn't tightened her arms around his waist.

''Don't. I didn't mean it that way. We've done nothing but fight all weekend. Let me kiss it and make it better until later tonight when we have time for each other.''

''One kiss will hardly do what needs to be done,'' he said as he gathered her close once more and suckled her bottom lip for a long indulgent moment. ''I seem to have lost what little control I had. I've been semierect since I woke with you in my arms this morning. I'd like to nothing better than to forget that blasted party and stay here with you, with the door locked.''

''Me, too. But it's a little too late for that. We've got to get dressed, but I promise to do my best to please you . . . later.''

''I plan to hold you to that promise.'' He took one more lingering kiss before he went into the bedroom.

Amanda wondered with a worried frown. Zachary was becoming a little more possessive with each new day while she was becoming more dependent on him . . . too responsive to his needs. She longed to please him in and out of bed.

How long before he demanded she move back to the Circle-M? It was bound to happen . . . probably sooner than later. The question was, would she be strong enough to refuse, knowing it would likely damage what they now shared?

Would their marriage eventually come down to her having to make a choice between him or her career? She had worked so hard to make a name for herself in the interior design industry. She had worked even harder to be able to stand on her own two feet. She could not weaken now . . . she could not become her mother's daughter.

Zachary was dressed before Amanda and came into the bathroom where she was standing in front of the mirror applying her makeup.

"Sugar, we're late. I'd better go down while you finish up here. I'll see you, no later than fifteen minutes, right?" he quizzed, having to drag his eyes away from her delectable curves. Her breasts were cupped in a strapless beige bra, her round bottom in matching bikini panties and her long shapely legs beautifully displayed in thigh-high, lace-edged, cream-colored hosiery.

"Okay. I'm hurrying."

She paused to study his reflection in the mirror. He wore a navy tuxedo, pristine white shirt and navy bow tie. "Mmm, you're very handsome tonight. I'm going to have to keep my eyes on you."

There was pain in his eyes when he whirled her around to face him. His hands on her shoulders. "When are you going to start believing in us? What must I do to convince you my feelings are for you alone? Why can't you trust me?"

Her eyes filled with tears as she recognized he had accurately read her thoughts. She caught her bottom lip between small white teeth, unable to push her doubts away once and for all. They had been with her for so long and went far too deep.

"I'm sorry. I . . ." A single tear slid down past her velvety black lashes.

He lifted her chin saying, "Our marriage cannot survive unless it's built on trust. We don't have time to get into all that. You and I need to have a long talk . . . later." He placed a kiss on her temple. "Hurry."

He was in the bedroom before he remembered and called from over his shoulder, "I left something for you on the dresser. It would please me if you wore it tonight." With that he was gone.

"He's right," she mumbled aloud.

She had to stop this. He had given her no reason to distrust him. It had been her father who had hurt her mother with other women . . . not Zachary. Returning her attention to the mirror, she saw that she'd ruined her eye makeup and had to start over again. Sighing, she reached for cleansing lotion.

He was right. Without trust they had nothing. The one thing she was learning about herself this weekend was that deep inside she truly wanted their marriage to work. She didn't have much faith in love. Was it ever enough? Could it last?

When she least expected it something from the past would creep in, undermine her confidence and arouse her fears. Amanda had no idea how much of herself she would have to give Zachary in order to stay in this marriage. Couldn't he see that she was really trying to make it work?

When she emerged from the bathroom, she smoothed her curly hair into a loose knot at her crown, leaving a few wisps of black curls to frame her face and nape. She pulled on the yellow beaded evening gown when an impatient knock sounded on the outside door, an instant before it swung open.

"Amanda! Where are you?" Rebecca McFadden called, before she paused in the open bedroom doorway. Her anger was palpable.

"Did Zach send you to hurry me along?" Amanda asked as she finished zipping the dress and stepping into dyed-to-match silk-covered high-heeled pumps. Zachary's mother's continued silence caused Amanda glanced at her.

"Your meddling sent me!" Mrs. McFadden snapped, as she crossed the carpet.

"Really?"

Determined to remain in control, Amanda went over to the dresser and opened a square black velvet box with an expensive jeweler's name in gold letters printed on the lid. Tucked inside was an exquisite necklace, made of delicate jeweled flowers linked together by a fine gold chain. The center of each floral bloom was a round diamond, the petals were crescent-shaped rubies and the stems were channel-set emeralds. There were also matching floral motif lever-back earrings. They were a perfect match to the lovely bracelet he'd given her for their anniversary. She stifled the gasp that rose in her throat to concentrate on putting them on.

"Is that all you have to say? How dare you interfere in Roger's life?" Mrs. McFadden fumed hotly, displaying none of the warmth and charm she used when her sons were around. "Peggy has talked Roger into building a house of their own once the baby has come. I'm suppose to be pleased that at least the house will be on the Circle-M!" She hissed, "It's all your doing. Don't deny it! I know you're responsible."

"I'm not denying anything." Amanda turned around to face her mother-in-law, the sparkling circle of delicate jeweled flowers resting on her collarbone. Amanda did not bother to conceal the joy she felt for her friends.

"Roger and Peggy have a right to live their own lives any way they please and without any interference from either of us, Mrs. McFadden. Your sons are hardly babies. Don't you think it's time to let go?''

"You little bitch! I'm warning you, I will make you regret the day you ever married my son. It won't last much longer. Zachary will eventually grow tired of running back and forth between here and Denver. We both know you will never be welcome in this house, not as long as I'm alive. I'll make your life unbearable.''

"What more can you do?" Amanda asked curiously.

"Don't push me. I'll never let you forget that you tricked my son into marrying you. If you hadn't gotten yourself pregnant, he would never have married a little nobody like you in the first place.''

"You know nothing about me or my marriage.''

"I know you got what you deserved. You lost that baby on purpose. I'm sure you don't want my son to know that.''

"Mandy, are you ready?" Zachary's voice penetrated the heavy silence that had fallen between the two women.

The two women stared at each other, both wondering the exact same thing. Had Zachary overheard?

"Yes, I'm ready," Amanda called, having recovered enough to face him when his big body filled the threshold. "Your mother was just admiring my present. Thank you, honey. They're beautiful." She smiled up at him.

The last thing she wanted him to know was how intensely his mother disliked her. What she knew about her own parents had done nothing but cause her pain. Amanda did not want him hurt. Besides, there was nothing she could do to soften his mother's feelings of resentment. A rift between mother and son wouldn't help any of them.

"I'm glad you like them. You're the beautiful one, my love." Zachary dropped a warm kiss on her cheek, close to red-tinted lips. "Let's go, ladies, the guests will be arriving soon. We need our hostess." He offered both women an arm.

When they reached the hallway, Amanda said, "You two go ahead. I promised Peggy I'd stop in to show her my dress."

"Hurry," Zachary said before he escorted his mother down the stairs.

When Amanda joined the family a few minutes later they were stationed in the foyer welcoming friends and neighbors.

The birthday party was lavish. The dining room had been beautifully decorated and held an elaborate buffet with delectable dishes from smoked salmon to prime rib. A lovely decorated birthday cake had been provided and a fountain of champagne flowed. A small band played in one corner of the spacious living room.

Barbara seemed thrilled, Amanda decided several hours later, judging by the way she fluttered from group to group. She was the center of attention and her happiness showed on her pretty features. She had been hanging on to one young man most of the evening, while Bradford brooded in the background with a whiskey glass in hand.

Amanda had managed to visit with Peggy for a short time, using an excuse of bringing up some of the rich canapés for her to nibble on. But eventually, she had to rejoin the party.

Most of the Glenwood Springs ranching families were represented. Zachary introduced Amanda to the guests she did not know, some who were neighbors that she hadn't seen since her grandfather's funeral.

It wasn't that she expected Zachary to ignore her, but she was surprised that he went out of his way to entertain her as if she were his date rather than his wife. Amanda suddenly realized that was something they had never done . . . dated. They had gone from friends to lovers in one short night. She would be lying to herself if she did not admit how much she enjoyed the attention.

Not long after Zachary had been summoned to the telephone, Miles Stevens approached Amanda.

"Alone at last." Miles beamed at her. "That husband of yours has not let you out of his sight all evening."

"Miles. It has been a long time. How have you been?" She smiled, undecided whether or not she was pleased to see him.

He was an attractive man, above average height with smooth, dark caramel-brown skin. Although she'd been dating him during the time her grandfather had first taken ill, it was Zachary that she had turned to for comfort and support. She had married him in a matter of weeks.

Amanda still remembered the awkward lunch with Miles when she had told him of her plans. It would be a gross understatement to say it had not gone well. She had no idea that he wanted more than the casual friendship they had shared. And she would always regret that she had hurt Miles.

"Busy." He shrugged. "The construction industry has been booming of late. You look stunning in that dress. May I have a dance with the most beautiful lady in the room?"

"I'd like that." Her smile was generous. She was unaware how closely her mother-in-law was observing her.

The band had switched to a slow, romantic tune when Miles held her a bit too close to his lean frame.

"It's getting crowded," she noted, glancing around the foyer.

The large front hallway was being used for dancing and it was filled with guests moving between the library and the dining and living rooms.

"Yes," he said, pressing her closer still. He bent his head so that he was able to whisper into her ear, "I've missed you, Amanda. It's been a long time since I've held you. For a while, I'd heard rumors that you and Zach had split up. Judging by his possessiveness tonight, I'm wondering if I heard wrong? Have I waited too long in contacting you? Did I miss my chance?"

Finding his closeness uncomfortable, Amanda tried to

keep as much space between their bodies as possible. She faltered, nearly stepping on his toe. Miles steadied her. Both of his hands were on her slim waist.

"I can't believe you asked me that." Her entire body stiffened.

"Why not?" he asked quietly. "We were once very close."

"Miles, we were friends. We were never intimate." She looked into his eyes when she said, "Don't read more into the past than what was really there." She pressed her hands on his chest, but he held her fast.

Neither noticed when Zachary emerged from the direction of his office, nor did they see his mother stop him and whisper into his ear.

"You married so quickly. You couldn't have been in love with Zach. You weren't even seeing him at the time. Why did you marry him?" Miles demanded, his hand coming up to caress her nape.

"I believe this is my dance," Zachary said from behind the other man.

Nineteen

Zachary sounded as if he had issued an order as he stared pointedly at the other man. He didn't wait for permission, but took Amanda's hand and swung her into his own arms.

"Why did you—" she began.

"We'll talk later," he said tightly, pulling her against his long length. His mouth was taut with anger.

"Zach?" she questioned softly, lifting her hand from his shoulder to the back of his neck. She ran her fingers over the tight muscles there. "What's the matter? Something to do with that telephone call?"

He was upset and she wanted to know why. Her heart overflowed with love for him as she inhaled his pine-scented aftershave and felt his thigh glide between her own as he moved her in time to the music.

Zachary looked down into her eyes. "You should know what is bothering me. Miles was holding you as if you two were lovers. How do you expect me to react when I find you in his arms . . . his hands all over you?''

"Did you say lovers?''

He was acting as if he were jealous of Miles. Why? Zachary had always been a self-assured man, confident of his own masculinity.

"Let's get out of here," he whispered, clasping her hand in his as he practically dragged her through the crowd toward the staircase.

"No!" she said in a sharp whisper.

"What's wrong?''

"You're not going to pull me up those stairs, not with all these people down here. They will think you're taking me to bed.''

Zachary's hand tightened on hers but he changed directions. He urged her ahead of him down the hall, past the dining room toward his office. Once they were inside with the door secure, thanks to the new lock he'd had installed, Amanda glared at him, folding her arms beneath her breasts.

"What is wrong with you? You know perfectly well I hadn't slept with anyone but you before or after we married!''

He ran his hand over his hair, turning to the liquor trolley near the window. He quickly filled a squat tumbler.

"I'm waiting!" Amanda tapped her foot impatiently against the hardwood floor.

He slammed down the glass without touching what was inside; then he hauled her against him. "Yeah, I know. I hated seeing you in his arms, especially knowing he's still in love with you. Don't deny it. I heard what he said!''

His kiss was hard, almost brutal. Amanda's soft mouth was pressed against her teeth. When she whimpered in protest, he instantly eased the pressure.

"I'm sorry. I didn't mean to do that.''

She pressed her mouth to his, opening to him and offering

him the moist sweetness within. Her tongue caressed his, forging a tantalizing assault on both of their senses.

"Oh, baby . . . I love you so much. Why are you doing this to me?" he muttered hoarsely, as if he were in pain.

He kissed her again and again, each new kiss deeper, hungrier than the one before, until she was breathless, almost drunk from the excitement he generated inside her.

"Did you go out with him while we were separated?" he asked with his cheek against her forhead.

"What did you ask me?"

He had the gall to repeat it.

Amanda reacted as if he had thrown ice water into her face. "I don't believe you had the nerve to ask that question again." She pushed against his chest. "Let go!"

Zachary held on to her. "Never. It's Miles I don't trust. The instant I left the room, he went after you." He moved a caressing knuckle down her cheek. "You're right. I am jealous."

"Sometimes you make me so angry!"

"What did he say to you?"

"Does it matter?"

"Hell, yes! Tell me."

"He heard we had separated. He wondered if he'd missed his opportunity."

Zachary swore, and Amanda caught his arms before he could leave the room. "Will you stop? You know perfectly well that when I needed support after I learned of Granddaddy's illness, I called you, not him."

"I'd like to smash his teeth down his throat."

"I don't like you like this."

Zachary dropped his head until his forehead touched her. Sighing heavily as his temper cooled, he ran his hands up and down her bare arms.

"Mandy . . ."

"No . . ." She said as he kissed her throat, "I'm angry

with you," yet shivered from the contact. "You make me crazy."

"The feeling is mutual," he whispered, as he took her arms and placed them on his shoulders, then tightened his hold, forcing the softness of her breasts against him.

She closed her eyes, wishing so many things were different. She had spent most of her life angry with her father and resenting her mother because she had failed to shield them from her father's violent drunken rages.

She often wondered how her life would have been different if she had not been Sebastian and Darlene's child. Would she have been able to love her husband the way he deserved to be loved?

"Tell me something. . . ."

"Anything." His head was bent toward hers, their mouths mere inches apart.

Trying to ignore the way her heart raced, she asked with candor, "Do you honestly think we can make a go of this marriage?"

"You don't?"

"I wish I knew. We married because I was pregnant. And now we are surviving on sexual need. It's not enough."

Zachary lifted her chin until he could look into her dark troubled gaze. "We share more than desire. And if I didn't think we could make it work, I would never have come back into your life. I would have let the divorce go through without protest. That would have been the end of it."

"But—"

"You promised me a year and I intend to hold you to that promise. Sure, we have problems. Everyone does. We can work through them, if we want it bad enough. It's not simple, but nothing worthwhile is." He gave her a hug. "We have to get back."

"Do we have to?"

He grinned. "Yes, remember our appointment after this is over."

When he ushered her back to where the party was in full swing, Amanda had plastered a smile on her lips. Like him, she was relieved when they could finally close the door to his suite behind them.

Pulling her against him, he dipped his head to explore the length of her soft neck. She trembled in response, losing sight of all their problems. Only this tall, bronze man mattered as he quickly unhooked and unzipped her dress.

She pressed her mouth against the base of his throat, tonguing the warm hollow. Freeing the onyx stud from his shirt, she placed kisses down his deep chest.

Desire mingled with long-denied hunger caused him to leave a trail of clothing behind them as he carried her into the bedroom.

Instead of letting her slide down his body as she expected, Zachary lifted her until he could take the engorged tip of one breast into the heat of his mouth. He leisurely laved her nipple, tantalizing her with the gentle scrape of his teeth. He didn't move on to suck in earnest until she asked for it.

His strength kept her upright while the tug of his mouth sent sparks of need racing through her bloodstream to pool in her woman's center. She sobbed at the pleasure, arched her back and offered him even more of herself while she tightened and released her inner muscles. She was so empty inside . . . she needed him. She called out his name, dazzled by the intensity of his mouth, before he turned his attention to the other breast.

She was moaning his name by the time he let her slide down his body and her feet touch the carpet. Her legs were too weak to support herself and she would have fallen if he hadn't been holding her. Her soft hands glided over his chest, lingering on his taut dark nipples, teasing them with her fingernails; then she warmed each in turn with the velvety heat of her tongue.

Her hands dropped to his waist and began to unfasten his trousers, then pushed them and his briefs away from firm buttocks, down past heavy-muscled thighs, long strong calves to his ankles, and he stepped free. Slowly, she rose, stroking the sensitive inner length of his long legs. He shuddered, capturing her hands before she could do more than cradle the fleshy sacks below his thick, jutting sex.

Zachary was the one trembling when he groaned, "No, love. Don't ..."

Reluctantly, Amanda stopped, but didn't try to conceal her disappointment.

As if he could read her mind he whispered, "It's not you, my love. It's me. I'm already so hot for you ... I can't take your soft hands." He kissed her hungrily, before admitting, "I don't want to disappoint us both."

"Honey, I enjoy touching you ... pleasing you," Amanda confessed, burying her face in the warm place where his neck and shoulder joined.

Zachary could not control the tremor that wracked his big body. Just the thought of her taking him into her soft hands touching him so intimately had nearly unmanned him. Pushing the coverlet and top sheet to the foot of the bed, he urged her into the center of the king-size bed.

Instead of immediately joining her, he stood staring down at her for a time, recalling how often in the past year he had longed for nothing more than to have his wife right where she was ... soft and willing to accept his love.

"Finally ..." he said around a heavy sign.

He covered her body with his own, before he licked her lips. "Open for me."

She complied, parting her thighs even more and gasping his name when he caressed between her legs, squeezing her feminine folds. He'd left the lamp burning so that he could see her responses.

After parting her softness and detecting her readiness, he shifted in order to tantalize her with the broad crest of his penis. Again and again he caressed her until she arched her back, pressing forward, needing more. He shuddered at the feel of her creamy heat, thrusting fully until he was buried full length in her tight sheath.

"Zach!" she cried out when he pulled away, but he was soon back.

She sighed as he repeated the process, taking more and more of her heat and giving more and more of himself. He quickened his pace when Amanda tightened around him, massaging the entire length of his penis. He groaned heavily, fighting for control.

He said her name before he dipped his head to kiss, then laved his way down her throat, lingering at the scented base. He tongued both nipples, before taking one taut peak into the warm depth of his mouth while quickening his thrusts. When he lifted her legs up around his waist she had to bite her lip to hold in a scream of pleasure.

"Honey . . . now," she begged, close to completion.

"Yes . . . now," he whispered as he reached between their bodies to repeatedly worry her clitoris.

Unable to control her responses as her senses took flight, she called out as she reached one heart-stopping climax after another. All too soon he sought his own shatteringly sweet release. Her arms tightened around him as he shuddered spastically. She rained kisses from his high cheekbones to his mouth.

Much later, as she rested, curled beside him, listening to his deep even breathing, her fears began to surface. She could not stop herself from wondering how she was to survive loving him so desperately.

She had just realized how she felt, yet her love for him

had kept growing, deepening to the point she couldn't seem to slow her own need. She literally craved his touch . . . his loving. She hadn't been able to say no to him, not since the night of the storm. And she had tried, even though she wanted him desperately.

Where would it end? More importantly, how would it end? There was no doubt in her mind that it would end. Would she survive his loss? Or would she some day wind up clinging to him, unable to let go? She cringed at the thought.

"Get real," she mumbled to herself. Was it already too late? She knew that if she lost him, she would lose not only her husband, but her dearest friend as well.

After carefully disengaging herself so as not to disturb him, she picked up their discarded clothing. She folded them and placed them in an armchair, all but his white silk shirt. She took a quick shower, dried off before she pulled on his shirt and buttoned it. It reached her midthigh, and the smell of his aftershave and his own scent lingered on the soft cloth. She tiptoed past the bed and into the sitting room.

Moonlight spilled through the open drapes, providing enough light that she need not worry about walking into furniture as she wondered aimlessly around the room.

For so long, she had done everything within her power to protect her tender emotions. She hadn't wanted to fall in love with Zachary. Yet, she had done just that. How long did she have before he recognized her vulnerability? Would he take advantage of that knowledge and use it against her?

Although she was tired, it was close to dawn before Amanda returned to bed, still without any clear answers.

Amanda accompanied Zachary and his family to the early church services. He voiced his disappointment when she turned down his invitation to go skiing with them. He kissed her good-bye with a whispered promise to make up for falling asleep on her last night.

She deciphered the knitting pattern while Peggy did the actual knitting. They were working on a baby blanket, doing more laughing and talking than working. Peggy chattered enthusiastically about the new house that she and Roger planned to build. The two old friends planned the color scheme, wallpaper, carpets, furnishings for most of the house, including the nursery. After a shared lunch, Amanda left, insisting that Peggy follow her doctor's order and nap until dinner.

Amanda changed into black slacks and a square-neck sweater and then packed her case. They would return to Denver later that evening and she was looking forward to it.

Even though she was tired from lack of sleep, Amanda was too restless to nap. She decided to go for a walk. Having collected her coat and boots from the closet in the foyer, she followed the gravel road toward the distant series of stables. She had no real interest in seeing the horses. In fact, she had not been on a horse since she had been thrown and had miscarried.

She had always enjoyed riding but she had never been an enthusiast like Zachary with his love of this land and the animals. It was surprising considering his father's lack of interest in ranching. Maybe it was in the blood, for his brothers spent hours in the saddle every weekend. They loved the land, and the physical labor involved in working the range, but they lacked the drive that was so much a part of Zachary.

She toyed with the idea of driving over to the Double-D. She should at least see the changes Zachary might have made since her grandfather's death. Yet, she had not been able to go back. It still hurt knowing that her grandfather would not be there to welcome her. The Double-D was the only real home she had had since her mother's death.

The sounds and smells connected to the ranch brought back memories of a happier time, sitting on the front porch in the evening with her grandfather. He had always asked her about school and would share his day with her. There had been so much love between them. With a heavy heart, Amanda pushed the memories away.

She couldn't help wondering if her father had driven out to the Double-D. Then shook her head. She doubted that he felt the way she always had about the old place. How could he when he hadn't come for a visit not once during the years she'd lived at the ranch?

She had made a point of not taking his calls, so she had no idea why he was still in the area. She hadn't expected him to remain, especially after he'd gotten the money. Her grandfather had been very generous with his wayward son.

There was nothing unusual about the fact she had not told Zachary about her father's calls. Over the years she had gotten quite good at avoiding talking about the man. She didn't welcome the painful memories connected to her parents. Nor did she want to admit that he still had the ability to shame her.

If she lived to be a hundred, she could never forget the time her father had came to school with her mother for a parent-teacher conference. She was nine or ten. And her father had been drinking, not enough to be belligerent, but just enough to be surly and smell like stale liquor . . . enough to embarrass her.

She hated him that day . . . hated how it made her feel, knowing that all the kids would finally know why she came to school with bruises. She'd wanted to hang her head that day and not meet any of her friends' eyes or even her teacher's gaze. Instead she had stubbornly lifted her chin

. . . pretending that the shame that came from being Sebastian's child couldn't touch her.

Amanda wrapped her arms around herself, but it was not the cold temperature or even the crisp breeze that caused a chill to rise on her skin. It had been a beautiful day, heavy with the scent of pine. It was a perfect day for skiing.

That thought naturally brought Zachary to mind, not that he was ever very far from her thoughts. His deep vibrant laugh, his masculine scent, his black eyes gleaming with amusement or heavy with passion.

Thank goodness the weekend was nearly over. A glance at her watch reminded her it was time she turned back. They would be leaving right after dinner.

She wasn't sure if it was just her imagination or if his mother had seemed upset. Whatever the reason, Rebecca McFadden hadn't shown her face since breakfast. Amanda couldn't help wondering if it had anything to do with what happened after the meal.

When Amanda walked into the library Zachary and his mother were talking privately. His mother's cool demeanor hadn't given Amanda pause but there had been a difference in the almost hateful look she had sent Amanda's way before she left the room. Mrs. McFadden had done it while Zachary looked on.

Mrs. McFadden had always made a point of being cordial in front of her sons. Before Amanda could question him, he had taken her into his arms and given her a warm and possessive kiss. Despite his declaration of love, she had purposefully held back, not voicing her tender emotions. She had no faith in those emotions.

It was at her mother's knee that she learned that love meant many things and not necessarily the sweet desire and gentleness she experienced in Zachary's arms. Her parents had married because of love. Love had not brought either one of them happiness.

Amanda was surprised to see the Jeep parked in the drive. Zachary, his brothers and Barbara were back early.

She had barely stepped inside and closed the door behind her when Mrs. McFadden said, "Where have you been? I've been looking all over the house for you!"

"I went for a walk." Taking in the other woman's red-rimmed eyes, Amanda asked, "Is something wrong? It's not Peggy, is it? She was sleeping when I left. She hasn't started bleeding again, has she?"

"It's Zachary," Mrs. McFadden said as she pressed her hand to her mouth, holding in a sob.

"What happened?"

"There was a skiing accident and he has been taken to the hospital. We have to hurry. Bradford and Barbara are waiting at the hospital," Mrs. McFadden explained as she pulled on her coat that had been conveniently draped over one of the hall chairs.

Amanda choked on the words rising in her throat and her vision blurred from tears. She formed a mental picture of him lying in the snow, his long powerful body broken and twisted. Hadn't that famous singer-turned-congressman been killed while skiing?

"No!" Her legs suddenly weakened. *Dear God ... please.*

Roger, who had been coming down the stairs, raced ahead when she saw her sway. He swung her off her feet and carried her over to the nearby chair.

"Mandy? Can you hear me?" he questioned, forcing her head down below her knees. "Mother, get her some brandy."

"I—I—I am fine," Amanda mumbled as her head cleared, but her heart was pounding with dread. "Is he ... how bad is it?" she managed to say when he let her sit upright.

"Drink this." Roger took the brandy snifter from his mother and held it for Amanda.

"Just tell me." She began to sob, pushing the drink away.

Roger questioned his mother, "You didn't tell her?"

"We don't have time for all this talking, son. We have to get to your brother. We'll have to leave her here. Joe, or one of the other men, can bring her later. We must get to the hospital now."

"Mother, please! We're not leaving until Mandy is able to come with us." He turned his attentions back to her when he said, "Come on, honey, drink this. It will steady your nerves."

Amanda sipped obediently, as eager to leave as her mother-in-law. But first she had to know the truth. "Roger, how bad . . . " She coughed, nearly choking in her haste to finish. " . . . is it?"

"He has a bad break in his right leg. He may have also cracked some ribs and he hit his head on a rock when he fell. We don't know how he is yet. It's too soon. He was on his way to the operating room when I left to get you two. Now finish that so we can get going."

Ignoring the tears spilling down her cheek, Amanda downed as much as she could. The heat of the drink burned all the way down to her stomach.

"I'm ready," she said, wiping impatiently at the tears with the handkerchief Roger had given her.

Twenty

When Roger escorted them into the hospital's waiting room, Bradford was anxiously pacing the floor and Barbara sat tapping her foot.

"Any news?" Roger prompted as he helped his mother into the chair beside his cousin.

"Nothing. He's still in surgery." Bradford kissed his mother's cheek before his troubled gaze moved to Amanda. "He's going to be fine, Mandy," he offered by way of a reassurance.

Amanda nodded, thankful for the firm support of the chair beneath her. She absently heard Mrs. McFadden demanding to know how this could happen. Zachary was an expert skier.

Bradford explained that an inexperienced skier had cut Zachary off on a steep downhill run, plowing right into him.

The other man had walked away with barely a scratch while Zach had to be rushed to the hospital in the ambulance.

"I want to see him now!" Mrs. McFadden insisted. "Where is Henry? You did call Henry, didn't you, Bradford?"

"Yes, Mother. He's with Zach," he explained patiently as he came to take her hands into his. "Getting yourself upset will only raise your blood pressure and won't help Zach. He's tough. He'll be fine."

"I agree with Aunt Rebecca. It's taking too long," Barbara said to no one in particular.

"I'll get you some coffee. Too bad this place doesn't provide hard liquor. I could use a drink." Bradford asked, "Mandy? Barbara? You care for something to drink."

Amanda looked up at the sound of her name but she had not been listening to the others. She'd been praying. "Sorry. What did you say?"

"Would you like something to drink?"

"No, no, thank you."

Amanda hastily wiped away a tear. All she knew was that it hurt having him here and not knowing how he was doing. How long before they knew something? How long until she could see Zachary . . . see for herself that he was going to be all right?

She was unaware of when Bradford left, or when he returned, for that matter. She stared without really seeing what was beyond the windows. She detested this place.

She knew every inch of this room, probably had sat in every chair, seen every snag in the carpet, counted the number of flowers in the wallpaper. Nothing had changed, except for the magazines on the side tables.

She'd spent so many hours in this very room while her grandfather was growing weaker with each passing day.

Jake Daniels had died in this hospital. Zachary had waited with her. He'd held her, talked to her and comforted her. Sometimes he'd simply sat next to her. The last time she had been here she'd been the patient. It was the day she had lost their baby.

"Oh, Zach . . . please be all right. Please," she silently chanted.

The sun had slipped from the sky, leaving the room heavy with shadows when Roger switched on the lamps while Bradford continued to pace.

"Good evening, folks." Dr. Henry Coleman's appearance brought them to their feet. "Rebecca, Amanda, I'm glad you both were able to make it." This elderly gentleman had been a friend and doctor to both families for many years.

"Sorry, it took so long. Doctor Vermin was called in to repair the damage to the leg. The surgery went well, even though there was quite a bit of damage to the leg."

"How is he?" Barbara rushed forward, voicing the most important question.

"He's still in recovery, but the surgery went well."

"Get to the point, Henry," Roger demanded. "Just how extensive are his injuries?"

Dr. Coleman smiled indulgently before saying, "It looks good. He also has a few bruised ribs, but there is no damage done to the lungs. We were really lucky with that but he does have a concussion."

"A concussion!" Mrs. McFadden exclaimed. "No one told us about a concussion."

"It's not as bad as it sounds. I want to keep him here and still for a few days. Give the leg time to knit together. Knowing Zach, that's not going to be easy." He chuckled.

"I want to see my boy," Mrs. McFadden insisted.

Amanda was weak with relief just knowing that he had made it through the surgery and was on the mend. But the doctor's reassurance was not enough. She needed to see for herself that he was going to be all right.

"It will be a while, Rebecca. He's still in recovery now. When he's awake and moved to his room you all can see him, but only for a short time." He gaze went to Amanda. "You all right, my dear?"

"I will be, once I've seen my husband." Her voice was barely above a whisper.

Dr. Coleman nodded, then excused himself. True to his word, in a little over an hour, the nurse came to show them into the waiting area, closer to Zachary's room.

Amanda was permitted to go in first, despite his mother's objection.

"He's heavily sedated, Mrs. McFadden," the nurse cautioned Amanda outside his door.

She nodded her understanding as she walked inside. Zachary's eyes were closed, and he had a bandage on his forehead. Although the lower half of his body was covered, the cast on his right leg started above his knee and went past his ankle to the middle of his foot, and it was supported by a pulley mounted above the bed. His normally bronze skin had taken on a gray tinge.

She was forced to blink back tears, her heart aching with love for him alone. She quietly crossed to the bed, taking the chair closest to the bed. She wanted to touch him, to run her hands down his lean cheeks and to press her lips to his mouth. She longed to feel his strong arms wrapped reassuringly around her.

She did nothing to disturb him; instead she was content just to sit, touch his hand and watch him sleep. She whispered a prayer of thankfulness that he had not been critically injured.

When his heavy-lidded black lashes lifted, he focused on her. "Mandy . . . " he whispered.

She squeezed his hand while forcing a smile. "Hi, sleepy-head. How do you feel?"

"Better . . . now that you're with me," he said groggily, then closed his eyes again. "Sorry . . ." he mumbled. "They have me so doped up, I can hardly keep my eyes open." He drifted off again.

The nurse notified her a few minutes later it was time for her to leave. Zachary woke when she tried to ease her hand away.

He held on to it. "Stay . . ."

"Honey, your family is waiting to see you."

"Stay with me."

The nurse smiled. "I'll send your family in one at a time, Mr. McFadden. Your wife can stay but you have to rest," she said before leaving.

Amanda sank back into the chair, relieved that she wouldn't have to leave him just yet. He barely managed a smile before closing his eyes again.

Refusing to dwell on the fact that her vulnerability to him grew as her feelings intensified, she focused on him. There would be time enough for that later. Time to acknowledge her doubts.

Each member of the family was allowed to stay for only a short time. His mother didn't even try to hide her resentment that Amanda was allowed to stay with him. It was in the pointed look she sent Amanda's way. Zachary was asleep when Amanda finally left, late that night.

She tossed restlessly, unable to sleep. She missed Zachary. She was pleased to find that he looked much better the next morning. He still had a terrible headache, was badly bruised, and his leg throbbed.

His family dropped in for visits during the course of the day. Amanda was grateful that Mrs. McFadden planned her visits during meal times, thus allowing Amanda an excuse to leave under the pretext of eating her own meal in the hospital cafeteria. Amanda kept her thoughts to herself. The last thing she wanted was to arouse his suspicions that there was something wrong between his wife and his beloved mother.

The next day when he began complaining about everything from the food to his forced confinement, Amanda was relieved. He wasn't so deadly still and he was definitely on the mend.

Just knowing how much the older woman resented her made it extremely difficult for Amanda to stay on. She had already prolonged her stay into the following week.

Even while hospitalized, Zachary managed to make arrangements for Amanda to have a car and driver at her disposal. Touched by his thoughtfulness when she tried to thank him, he claimed his motives were selfish. He wanted her to be able to visit him, frequently.

He slept through much of the first two days. On Wednesday morning when Amanda arrived she was pleased to find him sitting in one of the bedside armchairs with his leg propped on pillows. Each day he slept a little less and was getting stronger.

When she returned from her evening meal, he was on the telephone with his foreman giving orders for the next day's work schedule. Although she fussed at him for working when he should have been resting, she was delighted with his progress. He wore his own navy pajamas, the right leg seam split to accommodate the cast.

While preparing to leave, she mentioned, ''Honey, I won't be in until late afternoon tomorrow.''

''You're going back to Denver?''

''Yes, just for a few hours in the morning. I'll catch a ride in with Roger in the morning and drive back to see you after my luncheon appointment.''

"Where are you planning on spending the night?"

"Honey, I have a business to run, remember?" She smiled, attempting to ignore the frown forming between his dark brows. "Besides, you're doing so much better that you don't need me here all day and I'll be here every afternoon until you're out of this place."

She knew what had caused his frown. He wanted her to stay on at the ranch. She swallowed back her frustration. She simply couldn't spend another night under the same roof as Mrs. McFadden, especially when she was in danger of strangling the woman. His mother looked at her most days as if she couldn't stand the sight of her. The strain wasn't good for either of them. It was plain that one of them had to go, and it was going to be Amanda.

"I repeat, where are you planning on spending your nights?"

"My weekend stay has already been extended. I've imposed on your family long enough. Besides, now that you're so much better, it's time I went into the office." She leaned over from where she sat beside him on the bed to brush her lips against his in the hope of softening his mood. "Honey, I promise to spend every afternoon and evening with you until you're out of here. If we're lucky, you should be home by Friday."

He caught her chin, angling her face until she had no choice but to meet his dark penetrating gaze.

She smiled at him. "Honey, don't scowl so. You look quite fierce with that ugly purple bruise on your forehead."

It was the firm set of his jaw that announced that he expected an answer.

"Okay, okay. I'll be staying at the condo."

"Has my mother been rude to you again?"

She wasn't quick enough to conceal her shock. "What do you mean?" she hedged.

He caught her hand and placed it over his silk-covered chest. "You know perfectly well what I mean, Mandy McFadden. I overheard what my mother said to you on Saturday evening. She and I had a long talk before the ski trip."

He toyed with her wedding rings before he lifted her hand and placed a kiss in her palm. "I'm sorry, pretty girl. I had no idea that she has given you such a hard time. I never realized how much she resents you. I wish you had come to me with this."

She shook her head. "How could I tell you when I know how much you love your mother? Besides, I wish you hadn't spoken to her."

"Why not?"

"It only placed more strain on both of us." She suddenly realized that was exactly what had happened. It certainly explained why their pitiful relationship had deteriorated even more.

"The Circle-M is mine. I own the land and the property. If my mother can't treat you with the respect and courtesy due you as my wife, then she will have to leave."

"You told her all this?"

"Exactly."

Amanda couldn't believe it. No wonder the woman had taken to her bed much of the day on Sunday, until she heard of Zachary's accident. It certainly explained why his mother had barely spoken to her.

"Has my mother said something more to you? Has she made you feel less welcome since I've been in here?"

"Zach, have you lost your mind! You can't ask your mother to leave her own home because of me!"

"I had no choice."

"You want her to hate me for the rest of my natural life?

Because she's going to blame me, not you." She began pacing and mumbling to herself, "This doesn't make any sense. I have my own place. I can't believe you're being so cruel to your own mother."

"Calm down, baby. You know I love my mother. I'll see that she is always well provided for, even build her a new home on the property, and she can keep the staff. But she can't remain where she is, if she's going to mistreat you."

He looked tired as he leaned back against his pillows. Yet Amanda could tell by the set of his jaw that Zachary wasn't about to change his mind.

"Your mother has not been unkind to me." Amanda lowered her eyes so he couldn't see the lie in them.

"Then why did she say what she did?"

"She was upset because Roger and Peggy plan to build a home of their own. So what if she lost her temper? We've all said things we regret in a moment of anger."

"Are you sure that was all it was?"

"Of course, I'm sure. It was nothing! Besides, you know I prefer living in Denver. Enough of this. Honey, you're exhausted." Coming over to him, she said, "Please try and get some rest. I'll see you tomorrow as soon as I can get away."

Her intent was to kiss his cheek, but Zachary had other ideas. He cupped her nape, bringing her mouth to his. The kiss was undemanding, but thorough.

Inhaling her floral scent, he whispered against her throat, "I hate not being able to hold you during the night. Have you missed being in my arms as much as I've missed having you there?"

"Oh, yes." She sighed softly. Despite her best efforts she ached for his touch, for more of his kisses, yet she moved away. She laughed. "Let's not start something we can't finish. Besides, it's late and you need to rest."

Grabbing her coat, she slipped it on and tucked her purse over her shoulder as he said her name.

"Huh?"

"I'd feel much better about you staying in Denver if you continued to use the car and let Alex drive you."

"Zach, I'm not some rock star. I'm not used to having a limousine and driver."

"Get used to it or stay at the Double-D."

Her entire body stiffened with tension, her hands clenching into small fists. "You know I can't stay there, not without my . . ." Her voice trailed away, unable to say her grandfather's name.

"I know it's been hard, but don't you think it's time? Maybe, if you saw the place again, it won't be quite as painful as you're anticipating."

"I can't . . ." she said around a sob. "It's too soon." All she could think about was that her beloved grandfather would not be there to greet her.

"Don't agonize over it. When you're ready we'll do it together. Okay?"

She nodded, biting her trembling lip.

"In the meantime, you have a driver. Think of all the work you can get done during the ride, which means less for you to deal with at home later."

"I thought we had decided."

"No, Mandy. I don't want you driving that far alone, especially at night. It will only be until I'm out of the hospital and back on my feet."

"I'm not helpless!" She was so annoyed by his insistence that she overlooked the fact that he had qualified her living in the condo for only the present.

"I'm aware of that, but it's not the problem. My peace of mind is what's in question. I might not be out of here until the weekend. How do you think it makes me feel, knowing I can't do a thing to help you if you run into trouble on the road?'' His eyes never left hers. ''Even when I get out of this place, I won't be able to drive or fly until this cast comes off.''

''I hate riding in that limousine. I feel pretentious.''

Alex Jenson was her driver. He, like his mother, Kate, and all of Jake Daniels's old employees, were now on Zachary's payroll since he took over the running of her grandfather's ranch.

She had no choice but to accept the full extent of her own selfishness since her grandfather's death. She had been caught up in grief, so much so that she had not even thought of, let alone concerned herself with, the needs of Jake's employees, most of whom were old friends. Seeing Alex every day was a constant reminder of her shortcomings. Wasn't it bad enough that Zachary knew of her failings?

She wasn't only upset with herself but aware that her grandfather would be ashamed of her thoughtlessness. If not for Zach, her grandfather's people would be jobless or worse.

''Both my brothers have busy schedules. They may not be available when you want to come to the hospital. A driver is the solution, and Alex is the best. I shouldn't have to tell you that, Mandy, since he has been Jake's mechanic and handyman for years. Use him, if not for any other reason than for my sake.''

Amanda knew she had lost that round.

''All right. Night,'' she conceded, then hurried out.

Two days later, Zachary told Amanda he would be released the next day.

''Honey! That's fantastic!''

She was perched on the side of his bed, dressed in a cream turtleneck and brown leather slacks. She leaned forward to caress his cheek. When she straightened, she realized he didn't seem pleased.

"What's the matter?"

"I'm going back to the ranch, Mandy."

"I know. You don't have any choice. Even I don't expect you to run the ranch from Denver. And you won't be able to fly until the cast is off. Of course there'll be some physical therapy."

"This is not only about me."

"We have a logistic problem. What's new about that?" She rose to her feet, saying with a smile, "Six weeks isn't so long."

She had refused to dwell on the changes that may occur once he was discharged from the hospital. Why borrow trouble? Since his accident, she had been determined to take things one day at a time and not dwell on the future. It was less stressful that way.

So what if it looked as if they had to live apart for the time being? She assured herself that she could handle that. She could handle anything short of having to move back to the Circle-M until he recovered.

Six to eight weeks under his mother's roof was more like several lifetimes of turmoil from where she was standing. After only two days back in her home, she didn't want to so much as think about his mother's place.

"I want you with me, Mandy. Nothing has changed. You gave me your word when we reconciled that we would both give our marriage a chance. I expect you to keep that promise."

"What I promised was that you could stay with me, not the other way around."

"I'm not about to argue with you. We have an agreement. And we've been closer than we've ever been before. I don't want that to end, do you?"

"No, but—"

"Mandy, if you expect me to go back to the way it was with you in Denver and me on the ranch, you can forget it!" Even though he rested against the pillows in the upraised hospital bed, the strength of his personality hadn't diminished. "We'll only be at the ranch until I'm out of the cast and able to fly."

"Who are you trying to kid?" She jumped to her feet. "We're talking about a few months now, but when our year is over, we'll be right back to this same dilemma."

"For now, we're talking about two months at the most."

She saw the hurt in his eyes and couldn't bear it. She found herself softening. She didn't like him thinking that she did not want to be with him as much as he wanted to be with her.

"What if I came out on the weekends?" she reluctantly offered.

"Not good enough."

"Why?"

"It's not nearly enough. I need more, don't you?" His voice had taken on a husky tone.

"You're talking about sex," she accused, fighting the sensual memories his last declaration provoked . . . memories of the two of them lost in sweet intimacy.

"That's a part of it. I'm also talking about our commitment to each other." His voice was gruff when he said, "I'm not asking for any less than I'm willing to give."

She had no idea what to say. She felt as if she were trying to balance on a tightrope without a net. She couldn't let him know how much he meant to her . . . how much she needed him in her life. Nor could she risk losing him. Being apart after the snowstorm had been downright painful . . . this past week had been no picnic, come to think of it.

"Zach, please. Don't force me to decide now. I promised a year and I intend to keep that promise. Surely we can wait a few weeks to live together again. I promise I'll come out for the weekends and when you're able to travel—''

He interrupted, ''If it's not the ranch or my mother, what is it, Mandy?'' He ran a hand over his hair in obvious frustration. ''You don't want to move back to Jake's place. What in the hell is going on with you?''

Twenty-one

Amanda stood at the window. She couldn't see much in the darkness beyond the streetlights other than an occasional passing car. It was a quiet night, no snowflakes or even clouds in the sky. By Colorado standards, there was nothing to be concerned about.

It was her emotions that were in turmoil. She wrapped her arms protectively around herself. Zachary was right. This was not just about where they lived.

The knowledge that she wanted to be with him as much as, if not more than, he wanted to be with her was tearing her apart. No matter how hard she tried to control her feelings for him they continued to mushroom. If she had any doubts, all she had to do was recall her reaction when she learned about his accident. She had fallen apart. She couldn't think, she could barely breathe, she couldn't do anything until she saw for herself that he was going to be all right. She had been plain pitiful.

She closed her eyes against the bitter truth. There was no difference between her and her mother. She was just as vulnerable to Zachary as her mother had been to her father. That knowledge terrified Amanda as nothing else could.

"Damn it! Just tell me!"

"Zach, I just can't see why all of this has to be decided tonight. We can talk about this again after you're home. I'll come down in the morning and stay the weekend."

"No. We've put our marriage on hold long enough ... never again. Since I can't come to you, I'm asking you to live with me. If you want, we can start looking for a house of our own as soon as I'm back on my feet. Somewhere between the ranch and Denver."

"What's the rush?"

He swore heatedly before demanding, "Why don't you come right out and say it? You don't want our marriage to work, do you?"

"That's not true! Okay, I've made mistakes but so have you!"

"Not talking about it is your idea of a compromise?"

"You're acting as if I'm giving up!"

"That's what I call it." Zachary's voice was laced with bitterness. "You're so terrified of being hurt that you won't let yourself love me."

"I'm never—"

He went on as if she had not spoken. "Mandy, life's a gamble. Sometimes you win, sometimes you lose, but if you're not willing to take a risk, you're assured of getting nothing in return."

She felt as if she had been backed into a corner. Even though she knew she was hurting him, he was not the only one hurting. How could she make him understand? Why did she feel so compelled to try?

"Zach . . ." she said as she slowly moved to his side and sat down next to him on the bed, "if you would just give us some time, I'm certain we could work this out somehow."

"Sugar, we've been married for over a year and have spent less than three months of that time together. That's not good enough. Let Alex drive you back and forth every day to your office and give us a fighting chance. Given time, we will find a resolution to our housing problem."

She could not look away from the intensity in his gaze. She also knew that no matter how sincere he was, he had no idea what tomorrow or next month would bring. How could she do what he asked when he was talking about blind faith? What he wanted was for her to turn her life and heart over to him for safekeeping.

"I'm in love with you, Mandy McFadden. What's more, I think you're in love with me." He took her hands into his. "Trust me with your love. Trust me not to hurt you."

She nearly choked on a sob. He made it sound incredibly simple . . . there was nothing simple about it. How could it be when he expected so much of her? How many times had she seen her mother face danger with nothing more than blind trust. Over the years loving her father had bit by bit destroyed her mother's self-esteem . . . in the end it had destroyed her life.

"Monday . . ."

Unable to bear his closeness without clinging to him and begging for reassurance, Amanda pulled free. She hurried from his side into the connecting bathroom, pushing the door closed behind her.

Turning on the taps before she dropped down on the closed lid of the commode, she covered her face with her hands. Hot tears burned her lids and rolled down her cheeks. She had no idea how long she cried but eventually she calmed herself enough to splash cold water on her face.

Nothing either one of them said or did could contain the

fear and longing deep inside. After drying her face and hands on paper toweling, she angled her chin upward, then walked back into the room.

He studied her as she stopped at the foot of his bed.

"You want too much."

"Evidently," he said dryly.

Biting her bottom lip to hold back the tremors, she whispered, "You're asking to me to give up my home, more importantly, my life as I've known it these past five years."

He said, his jaw tight with frustration and need, "I'm asking you to be what you are, my love . . . my wife."

"Can you promise that you won't ever change?"

"You know I can't! I've no crystal ball or tarot cards to predict the future. You've already decided, haven't you?"

"No!" She shook her head vehemently. "I don't want to be hurt the way a man can hurt the woman he has pledged to love." Fresh tears sparkled in her dark eyes.

"Damn it! All men aren't like Sebastian Daniels. Jake loved your grandmother until his dying day, even though she had been gone since his sons were born. My parents loved each other for nearly thirty years. Do you think Roger is going to walk out on Peggy? He has never looked at another woman in the six years they've been married."

Zachary didn't hesitate when he vowed, "I have every intention of loving you until there is no more you or me. But this isn't about any of them. Admit it, it's about your parents, your father specifically." His voice was ripe with bitterness when he demanded to know, "Has he done something new to remind you of the past? Is he still calling you?

"I don't want to talk about my father. And you're wrong." Overwhelmed with nerves, tension and the inevitability of approaching doom, she insisted. "I know this is my fault. I'm the one who should never have married despite the circumstances. I'm not suited for marriage."

"That's your excuse for giving up?"

She stared at him. He looked furious, angrier than she ever remembered seeing him, more so than the day he received the divorce papers. But it was the raw pain in his eyes that disturbed her the most.

"I have to! I am what I am. Divorce is the only answer for us. It's the only way either of us can ever find any kind of happiness." In a whisper filled with misery, Amanda said, "I can't give you what you need."

"Can't or won't!"

She was openly sobbing as she grabbed her things and headed for the door. "I'm so very sorry."

"Taking the easy way out again, Mandy? I'm not coming after you this time. I've had it with you punishing me for something I had nothing to do with!"

Amanda ran out, right into Roger in the hallway. She murmured a quick apology before she ran past him.

Amanda was still blaming herself hours later. Alex had dropped her off in front of her condo and she had spent most of the evening restlessly pacing. She didn't have to remind herself that she'd run from all that had been and all that might have been because she was afraid to believe.

"It's for the best," she announced to the silent room.

She had done the right thing and the only thing she could have done under the circumstances. He should be thanking her for saving them both from a lifetime of heartache. The realization offered not one bit of relief. Knowing that Zachary wouldn't thank her brought on a fresh bout of tears.

At this very moment he, no doubt, was condemning her for her weakness as well as hating her for the dissolution of their marriage. She released a wrenched sob. Well, it was finally over. There was nothing left to save. No reason to look back . . . not now . . . not ever.

He wasn't blameless in all of this. Why did he have to

push her into a decision? Why did their future have to be settled today? Hadn't she offered to come every weekend until he was well again? Oh, no, that was not good enough for him. He wasn't really interested in a compromise! He wanted her to move back to the ranch . . . period . . . end of discussion.

In two short months, maybe less, he would be back on his feet again. But no, he would not accept that! He just had to push and push until she had no choice but to walk away. He expected too much!

"Congratulations, Mrs. McFadden. You won. You've gotten your precious son back," she said aloud as she tossed a fashion magazine aside. Just then the downstairs buzzer sounded. "Now what?"

She went into the foyer and picked up the wall-mounted telephone. "Yes?"

"Ms. Daniels-McFadden? This is Dave," the guard at the front desk in the lobby said. "There is a gentleman here to see you. Mr. Sebastian Daniels. Shall I send him up?"

She hesitated before she said, "Yes. Thank you." Returning the receiver to its cradle, she ran her hands over the goose pimples that had suddenly risen on her arms. Why had he come? More important, what did he want?

Why didn't he just take the money and go? What more did they have to talk about? Hadn't it all been said at lunch? Perhaps he was right. Maybe it was time to get it all out in the open once and for all. Then they both could move on.

She went into the kitchen and damped a paper towel with cool water and soothed her face and swollen lids. By the time the knock came, Amanda had decided she owed it to her mother to at least listen to what he had to say.

As she opened the door, her eyes collided with eyes as deep and dark brown as her own.

"Little bit, thanks for seeing me tonight."

"I'm surprised. I thought you'd be halfway to"—she

waved her hand in a vague gesture—"wherever." A shiver of apprehension trailed down her spine. Although he wasn't as flawlessly turned out as he had been at their lunch meeting, he seemed sober.

Nothing he had said or done since his return had persuaded her she'd been wrong about him. How could it when she knew that he had never so much as apologized for the physical and emotional pain he had caused her and her mother, let alone his abandoning her after her mother had passed?

"Why did you come? Hasn't my refusal to take your calls told you anything?"

"May I come in, princess?"

"Don't call me that. It's what Granddaddy called me."

"We need to talk face-to-face. I deserve that much."

She was not about to get into what she thought he deserved. All she wanted was this discussion behind her. She had been through enough for one lousy day. Instead of inviting him inside, she walked away from the door, leaving it up to him whether he stayed or went. She didn't really care anymore. She had lost everything she cared about today, when she walked out of Zachary's hospital room.

Amanda moved into the living room and sat down on the edge of one of the armchairs near the French doors. It wasn't long before she heard the door close and saw her father approach.

"This is nice."

"Just say what you have to say."

"Not going to offer me a seat, or a drink, for that matter? I know your mama taught you better."

She pulled back her shoulders and stiffened her spine, then folded her hands in her lap, offering no apology. "A drink? It was my impression that you were embracing sobriety these days."

A muscle jumped in his golden brown cheek. "You know

nothing about me! All I wanted was to talk to you. Did you get my messages?''

''It's a little late for talking. If it hadn't been for Grand-daddy I would have wound up in foster care. Just say what you came to say, then go.''

''You're in a hurry to see the back of me. Why? I read in the newspaper that your man had an accident on the slopes. Thought you might appreciate the company tonight.''

''Zachary is much better, and he'll be leaving the hospital tomorrow.'' Amanda stopped abruptly, knowing perfectly well he had no interest in Zachary.

Sebastian looked around the room expectantly, then peered inside the armoire. He grinned when he saw an array of crystal decanters filled with hard liquor and glasses tucked inside.

''What do you think you're doing?''

''Doing what you should have done, getting the liquid refreshment you should have offered when I arrived. First Darlene spoiled you, girl, then the old man finished the job.''

Angry, she said, ''That's the second reference you've made to my mother. Don't make another.''

He paused in his rush to fill a glass to glare at her. He took little care with the fine crystal in his hand but grabbed it and lifted it to his mouth, closing his eyes when he swallowed.

Disgusted, she acknowledged to herself how thankful she was that she had been left in her grandfather's care. ''What do you want!''

''Who do you think you're talking to, little girl? I'm your father, damn it! I won't stand for any lip from you.''

Amanda's laughter held no humor. ''This is my home, not yours. And I'm not your little girl. I have not been for a very long time. You, Sebastian Daniels, can't toss me around like you used to when I was a child. You're not even a man. You're nothing more than a mean drunk, hurting the people you claimed you loved the most."

"You shouldn't have any complaints. All grown up and married to a McFadden. Judging by this fancy place you got here and your own business, you got money to burn." He gestured wildly. "What do you need with the Double-D?"

"So that's why you're here. I should have known it wasn't sudden paternal concern. You've never really cared about me or my mother, or even your own father, for that matter. Have you even seen the place since you've been back?"

"Why should I? It belongs to you now," he returned angrily.

"What's your problem? Granddaddy left you one hundred thousand dollars, wasn't it enough?"

He swallowed the remaining liquor in his glass before he banged it down on the desk. "This is not about money! If it wasn't for you, the ranch would have been mine! I've always cared about that old man. He was the one who wouldn't let me forget my mistakes."

"If you cared about him, you would have done more than ask for money whenever you were down on your luck. Not once in the more than ten years I lived on the ranch did you show your sorry face. Not one time!"

"What in the hell do you know about it?"

"It's true. Most of the time, Granddaddy didn't know if you were dead or alive. I couldn't find you when he first got sick, and he asked for you. That's right. He wanted to see you before he died. Even the private investigator I hired couldn't find you."

She stopped only long enough to catch her breath before she said, "Granddaddy has been gone over a year and you're just showing up. You, Sebastian Daniels, don't know the meaning of the word *family*, or *love*, for that matter."

"Shut the hell up!" he roared angrily. He reached for the decanter with less than steady hands.

She stood in order to face him down. "My name is Amanda, not Darlene. You can't control me by yelling at me or even with your fists. Nor can you stop me from telling the truth. What I would like to ask is, how can you sleep at night knowing that you're responsible for my mother's death?"

"Damn you! You don't know what you're talking about. You were only a kid back then. You had no idea what went on between Darlene and me." He held the glass with both hands as he steadfastly drained every drop.

"I know you beat her up so badly the last time that even you got scared. You thought you had killed her that time, didn't you?" Amanda did not wait for a response before she said, "You broke my arm when I called for an ambulance. And then you ran like the coward you truly were. From what I can see, nothing has changed over the years."

Sebastian looked at her with hard, cold eyes as he poured more liquor into his glass. Only this time he slowed enough to sip the contents. "I said—"

"Like I care?" Restless and angry, she began moving back and forth between the living and the dining areas. Eventually, she stopped in front of him. "You didn't kill her then. It was later when you did not come back that she decided she couldn't live without you." She was quaking with rage when she said, "My mother slit both her wrists and bled to death because of you . . . you worthless drunk!"

Struggling to control her tremors, she placed a hand against the back of the sofa to steady herself. She was forced to brush away bitter tears, which temporary blinded her. It had taken years but she was able to voice the anger and hurt that had been locked inside her heart for too many years. At last, she had placed the blame where it belonged, in Sebastian Daniels's lap.

"I said shut up!" He walked toward her, his lined face a network of rage. He was not exactly steady on his feet, a glass clenched in his hand.

"Did you so much as think about her even once after you left?"

"Of course I did. I loved your mother!"

"Really?" Amanda crossed her arms beneath her breasts, lifting her chin. "Just like you loved Uncle Danny?"

He stopped at the mention of his twin brother's name. "What do you know about my brother?"

"I know Granddaddy loved you both. I also know that he could not forget that you were behind the wheel or that you had been drinking. In all that time since Uncle Danny's death, you never came back to the ranch . . . not even after Granddaddy took me in. You never came to see either one of us."

"The old man didn't want to see me."

"You're wrong."

"It's the truth! As for you and your mother . . . " Sebastian was breathing heavily, his eyes somewhat unfocused and glassy. ". . . loved you both, not that it matters now. I always planned to come back. Then Darlene was dead and you were at the ranch wrapping the old man around your finger until he would do anything for you." He drained what was left in the glass, then said, "The Double-D should have gone to me! What do you know about running a ranch?"

"I know it was what Granddaddy wanted. You can always contest the will, not that it will do you much good now. The will is airtight. You'll never get your hands on the Double-D."

He snarled, "What in the hell do you know about running a ranch?"

"Nothing, but my husband knows what he is doing. Jake wanted the ranch to someday go to his great-grandchildren. And I promised him that I would do my best to carry out his wishes. I don't think he believed you would take care of it.'' When he went to refill his glass yet again, she said, ''Don't you think you've had enough?''

Sebastian ignored her. After a long sip, he swore. His words were slurred when he said, ''The old bastard held a grudge against me until the day he died.''

''How can you say that? I think he wanted to make peace with you before he died. Why else would he ask to see you?''

He shook his head, the glass to his mouth.

''If you ask me, you should be grateful that Granddaddy remembered you in his will.''

''Grateful! That bastard . . .''

Clearly fed up with the entire conversation, Amanda gestured toward the door. ''I've heard enough. You said what you came to say. I want you to leave and I don't want to ever hear from you again.''

Sebastian stared at her as if he didn't believe his own ears. She held herself perfectly erect, determined not to let him see her discomfort. His eyes were cold, filled with rage, glazed in a way she remembered from her childhood and had never forgotten. It sent a chill racing down her spine.

What had she been thinking? This man was nothing like her husband. How could she have measured Zachary against her father? She had seen anger, acute frustration, even resentment in Zachary's eyes. What she had never seen was hatred.

Sebastian grabbed her by her upper arms and shook her so hard her teeth rattled and her head jerked back and forth. ''That ranch is mine! Do you understand me? I'm not leaving here until you sign it over to me!''

Although she tried, she couldn't break his hold. Near panic, she cried out, ''No! Take your hands off me!'' She was furious with herself for letting him corner her like this. She knew better . . . knew what he was capable of and that he could not to be trusted.

"I said—"

Sebastian shook her again just to make his point. "Damn you! I'm not letting go until I've knocked some sense into you. You're my daughter! I ain't leaving until you do what I tell you!"

Determined not to show the fear escalating inside her, she yelled, "You're hurting me!" as she struggled to break his bruising hold. "You can't make me do anything! Let go!"

He shook her as if she were nothing more than a rag doll. "You will do what you're told, little girl."

"Not in this lifetime! Now get out before I make sure you live to regret it!" Using the heels of her palms, she pushed as hard as she could to break his hold.

Sebastian jeered, as he jerked harder. "You're not in a position to make me regret anything."

Amanda screamed, not thinking, she just reacted. She kicked him in his shin as hard as she could with the pointed toe of a high-heel shoe, then stepped up and down using her full weight on the tops of his feet.

He swore as he raised his right hand and slapped her hard enough to send her flying across the room. She landed hard, the armchair in the foyer breaking her fall as she collapsed in it. Even though her eyes were filled with angry tears she never took her eyes off him.

Wiping the blood from her mouth and nose, she screamed, "You're less than a man! No wonder your own father disowned your sorry behind!"

He balled his hands and Amanda scrambled to get to the door when the doorbell sounded, followed by a loud knock on the door.

"Mandy? What is going on in there?" Roger yelled through the door.

"Roger!" she screamed as she fumbled with the lock and then the knob before she managed to get it open. She flung

herself into him, her face streaked with blood and tears.
"Help me!"

"Mandy? What's going on?"

She clung to him, burying her face against his shoulder,
her arms around his waist.

"I heard your screams when I stepped off the elevator."

She gestured wildly, unable to collect her scattered wits.
She was shaking so badly she could hardly stand.

He took one look at her cut lip, her puffy cheek and the
blood pouring from her nose. Pressing a handkerchief against
her nose to stem the flow of blood, he demanded, "Who
did this?"

"My father . . ." she said, struggling to catch her breath.
"He's been drinking and is angry. I asked him to leave but
he wouldn't go."

"Stay here." He walked inside and guided her over to
the armchair.

"Who are you?" Amanda heard her father demand, an
instant before she heard a grunt of pain and someone fall
to the floor. She rushed in to find Roger standing over her
father, lying on the carpet.

"I'm Roger McFadden, Mandy's brother-in-law," he
snarled as he slowly opened his balled fists. "Get up so I
can knock your sorry ass down again."

"What in the hell do you think you are doin'? This is
none of your damn business." Sebastian groggily stayed
where he was, eyeing Roger wearily.

"You've forgotten something, Daniels. Mandy is a
McFadden now. We protect our own. Now get the hell out
of here while you can still walk."

Sebastian managed to get to his feet, but he had to use
the back of the sofa for support. "This is no concern of the
McFaddens. It is between me and my girl!"

Amanda explained, "He's angry because Granddaddy left

the Double-D to me. He was trying to make me sign it over to him.''

''Mandy asked you to leave.'' Roger took a menacing step toward the other man. ''If I were you, I'd get the hell out of town. When my brother comes after you, and believe me he will, you'll get more than a few punches in your gut.''

''You're not welcome in my home,'' Amanda said. ''Anything else you have to say to me can be said through my attorney. I don't ever want to see you again.''

''Little bit, you can't mean—''

Grateful that her nose had stop bleeding, she lifted her chin and squared her shoulders when she said, ''I will be filing a police report tonight. Roger is right. It will be best if you leave the area, while you still can.''

''Amanda—''

She shook her head. ''I'm going into the kitchen to put on a kettle for tea. When I come back I want you gone.''

Twenty-two

Amanda's hands were far from steady when she wet paper toweling and cleaned the blood from her face. She turned the gas flame on beneath the kettle and began gathering what she needed for tea. She was slicing lemon when she heard the front door close and she closed her eyes with genuine relief.

A few moments later, Roger appeared in the doorway. "Sit down. I can do that." He went to the refrigerator door and filled a dish towel with ice cubes. "Here." He placed it on her bruised face. "Are you okay?"

"I'm fine now that he is gone." She brushed at her tears. At the look of concern on his face, she insisted. "Really. I have no idea why I'm crying. I've blamed him all these years for the way he treated my mother. And he actually thought he could do the same to me." She said tiredly, "It's been a tough day."

"I can imagine. Sit down before you fall down." Roger
guided her into one of the chairs around the polished oak
dining table.

"He's drunk. How is he going to get back to his hotel
without killing himself or someone else?"

"Where are you going?" Roger called as she jumped up
and rushed toward the foyer.

"Calling down to the front desk," she explained, reaching
for the wall phone. "Hello, Dave. Mr. Daniels is leaving
now. Would you see that a cab is ordered for him? He is
in no condition to get behind the wheel. Thank you. Bye."

Roger shook his head in wonder. "Why do you even
care?"

"If you're asking if I care about him, the answer is no.
He's already caused more than enough unhappiness. But I
don't want anyone else to suffer because of him." With that
said she realized just how tired she was and sat back down,
wincing when she placed the ice pack on the swelling.

"How bad is it? Do you need a doctor?"

"No, I'll be fine once the swelling goes down. When he
grabbed me and shook me, I realized I couldn't get free so
I kicked him, stepped on his feet and pressed my heels down
as hard as I could. That's when he hit me."

"Good for you. Are you really planning to file charges
against him?"

"Absolutely. I won't let him get away with hitting me
ever again. I can't go backward."

"Good girl. Let's go."

"No. This is something I need to do on my own. I have
to show him that he won't get away with hurting this Daniels
woman."

"Fine, but I'm the one who will be driving you. I'll turn
off the kettle, you get your coat and purse."

She was too tired to argue and nodded her consent. As
she walked with him to the car, she realized that her head

was spinning from all the things that had happened in this one day. First there had been the breakup with Zachary and now this.

Despite her dwindling energy, she answered every question and filled out the necessary paperwork. And despite all that had happened, she was proud of herself, genuinely pleased that she had done what should have been done a long time ago. Although she was saddened that her relationship with her father had deteriorated even more, she knew it could not be helped. If nothing else, he had proven that he was still capable of causing violence.

"I thank you for going with me to the police station, but you don't have to come in with me," she said as she unlocked her front door.

"Yeah, I do." Roger smiled, helping her with her coat and hanging it with his own in the closet.

She gave him a quick hug, then looped an arm through his as they walked inside. "It's finally over. It ended when I filed that police report."

"I'm proud of you, kiddo. You did what your mother couldn't do. I know that was not easy."

"Thanks." She went into the kitchen and turned on the flame under the kettle, for that long-awaited cup of tea.

"What I don't understand is why you let him in when he was in that condition. He could have done some serious damage."

"I know, but he seemed sober when he came to the door. And you're right, I never should have let him in. I was so distracted by . . . " She trailed off, thinking about her fight with Zachary. "Anyway, you don't have to worry. I won't make that mistake again."

Roger filled a fresh dish towel with ice and gave it to her.

"Can I get you something?"

"No, you sit down."

She was both physically and emotional drained. It was all she could do to remain upright. What a day.

When the kettle began whistling, Roger volunteered, "I'll get that." He brought in the tray she'd prepared earlier and placed it on the table in front of her.

"Thanks." When she tried to smile, she ended up wincing in pain. "I see you don't want a cup." She referred to the bottle of imported beer that Roger carried. "I do have glasses."

She looked away unhappily. He was drinking Zachary's favorite brew and now sat in his brother's chair. The last thing she wanted to be reminded of the man she loved and lost. She had never felt more ashamed or miserable as she thought of the way she had left him.

Roger loosened his tie and the top two buttons of his starched white shirt. He raked a hand over his close-cut hair in much the same manner as his older brother. Amanda bit her tender lip, despite the pain.

Her hands were trembling when she lifted the cup to her mouth and winced at the heat on her mouth, but drank it anyway. They had been friends for too long for her not to know that Roger had something on his mind.

"Why did you come tonight? Did Zach send you?"

"No. When I left him, he wasn't exactly calm. He's hurting. Do you mind telling me your side?"

"No! I don't want to talk about it."

"Too bad! I am not leaving until you tell me what is going on with you. What were you trying to do?"

"He was the one who forced the issue. He wants what I can't give him. And there's nothing I can do about it."

"Couldn't you have waited until he was at least out of the hospital? I don't know when I've been this angry with you. What were you thinking, girl? Mandy, how could you just walk out like that?"

Roger had never spoken so harshly to her before. She certainly didn't need a reminder that she had been the one to walk out, yet again. Nonetheless, she had done what she felt she had to do under the circumstances.

"Stop judging me! You don't know all the facts. You haven't even asked to hear my side of things."

"Hell, I know all I need to know. I damn sure know my brother. What were you trying to do to him? Break him?" He didn't give her a chance to respond before he said, "You treated him as if you hate him. Do you?"

"How can you even ask such things?" Amanda's troubled gaze filled with hurt. "Our marriage was doomed from the first. We only got married because I was pregnant and he felt guilty about it."

"Guilty!" Roger snarled. "If Zach hadn't loved you, there would have been no pregnancy."

"You don't know that!"

"The hell I don't! Zach's mistake was in not telling you how he felt years ago. He has been in love with you since you were seventeen!"

"That's not true and you know it!" Amanda jumped up, stalking into the kitchen. She placed both the wet dishcloth and her cup in the sink. As she walked through the dining room toward the living room she tossed back, "Go home, Roger."

Roger was right behind her, beer in hand. "The hell it isn't! Zach gave you time to grow up, time to have the kind of education, the career and independence you wanted. He never pushed you or even tried to persuade you one way or another. If you ask me, that was a serious mistake. He gave you too damn much time."

"What are you talking about? Your brother never said or did anything to make me think there was anything but friendship between us. You're wrong! Zachary McFadden married me because I was carrying his unplanned baby. He knew how I felt, knew I didn't really want to raise our child without a father. That was it!''

Placing the drink on an end table, Roger turned her around and took her hands into his own. "I know that's what Zach wanted you to believe. Even Jake knew how Zach felt about you. In fact, he encouraged my brother to marry you. Jake was afraid you would never marry because of what happened with your parents. Your grandfather urged Zach to start dating you the summer you graduated from high school."

"What?"

"Yes."

Amanda pulled her hands free, gesturing wildly. "It can't be true!"

"Why not?"

"Because it would mean I married him for one reason and he married me for another." It also meant she had been terribly unfair to him right from the first. She shook her head, not wanting to believe.

"Mandy, just think about it. If Zach only married you because you were pregnant, why has he stayed in the marriage so long after you'd lost the baby?"

No easy answer came to mind. She had never thought of it that way. Why should she when she knew the reason they got married? But what if Roger was right? What if Zachary had been in love with her when she turned to him for support?

She'd just learned about the seriousness of her grandfather's illness and she had been hurting. All she truly remembered was her concerns for her grandfather and the very real possibility that she would lose him. Her tears and Zachary's hugs of reassurance had led to gentle kisses, and eventually to sizzling-hot, overwhelming need. She longed to forget everything but the way Zachary made her feel.

Love had changed everything. It certainly had changed her. She was no longer afraid of the loss of control involved with making love to her husband. Gradually she'd learned to trust him in their bedroom. Her love for him allowed her to accept Zachary as both a lover and friend.

"You and Zach would have had a future together if you could've trusted him and stopped blaming him for something that happened between your parents."

"He told you?" she murmured in dismay.

"Yeah, he did. What I'd like to know is, what is there about my brother that reminds you of that weak, spineless drunk that was here tonight? I don't get the connection."

"Zach is nothing like my father. I've never intentionally confused the two of them."

"Then why are you punishing him?"

"I'm not ... not really." She looked pleadingly at him for understanding. "It's so hard to explain."

Roger leaned a shoulder against a wall. "I'm not in a hurry."

"When I was little I asked my mother why she stayed. She said it was because she loved him. All my life I've avoided falling in love. I never wanted to be like her."

"Mandy, no one really knows what happened between those two. There's no way of understanding why your mother stayed when your father was abusing both of you. And, you aren't like her. You stood up to your father, remember. You fought back. I've seen you stand up to my brother. I shouldn't have to tell you that Zach isn't a cruel man. He could never harm you."

"I know that."

"Do you? How many times have you kept yourself from getting too close to him because you didn't want to make the same mistakes that your mother made?"

She dropped her head. That was exactly what she had done whenever she felt he was getting too close.

"You've treated him as if he were unworthy of your trust and your love. You ran from him as if he were your abuser.

Tell me, what has he done wrong other than loving you and asking for your love in return?"

Amanda closed her eyes, unable to deny the truth. Wringing her hands in frustration, she accused, "You act as if this were easy for me. Well, it isn't. I love him so much it hurts. I can't help it." Struggling to hold on to her emotions, she whispered, "I've been trying so hard not to repeat my mother's mistakes I guess that I've been responding to Zach as if he were my father. Whenever I thought too hard about loving him, I would remember how deeply my mother loved my father and it would scare me. Honestly, I never meant to hurt him. All I was trying to do was protect myself." She brushed away a tear.

"I know, but it all comes back to why you two got married. Zach has waited years for you, my friend, to grow up. I don't honestly know if I could have done the same for Peggy, if she had been ten years younger than I am. I'm afraid I'd come up short. I don't have that kind of patience." Roger seemed to recognize his advantage and pressed on. "Just when Zach thought he finally had you . . . you needed time to adjust to the loss of your grandfather and the baby. And because Zach was in love with you, he gave it to you."

"And I repaid him by asking for a divorce," she said unhappily. "I've always known that Zachary loves me, but in love with me . . ." She stopped and glared at Roger. "How was I supposed to know? He has always had some gorgeous woman on his arm. Are you telling me that Zach was in love with me while he was sleeping around? Do I look that dumb?"

Roger laughed. "I never told you he was a saint. What did you expect? He's a man. He would have to be sporting a halo to survive that many years without sex."

"Then he wasn't in love with me or he would have waited."

"Girl, he did wait! In fact, he's still waiting for you to

put the past behind you. Jake was far too protective of you."
Roger shook his head. "Your understanding of men leaves
a lot to be desired, honey."

"Well, explain it to me!" Amanda snapped.

Roger flashed a smile. "Gladly. A man has certain needs
that must be met, no matter how much he loves a woman.
Oh, hell!" he said as if realizing he was putting it badly.
He started again, "Take me for instance, I love my wife
with all my heart. That doesn't mean when I see a good-
looking woman I don't look, or I don't appreciate her beauty.
If I do have a few lustful thoughts, that's about as far as it
goes because I'm in love with Peggy."

"What does your loyalty to Peggy have to do with me
and Zach?"

"Even though we haven't made love in months, I haven't
had a problem keeping my pants zipped. I know that one
day we'll be able to make love again and that is enough,
but then I'm married to the lady. On the other hand, if we
weren't married and I thought I could never have her, I
would have to satisfy those urges elsewhere."

"Are you saying that sex is okay with someone else as
long as you're not married?"

"Not exactly. No matter how much my brother loved you
until you became his wife, you couldn't claim his fidelity."

"We were apart most of last year. It's hard to believe he
was celibate that entire time."

"Believe it. Zach didn't fool around on you during the
time you were separated."

"I tried not to think about him at all."

"The hope that you two would be together again was
enough for him. Just as hope is enough for me. For all I
know Peggy may have some kind of complication after the
baby is born and I won't be able to touch her for who knows
how long. Sex is only a part of loving. There is so much
more. Peggy is my heart . . . she's all I want." Roger was

looking directly into her eyes when he said, "Zach feels that way about you, my friend. If you don't believe me, ask him."

Amanda wanted desperately to believe. Years of being afraid to love and receive love had scarred her heart. They left her afraid to accept what had been right in front of her all along.

"Zach was so angry, I don't think he wants me back," she mumbled unhappily, remembering the things he'd said just before she'd left. "And I don't blame him."

"Yeah, he's furious! So that means you're going to give up? What, you want a guarantee? There aren't any. There aren't any assurances that any of us will be here tomorrow, next week or next year, for that matter. It comes down to one thing. Do you want him? If you do, then you're going to have to give him your love on blind faith, just like the rest of us poor fools."

Roger hesitated before saying, "If you don't go back and at least tell him how you feel, don't think some other woman won't try and grab what you let go so easily."

"Never easily," she said quietly.

"Mandy, you'll be handing him over to some other woman to love, to have his children and share his life. Is that what you want?"

She flinched as she accepted that that was exactly what she had done. She'd thrown away his love as if it didn't matter. Tears burned the backs of her eyes but she refused to give in to them. The thought of someone else in his arms, someone else as his wife, bearing his babies, was too painful to consider.

Unable to remain still, she moved restlessly around the room. There was no doubt that she had run from love, yet again. Would he give her one more chance? Did she have the courage to even ask for it?

There had been so much left unsaid between them. She

loved him and wanted him, yet she had never told him, had kept that buried deep inside, letting fear shadow other considerations. She'd turned her back on their marriage, not once but twice. Only this time it was much, much worse.

She had left while he was still in a hospital bed . . . talk about being a coward. She couldn't blame him if he didn't want to see her again. She was proving to be Sebastian Daniels's daughter in more way than one. She had left Zachary just as her father had left her and her mother when they needed him the most. The reason was different but the sense of betrayal had to feel the same.

"He was so angry." Tears that had been burning her eyes began spilling down her cheeks. "Oh, Roger, I've lost him this time, haven't I?"

"I hope not. Do you love him?"

"You know I do. I didn't want to walk away like I did, but he insisted that I move to the ranch until he's better. How can I live there? Your mother and I just don't get along."

"So that means you're giving up?"

"You don't understand," she said, in misery. "I don't think I've ever seen Zach so angry. What if he won't even listen to me?"

"If he doesn't cooperate, you just let me know and I'll punch him in his sore ribs, then sit on his injured leg. How's that for brotherly love?" Roger quipped with a wicked grin.

"You're terrible, but I love you." She gave him a hug. "Thank you for coming tonight. I appreciate all your help."

"Well, you are my favorite sister-in-law."

"I'm your only sister-in-law." She laughed.

"We're family. Besides, I love you too. And I'm so glad you've spent so much time with Peggy. She's really enjoyed it."

Amanda smiled. "She's going to worry about you if you don't get going."

"Yeah." Roger squeezed her hand. "I'm going to need you in a few months when it's time for the baby to come. Will you help, Mandy? Keep me from coming apart? I start sweating whenever I think of what Peggy has to go through in that delivery room."

"I'll be there, my friend, regardless of what happens between me and Zach." She soothed, "Try not to worry. You and Peggy are going to have a beautiful and healthy baby."

"Thanks. I'd better go." Roger grabbed her hand. "Walk me to the door." When they were in the foyer, he asked, "Are you going to be okay tonight? You can always come home with me, if you feel uncomfortable about being here alone."

"I've stopped running, remember? I'll lock the door and not let anyone in. Besides, after what happened, I seriously doubt my father is coming near me ever again."

"I hope you're right about that. I'll check with the police in the morning. Try not to worry."

Her smile was a bit shaky when she confessed, "I'm going to the hospital in the morning. I'm hoping your brother will at least hear me out."

Roger leaned down to kiss her cheek. "Start with telling him how you feel about him."

She nodded. "Give Peggy my love."

"Will do. Good luck. I'm praying for you two."

"Thanks. We need it."

"Be sure and lock that door behind me."

"I will." Amanda waved from the open door, waiting until he disappeared into the elevator before closing, then locking her door.

Twenty-three

Amanda was in the foyer preparing to leave the next morning when the telephone rang. It was Roger letting her know that her father had taken her advice, he'd disappeared during the night. He had checked out of his hotel without leaving a forwarding address. She wasn't surprised. Her father always disappeared when things got rough.

Her driver, Alex Jenson, was waiting in front of the building when she emerged. This once she was grateful that she did not have to concentrate on the road. She'd slept fitfully the night before and done little else but think about seeing Zachary today.

She sat with her hands clasped tightly in her lap, staring out the window. She'd taken particular care with her appearance, doing her best to conceal the bruises and swelling on the side of her face and her cut bottom lip with makeup. Nothing she did could ease her mounting tension. She was terribly afraid that this would be the last time she saw her husband outside of a divorce court.

Zachary might not be willing to listen to anything she had to say. Her walking out yesterday had said that where they lived was more important to her than if they were together. He could consider himself better off without her. And she wouldn't blame him if he felt that way. After all, he had shown an exorbitant amount of patience from the first. He had dug in his heels and refused to give up on their marriage. He'd even moved to Denver, in hopes of a reconciliation.

Zachary was a very special man and certainly didn't deserve what she had said and done to him. She had been haunted by the look of hurt and disappointment she had seen in his eyes. She shuddered at the painful memory. He'd accused her of giving up on them. And he'd been right.

Was it already too late? Was there anything she could say at this point? How could she explain her change of heart? What if he refused to listen?

She searched for the right words as the powerful car eliminated the miles between Denver and the hospital in Glenwood Springs. The only thing she was certain of was that she wasn't leaving until she at least told him how she felt about him.

When the car slowed to a stop at the hospital entrance her heart pounded at an alarming rate. The decision would ultimately be his. Their marriage could end today.

"Good morning, Mrs. McFadden. You're early. I bet you're anxious to get that handsome husband of yours home." Mrs. Johnson, one of the nurses on duty at the nurses' station, said with a smile.

"Good morning, Mrs. Johnson. Is he awake?" Amanda had to force a smile.

"Oh, yes. He's with the doctor, but you can go on in."

"Thank you." Her high heels tapped on the gleaming floor as she approached Zachary's room.

"Good morning, Amanda," Dr. Coleman said as she came through the door. He leaned forward to kiss her on the cheek. "My, you look pretty today. I bet you can't wait to get this man home. I must say, Zach has been one of my worst patients." He roared with laugher. "But then, most active people usually are."

Zachary had looked up at the sound of her name. He was seated on the side of the bed, dressed in a blue chambray shirt and navy cords, the right leg of which had been split to accommodate the cast. A set of crutches was propped against the wall.

"Good morning." She managed a smile. Her gaze collided with his before she quickly turned back to the doctor. "How is he?"

"He's mending well. Just has to exercise a little common sense. Zach, your release forms should be ready before too long. Remember, stay off that leg as much as possible for the next couple of weeks. That means no riding or ranch work other than shuffling papers from one side of the desk to the other. I want to see you in two weeks at my office. I'll leave a couple of prescriptions with the nurse. My dear, you make sure he follows orders." Dr. Coleman squeezed her shoulder on the way out, pushing the door closed behind him.

Zachary's gaze raked over her from the top of her perfectly groomed curls caught in a smooth knot at her nape to her legs and small feet covered by black soft leather boots.

He didn't say a word as he watched her slide out of her fur coat and place it and her purse on the chair near the door. He looked away from the fullness of her breasts and softly curved hips covered by a black cashmere sweater and matching calf-length knit skirt, both trimmed in pink.

He broke the tense silence when he said, "Why did you come? Guilty conscience?"

"I know you're angry with me," she said quietly, "but we have to talk."

"About what? I thought we said all that had to be said last night? You want out and don't value me or our marriage. What? Did you bring yet another set of divorce papers? If so, show me where to sign," he snarled.

Hurt by the harshness of his tone, she forced herself to look into the depths of his dark eyes. They were hard, simmering with anger, with none of the tenderness she had grown accustomed to.

"Please, Zach," she pleaded, "just listen."

"Say it; then do me a favor and get the hell out."

She tilted her chin upward, taking care not to bite her swollen lip, despite its betraying tremor. Her limbs were not exactly steady as she said, "I'm sorry, I was wrong to leave the way I did."

He glared at her.

She whispered unhappily, "I've never seen you this angry before."

"What did you expect? You made your point. I finally got the message. You want out. Fine! I'm not about to beg you to stay and start acting like a wife," he grated harshly. "At least, this time there is no baby to consider. You made sure of that."

"What is that supposed to mean?"

"Birth control pills, sugar. No possibility of a slipup." There was no question that he was still furious. It was up to her.

Amanda rushed in before she lost the nerve. "I don't want a divorce. I never did . . . not really. I was so scared of being hurt I didn't give our marriage a chance. Because of my fears I ended up hurting us both."

"Did it ever occur to you that I might also have been scared?"

"No . . . you never seemed . . ." She stopped, searching for the right words. "Roger told me that—"

"Roger? What does my brother have to do with this? Is he the reason you're here?" Zachary demanded, a muscle jumping in his tightly held jaw.

"No!"

"What did he do? Beg you to come here today?"

"Of course not! I'm not here because of Roger. I'm here because I happen to be in love with you! Now will you shut up long enough to listen to what I have to say?" Her hand was on one hip while one high-heeled, booted foot tapped furiously on the linoleum floor.

Zachary looked doubtful. After a prolonged silence, he asked, "You mean it?"

"About wanting you to shut up and listen? Absolutely."

"No. That you're in love with me?" His eyes searched hers.

"Yes," Amanda said quietly, ". . . very much so." Afraid to make a move toward him, she waited with her heart racing and a mounting sense of dread.

"Then why in the hell did you give up on us and walk out on me yesterday?" His arms were crossed over his chest.

"You expect so much from me. I was overwhelmed with fears and doubts. Honey, I'm so sorry. I never meant to hurt you." She forced herself to ask while fighting back tears, "Am I too late?"

"I don't know. I've waited a long time to hear you say that. I don't know what, if anything, can change," Zachary said around a heavy sigh. "I've tried everything I could think of to show you how important you are to me. Yet, it never seemed to be enough. Mandy, I've been in love with you for so long. You were only seventeen when I realized how I felt. You were so young. It's been more than ten long years of waiting for you to love me back. I'm damn tired of it. And I sure as hell have no idea how to fix what's wrong between us," he ended solemnly.

With eyes shimmering from unshed tears, she said, "Zach, please, don't give up on me. I do love you ... so much it hurts. I've been afraid of how loving you makes me feel. That's what I have been running from."

He dropped his lids, effectively shielding his thoughts. After a while, he said, "Love has never been enough, has it? You don't trust me, or my feelings for you. So tell me what you expect to change now that you've told me how you feel."

"Everything," she murmured wishfully.

He quirked a brow. "Our problems haven't disappeared."

"Zach, it will be different this time. I'm no longer running."

"What happened in one night to bring about this miraculous change?"

"I did quite a bit of thinking. After seeing my father, I—"

"You saw Sebastian?"

"Yes. He came by last night. After see—"

"You let him inside the condo?"

"He seemed sober. Of course that didn't last long once he found where I kept the liquor. That's not the point. I'm—"

"Wait one minute. Are you telling me that you were alone in the condo and he'd been drinking?"

Reluctantly, she nodded. "Let me expla—"

"Mandy! What were you thinking? Did he put a hand on you?"

"He didn't really hurt me, if that's what you're asking."

"You're damn right that's what I'm asking. What happened?"

Frowning, she said, "He was angry about Granddaddy's will. He felt the Double-D should have gone to him." She took a deep breath before she admitted, "He grabbed me when I told him what I thought of him. It got a little out of hand.''

''Out of hand? What happened?''

''I lost my temper. I've kept so much resentment and anger inside for too long. It came out last night. I told him how I really felt about him and the way he treated us. Told him that I hold him responsible for my mother's death. He was furious. He tried to force me to sign the ranch over to him. When I refused he grabbed me and started shaking me.

''When he wouldn't let me go I panicked. I kicked him hard and stepped down on his feet, pressed my high heels down as hard as I could. That's when he slapped me—''

''Hit you!'' Zachary roared. ''Where are you hurt?'' He didn't wait for an answer. ''Just wait until I get my hands on that weak son of a bitch!'' Balancing on one leg, he made a grab for his crutches, missed and nearly fell in the process. Hanging on to the nightstand, he ordered, ''Hand those to me. We're leaving now.''

''No!'' She raced to steady him. She slipped a shoulder under his arm and encircled his trim waist. ''Will you calm down? Let me finish telling you what happened.''

''I'm going after him! Now get me those damn crutches!''

''No!'' Amanda eased him back toward the side of the bed. ''Sit down and stop swearing at me, Zachary McFadden!''

''Sorry, but I'm—''

''You aren't going anywhere until you have listened to me.''

A muscle played in his cheek, but he did sit back down on the side of the bed. He took a good look at her. He cupped her chin so he could see where she'd used makeup to conceal the damage. He swore heatedly.

''When I get my hands on him . . . ''

She kept her palms spread on his chest until she was certain he wouldn't move. ''Honey, it's over. Roger came by in time before anything more could happen. In fact, when your brother realized what my father had done he went after him with his fists. Even more important to me was that I did what my mother could never do. I went to the police station last night and filed a report."

"Good. Tell me, how badly did he hurt you? Did you go to emergency?"

"No, it's not that bad. I have some bruises on my arms and face and a cut lip and I'm sore. I know I shouldn't have let him in. I won't ever make that mistake again."

He nodded, taking deep breaths to calm himself. He watched as she moved over to the window. "Remind me to thank my meddling brother the next time I see him. Come here."

She shook her head, needing to keep some distance between them. "I need to say this. All of it."

"And I need to know that you haven't been badly hurt. Come here."

Amanda welcomed his concern, she desperately wanted his love and she longed to be in his arms. For now, it was more important to her that he listen to all she had to say. She did move to the foot of the bed, just out of reach.

"I was shaken up, but nothing serious. I'm fine."

She could tell by his expression that he didn't like it but offered no further objections.

"It wasn't until I looked into my father's eyes ... they were cold and filled with rage ..." She shuddered at the memory. "That was when I realized what I had done. I've been comparing the two of you, treating you as if you were like him. That was wrong." She took a shaky breath and then hurried on before she lost her nerve. "It's hard to explain but I've been protecting myself the way my mother couldn't seem to do. I've worked so hard over the years not to make the same mistakes. I wanted an education so that

I could always take care of myself, no matter what life brought.

"Zach, I loved her with all my heart but not once have I ever wanted to be like her. My father hurt her over and over again, yet she never fought back. After we married, I started to worry because I cared so much for you. When you moved in with me . . . I was so afraid of falling in love with you."

She wrung her hands, struggling to put her feelings into words. "Whenever you said you loved me I remembered how my father said those same words to her, usually after a beating. Love was a weakness . . . something I wanted no part of. I had such a difficult time accepting that the kind of love they had is nothing like what we share. I've pushed you away time and time again. I know I hurt you and you've been so patient with me. I've been so unfair to you, honey. But, I do love you. Can you ever forgive me? Please, my love, will you let me try and make it up to you?" She brushed impatiently at the tears in her eyes.

"Are you coming over here or do I have to come get you?"

Amanda was not conscious of moving, but when his fingers connected with hers, he tugged her forward until her breasts collided with his chest. He wrapped his arms around her and held on to her.

"Mandy . . ." he groaned as he buried his face against her sweet-scented throat.

"Can you—"

"Sssh . . ." he sighed, pressing tender butterfly-soft kisses down her bruised cheek and sore mouth. "Know that I love you, my heart."

"As I love you," she whispered against his mouth. "Hold me and never let me go."

"Never," he breathed against her skin. "I'm sorry, too.

I lost my temper yesterday. And I was still furious when you walked in here today.''

"You had a right. I hurt you needlessly. It was my fault . . . I was just so scared I didn't know what to do, so I ran.''

"It's over." His voice was brimming with emotions when he said, "We'll work it out . . . all of it. As long as we love each other, nothing else matters.''

"Nothing," she agreed.

He groaned deep in his throat, seeking more of her sweetness. He traced the outline of her lips with his tongue. Amanda trembled, opening for more of him, but when he pressed too hard, she winced in pain. He soothed, "I'm sorry, baby." He kissed her with tender care.

She whispered, "I've never been in love before. Have never come close to it . . . not until you.''

"When did you know for sure?''

She laughed. "That's easy. I suspected that I was in love with you the night of the storm when you were so late coming home, and we made love. But after Peggy's accident when we'd been apart for so long I knew. Then seeing you so unexpectedly jarred me into facing the truth about how deep my feelings went for you. All that time I'd been lying to myself . . . pretending I could control my feelings. I wanted you even when I said no. I wanted you to make love to me every bit as much as you wanted to . . . only I couldn't tell you how I felt.''

"Oh, Mandy," he whispered hoarsely.

He pressed his lips tenderly against the sensitive place where her neck and shoulder joined. She held on to him, her arms circling his neck, resting on his broad shoulders.

"I'm surprised you didn't realize.''

"How?" He chuckled. "When you were so good at pushing me away? For years you treated me as if I were your big brother. I hated it. When you really started dating after high school, I was a mess. I detested every guy who tried to take you out. There was nothing I could do about it. You were far too young for me. You couldn't handle me or know how deep my feelings went for you. I had no choice but to stay away," he confessed. "Your college years were the worst for me."

He kissed her bruised cheek, then found the enticing corner of her soft plum-tinted lips. He tenderly licked her lips, soothing the hurt.

"Zach . . ."

"I'm so sorry that your father hurt you. I wanted the two of you to heal the breach between you and to get to know each other all over again. But I never believed he would touch you in anger. Not that I trusted him, but I did not see him as a threat to you. I should have known better. I'm sorry I didn't make sure you were protected."

"Stop." She pressed her hand to his lips. "You were not to blame."

"You're mine. It is my job to keep you safe. Why last night? How did he know you were alone?"

"He read about your accident in the paper. I should have told you that he has been calling me at the office for some time. That they were persistent calls. I stopped taking them and ignored them. As hard as I tried, I could not forget how badly he treated my mother and me."

"Mandy, I'm going after him. When I get through with him, he'll know whose fists he will be facing, if he ever comes near you again."

"He's gone."

"What? Are up sure?"

"Roger called this morning to say that the police couldn't find him. He'd checked out of his hotel room without leaving a forwarding address."

"I'll find him. A private investigator can track him down."

"For what? He's a bitter, angry man. And he is alone.

He has lost all the people who love him. He has nothing but the money Jake left to him. And, he knows he's out of my life for good.''

''Are you sure about that?'' he asked, smoothing back her hair.

''Absolutely. It's finally behind me.'' She kissed him. ''Thank you, my darling.''

''Mandy,'' he said throatily, ''I love you so much.''

He gently kissed her, his tongue moving against hers, causing sparks of pure passion to flow throughout her system. He stopped abruptly, tilting her chin so she could meet his gaze.

''Don't ever put me through this kind of hell again. I won't put up with it. If you're upset with me or hurt by something I've said or done tell me, damn it, so we can talk it out. We'll face our problems together from now on. Okay?''

''Yes.''

He let out a deep sigh of heartfelt relief, then whispered into her ear, ''I feel as if I waited a lifetime to hear you say you love me. You're not the only one who's made mistakes. I was in a bad way when you left yesterday. I thought I'd lost you.''

''I know. I felt as if I'd lost you . . . it was horrible.'' She stroked his cheek. ''I know we married because I was pregnant, but . . .''

He pulled back enough to study her small African features. ''I married you because I loved you. Yeah, I lost control when I should have been concentrating on consoling you because of Jake's illness. It was something that never happened to me before. All I remember was one instant I was comforting you, the next I was taking advantage of the situation. My only excuse was that I'd waited so damn long to have you in my arms that I couldn't stop myself from touching you . . . making love to you.''

"It wasn't rape!" she insisted. "Honey, you didn't take what I did not want to give. I wanted you that night. I needed you. Making love with you helped me forget for a time the illness that was taking Granddaddy away from me."

"I got you pregnant."

"Yeah." She smiled. "And you also made me very happy. I loved our baby so very much. Zach, I have no regrets about what happened or how it happened. I don't want you to have any either. Our baby was created from love and nothing will make me believe differently. It was not meant to be. God's choice, not ours. I think we've both come to terms with that, don't you?"

They gazed into each other's eyes with understanding and simply held on to each other for a time.

She broke the silence when she said, "I'm ready to be your wife . . . the wife I should have been from the beginning."

Zachary closed his eyes and held Amanda tightly, despite the discomfort it caused his still tender rib cage. Eventually, he pulled back, asking, "What are you saying? That you're ready to come back to the ranch with me? Stay there with me until we can solve our housing problem?"

She nodded. "My bags are in the trunk of the car. I will learn to adore your mother, even if it kills us both." Amanda laughed, playfully nipping his earlobe. "I can't wait to get you alone, Mr. McFadden. Show you how very much I've missed you."

He laughed huskily. "You have a deal, Mandy McFadden. But I don't think I can wait that long. We can put the armchair in front of that door and turn out the light."

She giggled. "In the hospital? I want you, but not quite that desperately. I can wait until we're locked inside your bedroom."

He chuckled. "Maybe you have a point."

Her face was flushed from happiness and her eyes sparkled like diamonds. "Roger told me something that puzzled me."

"What did my meddling little brother say this time?" Light danced in his dark eyes.

"Did my grandfather really encourage you to marry me the summer I graduated from high school?"

"Yeah. Jake knew how I felt about you. He wanted you happy, loved and protected. He was an old-fashioned kind of guy. I was the one who decided not to pursue you. You wanted to go to college, have a career and have a taste of independence."

He shrugged. "So I kept my feelings from you. After a few years you became too independent, frightened of commitment. It was then that I realized it wasn't going to happen for us. I tried amusing myself with other women. It didn't work. I only wanted you."

He admitted, "You had me worried a few times, especially when you were dating Miles Stevens. He made no secret that he wanted to marry you."

"You knew I wasn't in love with Miles and that we were only friends."

"Yeah, but that didn't make it any easier to take. I felt the same way about you that he did. When you called about Jake, I was at the end of my patience." He shook his head ruefully. "No matter how many evenings I just happened to be in Denver and took you out to dinner or to a play or a concert, you continued to think of me as your friend."

He gave her a playful little shake that made her laugh before he said, "Oh, man! I needed you so badly that night. After we made love my need for you only got worse. If you hadn't married me and put me out of my misery when you realized you were pregnant, I don't know what I would have done."

She sighed wearily. "Only I married you and left you a few weeks later. Zach, how could you keep on loving me?"

"It wasn't a choice. My feelings didn't stop. You were lodged in my heart . . . a part of me." He admitted, "Once

I had your sweetness, I couldn't let you go. The worst was the months we lived apart. I wanted you so badly that I spent my nights dreaming of you, aching for you. That hasn't changed. No more nights apart, okay?''

"No more."

They shared a searing, hungry kiss.

Neither was aware of the nurse entering the room until she cleared her throat loudly, saying, "Excuse me. I have your release papers ready, Mr. McFadden."

Amanda took a step away from him. Her face was warm with embarrassment while Zachary grinned, not the least bit uncomfortable.

"Great, Mrs. Johnson." He accepted the papers attached to a clipboard and a pen.

"As soon as I have your signature at the bottom and gone over the doctor's orders, you're free to go."

Zachary quickly read the papers before he signed them and handed the clipboard back.

Mrs. Johnston reviewed the doctor's instructions, handed over two prescriptions, one for pain medication and the other an antibiotic. She smiled, asking, "Are you packed, Mr. McFadden?"

"Packed and ready to go, Mrs. Johnson."

His glance told Amanda that he couldn't wait until they had some privacy. Just then a male hospital volunteer brought in a wheelchair. Zachary started to protest, but Mrs. Johnson explained it was hospital policy.

He wasn't thrilled, but he was ready to leave. He nodded, pulling on a heavy, soft leather jacket before he was settled into the wheelchair. Amanda put on her own coat, put her purse over her shoulder, as well as his leather duffel bag and then grabbed his crutches. After thanking the hospital staff, they were soon on their way.

As soon as Alex Jenson saw them coming, he rushed forward to collect Zachary's things. He enthusiastically greeted them before he left to get the car. While the volunteer helped Zachary into the back of the sleek black limousine, Amanda settled on his left side, taking care not to jar him. Alex set the car into motion while Zachary closed the smoke-colored glass partition between the seats.

Twenty-four

Zachary's dark head dipped toward hers as he enclosed her in a warm hug. "I'm glad to be out of that place."

Amanda smiled, then asked, "Did you know that my father was behind the wheel in the accident that killed his twin brother Danny? Or that he had been drinking? Granddaddy never talked to me about it."

"No, I didn't." He brushed a finger over the shadows beneath her eyes. "Did you get any sleep last night?"

"Not much. I was worrying about us. I just knew you would never forgive me for walking out on you, yet again."

"I didn't get much either. It's behind us now." Using a forefinger, he traced the outline of her mouth. "Got any of that sweet sugar for me?"

She stroked her lips against his, urging his lips apart with the tip of her small pointed tongue. She explored the hot interior of his mouth before he groaned and his tongue began to move against hers. She pressed even closer to him. Her hand slid inside his jacket to caress the broad planes of his chambray-covered chest. He tightened his hold on her, intensifying the kiss as he pulled the pins from her hair, threaded his fingers into its thickness.

"Oh, baby. It's been too long." His mouth was warm against the slender column of her throat once their lips parted.

She eased back enough to lightly stroke the fading bruise on his forehead. "No more headaches?"

"I have an ache, but it's not in my head. I'll give you one guess as to where it is."

"Zach!" She blushed.

He released a deep throaty chuckle. "I wasn't looking forward to going back to the ranch without you." Resting his cheek against her dark curls, he added, "You've changed all that, my love."

She was silent, thinking about her grandfather. He had somehow known that she loved Zachary and had understood how very frightened she was of marriage. She recalled how happy he had been on their wedding day. He had always taken such good care of her during the years she had lived on the ranch with him. The Double-D had always been filled with love. Her grandfather had put so much of himself into that place. He started it on his own and was proud of what he accomplished.

"Zach . . ."

"Huh?" He'd been watching the passing scenery.

Safe and protected by his strength, confident in the love they shared, Amanda said, "I want to go home. To the Double-D."

"Okay. We'll go tomorrow."

"No, now. Will you come with me? I'm not sure I can do it alone."

He eased back enough to study her face. "You don't have

to go alone. But we don't have to do it today. We can wait until you're ready.''

"I've put it off for over a year. Granddaddy left the ranch to me and I haven't been back since his death. That's wrong.''

She didn't add that she had to go now, before she lost her nerve. She owed it to the wonderful man who had not only opened his home but also his heart to a frightened little girl.

"We'll go,'' Zachary said as he picked up the telephone tucked into the armrest and told Alex of the change in plans. When he finished, he stroked her cheek. "Don't worry. It's going to be fine.''

She dropped her head until her cheek rested on his shoulder. "I've been such a weak little fool.''

"You're being too hard on yourself. Jake left the ranch to you, but he also knew I would take care of it for you.''

She smiled, rubbing her cheek against his. "I'm being selfish, aren't I? You just left the hospital. It doesn't have to be today.''

"There is no need to wait on my account. I may have trouble getting in and out of the car, but I'm getting pretty good with those crutches. Don't worry about me. Alex can walk behind me, catch me if I fall on my behind. It certainly won't be the first tumble I've taken lately, now will it?''

She nodded absently. "Have there been any problems on the Double-D that I should have been paying attention to?''

"Nothing out of the ordinary. Relax.''

She really tried but she couldn't dismiss her feelings of guilt.

"How do you feel about throwing away those birth control pills?'' he asked.

Busy searching Zachary's gaze, Amanda failed to notice that the car had slowed to take the turn onto the gravel road that led to the Double-D.

"You want a baby?"

"I do. Is it too soon for you?"

"Oh, honey!" She threw her arms around his neck and hugged him tight. "I can't think of anything I would like more," she confessed breathlessly. "My doctor said I'm fine. There is no physical reason why we can't try again. Oh, Zach. You've made me so happy." She laughed, with tears sparkling on her dark lashes.

He grinned, kissing her carefully. "Nothing will go wrong this time."

"I know. I'll be especially careful. If necessary, I'm willing to stay in bed the whole time, just as Peggy has to do. Having a healthy baby is all that matters."

"You're going to be a wonderful mother, but let's hope it doesn't come to you being in bed. Have I told you lately that I love you?"

Her laughter rang out, rich with joy. "You know you have, but say it again and again. I'll never get tired of hearing it."

"Good. I'm more than willing to do my share of the work involved in making this new baby." He chuckled at her expression before he said in her ear, "It's been too long since I've been inside you . . . a part of you."

Shivers of desire raced over her skin as she pressed her breasts into his chest and her mouth against his. Her heart soared with love for him. There was nothing more she wanted in the entire world than to someday carry a child of their own to full term and hold that precious bounty in her arms.

"Mandy, what about your business? You've been showing a steady profit. This may not be the best time for us to start our family."

"You, my love, and our babies are more important than anything else. If necessary, I can always offer Yolanda a partnership."

"I want you happy. If you would rather wait . . . I'll

understand. As long as I have you, I don't need anything or anyone else. You're my heart.''

"And you're mine." She gazed lovingly up at him.

"Ready?" he asked as he reached for the door handle.

She'd been so engrossed in their love and plans for the future that she hadn't noticed the car had stopped in the wide drive.

It was time. Time for her to do what she hadn't been able to do in more than a year. She had to face the fact that her beloved grandfather would not be inside to welcome her back. He was gone.

"Sugar, we don't—"

She squeezed his hand. "Yes, I have to do this."

Alex waited with the crutches as Zachary eased himself out of the car, using the door and his good leg for support. Amanda quickly followed, standing behind him with her hands on either side of her husband's waist for additional support. Once Zachary had the crutches under his arms and gripped them, she walked beside him.

She noticed as they stood on the damp but well-salted drive that it, along with the curved front walkway and all the paths, was cleared of snow. Her eyes burned as she stared at the ranch-style house with its familiar rambling lines. She'd always loved the redbrick with black trim. It was the place she thought of as home.

They approached the wide front porch together and slowly mounted the stairs. Instantly, the rush of sweet memories flooded her. Nothing looked neglected, in fact, just the opposite. The oak flooring and wooden rocking chairs were free of snow, even the windows gleamed from a recent washing.

"Honey, do you remember this old swing?" she said with a smile. "We used to spend hours in the evenings during the warmer months here talking." She pulled back the heavy canvas tarp used to protect the redwood frame.

"If memory serves, we spent most of that time arguing.

It was John Wilkins, not me, who sat on that swing kissing you. There was more than one occasion when I almost cracked his jaw just for the hell of it.'' Zachary gave the swing a menacing look.

She giggled. ''What made you think of that? Besides, he only kissed me once. I'm surprised you even remember. Weren't you dating that empty-headed Gloria Gunston back then?''

He arched a brow but wisely kept his mouth closed.

''What did you see in her? She couldn't find her way out of a closet with a road map.''

He said, around a deep chuckle, ''It wasn't her brains I was interested in, darlin'.''

She purposefully turned her back on him. They'd reached the front door, but she held back. The front door opened and the storm door swung back. Jake's longtime house-keeper, Kate Jenson, filled the entrance with her sturdy frame.

''Mandy! Child, I have missed you so.'' Kate beamed at them.

''Mrs. Jenson. I'm so glad you're here.'' Amanda rushed forward to kiss the older woman's finely lined brown cheek, and she gave her a warm hug.

''Now, where else would I be, child?'' Kate quickly brushed away tears the same as Amanda was doing. ''Mr. Zach. Goodness! Look what you done to you'self. When my boy told me 'bout your accident, I couldn' believe it. Oh, I known you would break somethin' sooner or later. Just figured it a be on one of them wild horses you so fond of. You all come on in here. There be a nip in the air. May even snow again before mornin'.''

Amanda walked through the small foyer, amazed that not one thing had changed. Everything was exactly as it had been the day she had first come here to live in this house. She'd just turned twelve, her first birthday without her mother. She remembered being scared because her mother was dead and her father was gone. Jake had come for her and brought her to live with him on the ranch she had visited growing up.

The dark blue floral area rug covered the gleaming hardwood floor. The large sofa and armchairs were covered in a familiar worn blue leather. Her grandfather's favorite old tapestry recliner was in front of the big-screen television. The seat was still ripped, patched with tape. Her grandfather would not hear of recovering it, said it suited him just fine as it was.

She smiled, unaware of the three pairs of concerned eyes following her as she moved around the cozy room. She ran her hand lovingly over the old upright piano against the wall. No one had played it since her grandmother had died; nevertheless, it shone from a recent polishing, just as all the furniture did.

"Remember when Granddaddy insisted I take piano lessons?" She laughed, unaware of a tear trailing down her face. "He finally gave up when his poor ears couldn't take any more."

She walked beneath the archway into the formal dining room. The antique dining table and cushioned chairs gleamed with care. The hand-crocheted tablecloth her grandmother had made so many years ago had been lovingly preserved and covered its smooth surface. Her grandparents' wedding picture still hung on the wall over the china cabinet. A vase of fresh-cut flowers stood in the center of the table, Amanda noted with a smile. Her grandmother had always kept a flower garden and Jake insisted on having a fresh arrangement each day, another reminder of the woman he loved so dearly.

When she returned to the room her grandfather had always called the front parlor, she noticed the concern on the others' faces.

"It's good to have you home, child."

"It's so good to be home, Mrs. Jenson," Amanda said, and meant it.

The older woman had helped raise her over the years and had evidently continued to care for this house since her grandfather had been gone. She missed the look of relief on her husband's face.

"You two are staying for dinner, ain't you? There's plenty." Kate didn't try to disguise her eagerness.

"We'd love to," Zachary answered for both of them. Balancing on his crutches, he slid Amanda's coat down her arms and handed it along with his own discarded jacket to Alex. When Amanda lifted questioning brows, he grinned at her before carefully lowering himself into her grandfather's recliner. She moved to help him prop his injured leg on the upraised footrest.

"Are you in pain?" she asked as he let out a groan.

"I'm fine, my love. Alex and I'll just watch the basketball game on television while you ladies are in the kitchen."

Amanda sensed he was up to something, but had no idea what. He was awfully pleased with himself. It was almost as if he'd planned this visit . . . which was ridiculous. He had no way of knowing she would want to return to the Double-D today. She had not decided to come until they were under way.

He caught her hand, placing a kiss in the center of her palm.

"Come on, child," Mrs. Jenson urged. "You can help me set the table and finish the salad while I dish up the stew."

When she entered the large sunny kitchen, Amanda discovered that some things had indeed changed. It had been remodeled and enlarged to include a butcher block, center island with work area and prep sink.

There was a new professional cook top, double stainless

steel sinks, a new dishwasher, as well as built-in double ovens, a microwave and a new oversize refrigerator. There was considerably more counter space and new pine glass-front cabinets, complete with pullout storage bins. Gleaming copper pots hung from hooks above the stove.

A brick fireplace and a built in-desk area along with shelves were against the far wall. The round pine table and bright yellow, deep-cushioned chairs were tucked into a new alcove in front of curved bay windows. Huge hanging baskets of plants framed the windows.

"Oh, my goodness!" Amanda exclaimed.

"Do you like it?" Mrs. Jenson asked expectantly.

"I love it! But how? When?" Amanda questioned as she slowly moved around.

She paused to look through the yellow-curtained rear windows. There were even more changes. The old barn had been torn down and replaced by a redbrick four-car garage. The paddocks and feedlots were also gone. Now a rambling white fence separated the open range from the house and ranch yard. "Where's the ranch equipment?"

"Mr. Zach had it all moved, honey, after Mr. Jake died. He knew you don't know beans 'bout raisin' cattle. His men work both sides of the range now. There's no fence separating the Circle-M and the Double-D. He also hired all your grandpa's people.

"I still take care of the house and Alex takes care of the ranch yard and repairs. Well, that was until my boy started driving that fancy car for you. Mr. Zach had the kitchen done last spring, along with other things. Now, let's get busy, girl, our men are hungry."

The two women worked side by side, falling into the comfortable routine that had been established years earlier. They caught up on each other's news. The table was soon heaping with food, from savory beef stew, cream potatoes and green salad to deep-dish apple cobbler for dessert.

Amanda felt as if she was back where she belonged. She enjoyed the meal and didn't mind helping with the cleanup. She kept waiting to be overwhelmed by the painful reminders of her grandfather's last days; instead she recalled the happiness and love that were part of her life on the Double-D.

Suddenly, she knew beyond doubt that this was where she wanted to start anew with Zachary. Could she convince him to stay? Or that her desire had nothing to do with the strained relationship between herself and his mother?

"Care to see the rest of the house?" Mrs. Jenson smiled as she dried her hands on a dish towel.

"There are more changes? Zachary didn't say a word when I told him how much I liked the other changes over lunch."

"Come along. See for yourself."

Mrs. Jenson led the way, down the familiar hallway past Amanda's grandfather's bedroom on the left, her girlhood bedroom on the right, the bathroom and the guest bedroom. What should have been the end of the hall angled toward the right and continued on toward a new set of double doors at the end of a new corridor.

"The master suite," Mrs. Jenson explained, accurately reading Amanda's astonishment. "Mr. Zach had the builders and carpenters here all last summer."

Last summer? They had been separated during that time. He'd been updating her home while she had been considering divorce?

Her heart raced with excitement and her curiosity got the better of her. They entered a spacious, sunny sitting room, complete with one entire wall of floor-to-ceiling windows. A natural stone fireplace was flanked on either side by built-in bookshelves. There were interior doors on either side of the room.

"The bedroom is through here," Mrs. Jenson said, opening the door on the left.

"Oh," Amanda exclaimed. The bedroom was larger than the sitting room. A set of French doors opened onto a verandah. "Is that a pool?"

"Sure is and a hot tub. Come along, child. I'll show you the dressing room with built-in shelves and the gold marble bathroom."

The walls throughout the suite had been painted and the luxurious carpeting underfoot were done in her favorite, a rich celery green. She also looked into the small room on the opposite side of the sitting room and saw that it could easily be turned into a home office or a nursery.

Happiness sparkled in her eyes and her heart swelled with love as she took it all in. Zachary had thought of everything, and he had done it all during a very difficult time for them both.

"Well, child, what do you think?" Mrs. Jenson asked hopefully.

"I can't believe it! It's beautiful! It's as if Zach knew that one day we would live here." She brushed away tears.

What had she ever done to deserve his love? His faith in her? He was such a wonderful man and she knew she would do everything within her power to make him happy. This had been waiting for her . . . waiting until she was ready to come back home.

"Where else would you go? This is your home, child. Mr. Zach knows that. You the one slow to accept. I know it was real hard for you coming back to this place with Mr. Jake gone. Lord knows I miss him too."

She kissed Amanda's cheek. "He would have been pleased to have you here. "Well, it's time for my nap. If you need somethin' you know where my rooms are. I hopes you decide to stay on, Mandy girl, but if you can't, you made this old lady really happy by coming by." With that she pressed Amanda's hand. "You married you'self a fine man. Mr. Zach loves you. Course, Mr. Jake always knew that.'' Mrs. Jenson left her alone with her thoughts.

Amanda's heart was bursting with love as she wandered back through the empty rooms. Her imagination took flight. As she stood at the French doors gazing out at the pool, she couldn't contain her excitement. Zachary had not only made this possible, he loved and understood her, perhaps better than she understood herself.

Suddenly, she had to see him ... had to tell him what was in her heart. Hurrying back down the hallway, she expected to find him in the front parlor, but he called her name as she passed.

She found him resting on the double bed in her old bedroom. She grinned at the sight of him among the ruffle-edged pillow shams, and the pink and green floral coverlet.

"You seem to have made yourself at home," she teased, closing the door behind her.

She smiled as she looked around the room. Her old books still filled the white bookcases, along with her old stereo. There were pictures of her parents, her grandparents as well as much younger versions of both Roger and Zachary on the mirrored white wicker dresser top. Her favorite rag doll sat on the pink-cushioned bottom of the white wicker rocker beside the window. Even the lace-edged pink floral curtains were the same, as was the pink carpet covering the floor.

"Well?" Zachary prompted, one arm stretched comfortably behind his head, his eyes searching hers.

"Well what?" She unzipped and pulled off her boots. "Tell you that you should have told me what you were up to? Or that you changed my home, my life without even a word to me?"

He looked disappointed when he asked, "You don't like the suite?"

Approaching the bed on bare feet, she said, "The only thing I have to say to you, Zachary McFadden ..." She paused, watching him closely. "... is thank you. I love it all, I especially love you ... so much."

He let out the breath he'd been holding. His mouth titled in an engaging grin. "The changes were wishful thinking on my part. It helped me get through the months we were separated." He pressed a kiss into the center of her palm. "I'm glad you like it. Is there anything you want changed? It can be redone, if you like."

"Nothing." She laughed as she walked around the bed to curl up on his left side, careful not to jar his leg propped on pillows. "Oh, my love, I never expected anything like this. How did you know that some day I'd want to move back here?"

"I didn't." Zachary gathered her close, inhaling her womanly scent. "But this is still your home. And I wanted it ready in the event you decided you wanted to live here someday. As time passed, I had to accept that you didn't want to come back . . . not without Jake. I tried to understand and respect your feelings."

"You don't object to our living here rather than the Circle-M?"

"You are kidding, aren't you? My heart, I can see the joy in your eyes. As long as we're together I honestly don't care where we live. It certainly solves the problem with my mother."

"Yes, it does. Zach, I'm so happy." She kissed him, but before he could deepen the kiss, Amanda said, bubbling with excitement, "I'd like to use the furniture from both the condo and your rooms. I also want to finish redecorating the rest of the house so it reflects our taste. I think it's time I sold the condo, since I won't have any use for it. You can run the ranch from here, can't you, honey?"

In her excitement she didn't give him time to answer. "I think I can work out a way so that I don't have to drive into the office any more than a few days a week. I'd rather work here. What do you think?''

"Amanda Daniels McFadden, I think you are wonderful," he whispered, easing her up and across his chest until he could place tender kisses on her lips and down her throat. "Now, don't you think it's time you turned your attention to me?''

She smiled impishly. "Are you feeling neglected?''

"Very," he whispered, his mouth against her throat, his hands caressing down her back and settling on her lush bottom.

She licked the corners of his mouth before she slipped her tongue between his parted lips, sharing a hot caress. She heard his throaty groan before he hungrily ravished her mouth, enjoying her sweetness. Quivering from mounting desire, she moaned when he waded an assault on her senses.

Resting her forehead on his chin, she said breathlessly, "We shouldn't be doing this."

Combing his fingers through her thick curls, he said. "Why not? I'll be fine, once you take care of my little problem."

Amanda giggled, blushing. "There is nothing little about your problem." She stroked a hand down his chest to caress the hard length of his sex. "Seriously," she said as she reached up to cradle his cheeks. "I want to thank you."

He laughed huskily. "For kissing you? I plan to do an awful lot of kissing on you, Mandy McFadden . . . and much more."

"No, for keeping Mrs. Jenson and Alex on, as well as the other men who worked for my grandfather. I've been so caught up in my own problems that I neglected everyone, including you." She admitted with difficulty, "Granddaddy would be ashamed of me, if he knew."

"You're wrong about that. You've never been selfish. You've suffered two major losses in less than a year. Stop beating yourself up about what happened.'' He brushed her mouth with his. ''I've made my share of mistakes.

''All that matters now is that we have a home of our own. Most important, we're starting a new life together. I hope you discovered that you haven't completely lost your grandfather. Jake's memory is still in here, in your heart.''

Massaging the knot of tension he found at her nape, he continued, ''No, sugar, you have nothing to thank me for. I knew that you would start to worry about the Jensons and the others . . . once you had gotten past the grief. I merely did what I thought you'd want me to do.''

''I love you, so very much,'' she said, burying her face against his throat. ''I don't want us to ever be apart again. Not even for one night.''

''And I love you. Never doubt it.''

Tucking a soft wave of black hair behind her ear, he asked, ''Did you take your birth control pill today?''

''Not yet. I take them at night before I go to bed.''

''Are you planning to take one tonight?''

The smile she gave him radiated pure happiness. ''Nope.''

''Good.'' His eyes danced with pleasure as he gave her a hard, breathtaking kiss.

''Zach . . .''

''Did I tell you how proud I am of you, for standing up to your father? I know that couldn't have been easy. And then going ahead and pressing charges against him.'' He gazed into her eyes when he said, ''Don't worry about him. Sebastian will never get another opportunity to hurt you ever again.''

''I know. The past doesn't hold the power it once did. Confronting my father and telling him about how I felt as a child and how my mother died helped me let it go. It's over. I promise not to let my parents' mistakes affect our happiness again.''

"Don't beat yourself up about it. We have so much to be grateful for ... so much to look forward to."

They enjoyed a series of love-filled kisses. She sighed happily, her head on his shoulder.

"I feel sorry for him, Zach. I think deep down inside he really wanted to be a part of my life, but he was the one who took that away. It can't happen now, not unless he stops drinking for good."

Zachary was doubtful, but kept his thoughts to himself.

"If you have no objections, I want our children to grow up here in this house, just as I did."

"I'd like that, too," he said with a wide smile.

"Granddaddy would have been so pleased."

"Yes, he would." He cradled her in his arms, savoring their physical and emotional closeness.

"How long do you think it will take us to move in?"

He chuckled. "We've already moved in. It may take a little time before our clothing and furniture catch up with us." Feeling moisture on his open collar, Zachary looked at her in concern. "What's wrong, my pretty girl?"

"Happy tears," she explained. "I'm just so glad that things turned out the way they did. I was so worried when I left the condo this morning." She rained kisses down his face, lingering on his full lips. "Never forget that I believe in you and our love. Is that enough for you, Zach?"

"More than enough," he said an instant before his lips took hers in a deep, heartwarming kiss. "Show me how much."

"Happily," she whispered, before proceeded to do just that.

Epilogue

One year later

"Zach! Everyone's here," Amanda said, looking at all the cars parked on both sides of the drive as the car eased to a stop in front of the house.

He said with a wide grin, "What do you expect? My son couldn't come home without a party to celebrate his birth."

"Oh, really." Amanda laughed. "Your son is only three days old."

"Old enough to learn how very much he's loved." Zachary unbuckled his seat belt and leaned forward to undo hers before he pressed a tender kiss to her lips. "Thank you. He is so beautiful."

Amanda smiled. "Are you going to do this every day from now on? You've been thanking me since the day he was born."

"Yeah. Get used to it, sugar. Happy?"

"Very. How about you?" she said, caressing his cheek.

"Now that you're home, I couldn't be better. Come on, let's get our little man inside before everyone comes out here."

Amanda laughed, waiting until Zachary came around to help her out. He slid inside the backseat to unfasten and remove the baby's car seat.

"He is such a good baby. He slept all the way home." Amanda adjusted the soft blanket to make sure he was covered.

"You go on ahead, little Mommy. I'm right behind you."

Amanda smiled, pleased by the loving care Zachary took with their baby. She just knew he was going to be a wonderful father just by the way he was not put off by changing his son's diaper or uncomfortable handling him. Zachary held him while she gave little Andrew his first bath.

"Hurry up, you two. What has taken so long to get my nephew in here? You two been necking in the car, right?" Bradford said with a wide grin, holding the door open. Kissing Amanda's cheek, he said, "You got him so bundled I can't see him."

"He is supposed to be bundled, silly. It's cold out there," Barbara said from behind her husband of only two months. "Mandy, you look fabulous. I hope I look half as good when it's my turn." She gave her sister-in-law an affectionate hug.

The animosity between the two had long since disappeared once Barbara admitted to herself how much she loved Bradford and the two started dating in earnest.

"Thanks. Don't worry, you will."

"Barbara is right. You look wonderful," Peggy said as she greeted her with a warm hug.

"Where is Carol Ann?" Amanda asked as she slipped out of her coat. She referred to Roger and Peggy's ten-month-old daughter.

"Roger is putting her down for a nap. She wanted to see her new cousin but couldn't keep her eyes open. I'm hoping she'll be awake for the party."

Amanda shook her head. Everyone was wearing wild party hats. "I can't believe you guys."

"Wait until you see the cake I ordered," Mrs. McFadden said, coming from the kitchen. "Sit down, young lady, while you can. That little darling is going to keep you up more nights than not."

Amanda smiled at her mother-in-law. Many things in the past year had changed. It had taken time but once Zachary's mother knew that Amanda was carrying her first grandson, she had done everything she could to mend the rift between them. Mrs. McFadden had even taken to going with Amanda for her doctor's appointments. Amanda welcomed her concern and support. She did it for her husband, knowing how much his mother meant to him. She wanted their child to be a part of a warm and loving family.

"Let me see him," Roger said, joining the others around Zachary.

"Hey. What about me?"

Roger laughed, coming over and giving Amanda a kiss on the cheek. "You look great, little mother."

"Thank you." Amanda settled on one end of the sofa. Her doctor had said she had a relatively easy delivery, which had consisted of about ten hours of labor. Zachary was at her side, helping her through. They both cried with joy when little Andrew Jacob McFadden was born, all of nine pounds, four ounces, with a very healthy set of lungs and a sizable appetite.

"You boys, stop. You are keeping up too much noise for my grandbaby."

"And my god-baby," Kate Jenson said with a wide smile as she came from the kitchen, her customary apron around her waist. "Bring him over to his mama so she can get all those clothes off of him. He is wrapped up tighter than a Christmas package.''

''Did I put too much on him?'' Amanda asked anxiously. ''I just didn't want him to catch cold.''

Mrs. McFadden patted her hand. ''You did fine, honey. We are all here to help you when you need anything. Isn't that right, Kate and Peggy?''

''Absolutely.'' The ladies beamed.

Amanda smiled, not wanting to be an overprotective mother. But it was all so new to her. She knew she was bound to make mistakes.

Zachary kissed his mother's cheek before he took little Andrew out of his blankets and bunting, and handed his son over to Amanda. She kissed the baby's brow as he yawned, stretched and opened his large black eyes. Then she settled him in his grandmother's arms.

Mrs. McFadden cradled him with happy tears in her eyes. ''Thank you, Mandy. He is so precious. He looks just like Zach when he was born. Look at those strong little legs and arms. And that's a Hamilton chin.'' She looked over at his proud parents. Zachary stood next to Mandy with his hand on her shoulder. ''Thank you both, for naming him after his grandfather. It means the world to me.''

There was not a dry eye in the room.

''Enough of this. It's party time! Come on, Peggy and Barbara, you can help me put the food on the table. Come on, Brad and Roger, you can help, too,'' Kate Jenson said.

Amanda squeezed her husband's hand. She looked thoughtfully up at him and asked, ''What do you serve at a birth party?''

''What else but barbecue ribs and chicken and birthday cake?'' Zachary teased, leaning down to brush her lips with his. ''Love you,'' he whispered into her ear.

''Love you more,'' she whispered back.

Dear Reader:

I hope you enjoyed WHEN A MAN LOVES A WOMAN. Reading has been an important part of my life for many years. I read my first romance novel for a junior high school book report and was hooked for life.

I truly enjoy hearing from you. Please take time to visit my Web site at www.tlt.com/authors/bford.htm. I do receive all your comments, but if you would like a response, please write to me at P.O. Box 944, Saginaw, MI 48606, and include a self-addressed, stamped envelope.

Thank you,
Bette Ford

ABOUT THE AUTHOR

Bette Ford grew up in Saginaw, Michigan, and graduated from Saginaw High School. She obtained her bachelor's degree from Central State University in Wilberforce, Ohio. Bette began her teaching career in Detroit and completed her master's degree at Wayne State University. She has taught for the Detroit Public Schools Headstart program for many years. She is currently writing full-time.

More Sizzling Romance From
Bette Ford

__All the Love	0-7860-0350-2	**$4.99**US/**$6.50**CAN
__One of A Kind	1-58314-000-X	**$4.99**US/**$6.50**CAN
__Island Magic	1-58314-113-8	**$5.99**US/**$7.99**CAN
__After Dark	1-58314-175-8	**$5.99**US/**$7.99**CAN
__For Always	1-58314-180-4	**$5.99**US/**$7.99**CAN
__Forever After	1-58314-199-5	**$5.99**US/**$7.99**CAN